CAGES

CAGES

A Tale of Insurrection

Jeffrey C. Pugh

RESOURCE *Publications* · Eugene, Oregon

CAGES
A Tale of Insurrection

Resource Publications
An Imprint of Wipf and Stock Publishers
199 W. 8th Ave., Suite 3
Eugene, OR 97401

www.wipfandstock.com

PAPERBACK ISBN: 978-1-6667-9179-2
HARDCOVER ISBN: 978-1-6667-9177-8
EBOOK ISBN: 978-1-6667-9178-5

FEBRUARY 14, 2022 8:46 AM

To Jan Rivero
My companion on the journey

On a frigid January morning in 1536 three bodies in iron cages were hauled to the top of St. Lambert's Cathedral in Münster, Germany. Though the bodies are gone, the cages remain.

CONTENTS

PART III

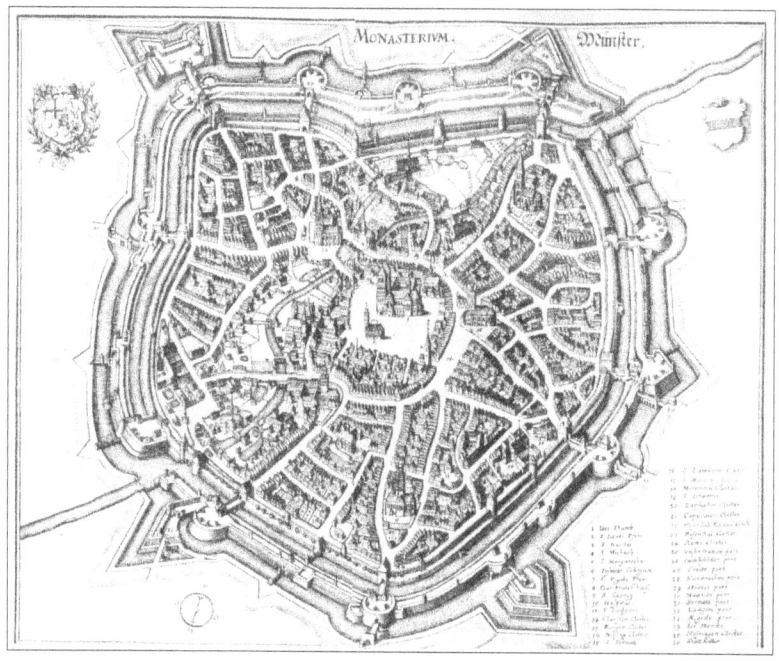

Topographia Westphaliae[1]

1. "Topographia Westphaliae" by Martin Zeiler, 1647; (https://commons.wikime-dia.org/wiki/File:De_merian_Westphaliae_124.jpg.

Acknowledgments

In October of 1995 I stood in the shadow of St. Lambert's cages in Münster, Germany contemplating the power of historical consciousness. Why keep these cages hanging through the centuries, even replacing them after the cathedral was bombed to rubble in World War II? What warning were these cages supposed to deliver that centuries later they still hang from the cathedral's towers? In that moment I was gripped with the desire to account for the events in Münster in a way different than the scholar's perspective. What could possibly motivate people to such madness as unfolded in Münster? How did such a powerful city fall under the spell of religious extremism?

It is easy for our age to dismiss such events as the consequences of religious delusion, especially when we see apocalyptically driven insurrections across the global stage in our time. We have ample evidence that when societies are in a state of flux, with communal guideposts and institutions eroding, religion functions as a place of salvation, a way to make sense of the upheaval one is experiencing. Religion can also be a place of rebellion and resistance to the orders that determine people's lives. Such was the case for sixteenth century Europe, and Münster is just one story among dozens that tell of people breaking loose from the political, economic, and religious orders that had shaped their identities for centuries.

This journey into the unknown could not have been taken without the help of those who were my teachers and guides. Their patience and expertise helped me overcome a lot of obstacles, though the greatest lessons I learned were from the many stumbles along the way.

My initial guide into this strange new world of writing fiction was Jaimee Garbacik of Footnote Editorial. Presented with an absolute novice, she was patient, longsuffering, and extremely insightful in teaching me about writing. It was like having a personal tutor shepherd me through a world I barely understood. My next guide, Catherine Adams of Inkslinger Editing, helped me refine the story, the characters, and the flow of the book. Her encouragement kept me on task, especially when I felt like giving up. If it were not for these two, I doubt I would have stayed with it.

I also found The History Quill, a company that works with historical fiction writers, to be enormously helpful in getting me over the finish line. Pippa Brush Chappell's content edit was extraordinarily helpful to me with the final shape of the book, though I still grieve some of those final cuts. Sarah Dronfield's edits strengthened the book and gave me the confidence to release it into the wild. Rachael Mortimer's proofreading was meticulous and saved me from many mistakes. I am so grateful for these skillful people and their invaluable aid and encouragement.

For a compelling reading of the Anabaptists, I have numerous scholars to thank, but it is William Paul Bergkamp's University of Chicago Master of Arts thesis *The Emergence of the Anabaptist Kingdom of Münster: An Examination of the Development of Christian Thought* that inspired me to continue with this project. At a meeting of the American Academy of Religion I told him I was working on a historical fiction book about Münster, to which he responded he had written his Masters thesis on Münster. He graciously sent me a copy, which helped me clarify new directions.

All along this path I was fortunate enough to have friends who gave me helpful insight and questions as they read through the book. Though I fear I have left someone out, I am incredibly indebted to John Billman, Bari Lynn Hein, Bizz Glover, Karla Kincannon, Tom Miller, Julie Carpenter, Tim Peeples, L. D. Russell, Tom Tiemann, Eileen McGrath, Jim McDonald, Dennis Pagano, and Russ Vandermaas-Peeler for reading early drafts of this and offering suggestions.

Without the support of Elon University through the years this book was taking shape I could never have finished. Tim Peeples was especially helpful, not the least because he did not tell me the truth about the first draft I gave him. My departmental family at Elon, who I am sure at times wondered why a professor was spending his time on writing fiction, were also incredibly supportive, listening to ideas, research, and living through presentations on this material. I am grateful to Lynn Huber, Geoff Claussen, Pam Wingfield, Michael Pregill, Toddie Peters, Amy Allocco, Brian Pennington, Ariela Marcus-Sells, and L. D. Russell for their support over the years.

Finally, the unwavering support of Jan Rivero strengthened my resolve in moments I wanted nothing more than to put this book away. Her continuing conversations and insights about the characters, the story, and the entire project have been invaluable. She even fell in love with Münster, which is easy to do.

From the days of John the Baptist until now the kingdom of heaven
has suffered violence, and the violent take it by force.

MATT: 11:12

PART I

PROLOGUE

Rottenburg am Neckar, May 22, 1527

THE SIGHT OF MARGARETHA SATTLER'S straw-colored braids floating on
the river paralyzed Andreas Wagner. Seconds before, her eyes locked on
his, she was screaming, squirming on her ducking stool as Rottenburg's
magistrates lowered her into the murky brown water. Now, only her dingy
white bonnet floating downstream spoke for her. When they lifted up her
body, slumped and lifeless, Andreas groaned. He mourned for her and
her husband, Michael, who had been executed a couple of days earlier. He
grieved the entire spectacle of human stupidity he had witnessed since
he left the monastery two years ago. Sparse tears etched streaks down his
grimy face.

Groans and tears were all the knot of priests and magistrates standing off to the side needed. They were on him in seconds, grabbing his
arms as Andreas begged them to stop. Ignoring his protests, they threw

him into a rolling iron-barred cage. One more heretic added to the pitiful figures huddled anxiously with him awaiting their fate.

Standing on the splintery floor of the cart, Andreas ran his hand up and down the rusty iron bars. His body twitched when he realized he was in the cage that brought Margaretha to the river this morning. *Why did you come?* His knuckles lost color as he clutched the crusty bars, trying to stop the screaming accusations in his head. How was he going to convince the authorities that he had nothing to do with Sattler's sect? What did he care about them, their beliefs? He should have stayed in Horb with his carpenter's guild where he belonged. Wood he understood. Humans were a bottomless mystery.

Arriving at the desolate wooden and iron door of Rottenburg's dungeons, Andreas confronted new terrors. Confusion engulfed him as the jailers dragged him and the others out of their carts and across the small stone plaza, hauling them down into the bowels of the prison. Monks' chanting in the distance mingled incongruously with the moans of prisoners as Andreas was dragged past their darkened rooms. The deeper into the narrow tunnel they forced him, the more his body betrayed him; resistance turned to helplessness and clothes drenched with sweat. The sticky smell of stale piss and vomit assaulted him as they pushed him inside of his cell.

Andreas's imagination flooded with images he had seen on woodcuts—prints of imps and demons pulling out arms and legs, of malformed bodies crying out in anguish as they perished in flames—visions of hell that were becoming all too real. Andreas wasn't afraid of the devil. Those who saw Satan in a thunderstorm, heard him in the creaking of a branch, or an owl's hoot, were the ones who really scared him. People who saw the devil everywhere usually ended up devils themselves. Worse than Satan—Andreas had fallen into the hands of the righteous.

He would be willing to confess anything to escape suffering. Before he could even catch his breath, two burly men lumbered into his cell, clutched his shoulders with hands strengthened by hundreds who resisted, and shoved him across the hall into a damp, dimly lit room, warmed only by the fires heating sets of tongs and pikes. Andreas choked on the acrid burning smoke hovering in the room; his stomach grew sour. They wrestled him onto a long table and fastened him with ropes, pulling his arms above his head and attaching them to a hook. Through the corner of his eye, Andreas caught sight of a man dressed in clerical robes sitting at a small table, dipping his quill into a pot of ink. What was a priest doing here?

"Your name?" The wrinkled old priest fixed rheumy blue eyes on Andreas, his shaky hand holding a pen above the paper.

"Andreas Wagner." The pen scratched out the letters.

"And your home?"

"Münster." The smoke irritated his eyes, causing them to water. "Westphalia."

The priest put down his quill and adjusted his floppy velvet hat. "You're a long way from home. Don't they have any heretics where you live? Did you have to come and join ours?"

"I'm not a heretic. I was an Augustinian monk in Münster." Andreas thought if he could just explain himself . . .

"Was?" the tart voice probed. "Did you desert your order?"

"No, my parents left me there; I was following a path I did not choose."

"Hmm." The priest drummed fingers on his parchment. "Sattler was a monk, a prior, even. Satan seduced him, probably with that woman of his." The priest crossed himself.

"I'm not one of them." Andreas shook his head in denial.

"They all say that," the priest scoffed. "Yes or no? Have you had the second baptism?"

"What does it matter? I don't follow them; I'm not one of them," Andreas protested.

"But you wept when the woman was freed from her sin." The voice softened. "Is that a tear I see?" The priest reached out and touched Andreas's cheek.

"I was crying for all the harm those people have done," Andreas croaked, his mouth dry. "Now . . . the smoke."

The old man shifted in his seat and pressed his bony fingers together. "Doubtful."

"I've nothing but the truth to tell. I'm a woodworker in Horb and heard about the trial. I was interested in seeing the heretic for myself."

"I hear uncertainty in your voice. If you don't tell us the truth, it'll go worse for you. Horb's an infected nest of heresy."

Focused on the priest interrogating him, Andreas barely registered the jailer taking glowing tongs out of the fire until he sensed the heat nearing his side. Tears and sweat streaming down his face, Andreas squirmed on the table, his back scratched and irritated by the ridges and splinters of the rough wood beneath him; Andreas cursed the careless craftsman who couldn't even bother to properly plane the board from which he plunged off the edge of the world.

1

*Jaberg, Bern Canton, Swiss Confederacy,
August 28, 1533*

Hunger drove Andreas into Jaberg. He had entered the village on his way to Bern and saw a large crowd gathered by the river. If it was a festival, a stranger might be welcomed and there'd be food for sale. He approached the noisy bustle as two voices sounded over the hum of the crowd. One, male, was a raspy, squawky irritation, squealing out accusations; the other, a woman, urgently beating back his charges. Weaving among the bodies, he peeked through a gap between the villagers. It was no celebration. On the edge of the roaring river, a woman sat tied to a ducking stool. *Everyone fears for their salvation, yet no one is safe.*

Images of others on these stools left him gasping. He'd worked hard to avoid this, knew he should slip away while he could, but he couldn't take his eyes off the woman straining against the ropes that bound her to the chair. The fire in her eyes immobilized him even as he tried to steady his shaking hands. Life had not yet worn her down, though it appeared her village was intending to rectify that.

Dressed in a dirndl, her thin frame was held captive in a crude seat fastened to the end of a thick log, resting on a fulcrum and manipulated by a rope tied to the other end. Andreas knew that soon the chair would be lifted up, swung out over the river, and then lowered—a lever of death. The men closest to the woman had been given the job of pushing the stool out above the rushing water and holding the chair steady when it submerged. Looking into the Aare river, Andreas figured they would need all their strength today. It flowed granite-grey and foamy, the Alps worn down into liquid.

"We can't suffer a witch to live." The squealing priest, ratty brown robe stretched across his ample stomach, grabbed the woman's blonde braid and pulled. "The Word of God is clear. We must cleanse ourselves from evil. She's the cause of the plague tormenting us."

"As for what God desires, I'm quite sure it's different from your desires, *priest*," the woman spat.

She hated priests too, or at least this one.

"Papa!" the woman said to the man cowering beside the slovenly priest. "I'm your *daughter*! How can you believe this rutting pig? You know I didn't do this."

The stooped man shifted from foot to foot, his head jerking back and forth between woman and priest. He moaned as his body bent over like he had just been punched in the stomach. The priest lifted the tormented man's shoulder and nodded at him encouragingly.

"Elsbeth, why would Father Kömmer lie? God's servants don't lie; they bring us the truth."

"Not this one, Papa."

Andreas's hands drew into fists. *They lie all the time.* He surveyed the crowd; the faces on several of the women gave him some hope. They had their doubts. After all, Elsbeth was one of theirs, and they may have succumbed to the priest's extortions.

The father called across the log, "Elsbeth, I'm in agony. Have you been using magic to bring men to your bed?"

"You can't believe that."

"But the priest showed me your potions, your amulets."

"The only thing I'm guilty of is telling that fat pus sack I wouldn't sleep with him," Elsbeth retorted.

Laughter rippled through the crowd as some voices yelled out encouragement to Elsbeth. The priest, swelling with indignation, screeched, "See? What more proof do we need? She speaks vile words against God's servants."

"You're no servant of God. Your breath alone smells like the gates of hell," Elsbeth shot back.

More laughter erupted from the crowd as sweat beaded on the priest's forehead. Elsbeth's eyes flashed with defiance as her gaze swept over the crowd. Then her eyes stopped and locked onto Andreas. He was not invisible to her.

A man, wrinkly hands resting on his cane, stood in a group of men off to the side. "Elsbeth!" he shouted. "We've prayed about this. We asked

God for direction. Father Kömmer said you'd deny the accusation. Once you've given yourself over to lust, Satan possesses you. Father read to us from the *Malleus . . . Male . . . ficarum.*"

Andreas grimaced at the man's stammering Latin. He was familiar with the book known as *Der Hexenhammer, The Hammer of Witches.* The priest's intent was clear; he wanted death. Andreas glanced around him at the confused faces. This was what unscrupulous priests did—threw sand in your eyes, clouded your mind with uncertainty until you agreed with them, because priests knew things. They were closer to God. That's what they wanted you to think.

When Andreas looked back at Elsbeth, she had slouched in the chair, her head lowered and her chest heaving to catch her breath. She appeared to be talking to herself, but then she erupted in mocking laughter.

"She's lost her head," a woman beside Andreas whispered to her companion.

"She's possessed," the other woman answered, fingering the walnut talisman that hung around her neck. "He's gloating at us . . . through her."

"You've known me since I was a child!" Elsbeth yelled. "You watched me grow up. You've played with me, taught me, cared for me. I've cut your cheese, sliced your bread, and poured you drink at the tavern. When would I have had time to consort with the devil? Mama died taking care of you through this plague, but now you make me your prey? Do you actually believe this miserable excuse for a priest over me?"

The priest lunged at her, holding out a cross and shaking a vial of water onto her. "Silence, Satan!"

"Go to hell!" Elsbeth screamed, twisting away from him.

"See? Proof!" The priest pointed at Elsbeth as he circled around her. "Pray Satan does not enter into you, or it will be worse for you than her."

Elsbeth scanned the crowd, imploring them for mercy. When her anxious eyes met their faces, several began crying, turning away from her. "Sisters," she pleaded, "you told me you've felt that bastard's hands on you. Kömmer's the liar, not me. You'll be up here next unless you stop this."

No one moved; no one spoke. Every head bowed away from her. The only sounds rising to Andreas's ears were the rushing of the river and the wind blowing through the pine and aspen trees.

Kömmer's eyes, however, were fixed on Elsbeth. A slight smile forming at the corner of the priest's lips. *He's getting what he wants.* Andreas struggled against the urge to shout out on her behalf. He searched the crowd for some sign that the uncertainty he sensed earlier could still win the day. One word from him, though, and he'd be their next victim. They may have agonized over killing one of their own, but a stranger wouldn't merit much remorse.

Met with silence and turned shoulders, Elsbeth slumped in her seat. "I go to God then, but the rest of you have to live with his lies. Don't be seduced by that mound of shit hiding behind his cloak. His words are like a fart from a pig's arse." She glared at the priest as he whispered into her father's ear.

"Elsbeth!" Her father's scream pierced through the murmuring voices. "There's still hope. If you repent, Father will pray with you in private confession. He'll ask God to forgive you."

All eyes turned to the priest, his hands clasped on his chest, his face a mask of benevolence.

"Papa, open your eyes," Elsbeth urged. "I'd rather die today and rot in hell if heaven contains the likes of him."

"As you wish." The priest motioned to the men around the ducking stool. But they hesitated when the father's wailing exploded in the morning air, shaking the crowd as small groups clumped together, holding one another and sobbing.

"This is wrong!" a man next to Andreas shouted. Other voices called out in protest as confusion covered the crowd like the thick summer fog that crept from the river, smothering the village.

"You must obey God, or else," the priest threatened.

Andreas turned away and started pushing past the knot of people who had formed behind him; he wasn't going to watch another execution. Then he heard Elsbeth weeping. His head dropped and his feet stopped. Cursing his body's betrayal, he tried to break from the crowd again but remained frozen, unable to move.

"Please! Don't do this!" Elsbeth begged.

He glanced back at the men around the chair. It was foolish to think he could do anything about them. They pulled on the rope end of the log and lifted her off the ground. She hovered a few feet above the crowd as they swung her toward the river—the queen of death floating on her throne, looking down on her subjects. Her eyes, no longer defiant, widened with horror; the same look that haunted Andreas's dreams.

Trapped in his indecision, Andreas was carried along by the crowds surging forward as the chair went out over the river. When the throng stopped, he stood mere feet from the water's edge. Thoughts of what he was going to feel like when this was over propelled Andreas to decision. On the other side of the log from him the men started to lower her. Andreas saw a chance, a slim one.

He drew his knife from its sheath as Elsbeth's feet and ankles disappeared into the river and the water climbed to her waist. Screams and moans of protest broke out.

"I beg you," Elsbeth cried out, "Papa, don't!"

Andreas, knife in hand, took three quick steps, leapt on the fulcrum, and launched himself toward Elsbeth's chair. She screamed as his body collided with hers, jerking the rope quickly out of the hands of those lowering her as the chair smacked into the water.

"Hel—!" Elsbeth went under. Sinking down into the river with her, Andreas cut at the cords on her right hand, his knife laboring against the rope until he felt it cut through. She struggled, thrashing against him, trying to wrest her other arm free. His head throbbing, Andreas crossed her body, fighting against the current that worked to tear him away from her. He grasped her arm and started desperately hacking at the rope, his hand moving vigorously against the wet cord. He worried that he would jerk the knife so hard he might slice her wrists.

Andreas knew the men on the bank would recover the rope at any moment. When they lifted them up, he would have to let go and leave Elsbeth to her fate. His arm tired as he sensed the chair resisting the water, surging upward in defiance of the current, taking him with it. The knife cut free of the rope just as the sun warmed his back. Her mouth opened to scream, but he pulled her into the surging current before she could get the words out.

She quickly slipped from his grasp as he struggled to keep his head above water. Voices shouted over the roar of the river. A few of the women ran along the bank, calling them to return. Elsbeth, bobbing furiously in the water, held out her arm to the running women, but she kept going under as she twisted toward them.

"Turn around and go with the river!" Andreas shouted.

Elsbeth positioned herself so she could keep her head out of the water, allowing the river to carry her along. Andreas pointed downstream and yelled, "Bern!" She kept twisting around for one last look at her village disappearing in the distance, the figures running after them on the riverbank growing smaller and smaller.

Andreas watched Elsbeth struggle for one more glimpse of home, her outstretched arm an attempt to reach back and grab the fragments of her life. He knew they would never forgive her, would never accept her back into the fold after this. She had become their scapegoat, their sacrifice, the one into whom they poured their fears and anxieties before they murdered her, hoping somehow that their own sins would be forgiven. It was an old story, maybe the oldest story.

His world, too, had just changed. He had not thought about what would happen after he leapt onto the stool; he only knew that one way or the other, death or life, he hoped finally to be at peace with his failures. Two bodies, carried from a haunted and deadly past, surged toward an uncertain future.

The Aare swept them swiftly downstream until they neared the horseshoe-shaped bend curving around the city of Bern. The terra-cotta roofs climbing up from the river were a welcome sight, as was a slowing of the current, allowing them a chance to move toward land. Motioning toward the city side of the river, Andreas gestured to a place where they could climb out. Elsbeth nodded, following him toward the bank.

Pulling himself to the edge of the river, Andreas reached to help Elsbeth, but she brushed his hand away as she climbed onto land. Staggering toward a patch of sunlight in a clearing several yards away, Elsbeth collapsed onto the ground, coughing violently. Andreas followed, taking a place a few feet away, trying to catch his breath.

"Why . . . " she panted, " . . . did you do that?"

"I . . . don't . . . know." Andreas took in deep gulps of air.

"They . . . were going to kill . . . me . . . " Elsbeth's voice wavered.

"Apparently." Andreas turned on his side to face her.

"Why were you even there?"

"Chance. Passing through on the way home."

"My own village tried to kill me." Elsbeth sobbed, her chest rising and falling.

"There were some who tried to stop it." Andreas felt the futility of his words.

"They could've tried harder!" Elsbeth's fists hit the ground. "Goddamn them! Goddamn!" She sat up, turning her head toward him.

Andreas studied Elsbeth's grey-blue eyes. He had the feeling she was remembering everything, storing it up somewhere in case she needed the memory later. Falling back down, she was silent for a few minutes as Andreas listened to the rushing water of the river, contemplating his impulsiveness.

"I don't have anything." Elsbeth broke the silence.

"What?"

"I don't have anything to give you . . . for saving my life."

"There's no need." Andreas heard a distance enter Elsbeth's voice, as if she wasn't entirely present.

"It's only that most people would want something."

"You don't owe me." Andreas rose to his feet.

"That's not exactly true, is it? I owe you my life." Elsbeth struggled to stand. "I'm Elsbeth Joris. You are?"

"Andreas Wagner."

Elsbeth's face tightened, filling with shadow. "What am I going to do now?"

"Do you have anywhere else you can go? It's dangerous for a woman to be out in the world alone."

"I can take care of myself," Elsbeth bristled.

"Don't take offense. It's just that there're hard men about. If the cut-purses don't get you, the highway robbers will. The roads are littered with thieves looking for easy money."

"I don't have any money." Elsbeth patted her pockets.

"But they don't know that, and it may not be your money they're after when it comes down to it."

Elsbeth stood for minutes wringing the excess water from her dirndl. "Maybe I should go to my sister's house," she murmured. "She lives here."

"Your father surely is on his way there, probably with the priest in hand."

Elsbeth paced in a small circle, her face narrowing in concentration. As she drew her hands behind her head, Andreas recalled his confusion when his world first fell apart.

"Goddamn them all!" Elsbeth's body reared back. She wandered toward the river and stood on the edge, her feet inches away from slid-ing back in, her arms wrapping tightly around her. "What's to become of me?"

Andreas wondered if she were contemplating walking into the river, letting the current sweep her away. "I have some money," he offered. "For now, we can get a room and some food. We can figure out something tomorrow."

Elsbeth kept her eyes on the Aare, back in the direction of her lost home. Finally, she heaved a deep breath. "We may as well; I seem to be out of choices." She pushed past him toward the city, cursing her father under her breath.

2

Bern

THE GREASY LEFT HAND kept wiping the threadbare robe as the right held out the wafer. Elsbeth could smell the traces of cheese, onion, garlic, and beer beneath his long, dirty nails as her face neared the body of Christ. He wouldn't put the host on her tongue when she opened her mouth but held it firmly until she put her lips over his fingers, sucking the wafer away, causing him to shudder. In a flash, Father Kömmer was holding her head under water in the baptismal font, causing her to thrash like a fish caught on a hook. She bolted up, gasping for air, face wet with tears and sweat. Flopping back in the strange bed, it took a moment to get her bearings, her nightmare receding into remnants.

Abandoned.

Her mind raced back to when she plunged into the Aare, Andreas's body crashing into hers, crawling from the river into her new life. Standing on the bank yesterday, the reality of her situation sliced a wound into her she feared would sever her from sanity. Lacking options, she reluctantly agreed to go with Andreas to this inn on the edge of Bern. Andreas had told the innkeeper they were husband and wife. It just seemed easier that way. By the time they were huddled in their room, eating some food he'd bought from the market, they were both exhausted and said little. After eating, he fell asleep on the floor.

Elsbeth stayed awake most of the night, trying to make sense of the day. Why had they turned on her, willing to believe the priest? Why had Papa not listened to her? Why did a stranger risk his life to save her when her own people stood silent? She remembered seeing Andreas in the crowd, his straw-colored hair pulled back and tied with a string. The red scar on his cheek that disappeared into his thick beard marked him as wounded in her mind, but from what? It was only later in the day that he came more into focus for her. He had known hard work from the looks of him. The blue eyes, flecked with yellow, were disconcerting, like they saw into her somehow.

Elsbeth inspected the bruises on her wrists, still sore from straining to break free of that damned stool. An iciness burrowed deep inside her, trying to make a home. She feared the coldness of it. She stared at the floor where Andreas had slept. Where had he gone? Discomfort nudged her, like someone poking her chest. She threw off the cover, grabbed her clothes, and dressed, hearing muted voices below her.

Moments later, Andreas came in carrying a tray of bread, cheese, bacon, eggs, fruit, and a small cup of cider. He smiled and put the tray down on the table beside her. "Thank you," she murmured, reaching for the bread and cheese, hunger overcoming wariness.

"Good morning." Andreas stepped away from the bed.

"Nothing good about it," Elsbeth groused. She tore off a piece of bread and shoved it in her mouth.

"Any thoughts on what you'll do?" Andreas leaned against the wall beside the door.

"I thought about going to my sister, but I can't. You're right; that's the first place Papa will look. I can't go to my brothers in Thun. I'm an unattached woman; I'll be regarded with suspicion no matter where I go. People will probably think I'm a whore or, worse, a witch."

"True, but we can't stay here," Andreas offered.

"We?" Elsbeth snapped. "There's no 'we.'"

"I'm sorry. I was just trying to be helpful." Andreas moved down the wall to the corner of the room.

"This is my problem, not yours. I didn't mean offense. I'm still trying to sort all this out. Why'd they turn on me like that? Why did you jump on that chair?"

Andreas heaved a deep breath. "I wanted to make something right. I have other memories of those stools." A cloud passed over Andreas's face.

"I'm grateful. If you hadn't been there, I'd be dead by now, killed by my own people." Elsbeth drew her legs and arms into herself and lowered her head onto her knees.

Andreas sat in silence as tears dampened Elsbeth's clothes. "I've given this some thought," he said after a few moments.

Elsbeth jerked her head up, eyes flashing. "Have you?"

Andreas put his hands up. "I mean no harm."

Elsbeth unfolded her legs and took a strawberry off the tray. "I'm not sure who or what to trust anymore."

"I understand, but I have an idea if you want to hear it." Andreas grabbed a piece of bacon and popped it into his mouth.

Elsbeth remained silent, staring at the wall until her eyes turned toward Andreas.

"I'm on my way home, and you're welcome to come with me."

"Home?"

"Münster, in Westphalia."

Until yesterday morning, Elsbeth had a hard time grasping why anyone would leave home. Then she realized that home was lost to her. Perhaps to Andreas as well? "Why'd you leave? What takes you back?"

Andreas smiled. "You ask a lot of questions. I left to find my parents. I'm returning because I need to see a friend. I hope he can help me."

"How long have you been away?" Elsbeth pressed.

"It's been eight years since I left the monastery."

Elsbeth leapt up out of the bed and moved to the opposite end of the room, her back pressing into the wall. "Wait, you're a priest? A god-damned priest?" she shouted. "You could've mentioned that last night."

"Shh!" Andreas motioned with his finger. "The walls are thin, and curious ears are everywhere. I was a monk, not a priest. I left the order eight years ago."

Elsbeth pressed back harder into the wall, feeling like the wind had been knocked out of her. "What other secrets do you have?"

"Does it matter just this moment?" Andreas whispered. "Perhaps you need to give some thought to what'll happen if your father arrives in Bern and hears about the wet and miserable-looking strangers walking through the market arcades yesterday. I'm leaving as soon as possible; you're welcome to join me."

Elsbeth returned to the bed, struggling to calm herself.

"What happened to you is awful, horrible." Andreas finally broke the silence. "But what are your options? I can't see them. You're right to be concerned that you're unattached. I know a place in Münster that would take you in if you need some time to work things through."

"What place?"

"Überwasser Convent. The abbess there is a good woman, so you should be in safe hands. You could work there until you think of another path. You don't have to take vows. They hire housekeepers to help with the work. It would give you a safe place to make plans."

Elsbeth slumped back on the bed, her head cradled in her hands.

"I'm not forcing this; you can do as you please," Andreas said, holding out the plate of food to her.

Elsbeth took a piece of cheese. "How far is it?"

"Some distance, perhaps weeks away, depending on how fast we can travel."

"And do we have to be husband and wife on the way?"

"Only in name; it'd be safer. There won't be as many questions."

Elsbeth frowned at the thought of being seen as someone's wife. After yesterday, no one was going to have power over her if she could help it. She studied the man in front of her. Who knew what he really wanted? Still, she didn't have anyone else to trust. She'd have to take some risks if she was going to survive.

"Elsbeth?"

"Maybe my sister's husband will protect me." Even Elsbeth was unconvinced when she heard herself say it.

"And if he doesn't? What then? They'll kill you if they get you back. If I know the priest, you most likely won't even make it to the village. He'll kill your father, rape you, and leave you for dead. You wouldn't be the first woman found in a ditch somewhere. He'll blame it on robbers, say he tried to protect you and your father, but there were too many of them."

Elsbeth was up again, stalking the floor from wall to wall. "That's a dire story. There has to be another way."

"Stay or go"—Andreas crossed his arms—"it's your choice to make. I'm offering you the hope of a sanctuary. If you think of something better, do as you wish."

Elsbeth stood silently for a few seconds before she started trembling. Her body, locked tight since yesterday, a prisoner to fear and terror, loosened from the inside out. Trembling turned to shaking. She wanted to be held. Wounded, she wanted to howl at the heavens. There was no one she could trust, no arms for solace. Andreas reached out his hand to touch her shoulder, but when she flinched, he withdrew to a chair on his side of the room. She thought she would never know a greater pain than yesterday's betrayal, but the feeling of being severed from her former life filled Elsbeth with a heaviness she feared would drag her into darkness worse than drowning. Life had squeezed her into this moment, and she was at a loss as to which path to take.

3

September 23, 1533

IT WAS DANGEROUS, foolish, but in the end, what other option was there? Leaving Bern, Elsbeth harbored the hope that when her father couldn't find her, his guilt would eat at him. She wanted to scar him, leave a wound he wouldn't soon forget. The knowledge that she carried such anger was a revelation, but there had been other discoveries on this journey. She knew her back quickly grew sore riding in the wooden cart as it slogged over muddy ruts. She knew she hated biting bugs and sleeping outside, and eel was her least favorite food. Much to her surprise, Elsbeth realized that, despite those hardships, she had grown to embrace the uncertainty of her new life. Every new experience, even the dangerous ones, left her hungering to see what was around the bend.

They had only been on the road a few days before Andreas struck up a conversation with a man named Jost buying bread in Basel. When Jost found out they were going to Münster, he invited them to travel with him and his companions. Andreas didn't hesitate, even when Jost said they were all Anabaptists. He told Elsbeth they could be trusted. The priest had warned her village about the heretics called "Anabaptists," but Elsbeth knew he was a liar. Still, Elsbeth found them an odd sort.

At night, they would share stories around the fire of running from authorities, hiding out in barns and woods, hoping to stay alive. As she listened to their stories, it occurred to her she was just enough of a Catholic to be worried about anybody who wasn't. These people were hunted to death in the world because they baptized adults. She had never thought of how powerful ideas were.

Two weeks after meeting the Anabaptists, a merchant on his way to Münster joined them. It was his cart, full of sheep's wool and other goods for market, Elsbeth now rode in. She shifted her weight to find some comfort and found Andreas walking alongside of her.

"You're quiet," she said through the wooden slats.

Andreas raised his head, keeping his eyes forward. "Working out whether this was a good idea."

"You turn inward the closer to Münster we get."

Andreas's lips pressed together. "What I have to do there is hard. I'm fighting the urge to turn around."

"You can't do that," Elsbeth protested. "You've brought me this far; you can't desert me."

It was different now with Andreas, not like that first awkward evening. The sharing of their lives had closed the distance between them. Occasionally, they would touch one another, a hand on the shoulder, or an arm offered for aid getting out of the cart. In the small intimacies of those moments, Elsbeth sensed a bond being formed.

Before she could say much else, a man jumped in between them, pirouetting around, throwing his arms dramatically up to the sky. When they first encountered him a few days previously, Elsbeth thought him a handsome man with a neatly cut beard, full head of hair, and intelligent brown eyes. His silk blouse, purple velvet vest, well-tailored blue knee breeches, and white stockings hinted at a different life than the other pilgrims on this journey had known. He'd introduced himself as Jan of Leiden, but said everyone called him by his last name, Bockelson.

"Would you like to see my impression of Andreas?" Bockelson jested.

Elsbeth laughed and pulled herself up to look over the slats. "Yes, of course, show me."

Bockelson slumped his shoulders and started lumbering slowly along, his hands deep in the pockets of his pants, a dour look on his face. Every couple of steps he would stop, straighten up, and swivel his head alertly as if he were looking for wolves or bears. He kept this up for a couple of minutes before Andreas cupped his hand on Bockelson's shoulder.

"What're you implying?"

"You're much too serious, my friend." Bockelson patted Andreas's hand.

Andreas slipped away and kept walking, a slight smile appearing under his mustache. He looked at Elsbeth, winked, and quickened his pace without a word.

"Andreas," Bockelson called, running after him as Elsbeth sat back on the scratchy wool and contemplated the actor. His performances, laced with stories, impressions, and jokes, kept the others entertained and lightened the ardors of the journey. Still, likeable as he was, Elsbeth couldn't shake the feeling that something was slippery with him. For all his banter and joviality, Bockelson struck her as a man with plenty of secrets.

Since they could not make Münster by nightfall, they stopped to make camp, moving off the road and gathering firewood and food. Later, after a meal of rabbits and mushrooms, they sat and swapped stories of Münster.

"It's the carnivals I remember most," Andreas said as they warmed themselves around the evening fire, bodies pushed together. "So many different masks, and the smell of sausages cooking on open grills, the crowds of university students flowing through the streets, drinking and laughing. It was exciting. I looked forward to it."

"I remember those," said Jost, wiping his mouth on his sleeve, making yet another grease mark. "Crazy days. Men dressin' as women, women dressin' as men, costumes all around, torch processions through town. Those were some parties, but that's Münster—they wrap themselves up in their pleasures like muddy pigs in slop."

Elsbeth watched Jost throw his hands around as he talked. The bouncing of his massive belly and shaking of his thick beard accentuated his sense of drama and deep rumbly voice. She could barely make out his teeth when he smiled, though his brown eyes were always alight with humor. "That sounds harsh," she admonished.

"'Cause you don't know 'em," Jost replied. "They're not stupid people; they're sensible, yet vulgar. They work hard, but most despise learnin', or at least the liberal arts, even though they're proud of the university. They love to glaze windows or work with stone, metal, or wood, practical things, things you can use. Münsterites aren't tricky; they're straightforward, but they don't change easily."

"You can drive off nature with a stick, but it always comes back," Andreas quipped.

"They believe the planets influence 'em . . . the energies of places affect their bodies," Jost said, shaking his head. "Even the believers use astrology. Too much idolatry for me."

"How many of you are from Münster?" Bockelson asked, shifting his body. "My mother was from around there, and I didn't know any of this."

"You didn't mention that before." Andreas tilted his head toward Bockelson.

"I've been gone a year now," Jost interjected. "I grew up there."

"Why'd you leave?" Elsbeth asked.

"Kicked out of my order, the Knights of St. George."

All around the fire, eyebrows shot up, and people exchanged puzzled looks.

"I remember them." Andreas stretched out his legs and rested on his elbows. "Majestic white cloaks and massive embroidered black crosses. We were always jealous of that pleasant spot you possessed on the banks of the Aa. So much land."

"Why aren't you with them?" Bockelson asked.

"Goddamn Protestants converted me," Jost bellowed and began laughing. "Only those poor bastards didn't know how far I'd take it."

"How far *did* you take it?" Bockelson asked, leaning forward, eyes calling for more.

Elsbeth studied the faces of those crowded around the fire. Bockelson kept his gaze on Jost.

"I'm with this lot here, so that ought to tell you somethin'," Jost answered. "Sure, we and the other orders had all the money and lands . . . power to elect the burghers to run the city, collect the taxes. We answered to no one. But, for me, somethin' was missin'."

"I was in awe of the Knights," Andreas said, warming his hands over the fire.

"Me, too, until I heard the preachin' of Bernard Rothmann one day out in the market," Jost replied.

"Rothmann?" Elsbeth asked.

"Most important man in Münster," Jost claimed. "Hearing him is when I put away childish things. I didn't know how far from God I truly was. When the brothers found out I'd gone over to Luther, they tried to have me chained to the Stake of Disgrace at the cathedral. A touch of shamin' would put me right, they figured. A punch or two to their heads and I was out the door. Besides, by that time Münster had become so torn, the papists and Lutherans couldn't do anything 'bout one another. The city council'd gone to the Protestants, but they couldn't take over everything because the Catholics were still strong with the rich."

Elsbeth's mouth turned down. Jost's story unsettled her.

"Tell me more about Rothmann," Bockelson asked, rising to his feet and shaking his legs. "Is he important?"

"He was a blacksmith's son, wasn't he?" Andreas volunteered, looking at Jost. "Sang in the cathedral choir?"

"That songbird sings a different tune these days," Jost said, standing up to go relieve himself. "Now he sings the guilds and commons against the clergy and patricians. The cathedral canons sent him off to Köln, hopin' they could tame him, but he kept goin' straight to Luther and never looked back. By the time he was done trampin' around and came back, he was Protestant through and through. I hear he's gone beyond that now, maybe even turned Anabaptist."

"And he's not in prison or punished?" Bockelson asked.

"No. Every time the council tries to throw him out of the city, the guilds shout 'gospel' and 'freedom' and bring him back in another gate," Jost yelled over his shoulder as he stood against a large bush. "Makes exile hard because the people love him, especially the women."

Bockelson glanced at Andreas. "Was Münster always this interesting?"

Andreas shrugged.

"What do you think?" Elsbeth asked as she took a stick to stir the embers of the fire.

"About what?" Andreas answered.

"These tales."

"It's been a long time since I was there, but it sounds as if things are fraught." Andreas sat up and grabbed his knees.

"I suppose it depends on who's holdin' the torch," Jost hollered, adjusting his trousers and returning to his seat. "Though I hear it's safe for our people."

"Is that why you return?" Elsbeth asked Jost. "To be safe?"

"Münster *is* safe for Protestants, the way I hear it," Jost repeated. "The merchant Knipperdollin' sees to it."

"Knipperdolling? Dear God, now I'm totally lost," Elsbeth sighed.

"He's one of the most powerful men in the city," Jost replied. "Whoever he sides with has the advantage in who runs things."

"I'm thirsty," Elsbeth exhaled. She stood and stretched her body. "Can I have some of your wine?" she asked Tiemann, the merchant.

"'Course," he said, getting up to get her a cup. Elsbeth caught Andreas's eye and walked over to the cask of wine on the cart. While the merchant poured her cup, Andreas came to her side.

"These stories unsettle me." The memory of her village was never far enough away.

He took a sip of her cup and handed it back. "You'll be fine; we'll be fine."

Elsbeth's eyes focused on the group by the fire. "I hope you're right," she whispered, "because Münster sounds unstable." Finishing her drink, she returned with Andreas to the others as Bockelson and Jost talked.

"Tell me more about this Knipperdolling," Bockelson asked, motioning for more with his arms. "I'll perform if you tell me more." With that Bockelson jumped up, started singing a ditty, and danced around the fire.

"Some years back he called the Prince-Bishop of Westphalia a spindle-turner because he was making so much money on the looms of Nitzing Convent in the city," Jost said. "Knipperdollin' walked around town wearin' a hat on his head with spindles to mock the Prince-Bishop, who has no sense of humor."

"That's a dangerous game of bait the bear," Andreas said.

"It helped land Knipperdollin' in the Prince-Bishop's cell. Nabbed him when he was on a business trip to the Low Countries still wearing that insolent hat. He came out several months later with a limp. Somethin' about him having to spend a few months in an iron boot, if I remember correctly. Knipperdollin' started workin' with the guilds then, getting them more rights and power. In return, they gave him enough votes to sit on the council."

"Is he still on council?" Bockelson queried.

"You seem overly concerned about Knipperdollin," Jost said, suspicion lacing his voice. "What're you after?"

"You spin a tale; I'm only curious to see the garment your threads weave."

"You amuse me, man, but best be careful about the questions when you get in the city." Jost grunted and crossed his arms.

"Why *are* you so interested in all this?" Elsbeth asked, staring at Bockelson, who grabbed a few apples and started juggling them, feet shifting from side to side.

All eyes focused on him. "I come from here, don't I? At least my mother does. Curious about my beginnings."

"An interesting day tomorrow." Andreas stood up. "I need to rest, so good night to you all."

Elsbeth glanced at Andreas and noticed his right eye had partially closed, an expression she knew from experience echoed her own inner tension. She followed him away from the campfire.

"What're you thinking?" Elsbeth asked when they were out of earshot.

"About?"

"All of this. Bockelson, these people. What goes on in that city? You aren't keeping anything from me, are you?"

"I've told you all I know, Elsbeth," Andreas insisted. "I confess, things are different, but how so, I won't know until tomorrow."

Eagerness and anxiety struggled inside Elsbeth, making her stomach hurt. She had no idea what to expect, but something was happening in Münster that was drawing others to it. She wanted inside those gates to see for herself what this world she'd heard so much about looked like. Thinking about tomorrow and what awaited her, Elsbeth realized that her curiosity was stronger than her fear.

4

Münster, September 24, 1533

"Elsbeth! Up there, on the horizon." Andreas pointed as they crested a small rise.

She rose unsteadily to her feet, holding onto the side railings of the cart. In the distance, resting on the open rolling fields, she saw a patchwork of grains and grasses. The morning sun captured the rust and yellow hues of the rooflines of Münster. It appeared to her as a ship resting on a green and brown lake. First came the massive stone fortress that enveloped the city in a protective embrace. Behind the looming grey walls, numerous church spires rose up with soaring towers, dominating the skyline. Beneath those spires were the terra-cotta roofs of thousands of homes. The city projected power and wealth.

"Dear God! Andreas, it's magnificent. Why did you leave this?" Elsbeth said.

"Now that I see it again, I'm not sure."

"It looks impregnable," Bockelson added as he came up to join them. "I've heard stories about those walls, but seeing them in the flesh . . . "

"Münster's a center for trade," Andreas said. "They need to protect their wealth."

"What was it you told me a few days ago?" Elsbeth craned her neck to see ahead. "Something about cows?"

"Thin Danish cows come to Münster so they can fatten up for market."

"Ah, yes."

Elsbeth drank in the immense fields with their spinning windmills and wood houses. Pastures populated by cows, pigpens, and horses spread out in a fecund ring around the city. Terraces and orchards dotted the landscape, occasionally revealing a small stone church resting outside the walls. The scents of rosemary, lavender, and cut wheat filled her nose.

Drawing closer to the gate entrance, her view of the city disappeared behind the height of the walls. The Aa river, flowing from the southwest, channeled into a moat around the outer wall. Everyone in the party had grown quiet, their heads swiveling to take it all in. Elsbeth looked up. The sun glistened off the many cannon barrels jutting out from the prom-enade walls. They passed into a tunnel about twenty feet long that ran under the outer tower, emerging from the darkness to see a ditch and rampart with sharpened wooden logs and then another moat between the outer and inner walls. They passed over this moat and went through another guard tower, emerging out of the final gate into the city where guards were stopping all who entered. She slipped out of the cart and took a place close to Andreas.

"What's your business in Münster?" The guard's brusque voice ad-dressed the merchant Tiemann.

"I've come to sell my goods." Tiemann motioned to his cart. "These others have been traveling with me to protect me from thieves."

The guard studied the small company and pointed to Andreas. "What're you here for?"

"I was born here; I'm returning home."

"Wouldn't I know you if you lived here?" the guard challenged.

Andreas's face tightened. "I've been away a long time."

"And your religion?"

"What business is that of yours?" Andreas drew up his shoulders.

"I only warn those of you who might be Catholics." The guard opened his hands and bent his head down slightly. "They fare poorly in Münster these days."

"Why?" Andreas asked. "Münster has many Catholics."

"Not as many as we used to," the guard replied.

Andreas stepped closer to the guard. "How so?" Elsbeth followed, eager to hear the answer.

The guard waved the merchant and his wagon through as Andreas and Elsbeth remained. The guard dropped his voice as the others walked past. "Priests are mocked; people can't go to the cathedral, even on holy days. Baptisms of babies are prevented. Fights on the streets. Things are upside down."

"The Protestants do this?" Andreas asked.

"The worst don't call themselves by that name anymore." The guard chewed on the inside of his cheek as he watched another cart struggle toward the gate. "Too many factions . . . too much trouble . . . just thought you should be warned. Now move along." The guard motioned to the next group, his hand gripping the weapon at his side. Andreas and Elsbeth joined their companions.

They walked in silence toward the city center, the steel rims of the cart clacking out rhythmically on the grey stone streets, only pausing when Andreas froze in front of a pole where public announcements were hung. Elsbeth watched as Andreas's brow furrowed reading one of the pamphlets. He ripped it off the pole and stuck it into his tunic pocket.

Elsbeth ruminated on the guard's words. "Andreas? Is everything all right?"

"Don't know."

"News?" Bockelson asked, coming to their side.

"Unwelcome news." Andreas's pace quickened.

Bumping over the grey stones, the cart continued, the crowds growing denser as they approached the city center. Bodies flowed out from the side streets, joining them on the main road leading to market. One wrinkled old man wearing a cap with a jaunty feather came so close to the cart, Elsbeth could see the sores on his face. He leered at her, revealing brown teeth and empty gaps as he called out for money. The merchant brushed him away with a few harsh curses.

Entering the central market, they passed an ornate building with a façade of gables and steeples. Elsbeth studied the intricate stonework decorations on the ascending ledges. Two rows of arched windows drew her eyes upward to a sculpture in the middle. It stood on a crest, flanked by two other crests.

"City Hall. The council meets there," Andreas said, his eyes following Elsbeth's.

"It looks almost like a church."

"They intend it that way," Andreas replied. "Church and empire locked in one ordained order."

The marble and stone-fronted rowhouses lining the marketplace reminded her of high white and yellow riverbanks between which flowed a grey stream of stone. At the bottom of these homes, massive arcades hovered over the walkways, held up by arches carved with ornate decorations. Offering protection from rain and sun, the arcades covered the goods that tumbled out from underneath them into the marketplace.

"This is my stop," Tiemann announced, halting at the street leading down from City Hall to St. Paul's Cathedral. "Amulets and charms can protect you from the devil, but nothing can keep you from getting robbed, so mind the pickpockets. They love market days." With a wave, he was off to his business.

Bockelson eyed the market. He turned to Jost. "Where did you say Knipperdolling's house was?"

Jost pointed to one of the most ornate homes, up by the massive church at the opposite end of the market. "There, with the fancy stonework."

With barely a farewell, Bockelson slipped off, disappearing into the crowd.

"There you 'ave it," Jost said. "That one seems to have a nose for power."

"You were the one who told him Knipperdolling was a powerful man. Perhaps Bockelson has some introductions to make," Andreas said.

"This is where I've to part as well. My destination is up by Jew's Gate." Jost adjusted his sack and put out his hand to Andreas. "Will I see you again?"

"I'm not sure how long we'll be here," Andreas said. "We have some business, and I need to see an old friend, but after that I have no plans. I hope to be at the Augustinian house for a few days anyway."

"With the monks?" Jost asked. "They won't take married couples."

"Actually, we're not married," Elsbeth said. "We just tell others we are because it saves us questions. I'm destined for the convent."

Jost dropped his jaw, his mouth forming a huge dark ring of beard and teeth. "Coulda' fooled me." He laughed, his belly jiggling.

Elsbeth reached up and gave him a peck on the cheek. "Take care, Jost. Good life."

Jost smiled and put his hands on Andreas and Elsbeth's shoulders. "Then it's farewell for now. You two are slippery." He winked and waved as he ambled toward Jew's Gate.

Andreas and Elsbeth exchanged glances, and Andreas motioned toward the church at the end of the market as they set off in that direction. Elsbeth regarded the sumptuous fabrics arranged on tables in massive mounds of purple, red, yellow, and blue and imagined herself in a beautiful purple silk dress. Even though she had bathed and washed her clothes the day before, she feared she looked like a beggar.

Lace from Flanders, broadcloth from England, and tablecloths with delicate stitch work from Bohemia decorated the tables. From Frisia, samples of needlework that were more art than mere household goods rested delicately on boards straddling beer kegs. Exquisite cut glasses from France and china from Vienna sat on top of rough wooden shipping crates.

"Look at all this," Elsbeth said as they passed by open burlap bags of spices. She recognized the seductive smell of cinnamon, the earthiness of rosemary and fennel seeds. There was saffron and thyme, coriander and cumin. "That ginger dust is so . . . golden."

"Look closer," Andreas warned. "They added brick dust to make it heavier. You can spot it if you know what you are looking for. Some even keep their spices in damp vaults to increase the weight; others put sawdust in their food to get more money."

Elsbeth shot Andreas a skeptical look, but he kept walking toward the crowd at the end of the market. Bags of sugar, salt, and peppercorns lined the streets along the arcade. Casks of beer and wine sat among piles of leather, copper, metal foil, and tools. The spools and wedges of cheeses, pungent in the morning air, seemed endless. The closer they drew to the crowd standing in the shadows of St. Lambert's, however, the more nauseating the smells became. Butchered pig, beef, and chicken combined with odors from the adjacent fish market to create a stench that spoiled the pleasant feel of a warm breeze. A constant hum filled Elsbeth's ears from the yelling, laughing, bargaining, and haggling surrounding her. Groups of women stood gossiping at their stalls. Down a side street leading away from the fish market, a gaggle of people watched a man with small tongs pulling out the tooth of an old man sitting in a wooden chair.

"Tooth pullers, cutpurses, pickpockets, and quacks—market day really brings them out," Andreas muttered, continuing his path toward the church.

The crowds grew louder in that direction. People were shouting at a man standing in a wooden pulpit. Elsbeth had never seen anyone preaching outside before. *What a strange world this is.* Coming closer to the pulpit, the crowds pressed together so tightly she had a hard time getting through. Caught in a clump of people, strange hands jostling her, she lost sight of Andreas. As they pushed her harder, Elsbeth was struggling to breathe when Andreas's hand reached through the gaggle and pulled her out to his side. He maneuvered them just below the preacher who was bobbing up and down, yelling at the crowd.

"The devil's set up shop among us, and we can't see it! Is it hard to believe? The way we're made to live? But, beware, he who sups with Satan best have a long spoon!"

"Who is that man?" Elsbeth asked.

"Maybe one of those prophets Jost mentioned?" Andreas appeared befuddled.

The difference between the laughing crowds at the stalls and the fervor of this mob held in rapt attention by the man in the pulpit concerned Elsbeth. The louder they clapped their hands, the more excited the preacher grew. His hair, red and wiry, matched his fiery rhetoric. A slim tufted beard framed the thin face poking out of a long, plain black robe with a white ruffled collar. The edges of his mustache flipped up when he spoke, and Elsbeth sensed the flash of desire in his dark brown eyes. She wondered what it was this man craved so much that even she could see it.

"Those who bleed us will answer to the God who slew Ananias and Sapphira for withholding their goods. How much do they think they can suck from us? Did not the Virgin herself proclaim God would pull down the rich and mighty and lift up the poor and lowly? Did Mary not say God would fill the hungry with good things and send the rich empty away? Why should the rich tell us where we can fish, hunt, and draw water while they fill their bellies and take their ease? Mary called the wrath of God down on those who pressed on the helpless! God does not desire us to live in a world where the powerful take all our lands and goods after we die!"

Andreas stilled, his eyes riveted on the preacher, brows knitted in concentration.

"Andreas?" Elsbeth called to him. His head didn't move an inch. "What're we doing here?"

"Huh?" Andreas slightly shook his head, finally turning toward Elsbeth. "What?"

"Why are we here?" Elsbeth shouted. "I want to go."

"I just . . . uh . . . wanted to see what this was about. I think that's Bernard Rothmann."

As her eyes swept through the congregation, Elsbeth saw rough-looking men on the edges of the crowd holding axes, halberds, staffs, even swords. These were not peasant farmers with tools. Her breathing came faster, in quick bursts. Crowds could be propelled to violence with a word. The preacher's voice shifted up a register.

"We must be willing to offend others. Christ commands us to obey him, not man. Did he not say he came with a sword to divide a man from his family, a father from his son, mother from daughter, ruler from the ruled? We can't shrink back from the demands of our Lord!" The preacher lifted his arms, spurring the crowds to moans and cries that bounced off the outside walls of St. Lambert's Cathedral and into the marketplace. A group of women standing right below Rothmann seemed especially eager to catch his attention, each one outdoing the other in passionate expressions of closed eyes and open, inviting mouths.

"Rothmann! Rothmann! Rothmann!" they chanted, growing louder with each proclamation of his name.

"Now is the day of the Lord! Now is the season of our freedom! We worship God in freedom and truth!" the preacher shouted. He descended from his pulpit to a table at the foot of the stairs. Taking a large loaf of bread, he held it up and yelled, "This, this is the body of Christ given for you! Not with some incantations of black magic like the Mass, whose words you can't understand! This is true food for the soul!"

The crowd surged toward him, forming a tight band around the table. Taking a flask of wine, he poured it over the bread, soaking it, and held it over his head, purplish-red drops stippling his robe. "And this," he roared, "is the blood of Christ, shed for you, not withheld, but given that you may have life!"

As if by one voice, a guttural shouting reverberated throughout the square, echoing down the street as heads at the lower market turned to see what was causing so much noise.

Andreas clasped his hands behind his head. "Andreas?" Elsbeth asked. Was she imagining that the color drained from his face? "Are you well?"

This was an unwelcome sight—passionate crowds braying out to the sky, responding to the innovation of bread *and* wine. Centuries of sacred and ancient traditions dissolved in a moment. All those grasping at the wine-stained bread were clutching after a world devoid of priests who dribbled out mysteries one wafer at a time. This was bread that would fill the stomach and feed the soul for revolution.

"Let's go." Andreas pulled Elsbeth back to the market, but Elsbeth heard a voice over the din of the crowd.

"Andreas? Andreas Wagner?"

Andreas stopped dead, searching to locate the voice that called him. His face tightened as he scanned the crowd.

"Is it you?" Even in the tumult the voice arose, soft, inviting. Elsbeth could barely hear it, but the effect on Andreas unnerved her. He stopped and stood rooted to the spot like a statue.

"Ul . . . Ulrich?" Andreas finally found the source.

"It is you! I thought I would never see you again." The stranger now stood between Elsbeth and Andreas. With broad shoulders and long black hair, he was a bit taller than Andreas. He possessed a strong face, though Elsbeth could see where it would grow thick with age. His firm chin was marked by a triangle of hair just below his bottom lip. "I'd heard you were dead, but praise God, you're here in the flesh."

"Ulrich, I . . . how?" Andreas fumbled out a reply. "You're back?"

"It's a miracle, no doubt about it." Ulrich smiled and turned his attention to Elsbeth. "And is this your wife?" Ulrich grabbed Elsbeth's hand and raised it to his mouth, brushing it with a light kiss. "I'm Ulrich, Ulrich Schlatter."

"I'm a friend," Elsbeth said, fighting her attraction to the man.

"Only a friend? That news brightens my day, indeed."

"There are clouds," Elsbeth rejoined. "I'm destined for the convent."

Ulrich laughed quickly, then stopped. "Oh, you're serious? No matter, the doors of convents are swinging both ways these days. I'm sure we'll see one another again."

Andreas remained statuesque, mouth opened, eyes widened.

"Andreas"—Ulrich grabbed his shoulders—"wasn't that a wonderful sermon? Do you remember when we used to talk about how no one took the Gospel seriously? Now look what's become of us. People cheer the free Word."

"Why the axes and picks at worship, then?" Andreas found his voice. "What place do those have here?"

"Oh, those," Ulrich waved his hand. "We must protect ourselves. The papists don't want us here, and Lutherans fear Rothmann because the people are with him. We've been attacked. We must defend ourselves; wouldn't you agree?"

"No, I wouldn't," Andreas shouted above the cacophony.

"Trust me." Ulrich put his arm around Andreas. "We only protect ourselves from those who want to silence us."

"Who wants to silence you?" Elsbeth asked.

"Those who hamper the free course of the Word." Ulrich shifted his attention to Elsbeth. "Still, God's Word prevails while we drink good Münster beer." He laughed and clamped his hand on Andreas's shoulder.

"And who possesses this Word?" Elsbeth had come to distrust those who claimed to know what God wanted.

"Those who truly obey God keep the Word."

Elsbeth studied the happiness stamped on Ulrich's face. The focus in his bright green eyes as he examined her caused something inside her to shift between nervousness and excitement, like the early moments of a welcomed seduction.

"We have to go," Andreas said, breaking the gaze Ulrich and Elsbeth held.

"Do you have a place to stay?" Ulrich asked. "You can stay with me if you like. I've many friends who can house you. We can catch up, Andreas, share stories."

"We have other plans." Andreas put his hand on Elsbeth's shoulder and steered her quickly away as the crowd began a hymn.

"You didn't have to be so abrupt." Elsbeth struggled to keep up with Andreas. "He seemed pleasant enough."

"Yes, he can be very charming."

"You sound annoyed."

"Not annoyed, just surprised," Andreas said. "I didn't expect to see him here."

"Who is he to you?" She stopped, pulling Andreas to a halt.

Andreas drew his lips into his mouth before he spoke. "A voice that called me years ago, and I made the mistake of answering."

Elsbeth stood, expectant, waiting on Andreas.

"Ulrich came to the order after his parents died of the English Sweats. They found him by their bedside, curled up in a ball," Andreas said in a rush. "They brought him to the monastery because the prior looked after orphans. We took him in, treated him as one of us, but Ulrich never liked it there. When he was older, he ran afoul of the council and left."

"You're leaving gaps," Elsbeth protested. "How'd he turn from orphan to exile?"

"Maybe later, Elsbeth. Now we must get to the convent." Andreas strode away from her.

Elsbeth followed him, reaching for his shoulder. "Are you upset with me?"

"No, I'm sorry. I just . . . wasn't prepared for this." Andreas slowed.

They walked in silence back through the market to City Hall and then took a right turn down the street to St. Paul's Cathedral. Pale yellow walls topped with twin green copper spires towered over Cathedral Hill.

On the southern side of the cathedral lay a small chapter house, treasury, library, and gardens behind it. A smaller church, St. Margaret's, flanked it, both buildings surrounded by a vast expanse of stone and field. Majestic houses surrounded Cathedral Square.

"So many churches," Elsbeth muttered to herself. She tried to capture every detail of the cathedral as they walked past, but a growing anxiety picked at her. Her fear of being locked away, of not seeing Andreas again, of the unknown, confronted her. The future loomed like a huge beast threatening to devour her. Walking down the slight incline to a stone bridge spanning the Aa river, Elsbeth's legs grew heavy, resistant to taking another step.

"The convent's in back of Überwasser Church," Andreas said, leading Elsbeth by the hand. She gripped his hand, seeking reassurance.

"Are you sure this is going to be agreeable?" Elsbeth heard the tremor in her voice.

"Not as sure as I was," Andreas confessed. Arriving at the door, he tugged at the clapper. Nothing. He pulled it again. An iron bar slid open on the other side of the door, revealing a pair of pale blue eyes.

"What's your business here?"

"Good day, Abbess von Merveldt, may we have a word?" Andreas said.

"Who're you?"

"Andreas Wagner, I used to live with the Augustinians a while back."

"You don't look like him."

"I've changed since you caught me stealing food from the market." Andreas grinned.

The iron bar slid back in place, leaving Andreas and Elsbeth exchanging puzzled looks. Finally, the bolt was unlatched, and the door swung open.

"Wagner, you've changed." The abbess stood aside to let them pass into the courtyard, closed the door, and asked, "What brings you here?"

Dressed in her habit, her face framed by black cloth, the abbess kept her eyes on Elsbeth. Unnerved, Elsbeth thought Abbess von Merveldt must have been an intimidating presence in the most benign of situations. She would have been very beautiful when she was young. Her face was lean with high cheekbones and full lips and striking blue eyes. Her nose, bigger than most, conveyed strength. Elsbeth thought her elegant in her black robe and white apron.

"Abbess von Merveldt, this is a refugee from the Swiss Territories, Elsbeth Joris." Andreas broke the silence.

"Refugee, eh?" the abbess grunted, looking her up and down. "What're you running from, girl?"

Elsbeth's eyebrows rose when the abbess spoke in Elsbeth's dialect. She tried to catch Andreas's eye, but he stared at the abbess.

"A priest who wanted to kill me because I wouldn't let him hump me." Elsbeth tilted up her chin and squared her shoulders.

The abbess furrowed her brows. "A priest, eh? I see." She stroked her chin. "Well, it's not like you'd be the first."

Elsbeth rubbed her hands together and rocked slightly on her heels. She was suddenly so itchy in her skin, she wanted to leap out of herself. She smiled awkwardly, hoping to connect with the woman, or at least disarm her.

Abbess von Merveldt addressed Andreas, holding Elsbeth's gaze. "What do you want from me, Wagner?"

"Elsbeth needs a place to stay. I remembered you as a friend of hospitality."

"It's a dangerous thing to take in strangers these days. One never knows if you accept friend or foe," the abbess replied, her voice probing.

"Andreas . . . perhaps we shouldn't trouble the abbess." Elsbeth tugged on Andreas's sleeve.

"She's not yet given us an answer." Andreas smiled. "You know me, Ida; I'm no foe."

Ida examined them, eyes moving back and forth. She sighed. "This is still a place of refuge, no matter the madness that takes place outside. You're welcome to stay, Miss Joris, though you'll have to work for your food and shelter."

"I'm used to work," Elsbeth said.

"You're excused, Wagner," Ida von Merveldt ordered. "Miss Joris and I have things to attend to."

The abbess pushed Andreas toward the courtyard door as Elsbeth stood frozen, not sure how to say goodbye. When he turned to look at her one last time, all the moments of the past weeks washed over her. The stories they swapped, the confidences, sharing impressions of their companions—even the sight of Andreas's body when he washed; these images flooded her mind as she thought about what had happened to her since Andreas pulled her into the river. She had come to look forward to his company every day. They had shared this adventure together, and now she had no idea if she would ever see him again. He was being torn away from her like everything else in her life, and she was not prepared. Her hands wiped tears from her cheeks.

"Andreas . . . " She wanted nothing more than to run and hold him; he was the only familiar thing left to her. As much as she desired to touch him, however, she stood rooted.

"You'll be safe here, Elsbeth." Andreas went out the gate.

"But I—" Elsbeth called out as the door closed, leaving her alone with Ida.

Abandoned. Again.

5

Münster

BERNARD KNIPPERDOLLING LOOKED OUT his window at the crowds across the square gathered by St. Lambert's. Rothmann was in full form, arms and rhetoric flying. Perhaps he should step outside and walk over to listen; Rothmann was always good entertainment, especially when his congregation was enthused. Incendiary sermons were a small spark, but Knipperdolling knew that great fires had to start somewhere.

Stroking his beard and fiddling with the massive gold chain that rested against his ample chest, Knipperdolling contemplated his day. They showered him with praise for his virility and thick body at the brothels and bathhouses; perhaps a visit later in the afternoon? Silk shoes rocked as he debated whether to have something to eat or go watch Rothmann. The knock on his door interrupted him.

"Clara!" Knipperdolling called his daughter. No answer. More knocking. "Clara?" Evidently, she was out of hearing. He crossed his spacious living room and opened the door. "Yes?" Knipperdolling was doubly annoyed when he saw the straggly stranger in front of him. The man's clothes were presentable enough, green waist jacket over a cream-colored shirt with plain pants, but his beard was unkempt, and his hair only slightly brushed. "I've no money, go away."

"I'm not here because I need anything, my lord," the man said. "I'm here with a proposal, and I heard you might be the one to talk to."

"Proposal? About what?" Knipperdolling scoffed. "What could you possibly have that I would want?"

"Perhaps you could let me in? It's noisy out here." He pointed to the large crowd across the street.

Knipperdolling paused, sizing up the man in front of him. He wasn't dressed like a pauper, exactly, but the plain clothes didn't speak of wealth, and his eyes were hard to see under the brim of his floppy black hat. He twisted his face to the right, working out how to respond.

"If you just hear me out, I believe we have some common interests," the man said. "If you're unhappy, I'll leave. It'll only take a few minutes."

Knipperdolling sighed and stepped aside to let him into his hall. "Stay here and tell me what you want."

"I've heard you and the other true believers in this city may need some help to thwart the enemies of Christ." He took off his cap. "My name's Jan Bockelson, from Haarlem. I own the Inn of Two Herrings there. I've traveled here because my community has heard this is a free city for believers and I have news that might interest you."

Goddamn innkeeper. Might've known. Knipperdolling grew tense and started to push him out the door, but something about the man's eyes made him stop. "What do you know of my interests?"

"I hear you want a free city, liberated from the oppression of the Prince-Bishop." Bockelson studied his nails.

"And how would you be able to help us achieve that?" Knipperdolling asked, his hand reaching for the door. The man presumed too much.

"Offer me some refreshment and I can tell you." Bockelson smiled.

Knipperdolling stepped to his door and looked out at Rothmann, who was holding a loaf of wine-soaked bread above his head, the boisterous crowds roaring at his every word. What need had he of this odd innkeeper? Perhaps he should drag Bockelson over to St. Lambert's and show him that he didn't need anybody's help getting what he wanted. His man Rothmann could stir a mob to action. Knipperdolling shifted his head back toward Bockelson.

Bockelson leaned in closer to Knipperdolling. "If you could get what you wanted," he whispered, "you'd already have it."

Knipperdolling stopped. His eyes went over Bockelson top to bottom. Could he read minds? Maybe God had sent him? Caught between curiosity and intrigue, Knipperdolling closed the door to his house and pointed to his living room. What would it hurt? It was only a few minutes, and what if Bockelson had something to offer? The council was not pliable enough to Knipperdolling's desires. He wasn't mayor yet. Even in their weakened state, the papists still held strength in the city. He needed more people on his side. It wouldn't hurt anything to at least give the man a hearing. With one last look at Rothmann, he waved Bockelson inside his living room and closed the door.

"Clara!" Knipperdolling called to his daughter.

"Yes, Papa." Clara Knipperdolling appeared in a doorway.

"Where've you been? Didn't you hear me call you earlier?"

"No, Papa, I was out back." Clara gave only the slightest bow of the head to her father.

"We have company." Knipperdolling motioned toward Bockelson. "And he is in need of some refreshment."

Clara looked at Bockelson, starting with his face, and worked her way down. She smiled shyly, gave a quick curtsy, and went off to fetch food.

Knipperdolling motioned Bockelson to a purple velvet-covered chair in front of the fireplace and plopped down in the matching chair opposite his guest. The room was paneled in wood, with ornate marble arches and a massive fireplace. Huge windows, from floor to ceiling, looked out on the market, allowing a clear view of St. Lambert's and the crowds gathered there.

"How is it, Jan Bockelson, that you presume to understand me or what I want in the first place?" Knipperdolling asked.

"There are stories abroad of the wonderful things God is doing here. I've talked to people who sympathize with Münster's desire to see the Word of God prevail." Bockelson brushed some dust from his pants.

"Hmm," Knipperdolling murmured. "And what can you do for us to help us prevail over our foes?"

"What would you say if I told you I could bring hundreds, no, thousands of people to your city?"

"I would say they already flock here from all over the empire, knowing we offer them sanctuary from their persecutors."

"Yes, but I can bring you a prophet from the Netherlands, Jan Matthys; he sent me here. His followers hang on his every word, and they're bound to obey him and those he supports. We would favor you if you welcomed us here."

Clara brought a tray with fruit, bread, cheese, and wine and placed it on the table between them. Knipperdolling noticed Bockelson taking in his daughter's body. When she handed Bockelson a goblet of wine, he placed his hand on her arm. She coyly smiled. She was a plain woman, but a man could surely find comfort in the folds of her flesh. She possessed compliant blue eyes and luxurious brown hair, but even with these attributes, she had no current prospects for marriage, even with the potential of a sizable dowry. Knipperdolling thought perhaps it would be a good idea to get to know this visitor more.

"Tell me again about your master . . . Matthys?"

"He burns"—Bockelson put his hand to his chest and burped—"with a fever for God. He was a follower of Melchoir Hoffman, but he believes that Brother Hoffman's lost his way. Matthys has suffered for his faith. The magistrates in Haarlem put him to the tongue screw and awful beatings the last time they arrested him. His perseverance gives him trust among our people. I think he can help you here."

"I doubt that; we're doing well enough. We grow stronger on the council every day." Knipperdolling reached for a bunch of grapes and settled back in his chair. "It may take a bit more effort, but the fruit is almost ready to drop."

"Be that as it may, what happens when you have to face the Prince-Bishop? Will you have enough strength to defend yourselves? You've resisted him so far, but the time is coming when you won't be able to deflect him." Bockelson hunched over the table, closer to Knipperdolling. "And remember, I promised thousands."

"How do I know they would even fall in line once they arrived?" Despite his apprehension, Bernard Knipperdolling saw a path open to him that had been closed, a way to gain his desires. He glanced at Clara knitting in the corner. Maybe he should ask Bockelson to stay the night. She could see to his needs. Hospitality is a virtue.

"If you allow us to freely worship, we'll gladly support whoever gives us our freedom," Bockelson promised.

Knipperdolling observed him looking at Clara over his cup as he took a sip of wine. "I need some time to consider this, to talk it over with my companions, but if what you tell me is the truth, we may have much to share in the future." Knipperdolling's eyes flickered to his daughter.

Bockelson followed Knipperdolling's prompting glance, smiled, and turned back to his host. "Well, perhaps this journey is becoming everything I hoped it would be."

Knipperdolling motioned Clara to refill Bockelson's goblet. He reached over and put his hand on Bockelson's arm. "Then you must stay with me while you're in the city. Now, tell me more about your friend, Matthys."

6

Evening

LATE AFTERNOON SHADOWS CLIMBED the walls of St. Paul's as Andreas made his way across town, struggling with the day's revelations. He had been fifteen when Ulrich, a couple of years older, showed up. Things among the monastery boys were never quite the same afterwards. Bickering broke out constantly, and strife became part of the air they breathed. Ulrich kept posing questions that became like worms in Andreas's mind, breaking up the soil where firmly planted ideas and beliefs were no longer able to grow. He found himself questioning all the things he had been taught. Ulrich always posed the questions as if he was searching for answers: If God was so good, why did the innocent suffer? If God was so loving, why did people go to hell? Did Jesus really bleed in their mouths if they bit the wafer? On and on the questions came, relentless, until one day Andreas realized they had infected him with doubt.

The last time he had seen Ulrich Schlatter was eight years ago as Ulrich was being dragged to St. Mary's Gate, screaming curses on everyone who had a hand in his exile. Andreas thought Ulrich capable of anything that day. The wild, fierce look of a wounded animal on Ulrich's face unnerved him. Today, in the market, he seemed placid, almost serene. This worried Andreas even more than his horrific fury years ago.

Andreas stopped at St. Paul's and slipped through the slightly opened door of the cathedral's Paradise Porch. St. Peter, his blank eyes and gaping, agonized mouth, stood guard at the nave's entrance, as Mary and the Apostles peered down at him. Marble forms of Münster's history surrounded him, a gauntlet of austere and judgmental statues, protecting the entrance into paradise, representing life as people desired it: solid, secure, and, like God, never changing.

Walking down the right side of the nave toward the ambulatory, Andreas headed for the astronomical clock. He used to delight in the striking of the hours and the three wise men circling across the clock face, quickly disappearing from view. The whirl and clicks of hands and bells, planets and stars changing their course with each new hour, always fascinated him.

Red, gold, and blue tints of stained glass, muted in the late afternoon light, told the tales Andreas heard growing up: Jesus and the disciples, Jesus and the devil, the shepherd feeding his sheep, Mary feeding Jesus, and always, Christ suffering on the cross. These images had shaped his life, creating an interior world long evaporated by time and experience.

Passing around the ambulatory to the other side, Andreas recalled a church in Brussels he once visited. From the carved pulpit, a white marble skeleton lurched out from the wood, reaching toward the congregation. Death itself would grab anyone in a moment. Fear-soaked piety had long ago driven Andreas from God, but the memory of that specter made him shudder. He had entered the cathedral hopeful of feeling something, anything, but he felt . . . nothing.

Leaving, he skirted the fringe of the market as the merchants were packing up. He walked down to the ring road that ran along the inner wall, passed by Nitzing Convent, and continued until he arrived at the reception gate of the Augustinians. He recalled his first time at this gate. His mother held his hand that day, tears filling her eyes. His father constantly picked at his brown woolen hat while they waited for the prior. It seemed forever before Father Peter walked up and greeted them. Andreas stood behind his mother, clutching her simple grey linen dress. Peter looked directly at him. "What gift has God brought us today?" He smiled as he asked the question, but Andreas wondered why, if he were a gift, didn't his parents want him? Father Peter wanted him. Peter raised him, taught him, cared for him. Peter was the only person he could trust, but Andreas had deserted him. What was he going to do if Peter rejected him? His trembling hand rang the bell to announce his presence.

"Who is it?"

The voice was suspicious, not welcoming. "Andreas Wagner, a former brother. I was hoping to speak with your prior."

Locks and bolts sounded until, at last, the door swung open. Andreas stood back from the gaunt man, his body barely able to carry the robes of the order. Stubble and exhausted eyes framed his face.

"Everyone's in Vespers. You say you're a former brother? What color are the prior's eyes?"

"Hazel."

"His last name?"

"Droste. Why this questioning?"

"How long ago were you here?"

Andreas grew exasperated the longer the questioning continued. "Over eight years now. May I come in?"

The monk popped his head out of the doorway and looked nervously up and down the street. Pulling Andreas into the courtyard, he said, "You're welcome to wait until the prior can see you." The man latched the door behind him.

"Is all well here?" Andreas said.

"You can't be too sure of what's on the other side of the doors these days." The man motioned Andreas to follow him into the refectory. They entered the large reception hall and turned left toward the monks' quarters and refectory. Andreas peered down the hall toward the chapel, thinking he might catch a glimpse of Peter, but the brothers were all inside. Once in the refectory, the man pointed to a bench for Andreas to sit on before disappearing into the kitchen. In a few moments he returned with a cup of ale and a small piece of salt bread.

"I'll let Father know he has a guest."

Sipping his ale, Andreas watched the indigo-blue shades of twilight swallow up the room. Flickering candles projected dancing shadows on the floor. The refectory still had the musty smell that late afternoon thunderstorms leave in wood and stone, triggering a flood of nostalgia. His life had been peaceful here, governed by the rhythms of Divine Office, school, and daily work. Why hadn't he confided his doubts to Father Peter? Maybe there were answers to his questions, if only he had asked. Perhaps he was too hasty, too impulsive to find his own path. Had his desertion been worth it? He took a long drink.

Reaching into his pocket, Andreas took out the pamphlet he'd torn down that morning and opened it. The crude drawing made him queasy—a priest on his knees kissing the devil's arse as he defecated on the man's face. On the surface it seemed harmless enough, a bit of fun, poking holes in the pretensions of the powerful—but these images were often the first step on the road to a hatred that bathed the world in blood.

"Andreas? Is it really you?"

"Yes, Father." Andreas, startled by the man who had slipped up behind him, rose to face Father Peter. His light hazel eyes, perpetually smiling, seemed wearier than Andreas remembered. "Though according to Abbess von Merveldt, I'm not as easily recognizable as I used to be."

Peter enveloped him in a warm embrace. "It's good to see you, my friend. Welcome home."

"So, the prodigal son is forgiven?" Andreas whispered, comforted by Peter's deep baritone.

"There's nothing to forgive, Andreas. God is always at home; it is we who have gone for a walk."

Andreas fought back tears as Peter held him like a long-lost family member, the distance of years and betrayal dissolving in an instant. Finally releasing him, Peter stepped back. He was much the way Andreas recalled—tall and lean, with his aquiline nose and high forehead leading to a wreath of greying brown hair, cut in a tonsure. His beard, flecked in reddishbrown and grey, was closely cropped against his face.

"Where are my manners?" Peter said. "Are you hungry?"

"A bit, though the brother did bring me some bread with my drink."

"I'll get you some food." Peter headed for the kitchen, and Andreas sat back down.

After some clanging of pots and plates, Peter brought out a plate of cold sausages, more salt bread, and cabbage soup, along with another stein of beer. Making the sign of the cross over it, he placed the food on the table.

"What brings you back to us?" Peter asked, taking a seat opposite Andreas.

"A number of reasons. I've heard stories about Münster, about how you're becoming a sanctuary for heretics. I wanted to see for myself." Andreas gave Peter the pamphlet he had been studying. "This bodes ill."

"We slide in a dark direction, I'm afraid." Peter scanned the paper. "Hatred of us is shown openly on the streets."

"Things were troubled when I left, but this is . . . " Andreas shook his head.

"Disturbing," Peter finished. He rubbed the back of his neck. "At first it was just Catholics and Protestants fighting, but now—"

"Fanaticism changes the balance, I'm guessing."

"Some fan the flames. Is the name Bernard Knipperdolling familiar to you?"

Andreas nodded. "I heard he stirs the pot against the Prince-Bishop, but Knipperdolling is just one merchant."

"He's persuasive, rich, and has courted the guild council, not to mention he connives with the most powerful preacher in the city."

"Rothmann?"

Peter raised an eyebrow. "You know of him?"

"I heard him preaching this morning when we came into the marketplace." Andreas pushed the cabbage around his bowl. "Why's he not arrested for preaching outside?"

"Because he's protected. Rothmann is the spark that'll set us all ablaze, I fear."

"I saw men with axes and spears at his sermon."

"Mostly guild members, and some of the agitators from surrounding towns. They claim they need those for protection, but it shuts up those who would protest Rothmann's innovations."

"And Knipperdolling?"

"He has scores to settle, I suspect. The new Prince-Bishop, Franz von Waldeck, has been trying to clamp down on the city—blockades, tariffs, that sort of thing. Knipperdolling works to subvert von Waldeck's interests."

Andreas exhaled slowly. "This is a dangerous game; to what end?"

"I don't know the end. There's talk of freedom to worship, but that cloaks other desires. The poor have suffered for so long; it's hard to blame them when they get a whiff of being able to decide their own fate. Word has spread that Jesus returns here."

"Oh, saints, no." Andreas dropped his spoon and put his head in his hands. "That's a contagion that sickens all who embrace it." Andreas stretched out both hands and laid them on the table. "No good comes of this expectation; I've seen it drive men to madness."

"That's why your pamphlet worries me," Peter said, fingertips resting on his temples.

"I saw Ulrich Schlatter out there today." Andreas changed the conversation. "What role does he play in the city?"

"Ulrich has a stick of his own to stir with; I can only guess what he's up to. People listen to him, which makes him worth watching."

"Has he come here? To the monastery?"

"No. I'm sure his loathing of me has not run its course. Though I expect him to exact revenge on us at some point."

"But you were not the one who reported him to the authorities."

"True, but I didn't speak up for him at his trial, either. I don't think he'll forgive me for that. Truth be told, I wasn't unhappy to see him go."

"How'd he get back in the city?"

"The story he tells is that Rothmann invited him back. They struck up a friendship in Strasbourg after Rothmann left to join the Lutherans." Peter stood and gathered Andreas's plate and stein. "But you're not here because of events in Münster, are you, Andreas?"

Andreas gripped the edge of the table. "I was never able to hide much from you."

Peter looked at Andreas. "Your eyes tell a hard story."

Andreas bowed his head. "Father, will you hear my confession?"

"Meet me in my office; I'm going to clean these."

"Of course," Andreas mumbled and stood. He walked down the hall going to the back gardens, passed by some brothers standing outside the chapel, and entered Peter's office. There were even more books than he remembered. When he was young, Peter's books had fascinated him. He wanted to know what worlds they contained. Ibn Sina, al-Zarqālī, and Averroes were still on the shelves, along with Cicero, Aristotle, and Eusebius. Andreas ran his finger along the row. Tertullian, Athanasius, and Augustine sat in their usual place. Books on herbs and plants sat side by side with works on astrology and mathematics. Many of them were in Latin, but Andreas was surprised to find some of Luther's treatises sitting on the shelf, along with writings from the Swiss reformer, Ulrich Zwingli, and someone named John Calvin.

Peter entered the office and handed him a goblet of wine before sitting. He wore a stole over his black robe. Taking a chair opposite Andreas, Peter leaned in, and put his hand on Andreas's shoulder. "I'm ready whenever you are."

Andreas hung his head and took a deep breath. He thought he was done with priests, but he was so tired of carrying the weight of his life and just wanted to rest. "I should've remained here," he started, "but I was restless. I heard my parents were in Erfurt, that Father had found work there. That was the first place I went when I left, but the plague had taken them. They were already buried when I arrived."

"I'm sorry," Peter said. "Brothers from the cloister in Erfurt sent word they'd died after you disappeared."

Andreas ran his hands up and down his thighs. "I thought about coming right back, but I was too ashamed . . . the way I left. In Erfurt, I heard there was revolution in the south, so I went there."

"And what did you expect to find?"

"Certainly not what I discovered. It was mostly chaos. Everywhere I went, roving mobs were setting the torch to their world. Castles, churches, fields, nobles and their courts—the peasants turned everything to ashes. The wine cellars were always plundered first; then the fires and murders followed."

"Did you join their dance?" Peter asked.

"I was encouraged to, but I couldn't. I understood their anger, the frustration, but I couldn't run with the mob." Andreas paused. "Luther may have opened the door, but the peasants shit in the house. From Frankenhausen to Bern, preachers shouted 'Luther!' or 'Freedom!' at the masses, and off they dashed, crazed to right all the wrongs they had suffered. Of course, they used God to justify themselves—who doesn't?"

"If it isn't God, we usually find other reasons," Peter concurred. "Some even use the stars as justification."

Andreas nodded. "Their prophets were screaming about the 'Year of the Fish'; spreading tales that the stars foretold the apocalypse. If it's the end of the world, then anything's permitted. They preached that the poor shouldn't be sold for a pair of shoes, or the hungry bought with grains of wheat. It was a witch's brew of delirious hope, God, and revolution, but there was some truth in it."

"There *is* truth in it, Andreas, though in some circles helping the poor is not welcome."

"No, and among the rich it never will be. Eventually the fire burned itself out. The princes saw to that."

"I see no need for confession," Peter said.

Andreas held up his hand. "I was in Rottenburg, at the trial of Michael Sattler," Andreas continued. "Have you heard of him?"

"Former Benedictine prior who converted to Anabaptism and left the Church. He and his wife were executed," Peter said. "But that was years ago."

"I don't know why I went to his trial. I was curious, I guess."

"Curiosity is no sin." The men sat in silence until Peter spoke. "What happened at his trial, Andreas?"

"They kept yelling in the courtroom that Sattler was responsible for all the destruction and conflict, but he remained silent as they cursed him. That man seemed incapable of hurting anyone." Andreas grabbed the wooden handles of his chair. "After they announced his guilt and sentenced him to die, I followed the execution procession outside the city. It was like being in the grip of something I couldn't fight. I had to see how the story ended."

"It always ends poorly." Peter's head drooped slightly.

"Torture and death. The last thing I heard before the bags of gunpowder they'd tied around his neck exploded was Sattler blessing his executioner. I stumbled back into a tavern to get a drink and overheard some men talking about Sattler's wife and how they were going baptize her into hell in a day or two. I made the mistake of going to her execution." Andreas pitched forward and put his head in his hands, rubbing his temples with his fingers. After a moment, he sat up, clasping his hands to the back of his head.

"What happened?" Peter lifted his head and looked at Andreas.

"I was arrested, put in a cart, and taken back into Rottenburg."

"The dungeons of Rottenburg?" Peter whispered, eyes focused on the floor, his hands on his knees, rocking. "Not many come out of those."

Andreas nodded, his face a grim mask. "They took me down into a room where there were metal tongs . . . other instruments . . . pokers, ropes on pulleys, large wooden tables. The stench of stale vomit and piss was overwhelming." Andreas was on his feet, pacing into every corner of the room.

"Oh, Andreas . . . " Peter hugged his torso, his arms tightening their grip around his body.

"They thought they were getting the truth, but it was all a lie. I would've said I was sucking the devil's cock to escape the pain. It didn't matter to them what I said, as long as it was what they wanted to hear. When they heard what they were looking for, they praised God for revealing the truth to them." Andreas looked directly at Peter, his eyes rimming with tears. "What difference does truth make in a world like that?"

Peter stared back, wetness building in his eyes.

"How can something said with a hot poker pressed to the cheek, or a bucket of water flowing down the nose be the truth?" Andreas's voice cracked as he touched the scar on his face.

"Andreas . . . I . . . am . . . "

Leaning in closer to Peter, his voice an acid whisper of rage, Andreas growled, "Do you think they *enjoyed* it? Do you think God did? If they loved it when I screamed in unknown tongues, what does that make us?

If God allows this, what does it make Him? A cruel bastard?" Andreas took his seat and inspected his goblet. After a minute, he began to sob, his torso heaving in spasms, each tear a release from a hundred burdens. "Priests, Peter—goddamned priests—tortured me. They live by the logic of hell itself." Andreas's voice cracked with bitterness.

"Lord Christ," Peter murmured.

"They worked on me so hard I passed out. They figured I'd be out for longer, I suppose. When I woke, I saw them by the other table, working on one of the men brought in with me. They always worked in pairs, so they'd have a witness if they got the confession they were looking for." Andreas paused, his voice trembling. "I was still shaky, but I saw the iron poker resting beside my table. They must've gotten careless, thinking they were in control. They hadn't even tied me down after I passed out. Stupid of them."

Peter's face had drawn down, eyes unblinking, grief etched in every wrinkle on his brow.

"Their backs were to me; the other man was screaming so loud they never heard me get up and grab the poker. The bastard closest to me was dead with the first blow. I put all I had in it. The other man turned to me, and I hit him in his cock. When he bent over, I crushed his skull. The last thing I heard from him was a moan and a gurgle. The only noise after that was the sobbing of the man on the table."

Peter got up and walked around the room for a few minutes as Andreas stared at the bookshelves.

"I untied him, told him to be quiet," Andreas continued, his finger going to his lips. "We waited to hear if there would be reinforcements, but no one came. We opened the cell door and searched the tunnel leading to the street. Somewhere in the distance I heard Compline being sung. We stumbled through the tunnel and then outside. I was shocked there were no guards in the square. It felt good to breathe something other than the stench of those cells."

"What happened to the other man?"

"Not sure. As we parted, he said, 'Thank God for our deliverance.'"

"Thank God, indeed," Peter agreed.

"I told him it wasn't God's hand on the poker." Just then, the chants of Compline filtered through Peter's door. Andreas lifted his head, clenching his hands into trembling fists. "So, is there forgiveness for me?"

"There is always forgiveness, Andreas, though some wounds are hard to heal. You've seen hell, a hell I've never known, no matter how hard things have been in my life. It's a long journey back from where you've been," Peter said, placing his hand on Andreas's shoulder.

"I can't erase the thoughts that torment me," Andreas moaned. "Is there anything in that physic garden of yours for this?"

"I have plants to help you temporarily forget, but there's nothing that can permanently erase your memories. You need deeper healing than an herb might offer. There are ways back to life, but you have to know what's died first."

"I'm not sure what died, but I *do* feel dead inside," Andreas confessed, wiping his eyes with the palms of his hands. "Since that day, I've constantly wandered, never at home anywhere."

"I'm grateful you trusted me with this." Peter pulled Andreas to his feet and embraced him. "All is not lost, but you'll need to be patient; healing takes time."

"I'm sorry for giving you this burden." Andreas sobbed as his shoulders relaxed and the darkness in him dissipated a bit.

"I've had worse burdens, Andreas." Peter released him. "Let me show you to your room."

Later that night, Andreas lay on his bed in the monastery's guest quarters. His mind raced back to the day he entered Elsbeth's village and found her on the ducking stool. Had he thought saving her might right the scales? He recalled her abject despair after they crawled out of the river and she realized she had nowhere to go. He was glad she came with him to Münster, though he could never tell her that. His pleasure at her expense would have been cruel.

Elsbeth's laughter was a whisper in his mind; her smile a thing he treasured each day they journeyed. He was laconic, taciturn, but she made friends easily. He envied her light touch with people. Even after being betrayed by her friends and family, she was not shut off from others the way he was. Her absence unsettled him. Would he ever see her again? Had he done the right thing by bringing her here? As weariness sank deeper into him, pulling him toward sleep, more disturbing images forced their way in as he slowly lost consciousness: Rothmann's frantic voice, all the weapons in clutched hands, and most disturbing of all, Ulrich, grinning at him like a besotted fool. He was not prepared for what he witnessed—Münster teetering on the edge, poised on the brink of some unknown abyss.

PART II

7

Überwasser Convent, January 19, 1534

"THEY'RE HERE," INGRID SIGHED, peering out the window at the women and children huddled up below her in the courtyard.

"I told you they'd come," said Elsbeth, looking over Ingrid's shoulder.

The path to this day had been laid two weeks ago when Elsbeth's friends, Ingrid, Rachel, and Ursula cajoled Elsbeth to leave the convent with them to visit Bernard Rothmann's house. The sisters, who had been defiantly slipping away to the city center for weeks, reported to their friends in the convent that two mysterious men from the Netherlands, *apostles*, had come from Amsterdam to baptize Bernard Rothmann.

Adult baptism was a violation of imperial law, and those involved were challenging the authority of the Prince-Bishop. It was the transgression of it that seemed to excite her friends the most. They wanted to see the actual baptism for themselves, and after much arm tugging, Elsbeth yielded and joined them. It was the first time she had been out of the convent without Ida's permission, and the betrayal weighed on her. No one anticipated that going to Rothmann's baptism would lead to the mothers and siblings coming to collect disobedient daughters.

Two weeks ago, as Elsbeth ate honey cakes with all the other guests, it felt like the usual celebration of the Three Kings. Then the odd Dutch prophets called for water and poured it over Rothmann's head amid boisterous cheers and hymns. The sight of water attached to such emotion caused Elsbeth to head for the door before Ingrid intercepted her. All she could think about as Rothmann toweled off the remaining drops from his beard was her village gathered around her at the river, thinking they were doing God's will. Water kills as much as it gives life.

Now, watching Ida come out to greet the mothers, Elsbeth recalled the emptiness she felt on those stones as Andreas walked out of the gate. Once Ida took her inside and she settled, Ingrid, Rachel, and Ursula approached her door and struck up conversation. They immediately took her under their wing and taught her how to navigate her new home. Quick to share confidences, they expected Elsbeth to follow their lead, which she did, carefully at first, but then freely, as she came to trust them. The moment she told them the truth about why she was at Überwasser—about the lecherous priest, the attempted murder, Andreas, and their journey to Münster—they threw their arms around her and promised they would take care of her, no matter what. They were the only ones who knew what Andreas was to her.

Her new friends came from a world Elsbeth had never known: a life only imagined. Parents gave great benefices so the convent would shelter and educate their children. Überwasser was for nobility's daughters, yet despite their station, they accepted Elsbeth as an equal. She knew hard labor, but Ida also allowed her time to study, gave her books, even let her sit in on lessons. It was the first time she'd had the freedom to pursue life without the rule of men. Though she missed Andreas, in the last four months she had grown fond of her small world.

Ingrid chafed at being locked away. For Rachel and Ursula, the convent was a godsend, a sanctuary where they could be together every day. At first, Elsbeth was confused by their deep affection, but eventually she came to understand. Everyone wants union, and those two were made for each other. Sometimes their mutual doting almost made Elsbeth jealous. Surrounded by friends she loved, she missed Andreas. There were stolen moments with him at the market when she was shopping, but quick greetings and five minutes of talk only made her wish for more. Especially with the city falling apart.

After Rothmann's baptism, his flock of preachers pressured the whole city to be baptized. Catholics were steadfast in their refusal, and some of Luther's followers were wary, but just over a thousand did take baptism, which led to Prince-Bishop von Waldeck threatening to take over, abolish the city council, and reinstate his authority. The guilds responded by organizing and stockpiling weapons. Armed men staked out territory, carving the city up into factions. Von Waldeck ordered the families of Überwasser's disobedient nuns to take them back home until he could straighten out things.

Ingrid's strident voice turned Elsbeth's attention back to the room.

"I won't be caged up in that house again; I won't!" Ingrid cried. "I preached last night. Preached! I was nervous at first, but I'm good at it. I'm better at it than the men." She turned from the crowd outside to Ursula and Rachel, who stood behind her. "I don't care how many of my sisters they bring; I'm not going home."

Ursula and Rachel moved past Ingrid and Elsbeth to the window for a better look at the huddled women and children below.

"I got to eat what I wanted last night, not what I was told to." Ingrid's hands flew as fast as her words. "Rothmann and his men took me to a tavern. No rations on wine there. They want me to bring you all with me the next time. You must come. What's Ida going to do? Keep us locked in here? They offer us freedom."

"Perhaps we need to go a bit slower?" Elsbeth offered.

"I'm fine to stay put. Life's not so bad here," Rachel said, resting her headful of red hair on Ursula's bony shoulder. "I fear the outside."

"You'll get used to it soon enough," Ingrid said. "Besides, you don't have any longer to decide. Our moment of truth has come—mothers await."

Elsbeth looked out the window and suddenly wished it were her mother standing on the cobblestones as Ida motioned the crowd into the convent.

"We may as well get this over with," Ursula grumbled, moving toward the door.

"I'm not going anywhere with my mother." Ingrid's nose curled up. "I'll go to the market and scream that Ida is turning us over to von Waldeck. We'll see what happens then."

"He's a damn coward." Rachel spat on the floor. "He sends in our families to do his dirty work. Why can't we be left alone?"

Following her friends, Elsbeth remained silent, wishing she had it in her power to turn back the clock to the time before the two Dutch prophets showed up in town.

When they reached the reception room, Elsbeth passed by Ida. Drawn and wan, Ida's eyes were bloodshot and the lines on her face looked deeper. She sat still, keeping her eyes on the paper in front of her. She had faded in the shadows of the bickering, boisterous women in front of her. Elsbeth had to hand it to von Waldeck—bringing in the mothers was clever.

The room filled with chatter as the two groups faced one another . . . waiting. Now, Elsbeth was grateful she didn't have a mother to confront. Most of the sisters stood stone-faced, their arms folded tightly across their chests. Ida remained seated at a table between the two groups, dipping her quill absentmindedly into the ink well that rested at her right hand.

Finally, in the din of humming voices, a woman in a red velvet dress with silk taffeta sleeves took a step out of the mothers' crowd. Her cheekbones rested high on her face, accented by blond hair streaked with grey and tied back in a bun. Green eyes flashed with anger. Elsbeth looked at Ingrid, who cocked her head to look back at the woman. This had to be her mother.

"Dear daughter, I beg you, come back home with me." Ingrid's mother was strong, commanding. "This place is perilous. The Prince-Bishop called us to his estate to tell us how heresy has so infected your convent that some of you disobey your abbess. We hear of men calling themselves apostles and prophets, spreading all manner of lies. It's not safe for you. Von Waldeck gathers his forces, so come home with us until he's able to sort out this mess."

Ingrid stared intently at her mother, not betraying feeling, nor revealing her mind. Other mothers and siblings spoke up, imploring their daughters and sisters to return home, to flee the coming battles, but the nuns stood implacable against the entreaties of their families. Elsbeth glanced at Ida as she struggled to record the proceedings, but the cacophony of voices echoing around the room made that futile. The pleas continued until the clock tower on Überwasser Church struck the noon hour. The tone of the mothers turned to harangue, but the nuns remained defiant.

Finally, when parents and siblings had exhausted themselves first in entreaty and then condemnation, Ingrid strode out from her companions. "Go back to your homes! You're not true parents, else you wouldn't have thrown us into this place of death."

The words fell upon the intended targets. Ida's head bowed, her hand gripping her neck. Ingrid's mother swelled up against each indignant word. The turmoil between mother and daughter sank into Elsbeth's soul, her eyes filled with tears. She flipped back to wishing she had a mother she could argue with.

"How can you say this?" Ingrid's mother recoiled, stung.

"You neglected your parental duties. You handed us over to be burned by eternal fires when you placed us here. I know that now; I've been better instructed. You shut us away in order that we not bother you, but we've decided to choose an honest life, not one of popish superstition."

The grief in the voices took Elsbeth back to Jaberg. Was life an endless series of conflicts, set up between those who wanted to control the world and those who wanted to live freely? Elsbeth closed her eyes and could almost smell her mother's smokiness after a day of cooking. The estrangement building in the room grieved her, but at least Ingrid was making her own decision. She was not going to be put on the end of a ducking stool.

"When you locked us away in here, you sought to choose our family for us." Ingrid's arms flew in constant motion. "But now we choose our own life, with whom we live, to whom we give heed, what *we* believe. These 'heretics' as you call them tell us the truth. They give us the freedom to live our lives the way we want. They don't try to lock us away in some prison. They even give us freedom to preach, just like men. They've become our true family, a family that doesn't put our souls in peril."

Elsbeth heard Rothmann's cadences in Ingrid's voice. The moment Ingrid's words slammed across the room, the mothers' faces twisted in horror, their mouths spasms of anger. The expected docility of the nunnery rent like a poor curtain; payments of grand dowries and sacrifices of children offered to the convent no longer granted control. Sentences breaking into fragments echoed throughout the room.

"Ungrateful—"

"Renounce Satan—"

"Obey your parents—"

"You bitch—"

On and on it went, every harsh word a torch hurled onto the bridge between them, irrevocably burning their way back to one another into ashes, a conflagration of repressed rage and confusion. Others joined Ingrid and her mother on the front lines, imploring each side to repentance. Then, amid all the tumult, one of the mothers took her younger daughter in hand and silently walked across the room to where the nuns stood, putting her arm around her older daughter. The sight of one of their own, covered in brocade and jewels, standing with the disobedient children of Überwasser, left the mothers apoplectic with anger. They turned on one another, shouting and wailing until Ingrid's mother screamed.

"Stop this! Stop this now!"

A hush fell over the room, the only sound the labored breathing of the women.

"This is your doing." Ingrid's mother strode over to Ida, who cradled her head in her hands, fingers massaging her temples, no longer trying to keep track of the comments. "We trusted you with our daughters. The Prince-Bishop assured us that you kept good order and now this . . . this . . . defiance. Von Waldeck is going to be most displeased."

Ida's fingers stopped, but when her head rose, she merely stared blankly at the group of women before her.

"Unless you accept us, it would be better if you left," Ingrid demanded. "It would be preferable if you repent and join us, but if you persist in your lies, we can have no part of you. Satan may have you, but he'll not have us in the bargain."

Amid tears, wailing, and curses, the families filed out of the room. Elsbeth walked over to Ida and put a hand on her shoulder. These women were not going to live under the old ways anymore. They had been offered a way out of their imagined prison and they were eager to take it. Watching everyone stalk out of the room, Elsbeth could not escape the feeling that the new life so eagerly anticipated by her friends held much less promise than the one they presently possessed.

8

February 6, Morning

RUMORS CIRCULATED LIKE THE crows around St. Paul's towers: churches outside the city's walls smashed to pieces by rioting mobs; fights throughout city parishes; priests forbidden to leave their monasteries; and most ominous of all, Franz von Waldeck was building a siege army to take Münster in hand. Anxiety settled on the city the way winter clouds hung on the Alps.

Elsbeth still gathered provisions, but some of the sisters were stealing away from the convent to live in the city center, and her baskets grew lighter by the day. A few days ago, she spotted Andreas in the market, and they agreed to start meeting in a tavern on King Street to compare notes. It was Andreas who told Elsbeth that Bockelson had returned to the city, married Clara Knipperdolling, and moved into Bernard Knipperdolling's house. Elsbeth shared with Andreas the turmoil roiling the convent. On the days they talked in the tavern, Elsbeth welcomed the warmth of Andreas's thigh next to hers, the touch of his hand on hers.

She sometimes felt the weight of being confined, especially on mornings like this when she had to stand in Überwasser Church waiting for preachers to lecture the sisters. Scanning the small group of nuns waiting for Bernard Rothmann to arrive at morning prayers, Elsbeth wondered why he was coming to them this morning. Every day a new intrigue. In front of her, Rachel and Ursula locked their arms together, looking as if they expected to take on the whole world. Ingrid had tried to talk them into leaving, but they liked where they were and Ingrid, after heavy sighs, said she wouldn't go without them. She stared at the floor, shifting back and forth, while Elsbeth absentmindedly took in the statues of the saints lining the walls.

"Wonder what Rothmann has to say this morning?" Ingrid asked, wrapping her cloak tighter around herself to keep out the early February cold.

"Whatever it is, I'm sure Ida's not pleased," Elsbeth whispered, searching for the abbess. "She's the one to pick the preachers, but they've taken that from her."

"She may be unhappy, but from the looks of things, the rest of our sisters can't wait for him to get here," Ursula said.

Rachel, her arm in Ursula's, smiled. "At least we're immune to his charms."

"Shh!" one of the women in front of them chided. Rachel and Ursula giggled.

A commotion arose in the back of the church as the hum in the room elevated a register. Elsbeth didn't need to look to know that Rothmann had arrived. Slowly walking to the front, he bowed before the cross and ascended the pulpit. He stroked his mustache, lost in thought, looking at his pages. Elsbeth could understand the attraction he held for women with his expressive face and intense eyes. His impeccably groomed hair and beautiful clothes stood in sharp contrast to most of the city's men.

"That man is prettier than many of the women in this city," Rachel observed.

"Indeed," Ingrid said.

Rothmann flashed a sly smile to his audience. The sisters smiled back expectantly. Rachel and Ursula grabbed one another tighter. Elsbeth finally located Ida standing with her assistants, Sister Elizabeth and Sister Mary. Ida looked miserable as she focused on a statue of the Virgin Mary.

Rothmann raised his arms. The room quieted.

"Dear sisters, it was for freedom that Christ came. Jesus told his disciples that they would know the truth and the truth would set them free." Rothmann paused, a grin spreading across his face. "You were born for freedom, not servitude."

Elsbeth glanced at Ingrid, who rolled her eyes.

"We were created to obey the whole Word of God. You have been released from bondage in order to freely follow this word. Although the false church, the great Whore of Babylon, stole your lives, God wants to restore you to the fullness of life." The murmuring grew louder. "God knows you have been faithful. Our Lord understands that many of you have tried with all your heart to serve Him in this place."

With their fidgety hands and anxious faces, Elsbeth thought it looked as if the sisters were ready to take flight at any moment.

"But . . . the Bible tells us that we should be fruitful and multiply," Rothmann continued. "We were meant to create those who glorify God. We were made by God to fill the earth with the fruit of our labors, even the fruit of our wombs, were we not?" Rothmann paused, his eyes scanning the nave. "Yes, we were," he answered. "Now, in every endeavor, we know that men can better help other men, but there is one favor that God has granted you that He has not granted men."

Breaths bated, the women leaned forward to hear what God had withheld from men, for it was certainly not power, money, and autonomy.

"It is the blessing of childbirth."

Sighs released. Many of the women around Elsbeth signaled assent with bobbing heads. Babies. Gifts from wombs that, at least here, were never to flower. In the coldness of convent cells, few hadn't thought about the warmth of an infant. Voices knit a network of desire throughout the congregation, creating a babbling din.

"God has commanded the holy estate of matrimony that we might spread over the earth and be fruitful. Ask yourselves this morning, you who are imprisoned, are you being faithful to God's will? Were you meant to waste your gifts? How many of you truly think this life of being locked away is what God desires for you? You should live freely, as women outside do. You have been kept in this fortress not *for* God, but *from* God. Even at this moment, the Holy Spirit is pounding at your gates, seeking entrance."

Perhaps it was the word *pounding* that caused a chink in the solemnity of the moment. Rachel and Ursula snorted as Elsbeth's hand flew over her mouth to hide her amusement. Rothmann stopped and scowled at the three of them, which only made it more difficult to stay somber.

"You've been selfish, sisters," Rothmann continued, narrowing his eyes. "You claim to keep yourselves for God, but you haven't. Offer yourselves up to Him that He may plow your fields and scatter His seeds of holiness."

As tittering spread through the room, Elsbeth spied Ida and her companions stalk out of the church.

"God has revealed to me that you are to flee from this den of Satan." Rothmann leaned over the pulpit, aiming an increasingly loud voice at the retreating women. "You were put here by others to shrivel up and die, but Christ has come to set you free to blossom fully. I have been given a sign by God that what I tell you this morning is the truth."

That stilled the giggles. Elsbeth warily considered Rothmann. What sign?

Rothmann's left hand lifted above his head as his right fist held the pages of his sermon. "Before the clock of this church strikes the last bell of midnight, God will bring down the tower. Every living thing that remains will collapse before the power of God. Sisters, flee the wrath that is to come. There is time to save yourselves, but you must leave immediately. We will take you in and provide for you if you will cross the river and join us."

With that, Rothmann swiftly descended the pulpit's winding staircase. He positioned himself in front of the nuns and began chanting the Psalm appointed for the day: *The snare is broken, and we have escaped.* Rothmann repeated the chorus as the women joined in; the room filled with the singsong chant—a message of liberation filling everyone's ear.

Permission had been given for desires long pent up to find release. The sisters were not inclined to deny what came in a flood of longing on cold lonely nights simply because every noble family must tithe from convenience or piety a part of its flesh to the Church. To know the warmth of another body, the hopefulness of love—a new horizon of possibilities suddenly opened. It struck Elsbeth in that moment how doubly bound each of these women was by her high birth. They'd tasted of the pleasures of money and then were told to forsake them to save the souls of their spoiled siblings and relations.

Elsbeth made for the kitchen. She had no idea if anyone was coming to midday meal after this morning, but it was still her job to prepare it. She was surprised to find Ida vigorously chopping carrots and leeks and throwing them into a boiling pot.

"Ida, this isn't your job," Elsbeth protested. "You've more important things to do."

"Not anymore," Ida muttered, her hands moving furiously.

"Nonsense, this will pass." Elsbeth crossed over to the counter and picked up a knife.

"Perhaps, but I won't be here to see it." Ida's knife smacked rapidly against the cutting board.

"Ida?"

"I've been preparing for this moment, though I had hoped it wouldn't come to this. I've been sending our treasures out of the city for safekeeping. It's over. By tomorrow, I doubt there'll be a convent left."

"Rothmann said the towers would fall before midnight," Elsbeth said.

"Oh, I heard him from the back of the church." Ida's knife worked faster. "You need to think about what you're going to do, girl."

"What I'm going to do?"

"The convent's done for a bit; you need to consider your future."

"But you're staying, aren't you? Can't I still stay here with you?" Anxiety flooded through Elsbeth.

"No, I'm leaving. When von Waldeck gets wind of this, all the angels and amulets in the world won't protect us—not when his mercenaries arrive."

"Do you really believe it will come to that?"

"It's a certainty; his patience is exhausted." Ida put down her knife and rested her hands on the table.

"Where will you go?"

"I've made arrangements, and if you want, I also have permission to bring you with me," Ida said.

Elsbeth kept her head focused on the turnips she was slicing. The thought of being exiled again was too painful. Her hands trembled so much she placed her knife on the counter and threw her arms around the abbess. Ida's body stiffened, but then she put her arms around Elsbeth and breathed a deep sigh.

"I'm sorry, Elsbeth. Having you here has been a blessing to me."

"And being here has been a blessing for me."

"I wish it hadn't come to this," Ida said.

"All's not lost. If the towers don't fall tonight, no one will believe him."

Ida looked at Elsbeth and shrugged. "Maybe so. It *was* a bold prediction."

9

Evening

"Münster loves its spectacles," Ingrid said to Elsbeth as they gathered in the courtyard of Überwasser Church.

"It certainly seems that way." Elsbeth marveled at the crowds milling around, drinking ale and eating from the food carts that had arrived that afternoon. Word of Rothmann's prophecy spread fast through the city, and the crowds had filled the square below Überwasser's towers. Waiting for midnight, men played cards, prostitutes trolled for customers, and children ran around the legs of adults. Elsbeth pulled her cloak tighter over her shoulders and searched the swelling crowds for Andreas. Surely word of Rothmann's forecast had reached him at the monastery. Fires burned in braziers throughout the crowd, but she could not get warm. The remaining sisters from Überwasser stood huddled in groups—some with Rothmann's preachers, and others with nuns from other convents.

"Elsbeth." Ingrid pointed to the stone bridge straddling the Aa river. Elsbeth spotted Andreas coming over the bridge, accompanied by a hooded stranger.

"Andreas!" She waved as the two men drew closer to her.

"Elsbeth, I'd like for you to meet Father Peter." Andreas moved to the side so she would have a closer view.

Elsbeth broke into a large grin as her eyes rested on Peter. He was wearing a plain black woolen cloak that seemed too big for him. His hood obscured part of his face, but Elsbeth saw a flash of a smile from within the shadows of the hood.

"I had begun to wonder if Andreas made you up," Elsbeth said. "It's so good to meet you at last."

"It's good to meet you, Elsbeth." Peter's hand emerged from his cloak. "I've heard much about you since Andreas returned."

Grasping Peter's hand, Elsbeth smiled. "And I hear of you every time I see him, but it's so nice to meet you."

"And it is good for me to meet the woman I hear about daily."

"It appears we have much to talk about later." Elsbeth tilted her head to Andreas.

"The entire city turned out." Andreas deflected attention back to the crowd.

"You must admit," Peter broke in, "as far as prophecies go, this one is remarkable, though reckless."

"What would possess Rothmann to make such a claim?" Andreas asked. "He's been careful not to promise more than he can deliver."

"He's excited everyone." Elsbeth spied Ida and her companions standing outside the convent gate. "Though for some, this is not a welcome time—"

"Look, coming across the bridge," Andreas interrupted.

Ulrich Schlatter, Bernard Rothmann, Jan Bockelson, and Bernard Knipperdolling walked off the bridge and strode into the crowd with a man and woman Elsbeth had never seen before. Conversations trailed off as Andreas, Elsbeth, and Peter turned their attention to the approaching strangers. The man towered over everyone he passed. Dressed in a long black robe, with a greyish-white beard flowing in an unruly cascade down his chest, he seemed more specter than man. Strands of brownish-grey hair hung down the sides of his head, accentuating the enormous, almost-bald skull jutting out from his slumped shoulders. Elsbeth was reminded of gargoyles she had seen on the cathedral in Köln and pictures of death's reaper shown her as a child. A petite woman in a hooded white robe worked to keep pace beside him.

"Who are they?" Elsbeth wondered.

Ulrich approached, steps ahead of the others.

"I was hoping I'd see you, Elsbeth. Though, Droste . . . I never expected to see you out. It can be dangerous for priests on the streets these days." Ulrich eyed Peter for a long moment before he faced Andreas and Elsbeth. "Would you like to meet my companions?"

"Who are they?" Elsbeth probed as the group joined them.

"Andreas, Elsbeth, it's good to see you again," Bockelson said. "I want you to meet the man who changed my life. This is the prophet, Jan Matthys, and his . . . um, wife, Divara."

Elsbeth pulled back in the presence of the tall man whose eyes focused on her. Something wild and not entirely of this world stared at her when she tried to hold his gaze. Elsbeth noticed the woman studying her as well. She looked twenty years younger than the man. Her long black hair framed a doll-like face with delicate features and intense green eyes. She moved closer, staring at Elsbeth from under the hood that partially cloaked her face. Taking Elsbeth's shoulders, she kissed her on each cheek and whispered, "Peace be with you." Her dialect was so odd Elsbeth barely understood her.

"Wel . . . come." Elsbeth was dumbstruck by the couple standing before her. In a city that had its share of oddities, they stood out.

"It was good to see you both, but we have business to attend to," Bockelson said, taking Rothmann's arm and steering him toward the church. Matthys and Divara followed along, but as she passed Elsbeth, Divara looked back over her shoulder, a trace of a smile playing out on her lips.

"Looks like it's too late for Rothmann to turn back," Ulrich said.

"What happens if the tower doesn't fall?" Elsbeth asked, her eyes trained on Divara.

"If?" Andreas snorted. "There's no chance that happens."

"Don't sound so incredulous, Andreas," Ulrich said. "We don't know what will happen."

"We do," Andreas insisted. "Come midnight that tower will still be standing, and we'll all go home."

"But if it doesn't fall, won't Rothmann lose face?" Elsbeth asked, mindful of her conversation with Ida earlier.

"It's uncertain," Peter said. "If the pattern holds, those following Rothmann will find a way to excuse it."

"It would seem grounds for disgrace to me," Elsbeth said.

"Can't disagree with that," Andreas muttered. "I've seen it before, though. Once you've decided on your messiah, it's hard to let go of the delusion."

"Cheer up, Andreas. The truth of the thing will be revealed soon enough," Ulrich teased.

"If we're lucky," Andreas said.

"Elsbeth, as always, it's been a pleasure." Ulrich bowed slightly in her direction before slipping into the crowd.

"Why does he provoke you so?" Elsbeth asked.

"He doesn't." Andreas crossed his arms.

"He just did," Peter interjected. "He toys with you."

"He annoys me." Andreas's arms wrapped tighter around himself.

"Apparently," Elsbeth said. "Ulrich doesn't worry me as much as some of the other things I've seen in this city; it feels like warring camps. I'm stopped every day I go to market and told it isn't safe on the streets."

"The reign of the righteous is dangerous," Andreas declared.

"Reign of the righteous?"

"The ones most convinced of their own purity are the dangerous ones." Andreas shifted his feet. "The word *cleanse* makes me nervous. No good comes of that. Purity becomes a cloak for other desires."

"My friends are devout," Elsbeth protested. "I don't think they mean harm."

"Perhaps not, but they're probably not yet 'true believers.' Those you can't reason with. Once a man is convinced of his righteousness, his cause becomes God's. It's demonic."

"Demonic?" Elsbeth grimaced. "Surely you don't believe that?"

"I've seen the desire for purity drive men to utter darkness." Andreas relaxed his shoulders. "They destroy everything to gain a pure world. Look at those over there." Andreas pointed to men holding weapons on the edge of the crowd. "In the wrong hands, purity becomes a weapon and piety justifies murder."

Elsbeth stared at the men holding their axes, swords, and guns, expectant looks on their faces, and pondered Andreas's words.

"It's time." Conversation stilled all over the courtyard. Those who were drinking grew less boisterous, faces turned to the clock. Voices softened as people edged closer to one another and further away from the clock tower.

Minutes before midnight, Rothmann walked closer to the church. His face went from the tower to the crowds, guiding everyone's focus to the clock.

"Behold the power of God!" Rothmann yelled as the clock struck its first bell.

Several people screamed and ran toward the bridge, angling for a quick escape from falling debris.

But in moments, as the echoes of twelve bells faded, people looked at one another, confused.

"False prophet!" someone yelled on the other side of Andreas. "You're a false prophet!"

"Who said that?" Rothmann demanded, storming into the crowd. "Who challenges me?"

"Answer him; are you false?" someone else yelled.

"Brothers and sisters!" Rothmann shouted. "As it was when God called Jonah to prophesy against Nineveh, so it is today. He told Jonah that He would destroy that wicked city and Jonah went and proclaimed God's judgment. They repented, and God's wrath was turned away!"

Andreas's and Elsbeth's eyes widened—around them, heads on either side began to bob.

"The sisters of this convent are deserting their order, thus obeying God. All that remain are the hard-hearted," Rothmann said. A measured look over at Ida and the two older nuns underscored his meaning. "And God will deal with them as He desires."

"What a weasel," Andreas muttered.

Rothmann raised his arms. "God has spared this church for when we need it. Glory to God, who keeps His promises."

A cacophony of unconvinced protests rattled around the gathering until Bernard Knipperdolling strode from the crowd to Rothmann and thundered, "Thanks be to God!"

All heads turned toward the pair, expectant.

"Brothers and sisters, God has given us a sign tonight that if we are faithful, nothing can overcome us!"

Elsbeth glanced at Rothmann, his face as stunned as everyone else's.

"God did not fail us tonight!" Knipperdolling bellowed. "Pastor Rothmann's not a false prophet. He told me this afternoon that when God said the tower was going to fall, he wasn't quite sure what it meant, but he decided to step out in faith."

"But he told the nuns the tower would come down," a voice challenged.

"Yes, and as we pull the witches and heathens from their towers, they *will* fall, but today we have turned from unbelief, just as Nineveh did. Rothmann is right. If the nuns had not left today, God would've destroyed this place. We've been spared by the faithfulness of our sisters."

"Knipperdolling speaks the truth!" Rothmann paced in front of the crowd, his arms upraised. "God spoke to me, and His word is thus: those who desire to follow Him must leave the Whore of Babylon and join us. We'll take this church and redeem it."

Silence followed as the throng considered this interpretation. Some tried to convince themselves that a miracle had occurred; others were certain they had been deceived. Arguments broke out, chattering increased, and a few shouts of *Praise God* lifted above the clamor. Picked up by others, the chant scattered through the crowds until it rang out over the courtyard. A chorus of *Hosanna* broke out as Rothmann walked over to where Knipperdolling stood, grabbed his hand, and raised it to the sky. Cheering erupted.

"Fools," Andreas jeered.

"Don't mock this, Andreas," Peter warned. "There are things to learn here."

"What things?"

"How deep the deception takes them."

"I don't care about their deceptions," Elsbeth responded. "My friends suffer because of them." Elsbeth nodded at Ida and her companions who were holding their arms around one another. Searching for the other sisters, Elsbeth saw a few who had been spending nights in the city center, slipping off their habits, standing in the cold, clad only in thin underdresses. Men took off their cloaks and draped them over the shivering women.

"Andreas, I need a minute," Elsbeth said. Brushing through the crowd, she walked to Ida and hugged her. "I'm so sorry."

"That man takes shit and spins it into gold," Ida said bitterly.

"Yes, I'm afraid he does," Elsbeth said, holding her friend a bit tighter.

10

February 8

THE DISAPPOINTMENT OF FAILED prophecy had been managed, but Andreas knew that the suppressed desires of those hoping for a sign from God remained. Refugees had been filtering into Münster for months. Escaping the pastures carefully tended by magistrates and priests, they had broken the fences and fled their shepherds. Now, they wandered the streets, wondering if Knipperdolling's revelation was only a foretaste of the coming of the glory—the glory that would reveal to the entire world that it was they, not the rulers and mighty men, who had been faithful.

Pondering the deaths he'd witnessed in the last decade, Andreas felt some sympathy for the refugees who had been hounded and driven to Münster by the Antichrists of Amsterdam, Köln, Strasbourg, and the rest of the empire. In Münster the dispossessed had a place, a small piece of the world where they were safe, where one could believe what one wanted. Take all the years of being hunted, the pain of persecution—suffering jammed into a bottle—uncork that and worlds come undone. That brew made the most sober soul drunk, stumbling through the world looking for a sign, a sign from the heavens to obey. Andreas feared the explosion.

The past months had heightened his dread as he watched the newcomers strutting and gliding around the marketplace, weapons in hand, secure in the realization that behind Münster's formidable walls they were safe. They called themselves "wheat," waiting to be harvested in the last days; those who did not follow the truth were "chaff," ready for the fire. Münster was tinder, waiting for the match to set it ablaze. Peter told Andreas last night as they returned home that at some point it had to explode. He never expected it to be the next afternoon.

Andreas, his unease growing watching the milling crowds, stood with Elsbeth across the cobblestone square from Knipperdolling's house. An uncomfortable familiarity settled deep into him. A mob looking for direction could be a weapon in the hands of those skilled at inciting passions. Too many lines had been crossed, and the council was too divided, too impotent, to act. Catholics hid behind the doors of their houses, and the cabal in Knipperdolling's house sat and plotted . . . what?

"Ida makes final preparations." Elsbeth interrupted Andreas's thoughts. "She thought about staying longer to see if von Waldeck would negotiate, but she's convinced staying here is not prudent."

"Have you thought about what you'll do? You can't stay at the convent alone."

"Ingrid says that Ulrich has found a place for her, Ursula, and Rachel, just off the market. She told me there was more than enough room for me."

"So." Andreas frowned. "Ulrich's prepared."

"I was happy to have the offer."

"Ulrich's offers always carry a cost," Andreas warned. "Be careful with him."

"I'm grateful for his help," Elsbeth countered. "Ida begs me to come with her. Her brother urges her to leave because the Prince-Bishop is raising a siege army."

"Then the rumors are true." Andreas pondered what Peter had told him that morning. One of von Waldeck's chaplains was passing word to all Catholics inside the city to prepare for an attack and paint their doors with a cross.

"I'm staying with Ida until she leaves." Elsbeth blew on her woolen-wrapped hands to keep them warm. "Have you seen—?"

St. Lambert's bells rang out the third hour, absorbing Elsbeth's words.

Knipperdolling's front door opened, and he and Bockelson trooped outside, dressed in simple clothes with plain grey woolen cloaks, heads bowed. Then their piercing screams shot through the market.

"Repent! Repent!" Knipperdolling and Bockelson reared back and roared into the sky. "The hour is upon us!"

Everyone in the market froze, seized by the eerie cries.

"Prepare the way of the Lord!" the two howled in unison.

Elsbeth and Andreas exchanged bewildered glances. "God," Andreas said, "what now?"

Running through the marketplace, Knipperdolling and Bockelson pointed to the sky, howling, "Can you see them? The cloud of witnesses! Can't you see them?"

Elsbeth searched the afternoon sky. "It's just grey clouds."

The two men ran into shops up and down the market, pulling people out into the streets and imploring repentance before Christ returned. Drawn by the turmoil, others flowed into the marketplace from all directions, an agitated crush of bodies. They clumped together, excited voices filling the entire length of the plaza as several preachers milled through them, exhorting sinners to turn to God.

"What the hell's going on?" Andreas asked two men who rolled a barrel of water past him. They merely shrugged and went about their task.

When St. Lambert's clock struck four, Knipperdolling and Bockelson bolted out of the market, running toward St. Paul's. Groups of men and women followed, chasing them like baby geese running after their mother.

Elsbeth shook her head. "Your descriptions of Münster didn't do it justice."

Andreas wrapped his arm around Elsbeth's shoulders. "My descriptions of Münster didn't account for this. Probably just theater to get attention."

Elsbeth put her arm around Andreas's waist, pressing her body closer into his. "I'll grant it's entertaining, but what's the point?"

Shouting spread throughout the parishes, encircling the city in a ring of excited screams and roars. The louder the noise grew, the more people flew to the marketplace. They came from every street, expanding the crowd. With each new parish visited by Knipperdolling and Bockelson, more people joined the masses of yelping, yipping, crying men and women.

"I need to sit." Andreas dropped to the stoop of one of the shops. Elsbeth squeezed close, watching the white puffs of her breath. Torches were lit throughout the market, making it seem as if the dusky evening was ablaze. Andreas glanced up, directing Elsbeth to do the same. The evening clouds gathered in an odd formation of angry grey and black layers, dimpled with red and purple clumps that dipped toward them. The sky itself seemed to be signaling disaster.

Muffled hysteria wafted through the market as they awaited the return of Knipperdolling and Bockelson. A tall, gangly man jumped past Elsbeth, flapping his arms as if they were wings. Leaping, flailing, dancing, he vainly tried to propel himself skyward, but could not achieve his goal. Having failed to gain heaven, he chose humility and fell to the ground, first crawling, and then rolling, in a mixture of mud and dung. Young boys surrounded him and mocked, yelling in unison with him, "Oh God! Oh God! Oh God!"

A blind man ran up to Andreas. Looking directly at him with his filmed eyes, he screamed abruptly, "I can see! I can see!" and began dancing in the street. Several people gathered around him in celebration and together they moved toward Ludger Street, where the man slipped on a pile of horseshit and fell on the cobblestones. The crowd stood over him for a minute, and when he didn't get up, they turned back toward the market in search of a more reliable prophet.

Everyone stood dazed, unsure what to do. At first, most watched placidly, but soon, even the calmest among them started moaning as the crowds grew so large they filled arcade and street alike. Knees went weak and people slumped prostrate in lumps, draped over one another like slices of meat on a platter. Many in the crowd started howling, and soon some people took to all fours, barking, crawling, burrowing their noses deep into the piles of bodies that had formed on the street. It was as if they had not been allowed to be human beings for so long, they had become something more feral.

Some women twirled in circles, arms raised up to the sky, their faces euphoric. Others, arms splayed out, lay on the ground and moaned as if they were having orgasms. Andreas glanced at Elsbeth as she gripped him tighter, her face flushed with excitement. Beside her, a man tried to ascend an invisible ladder. Elsbeth's head moved from Andreas to a group who had taken off their clothes and danced together near a bonfire ablaze in the middle of the market.

Elsbeth pointed to the scene unfolding in front of her. "What is this?"

"Madness. This is madness."

"Yes, but exciting madness." She put her arms around his neck and pulled herself into him, her body mashed against his. "They seem so alive, so passionate."

"This is not life, though." Andreas sensed the invitation, felt his body respond and half wanted to strip off his clothes and take her. Who would notice? But fear overwhelmed his lust. The market had turned into one huge squirming mob of insanity; bodies were undulating, crawling, leaping toward the sky—souls trying to fly off to their own personal heaven.

Knipperdolling and Bockelson stumbled back into the marketplace, exhausted, sweaty, but exuberant. Hair matted and clothes soiled, sobbing and groaning as if they were in the last throes of the plague, they rushed through the crowds who parted to let them pass. Andreas noticed large barrels of water positioned in the center of the plaza.

The clock struck five.

Andreas touched Elsbeth's shoulder and pointed to the barrels. "What's this?"

"Water to slake the thirst I have?"

"No, something else is happening," Andreas said.

Rothmann came out of Knipperdolling's house and mounted the wooden pulpit beside St. Lambert's. Their attention diverted by him, Andreas and Elsbeth did not realize that Bockelson and Knipperdolling now stood beside them.

"Repent." Frozen sticks of snot and splotches of spit decorated Knipperdolling's unkempt beard and mustache, his eyes shimmering with an unsettling intensity.

Bockelson, face ablaze, grabbed them around the neck and kissed them both hard on the cheek, nuzzling against them. "Beloved of God, repent. The day of the Lord is at hand! Will you join us to prepare the way? God loves you. I love you." He pulled them closer to him. "We want you to be part of the elect."

Elsbeth drew back. "I thought we already were."

Bockelson moved his hand down to her hip, pressing his body into hers. "There is so much more. Come, join us."

Andreas broke the embrace, taking Elsbeth's arm. "What's going on here, Jan?"

"The Kingdom of God, my friend," Bockelson replied, quickly moving to the crowd at the next stoop, cajoling and exhorting others to prepare for Christ's return. Andreas noticed Bockelson did not grab the others quite the way he had Elsbeth.

"This is a fire that will burn down the house," Andreas said through gritted teeth.

"Maybe some houses need to burn," Elsbeth said. "I could use a little heat in my life."

"Not like this." Andreas grew more concerned about Elsbeth's attraction to the chaos.

"Repent! This is the time of repentance! Repent!" Rothmann's voice rose above the din. He called to the crowd from his wooden pulpit. Slowly, clutches of people walked over to him. "Repent, brothers and sisters!" Rothmann shouted. "Be baptized with the true baptism of Christ. Be faithful to God and the Word. Believe and be baptized!"

"Damn, that's it!" Andreas exclaimed.

"What is?" Elsbeth asked.

"Look around you . . . at the barrels." Andreas pointed to Rothmann's preachers standing by the water.

"Prepare yourself for our Lord Jesus!" Rothmann called. "Believe, and you shall be baptized this very night!"

"They're taking power!" Andreas cried out.

"What do you mean, *they're taking power*? How can that be?" Elsbeth wondered.

"They're taking power by baptism."

"I don't understand." Elsbeth's face scrunched up.

"Rothmann baptized over a thousand people, but many resisted. He didn't have the numbers he needed," Andreas said, agitated. "Now look at them." Andreas motioned to the people walking toward the barrels. "Believers' baptism violates imperial law. If they're baptized, they become outlaws to the empire. This isn't baptism; it's an initiation."

"Initiation into what?"

"I'm not sure . . . a new state? I don't know the game here, but it's an assault on the authority of the Prince-Bishop."

"We need something new." Elsbeth slipped her arm into Andreas's cloak. "We could use some comfort."

With each knot of people Knipperdolling and Bockelson passed, several would step away and walk to the water barrels. Rothmann's preachers directed them to form lines of shivering bodies as they waited for baptism. Water poured over hundreds of people and splashed into the street, washing away their sins like it did the dung and mud that clung to the paving stones.

"This is foul." Andreas looked across the street at Knipperdolling's house. "Come with me." He grabbed Elsbeth's hand and tugged her halfway out into the street, peering into Knipperdolling's open door. Through evening's fading light, he spied a crowd of men gathered around the newcomer, Matthys, whose body shook as he leaned against the wall. Beside him stood several men, their arms draped around Matthys's shoulders. Andreas was steering Elsbeth closer to get a better look when Divara appeared and looked outside. When she saw Elsbeth, she smiled and motioned her inside.

"Andreas," Elsbeth said, pointing to Divara. "She wants us to come."

"That's a pit of death," Andreas warned. "That isn't for us; please trust me. Let's go." Andreas grabbed Elsbeth's elbow to steer her away from Knipperdolling's door, but she pulled away.

"No! You don't get to make my decisions." Elsbeth hunched her shoulders and moved a couple of steps from Andreas. "That woman could be my friend, and right now I need all the friends I can get."

"Elsbeth, look around you; this is insane. We need to leave," Andreas pleaded as Elsbeth kept shaking her head.

"You do what you wish, Andreas. Divara asked me in, and that's where I'm going." Elsbeth broke for Knipperdolling's house.

"Elsbeth . . . No!" Andreas shouted, but she strode through the door, a smile for Divara already on her face.

Helpless, Andreas watched as Divara hugged Elsbeth and motioned someone to join them. Ulrich came into view and gave Elsbeth a warm embrace as she whispered something in his ear and pointed outside. Ulrich looked out in the street at Andreas, walked to the door, a triumphant grin spread over his face, and slowly swung the door shut.

11

February 9

"GODDAMN!"

The feed bucket sailed through the air, landed harmlessly, and rolled toward the inner wall behind the monastery. Andreas put his hands behind his head and tromped back and forth, cursing at the ground before he went to retrieve the pail. A tormented, sleepless night had left him exhausted as he tried to grasp the events of the last couple of days: Rothmann's prophecy, Matthys and Divara, the city going mad, and the most painful part, Elsbeth turning her back on him. Everything had changed in an instant. He wanted to escape before things got worse. But how could he leave Peter? How could he leave Elsbeth? Her new friends would destroy her. Picking up the bucket, he strode to the pigpen, threw it into the corner, and headed to Peter's office, barging in without knocking. Peter sat behind his desk, lost in thought.

"Peter?" His friend looked wan. "Are you well?"

"I was about to ask you the same, given your yelling outside." Peter motioned Andreas to take a seat. "I'm still thinking about the report you gave me from last night. It augurs ill."

"It does indeed." Andreas took his usual seat by the fire, grabbing a poker.

"I heard the commotion in the parish, but I had no idea what they were up to. I thought it was just another night rally."

"They were seizing power." Andreas jabbed at the wood until sparks leapt up from the fire. "I'm sure of it. They provoke von Waldeck to attack."

"Perhaps." Peter rose from his desk, walked over to the stack of wood in his office, grabbed a couple of logs, and placed them into the fireplace.

"They have no interest in tolerating others, Catholic or Lutheran." Andreas's fingers drummed on the arm of the chair.

Peter sighed. "You're probably right, though it seems ironic."

"Ironic?"

"The Anabaptists want to abolish infant baptism because it's not freely chosen. But last night's baptism was coerced. That's not freedom."

"So, the new order demands an outward sign as well?" Andreas rose from his chair and went to lean against the wall beside the fireplace. "Infant or adult—what's the difference?"

"From what you describe, probably very little; it looks like baptism has become an initiation into a different type of kingdom."

"That's what I thought."

"That doesn't concern me as much as their rhetoric."

"Rhetoric?"

"It's the way they use Scripture that reveals their intentions." Peter rubbed his eyes. "The attempt to go back to some imagined golden age that existed in the Bible and capture that for our time is a recipe for folly."

"You see that here?"

"To them, this is the New Jerusalem and the Church is the Whore of Babylon. In their minds, we live in the last days."

"Then they misinterpret."

"Yes, but suffering brings others to the city. Since the decree was issued to wipe Anabaptists from the face of the earth, they've been hunted down and slaughtered without mercy. You've witnessed it. Who wouldn't want a sanctuary, a place where they can make the rules?"

"If that's the case, we're in danger. If the workers' guilds and radicals make common cause with the refugees, they become the law. Any who don't live by their rules become the targets of their piety."

"I'm not sure matters have reached that point," Peter responded. "City council still holds the balance of power for now, and I don't see Mayor Tilbeck letting go of his power."

"If it gets to that point, would you think about leaving?"

Peter's eyebrow arched. "Why would I do that?"

"To be safe; you must know the rebels will come for you. They hate Catholics almost as much as they hate the nobles and magistrates."

"I'm where I need to be, Andreas. People depend on me. A true shepherd doesn't leave his flock defenseless, and Matthys's eyes burn with the fever of a rabid wolf."

"Do you think Matthys was behind Knipperdolling and Rothmann's performance last night?"

"I don't know, but from the moment he showed up, events have quickly escalated. Someone is playing the tune others are dancing to," Peter said. "I'm just not sure who it is."

"Maybe Ulrich sounds the notes," Andreas offered.

"It wouldn't be the first time Ulrich connived."

Andreas remembered Ulrich's face last night as he closed the door to Knipperdolling's house. "Father, excuse me, I need to go check on Elsbeth. She mentioned last night that Ida was leaving the convent, and I want to see if she has a place to stay." Andreas stood up.

"I'd heard Ida was leaving. That's probably for the best—and, Andreas?"

"Yes?"

"Tell Elsbeth she can stay in our guesthouse if she needs shelter."

"Here?"

"The old rules no longer apply."

Andreas kept his hand on the doorknob for a moment. "I suppose you're right," he agreed, pulling the door behind him.

Walking through the city, Andreas noted the preparations: men were piling up furniture to blockade the streets; others were drawing thick chains across alleys; children, overwhelmed with the weight of swords and guns in their arms, trotted past him. Piles of ammunition were being stacked behind wagons positioned to withstand assault. Lines of hatred drawn in hearts for months were now being manifested in barricaded avenues and stockpiles of weapons. It gnawed at him. He came back home thinking that he might find a place of rest, somewhere to hope again, but now hope seemed foolish.

He crossed the bridge to Überwasser and was headed for the convent when a man came out of a large group of people beside the church and intercepted him. "What're you doing here?" the hulking man with greasy hair and missing teeth demanded.

"Not your concern," Andreas countered, in no mood to be bullied.

"We're going to get rid of those goddamn heretics," the man cursed, spitting on the street. "Are you with them?" He pointed across the river. "Or are you with us?" His finger ran an arc to the mob behind him.

"I keep my own counsel," Andreas said. "I've come to see the abbess, so if you don't mind—"

"Maybe I do." The man moved to block his way.

Andreas stopped and looked over to the church courtyard where servant girls were pulling guns from under their dresses and handing them to men who gathered the weapons and stacked them in small piles.

"What's this?" Andreas demanded.

"None of *your* concern."

"Why are servants smuggling guns over to this side of the city?"

"If you know what's good for you, you'll stay on this side of the river," the man said before returning to his friends.

"Arse," Andreas muttered. He continued around the church to the convent gate where he found the door unlocked. Stepping inside, Andreas's heart sank when he saw Elsbeth talking with Ulrich, her hand resting on his shoulder. Ulrich turned and raised an arm in greeting.

"Andreas, we were just talking about you. I was telling Elsbeth she might be safer if she came to the city center. All alone in a huge convent, it could be very dangerous."

Elsbeth looked at the ground, not meeting Andreas's eyes.

"It could indeed," Andreas said, trying to catch Elsbeth's eye. "In my walk through the city center just now, danger's everywhere."

"You'll need a place to live soon when your monastery empties," Ulrich said. "I can help you, too."

Before Andreas could reply, Elsbeth interrupted. "Thank you again, Ulrich, but Ida needs me now."

"Today she does, but what about tomorrow?" Ulrich took Elsbeth's hand. "Please consider my offer; I only want to make sure you're safe."

"I'll keep it in mind." Elsbeth raised her head and smiled. "Thank you; you've been a good friend."

"Well then, good. Now, excuse me, I have things to attend to," Ulrich said. He put his hand on Andreas's shoulder and gave him a wink. "Convents and monasteries are not as safe as before. We must be careful."

Andreas's eyes followed Ulrich out the gate. He turned to Elsbeth, whose shoulders slumped.

"What's wrong?"

"Ulrich may be right. Ida's leaving, and most of the sisters have fled. Ingrid and the others have moved into their new quarters. This place turns bleak. It was so full of life when I arrived, but without my friends, it feels like a tomb."

"Peter told me you could stay in our guesthouse," Andreas offered.

"I can make my own way. I make new friends now." Elsbeth straightened. "I'm certainly not ready to live among priests. How could you even suggest such a thing?"

"I only meant—"

"What did you mean?" Elsbeth backed away. "To lock me up with priests? I could trust Father Peter, perhaps, but the rest? However bad this grows, I've been able to make my own decisions; I don't need you making them for me. I would've thought after last night you understood that. How many times do we need to fight this battle?"

Andreas stood silently, uncertain of his words. If she was slipping away last night, this morning she was a ship far out from shore, sailing quickly toward the other side of the lake. "I'm sorry. I meant no harm."

"No, I'm tired." Elsbeth's voice softened. "I didn't mean to snap. I've been out late the last couple of nights and have had little sleep. And then, this morning I woke up to the sounds of men gathering weapons outside."

Fatigue and fear hung on Elsbeth's body like the heavy woolen cloak she wore.

"I had better go, so you can get some rest," Andreas said.

Ida appeared at the convent's door. "Wagner, a word?" Ida said. "Elsbeth, would you go and attend to the older sisters? They need some help packing their things."

"Of course, I'm on my way." Before leaving, she took Andreas's hand and squeezed it. "I'm sorry," she whispered.

When she was gone, Ida studied Andreas. Feeling the weight of her attention, Andreas crossed his arms and rocked. "Wagner, it's cold out; would you step inside the kitchen for a minute?"

Seconds later, Andreas warmed his hands by the wood stove as Ida stood with her hand cradling her chin. It was a moment before she spoke. "She needs your help."

"What?"

"Elsbeth. She's going to need your help. The rest of us are leaving. We're too old for this nonsense, and I don't think I could survive a siege."

"Do you really think there'll be a siege?"

"Are you that stupid, Wagner? Did you not see the mob outside when you came across the river? Knipperdolling's forces on one side; Tilbeck's on the other. How do you think this goes? Von Waldeck won't let his crown jewel suffer this."

"Maybe they'll settle down," Andreas said, knowing the signs did not point in that direction.

"Your naiveté is touching, if misplaced. If things go as I expect, there'll be a war inside the walls, and once they've devoured one another, von Waldeck will sweep up the remains." Ida packed some more dishes on the tables into wooden boxes. "You should take Elsbeth and get out while you still can."

"I can't leave Peter."

"And she can't leave you."

"Pardon?"

Ida rapped her knuckles on Andreas's head. "Curious—it doesn't sound like wood. She cares for you."

Andreas's face flew open. This was news from an unexpected source. "And I care for her," Andreas said. "Peter told me this morning that if things go poorly, she can come and stay in the guesthouse."

"That's a relief, though honestly, he should leave as well."

"I asked him to, but he says he's needed here."

"Peter Droste was born stubborn and hasn't changed," Ida said.

"He can be stubborn, but . . . " Her words finally registered. "Wait—you knew him? When he was growing up?"

"Of course. We were playmates as children."

Andreas had never considered Peter and Ida's lives before they entered orders, had never asked Peter about his life before the monastery, or how he had become a priest. Now, he wanted to know everything. "What was he like? One hand in the herbs, the other in a book?" Andreas grinned.

Ida arched her eyebrows. "Peter Droste was the meanest little boy I ever knew."

"Wha—? God, Ida . . . " Andreas stumbled over his words, trying to absorb this revelation.

"Slow down, Wagner; take a breath." Ida rubbed her hands together. "You think he was born a saint? He was a rough boy, angry all the time, though I suppose he thought he had a right. Constantly got in fights. I had to smack him in the face one time when he got ugly with me."

Andreas stared at Ida, fascinated. Peter and Ida as children! He envisioned them running around the market, sneaking into churches, and getting into trouble. Where had Ida come from? Did noble parents stick her in a convent? Why had Peter become a monk? The questions overwhelmed him.

"Peter Droste lost his parents when he was about fourteen," Ida began. "They went quickly after they took the plague. He walked over to a neighbor's house to tell them his parents were dead. Can you imagine, fourteen years of age and you have to do such a thing?"

Andreas shook his head, contemplating this news. This must be why Peter took in so many orphans, why he took in Ulrich. He had suffered the same thing.

"He was looked after by friends of his parents who put him in a school run by the Brethren of the Common Life in Deventer," Ida continued. "By the time I saw him again, seven years later, he was different, more the man he became. He told me he was going to take holy orders and serve God. I was shocked. Never expected it. He chose it for himself, not like so many others. It wasn't forced on him."

Memories came to Andreas of his parents, the day they brought him to the monastery, and Peter's smile that morning. He thought about Peter's ceaseless patience with him, the long nights they had spent talking since he returned. Peter was the closest thing Andreas had ever had to a real father. And Andreas had not even had the guts to say goodbye when he left Münster— had not even taken time to thank Peter for all he had done. One day he simply walked out of the monastery, out of the gates, and beyond the walls. How incredibly selfish.

Shame overwhelmed him. His suffering was not unique, yet he had hidden himself away from others, thinking his pain was different. Others had lost parents, suffered unjustly, or were damaged. People he should have been attentive to, listened to, spent time with—he had ignored them all because he thought no one could understand what he had endured.

Andreas reached behind him for the table as his knees weakened. He sunk down onto the bench and wordlessly stared up at Ida, tears dappling his cheeks.

"Wagner, are you ill?"

He thought of Elsbeth—the way she laughed when something went wrong, the smile she wore when they shared a joke—it all swept over him as he realized how deeply he cared about her and how scared he was of letting her know. His life had been locked up in more ways than one. And now, he might never have the chance to tell her how much she meant to him. She was moving to another circle, one that cared nothing for him.

"I never knew," Andreas murmured.

"Wagner, you need to convince Peter he's in danger," Ida urged. "Beg him to leave, if you can, but don't leave him to the mercies of Münster's wars."

"I'll stay with him, no matter what happens," Andreas promised.

"And Elsbeth? What about her? You must realize that she stays because of you? If you don't leave, she won't."

"She's found others more important to her."

"God, Wagner, you wallow in pity like a pig in slop. She talks about you constantly. Frankly, I grow weary of hearing your name. Take your head out of your arse and look at something other than yourself. She needs you."

"And I, her," Andreas said. "I won't leave her."

"Good, because I've talked myself hoarse trying to make her see the sense in coming with me," Ida said. "Oh, Wagner?"

"Yes?"

"I have powerful friends. If anything happens to that woman, I'll have those friends find you, wrap you up in a burlap bag with stones, and toss you into the river." Ida smiled kindly, though her eyes held Andreas in a fierce gaze.

"I understand," he murmured.

"Good. You can let yourself out," Ida commanded. "And if I were you, I would step carefully. This city is turning into one stinking pile."

12

Evening

ANDREAS PUSHED HIS WAY through the crowds carousing, drinking, sing-ing, and celebrating like it was a carnival day. The tension of the morning with warring camps on opposite sides of the city ready to fight had given way to drunken crowds thronging the streets. Knipperdolling and the mayor, Herman Tilbeck, had reached a truce and agreed Tilbeck would not open the gates to von Waldeck's men. Open taverns with free food and drink sealed the deal.

Ida's words still lay heavy on him. He needed to find Elsbeth before it was too late. Maybe she was at the convent. Was she already lost to him? Desperate, he searched for her. Surely by now Ulrich had infected her with his poison. Andreas recalled the lies Ulrich used to weave about Peter in the dark nights as they tried to go to sleep. What do you think Father Peter is growing in that garden of his? Where does Father go when he leaves the monastery? Probably to a full flask and the arms of some woman in a tavern like other monks. Maybe some of the boys he housed were his own children? Maybe he wanted other things from them? Who knows what lonely priests get up to in the middle of the night? Ulrich was clever, the way he could plant the seed and wait for it to grow. Had he somehow pushed Andreas away from Peter? Was Elsbeth being pushed away from him that very minute?

Andreas hurried to Überwasser, breaking into a run when he saw the double doors of the outer gate standing wide open. But when he burst through the entrance, Ida, her face drawn and tired, was standing by a coach with two older nuns. The scene was unexpected, though no less frightening than if a horde of peasants were pulling apart the convent.

"She's not here anymore, Wagner. We depart, so I sent her away. She can't stay here by herself."

"Where did she go?"

"I'm not sure. Schlatter and some men came and took her a few hours ago."

Andreas stiffened, his hands locking behind his head. "No," he groaned.

"She said something about wanting to be with Ingrid and the others. She mentioned King Street?"

Andreas nodded to Ida and made for the marketplace. When he arrived, torches were being lit, illuminating a grey winter's eve. The smell of sausages on grills tempted him to stop and pause, but he hurried through the market and down King Street, asking if anyone knew where the sisters from Überwasser lived. Someone finally pointed out a rowhouse a block from the market. Moments later, standing in front of the door, Andreas took a deep breath and knocked. Ingrid opened the door. Past her, Rachel and Ursula sat by the fireplace.

"She's not here. She's with Ulrich and Divara," Ingrid said, opening the door wider. "You're welcome to wait for her, though."

Andreas mumbled thanks, but headed for the marketplace, where he found hundreds of people yelling and screaming, pointing up to the evening sky. The clouds gave the appearance of red-tipped clumps dripping toward the earth. An eerie combination of purple, black, and grey streaks painted the cloudy canopy—the hues heightened by burning torches—a reprise of a few nights ago.

Then, the screaming started.

God, not again.

"Ezekiel! Ezekiel! He comes in his chariot!"

Andreas looked for Rothmann or Knipperdolling, but when he located the voice in the middle of the market, it was a local tailor, his head tilted up, pointing at the sky. Others craned their necks skyward.

"He comes!"

"The rider on the white horse!"

"Prepare the way of the Lord!"

Shouts of gibberish and confusion filled the air. To Andreas, it was like reliving the horrible fever dream that had gripped the mob the previous night. People fell prostrate in the street, calling out supplications to the Lord they believed had come to claim them. A man beside Andreas ran over to a brazier and picked up a hot coal with a pair of tongs.

Holding the burning chunk up, he shouted, "Woe is me, for I am a man of unclean lips, and I dwell in the midst of an unclean people!" When he put the coal to his mouth, several closest to him knelt on the street, struck by the power of his shrieks. Andreas scurried away from the crowd forming around the moaning man lying on the ground, glowing coal and tongs by his side.

Finally, he spotted Divara's white cloak, her hood up. He moved toward her just as a naked man ran past him, shouting, "Naked for the naked truth!" Following along in his wake were several others who had stripped off their clothes. They ran in circles, yelling. A naked woman, her pendulous breasts flopping against her chest, passed Andreas. Her shouts smacked against his ears: "Naked I came into this world; naked shall I leave it!"

Pushing past the throngs, Andreas struggled to keep sight of Divara as the crowds swelled. One of the naked women grabbed Andreas as he tried to slip past her. Eyes widened, she screamed in his face, "He comes! He comes!" Andreas jerked back from her, his throat constricting.

Fighting the urge to vomit, Andreas stretched his neck up, searching for Divara as bodies once again piled on top of one another in the street. People collapsed in squirming, moaning heaps. Andreas remembered a painting he had seen where bodies were splayed over the canvas in various stages of dismemberment and lust. The sight of those tormented souls, locked between death and life, had filled him with dread and . . . attraction. He could not lift his eyes from the canvas. Something about the naked bodies grabbing one another fascinated him. Now, looking at the writhing mess in front of him, the crawling, grabbing bodies only horrified him.

The white hood came into view and Andreas approached Divara. He spied Elsbeth slowly swaying, holding hands with the people on either side of her. Her head was tilted back, eyes closed, mouth open, smiling. Despite his revulsion at the scene before him, Andreas's desire for her grew.

"Elsbeth!" he called.

She lowered her head, opened her eyes, and smiled when she saw him. Pulling away from her companions, she grabbed him around the waist. "Andreas, get a drink; come and join us."

Andreas looked at Elsbeth, baffled. The only thing he wanted was to flee the insanity around him.

As he struggled with what to say, a new group of about two dozen people entered the market, walking slowly, mimicking a saint's day procession. Münster was nothing but a carnival now. The revelers were dressed as priests, monks, and nuns, shouting as they pulled a cage on a wooden cart. A cold chill ran through Andreas when he spotted the cage, the memory of another cage indelibly burned into him. Inside the coop, a man dressed like the Prince-Bishop wore a long black robe. With a soldier's breastplate strapped to his chest, he held a sword in one hand and a shepherd's crook in the other. An ornate conical hat decorated with crosses perched precariously on his head. The crowds jeered and mocked, erupting into riotous laughter when he lifted his robe and farted.

Divara laughed and looked at Andreas.

"Come spend some time with us," Divara said, taking his hand. "You look like you could use some laughter."

"There was a time when I might have found that charming, but now it leaves me cold," Andreas muttered. Was it his imagination or was there an invitation in Divara's squeeze of his hand?

Elsbeth pulled at his sleeve, grabbing for his other hand. "You're the one who told me that a little mockery of the powerful is not a bad thing."

"In the right circumstances, but this is different; this incites too many passions."

"Is a little passion a bad thing?" Elsbeth said, kissing his cheek. "Didn't you say Münster loves its carnivals?"

Those dressed in robes surrounded them, raising their garments and exposing themselves, laughing and dancing little jigs. Others laughed and cheered as they skipped along. The group that had first disrobed ran past them, howling to the sky.

"For freedom has Christ set us free!"

"You shall know the truth and the truth will set you free!"

A naked man ran up to them and screamed, "No law for those who love God!"

Elsbeth cast her eyes at the man's thrusting crotch and then looked at Andreas and Divara. "It must be colder than I thought," she quipped.

"This is no cause for laughter," Andreas said.

"This happens all the time in the Netherlands," Divara said. "People who are free in God cast off the old ways."

"We're not Dutchmen," Andreas protested.

"Hello, friends," Ulrich said, stepping in between Andreas and Elsbeth. "Quite the display, eh? Brings back old memories, doesn't it, Andreas?"

Andreas, his mouth agape, his mind slipping deeper into quicksand, mutely stared at Ulrich.

Ulrich smiled, put his arm around Andreas's shoulders, and pulled him closer. "Isn't this marvelous? A man could have whatever he wanted." Ulrich's eyes went from Andreas to . . . Divara.

"Elsbeth." Andreas bent down and spoke in her ear. "I have to talk to you."

"Now? This very moment?" Elsbeth said. "Can't it wait?"

"Please, a word in private?" Andreas begged.

Elsbeth stood for a moment, her eyes moving all around her, taking in the spectacle. Finally, she took Andreas's arm. "Of course." Touching Divara's shoulder and Ulrich's arm, she said, "I'll see you later."

The two walked silently past the squirming bodies, the would-be prophets searching the sky for chariots of fire. Smoke from torches filled the square as the last bit of light ebbed out of the sky, leaving more darkness and, with it, more screams. Elsbeth put her arm in Andreas's, a sign of reconciliation. He put his hand on hers and steered them toward Cathedral Hill.

"Where are we going?" Elsbeth tensed slightly the further from the market they went. Andreas kept silent until they reached a point between St. Margaret's Church and St. Paul's. He pulled her into an alcove of St. Margaret's and leaned into her, holding her closer, feeling the warmth of her body. She slipped an arm around his waist, feeling for his face with her other hand. He bent down and kissed her softly, leaving his lips on hers, hoping she would respond.

"What's this?" Elsbeth tilted her head away.

"Something that should have happened in September, but I didn't have the courage."

"And you do now? I don't understand." Elsbeth squinted to see Andreas in the growing darkness.

"No," Andreas countered, not entirely certain he was telling the truth. "I've been afraid to feel anything, to get attached to anyone. But I realize that I can't live that way. I've loved you, probably since the day we met."

"You like your women tied to chairs?" Elsbeth teased. "Maybe I was wrong about you after all."

Andreas saw the smile form on her lips. "When we climbed out of the river, you were so vulnerable, so devastated. But you didn't hate the ones who wanted to kill you. Well, maybe the priest, but the others? You didn't want revenge as much as understanding for why they acted as they did. That's rare."

"I would've thought it isn't rare at all."

"And that's what won me. You see the best in people; I've lost that."

Elsbeth slid both arms around Andreas's waist, but an edge of suspicion crept into her voice. "Why tell me this now?"

"I've protected myself, but I want to be a part of your life. I'm afraid I'm losing that chance."

Elsbeth stiffened in Andreas's arms. "You should have told me this before. I'm not the girl I was coming here."

"I only recently found the courage. I've not been on good terms with myself," Andreas said. "You grow distant, and I fear losing you."

"Well, we should find ways to change that," Elsbeth responded, moving her body fully against him, enveloping him with her arms and nestling her head against his shoulder. "I've thought about you every day since we arrived. Those days when our paths crossed, I would hold onto the memories of you, remember our conversations until the next time we saw one another."

He stroked her hair, relieved his feelings were not in vain.

"But, as I said, I'm not the girl who came here." Elsbeth leaned back so she could see his face. "I won't be ruled by you or anyone else. I have new friends, people who care about me. I do love you, but I need all the friends I can get, because life guarantees me nothing."

"Which is another reason I've revealed myself," Andreas said. "There is nothing here for either of us. We should leave while we can. I've friends in Erfurt who can help us find a new life. I think I can convince Peter to find a safer monastery, and you and I can leave this behind."

"Why should we leave, though?" Elsbeth asked. "My friends are here; my life is here now."

"Everything aligns for disaster. We should flee before things fall apart," Andreas urged.

"You worry too much." Elsbeth put both her hands on his face. "Ulrich assures me things will be fine."

"And if they aren't?" Andreas took her hands in his. "Those outside our *paradise* won't tolerate anarchy; they never have."

"Well, that's for tomorrow. I don't know what that holds. For that matter, neither do you, but for now, come with me." Elsbeth took Andreas's hand and led him down the street from Cathedral Hill, across the bridge and to Überwasser's gate. Elsbeth pulled him toward the entrance, but Andreas stopped.

"You hesitate? Ida's gone. No one's here anymore." Elsbeth released his hand and slipped into the courtyard. "Are you coming?"

Andreas stood rooted. A door previously closed to him had just swung open, welcoming him inside. He knew that once he went to the other side of the gate, went to her room, felt her body next to his, the unleashed desire between them, the isolated life he had worked so hard to build would disintegrate. His thoughts raced back to the day they climbed out of the Aare. By the time they walked into Bern, she had already breached the walls he had built around himself, though he did not realize it at the time. He thought about the warmth of her flesh on his, the stirring in his body, her open mouth—there was no place left to go. He smiled and stepped across the threshold into Elsbeth's waiting embrace.

13

February 23

ULRICH ALWAYS ENJOYED A commanding view. Standing at the second-floor window of City Hall observing all that was going on below pleased him. He knew things others didn't, and that had served him well in life. Preoccupied by the crowds on the streets, he had lost track of the conversation in the room. Things were turning out far better than he'd dared to hope. Knipperdolling and Rothmann had not been hard to manage. He had even grown fond of Knipperdolling. Their time together in the bathhouses and brothels had been time well spent. He only had to agree with Knipperdolling's assessments, feed him the sweet praise he desired, nod his head knowingly when he laid out his plans, and Knipperdolling would quickly heed Ulrich's counsel.

Rothmann had been a bit tougher, though Ulrich remained inspired by his rhetorical skills. He might have been more powerful than Knipperdolling if it came down to a power struggle, but if it did, Ulrich would have to side with the merchant. You could only trust the self-deceived and power hungry. Rothmann was too devout, too prone to an inconvenient conscience. At least the duplicitous could be counted on to act predictably. Though, now that Ulrich considered it, Rothmann had been more than open to the suggestion that he and his gang of preachers take hatchets to the churches outside the wall.

Besides, better those two as allies than the hideous creature sitting at the table with the rest of the conspirators. *They should've cut out his damned tongue when they had the chance.* Ulrich stared at Jan Matthys continually running his tongue over his teeth and lips. *It's as if he knows that sucking sound maddens me.*

Ulrich's fingers cradled the side of his head. The very minute that man arrived in town, the stench of madness followed. How had that lunatic been able to seize control of so much so quickly? It exasperated Ulrich: the way people fawned over Matthys, hung on his every word. Ulrich had been working his charm diligently for months and had not been able to pull that off. The mad prophet was complicating his plan. Matthys's stories of his suffering circulated around the city as a sign of his holiness. Though his appearances on the streets were rare, his name was on everybody's lips. It was enough for even Ulrich to consider if the man was not capable of signs and wonders. Yet all that stood before him was a crazed old man wearing a tattered black gown with a strikingly beautiful woman trailing after him.

Of course, Divara was part of the attraction. Ulrich couldn't imagine what she could possibly see in the creature. Was there some hidden virtue that everyone was missing, some secret power that could attract a woman like that? Maybe Divara was the miracle. That at least would make sense. Ulrich couldn't figure out what her angle was. It just didn't fit. It was a mystery Ulrich wished he had the answer to.

The black prophet had brought over a thousand supporters to Münster, so sheer numbers gave him power, and more fell under his spell daily. Ulrich warned Knipperdolling that Matthys might get out of hand if they didn't do something to curb the man's growing strength. Then Bockelson confirmed Ulrich's suspicions one night during a long bout of drinking. He confided that Matthys was unpredictable . . . prone to fits of madness. Bockelson also revealed that before he took up with Matthys, he had run women at his Inn of Two Herrings. He regretted it now, of course, but Ulrich saw that the pimp didn't rest far beneath the surface. Ulrich suspected that Bockelson's allegiance to Matthys was as thin as a crepe.

"Ulrich, what do you think?" Knipperdolling called over to him, breaking his reverie.

"Um, sorry, what do I think about what?" Ulrich shifted his attention from the window to the enormous oak table where the men were sitting.

"About where to start after we take over the council. Don't you listen to anything?" Knipperdolling chided.

"The city will be yours to do with as you wish. There is still, however, the matter of von Waldeck to consider." Ulrich spoke so quietly that everyone else stopped talking. "He's sent out the call for mercenaries. I would move carefully."

"What can he do? We have control of the gates," Rothmann retorted. "The papists are lost, but Tilbeck has been warning the Protestants that von Waldeck will outlaw their creeds, so they're on our side."

"Some are," Knipperdolling cautioned. "More think the rebaptizers are heretics, but this changes every day. Tilbeck, have you told our friends you've taken baptism?"

Stunned, everyone looked at Tilbeck. Knipperdolling started laughing, saying in a theatrical tone, "The mayor of Münster has now passed through the waters of redemption."

The room erupted into a cacophony of excited voices. Tilbeck had come over to the true faith at last! Tilbeck made a slight bow, sweeping his hand toward Rothmann.

"We should cleanse the city of our enemies. They shouldn't be allowed to be here," Matthys spewed, dampening the mood. "It's not the enemy outside your gates that you should fear; it's the ones inside that can eat out your guts like maggots."

Something in Matthys's voice made Ulrich shiver with joy, no matter his concerns about the man. The tone was always low and growly at first, until the excitement came, and then he hit a certain pitch, darkly ethereal, as if the angel of death itself were calling for the harvest. The potential for destruction in that voice was breathtaking.

"No fear, Brother Matthys. No one will harm you here," Ulrich assured.

"Promises are empty. It's action that people respect." The tongue again, flicking in and out like a snake.

"When we have rousted the followers of Dr. Liar of Wittenberg, your people will be safe," Rothmann said.

"We are never safe—not as long as the heathen exist," Matthys growled, inclining his head toward the window. "You don't know them like I do. You don't know what they're capable of."

"You're here because we offered you and your people sanctuary. Have you been molested since you arrived?" Knipperdolling challenged.

"As long as the whore's priests and Luther's fools remain inside these walls, we'll never be safe!" Matthys started pacing.

"But after tomorrow, they'll have no more power," Rothmann said. "We'll have complete control, and the city will be ours. No more lukewarm Lutherans, no more papists; just true disciples on the council."

"I wasn't talking about the council," Matthys spat back.

Ulrich studied the room carefully. Tilbeck and Knipperdolling had put their heads together, probably conspiring about their next move. The rest of the room, however, could not take their eyes off Matthys. He had become larger than life, a projection of their own fears and desires. Ulrich wondered why they didn't realize how dangerous he was. How could they not grasp that expectation and anxiety, once planted in the head, sink into the heart, creating passions that are increasingly difficult to manage? The last several weeks alone should have taught them that. These fools expected Christ to plop out of the sky into their laps. Ulrich glanced around the room, his eyes fixing their gaze on Matthys. *They have no idea what that man is capable of.*

14

February 24

GUILD MEMBERS GATHERED in clusters outside City Hall. Hundreds of men tucked glazier's knives, huge leather straps, hammers, axes, and picks under their arms. The burghers had been meeting for hours now, voting on the next city council. The rumors favored Knipperdolling's gang. The council had always been moderate, levelheaded, but after tonight—who knew? Andreas could hear the shouts as the doors to City Hall opened onto the brightly lit portico. Knipperdolling and Tilbeck walked out together, arm in arm. Torches illumined their faces. Rothmann slipped in front of them and called for quiet.

"Co-Mayors!" Rothmann yelled. "The council is ours! Praise God! The Kingdom of God has come!"

Knipperdolling and Tilbeck clasped hands and raised their arms up to the sky. Shouting swept up and down the plaza. "Freedom! Freedom! Praise God! Praise God!" The cries and chants echoed against the walls of City Hall. Andreas watched Knipperdolling laugh and dance a jig as he clapped Rothmann on the back.

"They seem pleased," Andreas said to Peter. They had come to City Hall to hear election results, but Andreas grew uneasy at the weapons being brandished about.

"Knipperdolling has worked years for this moment," Peter said, his eyes on the portico. "He desires power the way a man desires a woman."

Behind Knipperdolling, Andreas watched other burghers, their faces drawn, filing out of the building and slipping away into the darkness. He caught a glimpse of Jan Matthys's black robe moving toward the steps of City Hall. Matthys ascended the stairs and stood, glowering, next to the new leaders. He raised his arms and swung around to face the crowd. His gloomy visage twisted from side to side, examining the mob. Andreas grew cold. What was he looking for?

"It's like Matthys won nothing today," Andreas said.

"He's already on to his next move," Peter replied. "He lives in the future, always in the future."

"They have control of the city. Why's he concerned for the future?"

"A man like that is always worried about what's coming next."

It caught Andreas short that he and Matthys might share something. He considered Matthys's pain. How is it that suffering ennobled some and crushed others? The chants and shouts grew louder. "These people scare me, Peter."

"Me too, people driven by fear can do great harm."

"But they say they're here because they love God, and their enemies hate them for it"

"True, but we often love God the way a farmer loves his cows—because it gives him milk and cheese."

Andreas spotted Ulrich talking to a group of men carrying axes and hammers.

"Wait here," Andreas said. "I'll be back in a minute."

"Don't take long. We should probably get home."

Andreas marched over to Ulrich, breaking into the circle around him. The other men stopped talking and stepped aside. "Have you seen Elsbeth?"

Ulrich smiled. "Not since we had dinner last night."

"Dinner?" Andreas's stomach churned.

"Yes, she was at Knipperdolling's house visiting Divara. When we finished our business preparing for tonight, I asked if I could buy her dinner. She looked like she needed some company." Ulrich's speech took on a humming tone.

"And you took pity on her, did you?"

"Wouldn't you?" Ulrich looked down at his fingers, and then clasped Andreas's shoulder. "We still haven't spent any time together since you showed up, Andreas. I'm beginning to think you're avoiding me. We're going to get something to drink. Come join us."

Andreas studied the men around Ulrich. He took in the way they joked, pretending to clobber each other with their hammers. For a moment, Andreas was tempted; it was an opportunity to learn something about the men around Ulrich. "Thanks, but I have to get back to Peter," Andreas said, setting off to find Peter.

"You look annoyed," Peter observed as Andreas settled again at his side.

"It was nothing. I was looking for—"

The piercing screams and explosion hit at the same time as the force of the blast threw Andreas and Peter to the ground. Shattered glass pierced people closest to the shop window. Stunned, Andreas looked over at Peter, who sat in the street, a trickle of blood running down his temple. Andreas reached his hand up to his head and discovered his own hand splotched with blood. People scattered in terror as rocks and pieces of wood and iron flew from the crowd into shop windows. Men ran up and down the square shouting in the empty holes where windows once were: "Out, Catholics! Out, heretics!"

"Saints!" Peter staggered to his feet.

Andreas, legs unsteady, pulled Peter toward the end of the marketplace, away from the flying stones and smashing windows. They passed a burning effigy of von Waldeck, as men with steins in their hands jumped over the flames, enthusiasm growing with each slug of beer. Several men loosened their trousers and started pissing on it to the cheering of the crowd.

"From bad to worse," Peter muttered.

"We need to get to the cathedral," Andreas said, thinking about the men surrounding Ulrich.

"Why?"

"A hunch."

They broke into a trot, circling down the street around the rowhouses fronting the market, and came to the east end of St. Paul's.

"Stop," Andreas called out abruptly, pulling Peter back into the shadow of St. Margaret's and pointing to where men carrying torches, ropes, hammers, and axes were entering the plaza in front of St. Paul's.

"They wouldn't," Peter cried.

"They would," Andreas said. "They couldn't do it before the elections, but now what prevents them?"

The charred ruins of a church he had witnessed burn outside Waldshut eight years ago crept into Andreas's mind. The peasants had swarmed over it like locusts, hacking, burning, and pillaging anything at hand. They pulled down the tower, chopped up the organ, and then they turned on the poor unfortunate priest. The man's screams had driven

Andreas into the woods. Those horrible screams still woke him up at night, his arms flailing. No matter how much he resisted the idea when he walked through St. Paul's last September, the cathedral had remained a symbol of hope to him that something good still graced the world. He and Peter froze as the men with their torches ran toward the Paradise Porch.

"No," Peter moaned.

"Follow me!" Andreas ran to the back of the cathedral. Reaching the courtyard, they slipped into the chapter house and from there entered the nave beside the altar. At the nave's other end, men streamed in from the Paradise Porch. Several were already attacking the side chapels, pulling down statues of the saints from their pedestals. Plaster and marble shattered on the ground.

"Oh, God," Peter lamented, putting his hand over his mouth.

A small group halted below the statue of the Virgin, unsure of what to do. Several of the men crossed themselves.

Then a gruff voice shouted, "For Christ and His kingdom!" A man threw a rope around Mary's neck. A couple of others grabbed the cord, and together they tugged until the statue crashed to the floor, breaking into pieces. Andreas and Peter helplessly watched as the marauders took heavy iron axes and hammers to the fallen stone, the clanging sound of mutilation echoing throughout the cathedral.

The pack of men continued their assault by pulling down the paintings and tapestries that hung in the side chapels, as dozens of marauders took their axes to the massive organ and chopped at the pipes, smashing the tubes and keyboard. Others went off to search the grounds. Andreas tugged on Peter's arm and pointed to a score of paintings piling up in the center of the cathedral. Men with swords sliced away the canvases and threw them in a small pile, while others used their axes to smash the frames. Shouting and laughing echoed throughout the cathedral as dozens of hands tore apart the rood screen separating the choir and altar from the rest of the church. A small party of four broke off from them and carried a triptych of Jesus's temptation in the wilderness out the front door.

Andreas and Peter remained still as the sacking grew worse. Stacks of wood and art littered the floor of the cathedral amid scattered pieces of stone and metal tubes from the organ. Some of the mob lowered their trousers and shit on the pile, while others relieved themselves of ale consumed earlier in the evening.

"Maybe these are the last days, after all," Peter said.

"It certainly feels like the end of something." Andreas's head moved around the cathedral, taking in the chaos.

Several men finished ripping out an altar panel and threw it on the floor as the astronomical clock chimed the hour. Three figures with axes ran over to it and started hacking away. Bits of metal clanged against the stone floor as they worked furiously to tear it off the wall.

"Not the clock," Andreas gasped.

The gang who had gone to the library returned, clutching ancient manuscripts to their chests. Books of meticulously copied pages, beautifully illustrated and lined with gold leaf, were casually thrown onto the stack of wood and canvas and silk. Someone brought a torch over and lowered it to the pile of manuscripts, paintings, and tapestries. They smoked a bit before erupting into flames.

As if in a trance, Peter stumbled out from the pillar they had been hiding behind.

"No, Peter—"

"The books," Peter wept. "Dear God!"

Andreas grabbed his arm and pulled him back.

More manuscripts were tossed on the pyre, the flames leaping toward the cathedral's ribbed vaults. Young boys jumped over the lesser fires, yelling and laughing at the older men's encouragement. Andreas gagged as the stench of shit, piss, and burning oils filled the cathedral. The smoke, having nowhere to go, formed a grey haze, rising to the top of the arches like a foggy morning mist lifting off a lake.

"It falls apart; the world comes undone," Peter mourned. "Dear Christ."

"Christ, indeed," Andreas said, examining the space where a massive statue of the crucifixion once stood. The crucified Christ was scattered in pieces on the floor. Glancing at the empty space where the statue of Jesus had been, Andreas noticed that the perfect forms of the two thieves crucified beside Jesus remained—unmolested.

Andreas and Peter's attention had been so focused on the rampage that they did not notice the figure that jumped up on the high altar. Above the excited shouts of triumphant men and squealing boys, the man on the altar shouted, his voice echoing through the cathedral, commanding attention.

"Brothers! Tear down the idols. Rejoice, for the great Whore of Babylon has fallen. Woe to her, and to all who follow her! Those who worship the whore and have bathed in the blood of the saints will be wiped from the face of the earth forever!"

Peter and Andreas looked at one another and then back at the altar.

Standing above them, Ulrich flashed a twisted grin, looking past them to the marauders. "Make straight the way of the Lord!" Ulrich shouted and looked directly at Andreas and Peter. "Cleanse the earth of its idolatries! Prepare the way for a new world!"

15

February 26

"AND SO, JUDITH SAVED her people by her faithfulness," Divara said, the Bible open in front of her. It had been two days since the sacking of the cathedral, and Divara invited a small group of women to join her in study. The story of Judith and Holofernes wasn't entirely new to most of the women. Ingrid said her father had a painting of it in his castle. Elsbeth, on the other hand, had never heard the tale before. It was from the Book of Judith and involved the Assyrian general Holofernes, who was going to destroy Judith's people, but under the pretense of sexual interest in the general, Judith visited her enemy's camp and managed to persuade guards that she was interested in Holofernes. The story made much of Judith's beauty. She was so attractive the general said it would be an insult not to have sex with her. She came to his tent one night, dressed to seduce him, but got him so drunk that he passed out. Then she took his sword, cut off his head, and carried it back in a sack to show her people that God had delivered them.

Divara smiled at the women arrayed around her. "She trusted God and He rewarded her."

Elsbeth considered Divara. She was a puzzle. The way she navigated the world fascinated Elsbeth. At first, she had thought Divara was at the mercy of Matthys and his moods, but soon Elsbeth saw the nuance in how she dealt with the man. Divara soothed his temper, smoothed the rough spots. Elsbeth thought she must have paid a price for this relationship with Matthys. Living with him had to be difficult. It gave her status, though. Women looked to her, and she enjoyed the attention.

"Sounds more like she trusted herself," Ingrid snorted. "God's not really acting; Judith is. She may ask God for strength, but it's Judith who acts. That's the point I'm making."

"Yes, of course, it was her action that won the day. But she had to have faith to go into her enemy's camp like that. She didn't know what would happen to her." Divara smiled, lips not a bit strained. Elsbeth thought her a compelling teacher. She felt the pull of the woman, but something made her hesitate.

"But she was used by God?" The question came from a young woman named Hille Feyken. Elsbeth had met her earlier when the girl first arrived from Frisia. Though she had a husband, she was very young. A headscarf usually covered her long auburn hair, but her slender figure and striking blue eyes accented her beauty. Elsbeth thought her extremely devout. She had come to the city with the other refugees and was like a sponge in Divara's studies, soaking up all she could. Her laughter was infectious, and she did not let her age prevent her from making contributions to the conversations.

"Yes, but 'used' can mean many things," Ingrid insisted. "It's a short path from 'used' to 'abused.'"

"I suppose, if you want, you could say that Judith's cunning and courage were the most important part," Divara conceded. "But the point is, she faced a much more powerful foe and didn't lose heart. Her people needed her. We may need a Judith if it comes to that."

"We should all have the courage Judith had," Feyken said, her shoulders straightening. "She passed the test of faith."

The room fell silent as the women contemplated such tests. Finally, Elsbeth broke the silence. "Does Matthys have a word for us? What can we expect?"

"He insists that Jesus returns here." Divara closed her Bible. "The prophet Melchoir Hoffman says Strasbourg, but Jan says here, in Münster."

"Do you believe it?" Rachel asked.

"All things are possible with God," Divara said.

"How did you end up with him?" Ingrid blurted out.

Divara responded like it was a normal question, not something of gossip—of something illicit, even. "I found him on the streets of Haarlem. He had just been converted by prophet Hoffman and was looking for instruction. I helped him out."

"You helped him out?" Ingrid repeated.

"I was a Benedictine nun. We were well educated in Scripture," Divara replied, looking around the room. "He really didn't know a lot. We used to spend hours together in study."

"Did you . . . you know?" Ingrid asked, thrusting her hips slightly.

Divara laughed with the women. "Not at that point, though his wife certainly thought we were. She told anyone who would listen that I spread my legs for Matthys so he could spread the Word of God."

Several women snickered, though Elsbeth thought about Matthys's wife. Where was she now? What did she feel when Matthys deserted her for Divara? It must have been difficult having this woman as a rival.

"Doesn't he scare you, though?" Ingrid, ever blunt, asked. "He frightens me to death."

"Jan?" Divara scrunched up her face. She posed like she was trying to figure out how to answer the question carefully. "It's part of being with a prophet. I used to be concerned when he started flailing around with one of his visions, but then I read the Bible, and those men were not easy to deal with either—locusts and honey, wearing the skin of beasts, dragging around a yoke over your neck—no, I get off easy. The thing is, he needs me."

Elsbeth looked around the room. Ingrid and the others enjoyed this back and forth. Divara had an easy way about her, but something still bothered Elsbeth. Perhaps it was her demand for loyalty that made Elsbeth hesitate to give herself to this woman the way she had to Ingrid, Ursula, and Rachel. She thought about Judith and Holofernes, about what the story didn't say about the lying, the deception. Was the lying part of God's plan? Maybe Judith seduced Holofernes—mounted him and rode him senseless as she poured wine down his gullet, getting him so drunk he passed out because God commanded it. Then, without a moment's hesitation, she chopped off his head. Would that be acceptable to God? And there was the matter of that head, carried back in a bloody sack to be dropped in front of her people. Evidently you could deal with your enemies however you pleased if God approved. As Elsbeth watched Divara happily laugh, she wondered if there were any limits, any place where even God might draw back and say, "Enough!"

16

Evening

"KILL THEM ALL!"

"What?" Knipperdolling sputtered.

"You heard me. Slay them all, every last one. They deserve it. God Himself will do it if we don't." Jan Matthys glared at Knipperdolling, who stroked his neck.

"We can't do that." Knipperdolling had called the meeting in his living room to discuss their next steps, but now he was regretting it. Matthys was off his chain and Knipperdolling could not get the leash back on.

"Are you questioning me?" Rising to his full height, Matthys stalked over to where Knipperdolling leaned against his windowsill.

"Not at all, but what you suggest can't be done." Knipperdolling straightened up to face Matthys.

"But we run things now; everyone has to obey us," Matthys insisted, pitch rising.

"It's not that easy. Besides, why do you want to kill them all?" Knipperdolling asked. "We have control of things. We have the churches, even St. Paul's; we own the council, and the guilds are with us. No one can touch you inside these walls. The others will have to live the way we want them to. We don't have to be murderous."

"Anyone who hasn't taken baptism can't be trusted. God has given us power; we should use it." Matthys tossed his arms up and down.

"If we kill them, we give our enemies reason to move against us," Knipperdolling countered. "We need friends. We spit in von Waldeck's eye and survived, but this would bring the whole of the empire down on us."

"So?" Matthys hissed.

Knipperdolling's hand rubbed his temple. "Brother, as more people flock to us, we'll be able to withstand anything the emperor or his popish fools throw our way. As it is now, we have too few to stand against them."

"Exactly why we can't trust the unbelievers." Matthys's arms waved faster.

"But wouldn't Jesus show them mercy?" Rothmann broke in.

Matthys slammed his fist on the table beside him. "When God told Saul to kill all the Amalekites, he stayed the sword instead. He disobeyed, so God took the kingdom from him and gave it to David. Saul failed God; I won't!"

Rothmann swiftly dropped his eyes from Matthys and sidled over to Knipperdolling. "He's popped out of the cuckoo clock."

"But our neighbors aren't Amalekites," Tilbeck said, standing near the fireplace. "We've brought many who were on the fence over to us. If we keep them inside the walls, we may be able to bring more to God."

Matthys was on Tilbeck immediately. "You presume to know how God thinks? I'm telling you, if we don't destroy these demons, they'll enter the house seven times stronger and destroy us. God demands sacrifice. We must give it to Him!" Matthys, inches away from Tilbeck's face, screamed, "Are you with me, or are you with them? Choose this day whom you'll serve! It's either God or Satan!"

"Do something," Rothmann whispered to Knipperdolling.

Matthys lurched around the room, flying from corner to corner. "We must be stronger than Saul! If he had killed the women, children, and livestock God commanded him to, he would've remained King of Israel! If we don't slay them all, God will take this city from us! We'll have shown ourselves unfit for His kingdom."

"But God has given us Münster to show His peace and compassion," Rothmann argued, throwing a glance toward the others who were gathered in the room.

Eyes narrowing, muscles tensing, Matthys's face contorted as the blue veins in his neck pulsed. He stood in place, pivoting in a circle to look at every person in the room. Knipperdolling's eyes registered the horror in their gaped mouths and widened eyes: Bockelson, Ulrich, Rothmann, Tilbeck, the other members of the council—even Divara and her friends appeared stunned by Matthys's suggestion of mass execution.

"Goddamn you all! I curse all those who stand in the way of God's will! Dogs and sorcerers surround us. We're drowning in an ocean of godless whores. Jesus says he comes at the end of days with a sword to separate and cleave those who follow him from those who don't."

"But the sword has been wielded against us; should we use it to strike down others?" Knipperdolling argued.

Matthys flayed his arms out toward the heavens, throwing his head back. "We fight the war of the saints. He comes to split the sheep from the goats, and we resist His will to our peril."

"Yes, brother, God did say those things." Knipperdolling took a step toward Matthys. "But Jesus also said we should be as harmless as doves and as wise as serpents. Perhaps it would be wiser to exile the evildoers out of the city instead of killing them."

"Bockelson!" Matthys called out, looking over his shoulder. "You're being very quiet."

Bockelson barely shifted as all eyes in the room turned to him. "Brother Matthys. Of course, you're right, but these people make sense as well. In due time, our numbers will increase as people flee to our New Jerusalem. No power on earth will be able to overcome us then, but Knipperdolling sees the matter before us clearly. We should exile the unbelievers, not kill them. Christ would give them an opportunity to repent of their sins."

Knipperdolling stifled a sigh of relief, hoping that Bockelson could tame the beast standing before them. He had put a lot of faith in Bockelson, and it was good to see it starting to pay off.

"It's godly to be merciful to our enemies." Knipperdolling reinforced the suggestion.

"Mercy thwarts God's will." Matthys's eyes drew into slits.

"God doesn't want us to kill all our neighbors," Rothmann said.

"Did they show us mercy when we were out there, in their world?" Matthys gesticulated wildly toward the windows. "Why should we show them any mercy here? At the judgment, snakes will crawl into their arse and out their mouth for the lies they told about us. They should fear us so that they will think twice before they persecute us."

"We don't have to kill them to make the world outside fear us. Forced exile will be painful enough," Knipperdolling said. "The stories the refugees tell will let the heathen know that something new is happening here. We send them away to spread our triumph, and then we'll close the gates and await the Lord."

Matthys cocked his head, looking like a confused rooster. Everyone else in the room looked at their feet. Without warning, Matthys burst out of the door and flew into the marketplace. A collective groan filled the room as everyone exhaled and looked at Knipperdolling. No one was sure what to do next, but they didn't have long to wait. Matthys, specks of thick sleet sparkling like diamonds on his black cloak, burst back into the room minutes later. Everyone moved closer to the walls.

"God said the land must be cleansed before the saints can claim it," Matthys proclaimed.

"There are many ways to purge the evil in our midst, brother," Rothmann offered, waving his arm toward the window. "We need to make sure we're blameless in the eyes of man so that the glory of God may be that much greater."

"We should at least offer them another chance to be baptized," Knipperdolling suggested. "If they refuse, we can say they're no longer welcome here."

"Then can we avenge the saints?" Matthys pleaded.

"If they don't accept our offer of holy peace, I'll be the first to bear the sword against them," Knipperdolling pledged.

"Then it's settled." Bockelson nodded at Knipperdolling. "Our mayor has given us his word, and he backs it up with a promise."

17

February 27

MORNING'S SUN WAS A pale presence, barely suggested by a smudged light in the leaden grey clouds. The wind had shifted overnight, bringing miserable weather to February's last days. Andreas put up his hood as he stood under the porch, looking out at a grim storm of freezing sleet and rain. Turning to go back inside, he was stopped by a commotion out in the street. Slipping and sliding across the courtyard, he opened the gate to see a blur of black and grey, coursing along the cobblestone street in front of the monastery.

"Repent! Repent! Repent!"

Andreas stepped back as Jan Matthys, black robe fluttering in his wake, swept past, screaming exhortations. *This grows tiresome.* Andreas closed the gate and went to inform Peter. Most of the other brothers had gone, departing to monasteries elsewhere, but Peter remained, and Andreas was not going to leave him. He walked through the reception area, down the hall, and entered Peter's study.

"What now?" Peter asked as Andreas opened the door.

"Matthys has slipped his tether." Andreas draped his cloak over a chair by the fireplace and took his usual seat.

Peter, face clenched in concentration, put down his book and drummed his fingers on his desk. A few moments later, he stood and grabbed his cloak off the hook on the wall.

"Peter, where are you going? It's miserable outside."

"I have to go to the market."

"Why?"

"Something is up, and I want to see what it is."

"Probably more of the same, don't you think?"

"I'm not sure, but everything that happens now is critical," Peter replied. He walked to the door, stopped, and looked at Andreas.

"Is it that important?" Andreas asked. "You know it will be more theater, another pretense to gain power."

"Precisely why we must go," Peter said. "I'm not sure I know what they intend. Are you coming?"

Andreas groaned, rose, grabbed his cloak, and tossed it around his shoulders. "Lead on," he said as they headed toward the marketplace.

Entering the fish market, they walked over to where Matthys was standing in the middle of the plaza. Scores of people were huddled against one another, staring at Matthys, waiting for the latest word from God. Soaking wet from the cold snow and sleet, Matthys's face was hidden behind the strings of hair hanging from his head. His beard was mottled with ice and mucus, and his eyes radiated a queer wildness as he whirled around, his arms spread wide.

"Repent! Repent! Repent!"

He slogged toward the center of the market, the expectant crowd trailing after him. He collapsed on the rough stones and remained motionless. A few people knelt in the mud and ice, praying fervently. Several dozen people closed in around him, but before they could touch him, Matthys leapt up and ran among the crowd.

"This is the Father's will, that you should be cleansed," he said, grabbing one of the younger women. "Be baptized and you shall be saved, Father." He clutched an older man.

Some people wore faces of absolute rapture, their expressions joyous, but others drew back when Matthys approached, their faces scrunching into fearful grimaces as his hands grabbed at them. Several men wearing thick black woolen cloaks, a murder of crows on a snow-covered street, skittered over the ice, trying to reach the prophet. Others hung back under the arcades, bracing themselves for the next explosion or tossed stone. Boards still covered the windows from the destruction touched off on the night of council elections. It only took a few seconds of listening to Matthys for many to quickly slip back into their homes and lock the doors.

"Nothing new here." Andreas tugged Peter's arm. "Let's go home; at least it's warm there."

"Not yet. We haven't seen the final act."

Matthys's hands flew up as he arched his back and bellowed, "We must be washed clean! Sinners must be baptized today! Those who pollute us must be driven from our midst!"

Scores of men standing beside Matthys formed into teams of three, going from door to door, banging on the homes lining the market.

"Come out! Prepare for judgment! Come out!" The cries echoed around the square as residents hesitantly opened their doors, like animals peeking out of their caves to see if predators were close by. When some were slow to come into the market, Matthys's men barged inside their homes and pulled them out.

"There are others not of my flock that must be brought in!" Matthys yelled, as confused groups of people came into the marketplace from all over the city and huddled together in the cold, damp street.

"They could've picked a better day for this," Andreas complained, wrapping his cloak around him, shoulders hunched against the sleet.

Peter pulled his hood tighter around his head. "There's never a good day for this."

Several men pushed and pulled a cart holding a huge copper pot from a local brewery toward Rothmann's preachers, who stood in the center of the plaza. The pot was carefully placed on the ground, water sloshing over the sides. The preachers gathered around it, waiting.

"Just like the night the madness started," Andreas said.

Huddled under the arcades, mothers tried to protect their wailing babies against the bitter winter storm, as elderly men and women, without cloak or coat, shivered in the cold, drawing closer to one another in a futile effort to stay warm. Despite the crying and protests, Bernard Rothmann spoke to the men and women quietly. Andreas watched as he kissed some of them, and they went to where the copper pot stood and were immediately baptized. Those Rothmann did not kiss were ordered down to the far end of the market by City Hall, where Matthys was haranguing all those sent there.

"Peter? What's happening?"

"It looks like we have a decision to make," Peter answered.

"Why?" Andreas asked. "What is this?"

"I can't be sure, but I think they're doing something with those who don't take baptism."

In a moment, Rothmann and Ulrich stood in front of them. "I'm sorry you have to be out here in such awful weather. You need to be baptized, or you'll have to leave the city." Andreas thought Rothmann sounded almost apologetic.

"I can't be baptized." Peter raised his hands to Rothmann and Ulrich. "You know I can't."

"Why not, Peter? You're a good man, not like some of those others. Join us. You don't owe the Church anything," Rothmann urged.

"I owe it everything."

"But, *Father*," Ulrich mocked. "Everyone knows the Church is a whore."

"That may be, Ulrich, but she is the only mother we have, and from the looks of things, you're an orphan once more."

"You tread on thin ice, old man." Ulrich brought his face to Peter's.

Rothmann interrupted. "Andreas, will you be baptized?"

"There's no need of my being baptized; I've been baptized in the spirit."

Rothmann's brows knitted. "In the spirit? What does that mean?"

"I came to true faith the day I saw Michael Sattler martyred."

"You were there when they martyred Sattler?" Rothmann looked astonished. "Why didn't I know this?"

"It made quite an impression." Andreas's hand went to the scar on his face. "Since I returned to Münster, I've been trying to lead Peter to the true faith."

Peter glanced at Andreas, raising an eyebrow.

"I have an idea." Ulrich flashed Peter a look of satisfaction. "We allow them to stay in Münster a bit longer. Perhaps Droste can be persuaded to repent. It's not his fault he was raised by a whore."

Rothmann considered the suggestion before responding. "Andreas, you and Peter can stay, but we intend on living a pure life. Join us soon or we *will* throw you out."

"Your graciousness is welcome," Andreas said, bowing slightly. He exhaled only when the men moved on to the next group of shivering people.

"You're trying to show me the true faith?" Peter shot Andreas a smile.

"It was the best I could come up with on the spot. Besides, how can you be sure that's not what I'm doing?"

"I finally get to see your plan."

The falling barrage of ice had stopped, but a heavy blanket of fear suffocated the marketplace. Andreas glanced toward City Hall and noticed Matthys heading toward St. Ludger's Gate along with the people who refused baptism.

"Do you think they meant people had to leave today? This very minute?" Andreas asked, pointing to the crowd following Matthys.

"There have been rumors; surely people have prepared for this."

"I think they're being thrown out of the city—they're exiling them now!"

"In this weather?" Peter protested. "They'll die."

"They're headed for St. Ludger's Gate. You coming?"

Nodding his head, Peter followed Andreas to the south portal of the city. They followed the inner ring road until St. Ludger's came into view. Hordes of people were lined up along the wall, waiting to be inspected before they were forced outside.

"Oh, God . . . they're not—" Peter cried.

"They are." Andreas guided Peter to the opposite side of the street, away from the line of exiles. Guards stood at the gate, taking everything people had brought before shoving them out of the city. Men, women, and children slowly removed their coats and gave all their satchels and purses to the guards. Wailing and angry shouting bounced off the walls.

"They're taking . . . everything," Peter gasped.

Andreas fought back the urge to attack a man commanding a mother to take off the cloak shielding her baby. He felt a hand touch his arm, pulling him back from his tunnel of rage.

"Andreas?" Peter's hand gripped Andreas's wrist.

"If I had a spear, someone would die," Andreas growled.

"You sound like them."

"I don't care."

"You should," Peter warned.

"Why?"

"Because anger consumes you."

"If that's true, it's because I've seen this before," Andreas lamented. "Those with power and money have the armies, while the poor have only swords and grievances. In the end, the powerful have the better of it. How can I not be angry?"

"Righteous anger needs to be tempered with mercy."

"I have mercy for my enemies," Andreas declared, "as long as they are swinging from a tree outside my window."

"Mockery is another expression of your anger, Andreas. It drags you into their chaos."

Andreas shook his head, wanting to destroy everything in front of him. He caught sight of Matthys with a spear pointed at the chest of one of the city's former patricians. The well-dressed man sat on a wagon containing barrels and boxes covered by a tarp. Evidently, someone had forewarned him of what was to come.

Matthys was yelling at his helpless victim. "You're not getting out of here free and clear, you filthy liar! Turn over the wagon, or I'll make you puke out your goods!"

"But I have a letter of safe conduct from the council," the man pleaded.

"And I don't give a shit if you have a letter from the pope; you're not leaving this city with what belongs to us!" Matthys shrieked. "Get off that goddamn wagon before I run you through!"

The man hesitated and Matthys called over some of his men. "Take off all his clothes, right down to the skin with this one."

"But I was promised safe passage out of the city," the man cried.

Matthys put his face so close to the man their noses were touching. "You *are* getting safe passage out of the city. You're still alive, aren't you?"

Whimpering, the man left his cart and shuffled helplessly toward the gate. Matthys turned his attention to others.

"Might as well start where the rot begins," Andreas muttered. He headed for Matthys.

Peter grabbed him. "No! Don't!"

"I don't have a choice." Andreas glared at Matthys.

"There're always choices. They would kill you before you reach him."

Andreas stood mute, pity stirring as old and young alike stumbled in tears out of Münster. A city built as a fortress to protect the wealth of its citizens—a place of safety for those within the walls—was fast becoming a prison. "There has to be something we can do."

"What would you suggest?" Peter asked. "Wisdom is knowing when you have nothing to win the battle. We can fight, but we'll join that line." Peter pointed to the exiles.

"At least we'd be free of these bastards." Andreas's hands drew into fists.

"And Elsbeth, what about her?" Peter reminded Andreas.

Andreas slumped slightly. He stomped away from the gate as Peter followed. They walked silently until Andreas said, "I don't know who to feel sorrier for."

"What's that?" Peter said.

"I don't know who to pity more," Andreas continued, "those who are leaving, or the ones who are left behind."

"That's a hard knot to untangle."

18

March 2

ELSBETH HAD NO INTEREST in Nitzing Convent, but Ingrid and her friends were convinced that the nuns of Nitzing needed liberation. Ingrid was quite persuasive, overcoming Elsbeth's resistance to accompany them to the convent. Walking with her friends, Elsbeth mused that in earlier times, the nuns of Überwasser would have cared little for the fate of the poorer nuns at Nitzing. Elsbeth entertained the thought that perhaps Nitzing's nuns had taken advantage of the city's chaos and had already fled. That hope was dashed when they arrived to locked gates, boisterous crowds, and frightened faces peering out the windows of Nitzing at the mob assembling outside.

Nitzing and her looms had escaped being sacked, but with the continuing purge and exile of Catholics and Protestants who failed to take baptism, those seizing control of the city had grown bolder. Elsbeth glanced around her. Almost every woman from Überwasser and some from the other convents were there, joined by a few dozen men. She spied Ulrich standing with a small knot of men engaged in discussion. Ingrid pulled Elsbeth into the line of women that had formed at the gate and were shouting at the fearful faces looking down on them.

"Sisters, dear sisters, we have come for you!" The chant grew louder and louder until Rachel and Ursula stepped forward from the line while others quieted.

"Sisters of Nitzing, put away your looms and lies, and join us!" Rachel shouted. "We have come to set you free!"

Some of the faces peeking out from the windows disappeared, drawing back into the convent.

"We want you to join us. We're your family now. No harm will come to you!" Ursula picked up the plea.

Amid the laughter and banging on the gates, Elsbeth thought it must be frightening on the other side of the convent's walls. She hated it when people were left without choices, forced to have their decisions made for them. Lost in her thoughts, Elsbeth did not notice Ulrich standing at her side, looking up at the windows.

"They've seen this before," Ulrich said.

"Pardon?" Elsbeth asked.

Ulrich's gaze stayed focused on the nuns. "The sisters—they've seen this before. This is not the first time people wanted to break in. Rumor is that they have enormous wealth inside . . . looms, wool. The weavers' guild complained they couldn't compete with cheap labor from the nuns. Blamed it on the Prince-Bishop's desire to build his wealth."

"Did they do anything about it?"

"Some men tried to break in one night. One of the monks at the Augustinian monastery had promised one of the nuns he would take her away if she wanted. Sweet words whispered through iron fences to seduce her to open the gate to him. He talked some guild members into joining his plan, but a servant girl discovered them and sounded the alarm."

"What happened?"

"The men were brought to jail and kept until the next morning. Council convened a hearing, heard testimony, and then decided to exile the ringleader."

"What happened to him?"

"You'll have to ask Andreas."

Elsbeth wheeled around to face Ulrich. "No," she exclaimed, "Andreas wouldn't do that, Ulrich. You tell tales."

"Do I?" Ulrich countered. "What did Andreas tell you about why he left Münster? Why was it so long before he came back?"

Elsbeth backed away from Ulrich, shaking her head. "That can't be. Andreas?"

Ulrich touched her shoulder. "How much do you really know about him? Why does he spend so much time in the monastery while the rest of us work to make things better?"

"Father Peter needs him."

"Does Father Peter need him so much that he neglects you?" Ulrich probed.

At this, everything stopped for Elsbeth. She heard the crowd cheering, saw a woman trying to climb over the gate, was faintly aware that the crowd around her grew more intense, but it all became muted as she worked out this new twist. Could she have been wrong? Ulrich sounded so sure, so confident. Had Andreas deceived her?

"What're you up to, Ulrich?" Elsbeth searched his face for a sign of joking, but no amusement rose to his eyes.

"Trying to help my friend not be deceived." Ulrich's eyebrows arched up. "You wouldn't be the first to be taken in by Andreas." Ulrich nodded toward the convent.

Elsbeth walked away from Ulrich, struggling with her thoughts. She thought she knew Andreas as much as a woman knows a man, but did she really know him? She believed him when he said he left to find his parents, but what if that was a lie? How could the man who saved her life turn around and keep so much hidden from her? Where *had* Andreas been since the night they spent together?

"Elsbeth? Are you well?" Ulrich cupped her elbow, drawing closer.

The muscles in her jaw tightened. "I have to go." She jerked her arm away from Ulrich and shot down the street to the monastery. Arriving, she vigorously rang the bell at the gate.

"All right, calm down; I'm coming."

Andreas opened the door and Elsbeth pushed him aside, stalked into the courtyard, and faced him, hands on her hips, trying to catch her breath. She stared at him for several seconds before she spoke. "Tell me again why you left Münster!"

"Why?" Andreas countered.

"Stop evading the question," Elsbeth demanded. "Why did you leave?"

"I've already told you . . . " Andreas replied. "What's this about?"

"You left on your own? Nothing to do with being exiled?" Elsbeth challenged.

"No, where did you hear that?" Andreas asked. They stood fixed, eyes locked. "Wait . . . did this come from Ulrich?"

"In fact, it did, but it should have come from you."

"Well, it couldn't come from me because I didn't do what you think I did. It was Ulrich who talked the guild men into helping him plunder Nitzing."

"That just makes it worse. I could respect some honesty, but this . . . you should be ashamed." Elsbeth folded her arms.

"I can prove it," Andreas said. "Ask Father Peter if you won't believe me."

Elsbeth shook her head in disbelief, confusion eroding her certitude. "I don't know who to believe anymore."

"And that's just the way Ulrich wants it." Andreas held out his hand.

Elsbeth smacked it away. "I won't be toyed with."

"Then just ask Peter," Andreas said, exasperated.

"Ask me what?" Peter ambled out into the courtyard.

"Father, did Andreas raid Nitzing Convent? Was that why he left?"

"Elsbeth, come inside where it's warmer." Peter turned on his heel and walked back into the monastery, leaving them both standing in the courtyard.

Elsbeth remained behind, hesitant, until Andreas said, "It's all right. All the brothers have left. We're the only ones here."

She looked at him, her anger dissipating slightly as he held out his hand, indicating she should go first. Her shoulders relaxed and she walked into the reception hall, following Peter into the refectory. He motioned to the bench, and Elsbeth took a seat while Peter disappeared into the kitchen. She had never been in a male sanctum before. Entering a world forbidden to women was disorienting, the thrill of the unknown mixing with the musky odors filling the room. This place smelled *thicker* than Überwasser.

Andreas took a seat on the other side of the table, staring at her, his hands in his lap. Peter set three steins on the table, pushing one toward Elsbeth. Andreas grabbed his and took a long gulp, wiping his mustache dry when he finished.

"Now, perhaps, you could tell me the tale you've heard?" Peter asked Elsbeth.

"Ulrich said Andreas had seduced a nun at Nitzing into opening the gate to him. He was going to rob the convent but was caught and thrown out of the city."

Peter and Andreas exchanged glances. "Andreas may have his reasons for not telling you everything," Peter said, "but he was not the one who instigated the attempt on Nitzing."

"Why would Ulrich say he was, then?" Elsbeth asked, her gaze shifting from Peter to Andreas.

"To drive a wedge between us," Andreas explained. "To turn you against me."

"Why would he do that?" Elsbeth muttered. "He has been nothing but kind to me since we arrived here."

A silence filled the room before Peter spoke. "It wasn't just the incident at Nitzing, but all the things Ulrich did that finally led to his exile," Peter began. "Nitzing was only the last transgression, but that one brought city council into it, and he forced their hand. They had to exile him. When he left, I thought I would never see him again."

Elsbeth cradled her head. "But . . . he sounded—"

"Convincing?" Andreas interjected.

"Yes."

"You would not be the first to find him so," Peter said. "I used to wonder if I had failed Ulrich, but I see him more clearly now."

"There's no reason to lie about Andreas. What could he gain?" Elsbeth was still perplexed.

"Much, especially if he thinks we grow close." Andreas reached across the table for Elsbeth's hand.

Peter glanced at their enclosed hands. "Elsbeth, men do all manner of things to their advantage. Ulrich was a moment in my life when I learned how deep deceit runs in the service of desire. He gives you what you want to hear because he wants something from you."

"I'm sorry," Elsbeth said. "It's been so hard to know who to trust in this city."

"The chaos is intended," Peter offered. "If we're off-balance, we're easier to control." With that Peter rose from the table and set off for his office.

Elsbeth and Andreas sat in silence, their heads pointed toward the floor. Finally, Elsbeth spoke. "At least Ulrich and his friends were there to help me move my things. You're close, then you're far away. You've become like a ghost ever since our night at Überwasser."

"I had to be here." Andreas caressed her arm. "Peter needed me."

"So did I." Elsbeth moved her arm away. "Some days I can't make sense of how mad things have become. I could really use your help."

"Peter did say you could come here."

"I like my friends and my freedom." Elsbeth shifted her hand closer to Andreas. "People watch out for me. Even Ulrich told me not to go out when the purge began the first night of the exile."

Andreas's brow furrowed.

"Don't look like that, Andreas. He lies to annoy you, but he's not evil. Besides, I must stand on my own. What if something were to happen to you? What if you left again? I need people who will help me if it comes to that."

Andreas rose and took Elsbeth's hand, helping her up. "I understand, but you would have the guest quarters to yourself here. I would be closer."

"I'll keep it in mind."

"We share something, something important," Andreas ventured.

The back of Elsbeth's hand touched Andreas's cheek. "I have to get back. Ingrid and the others may worry about where I've gone. We'll talk more." Elsbeth headed for the door, Andreas following behind.

They came outside the gate into a street full of people streaming from Nitzing. The revelers were laughing, carrying golden plates, candle-stick holders, reliquaries, even tapestries. Some had bundles of wool in their arms. A couple of men were rolling a cask of wine along the street. And trailing them all, Elsbeth spotted Ulrich carrying a massive, bejew-eled chalice lovingly in his hands.

He grinned. "Praise the Lord."

"Ulrich, what are you doing?" Elsbeth asked.

"Spoiling Egypt."

"What?"

"When Israel left Egypt, they took the Egyptian's wealth," Ulrich said, passing them with a wink. "We take Rome's."

Elsbeth watched Ulrich march up the street, occasionally raising his chalice over his head. She pondered a God who has His people steal. Is God a thief, taking from all those who were not chosen? It all seemed to have a certain sense to it, but Elsbeth shuddered when she considered where the path of the logic took her. A God beyond limits was capable of anything His followers desired.

19

March 3

"Andreas, come with me quickly," Peter called, poking his head in his office.

"What is it?" Andreas, startled, slammed shut the book he had taken off Peter's shelves.

"Don't ask questions, just come."

"Where to?"

Peter didn't answer as he rushed away and headed to the rear of the monastery, trotting through the back doors. "I want you to see something," he called back at Andreas, before he ran across the fields and gardens to the inner wall, quickly mounting the steps to the promenade.

"Slow down!" Andreas was surprised at how nimble Peter was at his age. By the time he climbed the stairs, Peter was leaning over the wall.

"Why are we up here?" Andreas asked.

"You'll see shortly." Peter concentrated on the horizon.

The two men focused their attention out into the countryside. It was hard to see past the thick fog that had formed over the moats, but slowly the sun peeked out from a gloomy sky. Eventually, the mists cleared to reveal hundreds of men moving massive amounts of dirt and building earthen defenses beyond the outer wall. Their wheelbarrows and shovels formed an unbroken chain of activity.

"So, it begins," Andreas murmured. "First the ditches and soon the ramparts. It's not hard to see what future takes shape out there."

Peter shielded his eyes against the morning light with his hand so he could watch the workers. "We've been blockaded before, but this is different."

"Yes, I'm afraid so." Andreas's stomach turned sour.

The fields that encircled Münster were fallow, but in past years they would have been busy with farmers planting crops, readying livestock pens, and preparing to feed the city. Though it was only days into March, in the coming months, plants and crops would have exploded into sheets of color, painting the countryside yellow and lavender. Now, brown dirt and mud marred the fields. Experience had taught Andreas what the coming days would bring. There would be trains of wagons arriving from Köln, Lübeck, perhaps even as far away as Amsterdam. They would be loaded with saltpeter, sulfur, iron musket balls, and heavy artillery shells to stuff into cannons. Following those wagons would be mercenaries, their families, and mistresses, their dingy tents sprouting like mushrooms from the barren earth. If nothing changed, Münster would be soaked in blood.

"So, Peter, will the Kingdom of Christ be stillborn?"

Peter surveyed the men laboring with their wheelbarrows and shovels. "Evidently it's in our souls to kill the things God creates."

"Ah, yes, well . . . *that* . . . " The back of Andreas's throat filled with thick drainage, making it difficult to breathe.

"I need to see what happens elsewhere in the city." Peter headed back to the stairs.

They walked toward St. Paul's, stunned to find the preparations outside were being matched by those inside the walls. Men hauled cannons and shells up the ramps leading to the promenade, ran weapons out toward the outer wall, and wheeled barrels of mud to stack against the wall in order to patch holes in the event of attack.

Peter stopped one of the men. "What happens here?"

"We're following orders to prepare for attack," the man replied.

"Who gives the orders?"

"Bockelson." The man picked up his wheelbarrow and headed toward this assignment.

Andreas wondered why Bockelson and not Knipperdolling or Tilbeck was in charge. Was Matthys too busy praying to organize things?

"I'm going to Cathedral Hill," Peter said.

They walked from St. Mary's Gate past Überwasser Church until they stood in the shadow of St. Paul's. Former knights and mercenaries, still wearing the clothing of their former lives, were showing others how to store gunpowder and saltpeter in St. Margaret's. Several men were pushing a large cannon across the field of stone and dirt toward the cathedral. Others busily stacked guns in front of St. Paul's as a man took count of the weapons in front of him. Everywhere Andreas and Peter looked, men were resolutely preparing for war.

"What was it you once told me about saints?" Andreas moved aside to let some men carrying a long box pass by. "I'm not sure I recall it, but when I was young, I remember you saying something about how the holier someone appears, the more concerned we should be."

"The more sainted, the more tainted?"

"Ah yes, that was it," Andreas said, nodding at the massive stacks of guns piled up on the cathedral steps.

"Life grows more perilous."

"I'm afraid so," Andreas replied. "But there is still time for us to leave."

Peter turned to Andreas, his face pinched. "Get behind me, Satan. Do what you must, but this is my home, the only home I've ever known. For good or ill, my fate is here, and I cannot leave. Take Elsbeth, go start a family, but give me some peace."

Andreas bowed his head. "I'm sorry. I guess I'm afraid."

Peter watched another cannon roll past them, men grunting in exertion. "We're all afraid, Andreas, but this is my life now."

Andreas put his arm around Peter's shoulders. "This is *our* life now."

20

March 14

THE TRANSFORMATION TO ARMED CAMP was far quicker than most expected. When the local peasants of surrounding towns and villages started digging the siege lines, Münster launched into intense preparations. Parties of men went outside the walls daily, destroying all that could aid the anticipated mercenaries. Windmills, churches, houses, anything that would provide advantage to the attackers was leveled. A ring of destruction now marred the view from the walls as everyone inside prepared to defend the city.

Bockelson was proving a surprisingly adept tactician, dividing the city into military units, assigning people to different gates, establishing a watch on the walls, and setting up communal meals among the workers. Preparing a home fit for Jesus's return was exhausting. Captivated with the joy of pulling down the old order, few had considered that their freedom would come with a cost.

Herbert Rusher, head of Münster's blacksmith's guild, thought about the cost as he stood watch in the cold March darkness with his two friends. "Why don't Matthys, Bockelson, and their gang ever take a night's watch? It's goddamn cold up here," Rusher complained. "Where are the prophets and preachers? Has anyone ever seen Matthys's arse up on the wall?"

"I'm sure the prophet has his reasons." Henry Mollenheck tried to mollify his friend.

"The prophet has his reasons?" Rusher jeered, refusing to be calmed. "Maybe the cold we suffer is the reason none of them ever come and help us."

"Rusher, be quiet. You never know who stands below the wall," Mollenheck warned. "There're itching ears everywhere."

"I'm sure of that. And why do they itch? To turn in anyone who questions our leaders? We're doomed is what it is," the blacksmith muttered.

"Shut up!" Mollenheck warned. "You want to get yourself killed, fine—but don't drag me into it."

The third man on guard duty, Henry Gresbeck, ale cup to lip, pretended to be occupied with the mercenaries and their carousing.

"I don't care anymore. They made promises, and none of 'em have been kept," Rusher groused. "They told us if we cleansed the city of papists, we were preparing a place fit for the Lord; that's what they said. They promised half the empire would run to us; that they'd come from all over to stand with us. Some of my best friends were driven out of the city with nothing but the clothes on their backs."

Henry Gresbeck stepped to the fire to warm himself. "Rusher, you need more patience."

"I had patience when this first started, Gresbeck, but they promised the Lord would come when we threw out the unbelievers. We did, and what happened? They took the best houses for themselves; they keep the goods they steal from convents and monasteries; and God wants this? Liars is what they are."

"Perhaps God wishes to vanquish all our enemies before He returns," Mollenheck said.

"Don't be stupid," Rusher shot back. "We've been deceived."

Gresbeck went over to the edge of the wall and looked to see if anybody was standing in the streets. "They're prophets. We shouldn't question their authority."

"Matthys is a shit prophet!" Rusher spat out.

"Goddammit, you stupid ass," Gresbeck shot back. "Shut up!"

"Why should I? Who do they think they are, these Dutchmen? They're asleep in their beds while we stand out here, our cocks ready to drop off from the cold, and where're they?"

"They run things now," Gresbeck argued. "We're not to question God's leaders."

"Wasn't that what we tried to overcome, the ones who told us to obey their authority because God made 'em the rulers?" Rusher scoffed. "How is this lot any different than the ones we got rid of?"

"You go too far, Rusher," Gresbeck said. "God doesn't call us to an easy life."

"That's fine for you, but not for me. Matthys is not worth a baker's fart. He's a lying shit prophet, and we eat the crap that falls from his mouth. I'm sick of having to take orders from strangers. I'm tired of having to live like this."

"If you keep saying those things, you won't have to worry about it much longer." Gresbeck took a long drink from his mug.

"How's that?" Rusher asked.

"Living—you won't have to worry about that part of things much longer," Gresbeck said, as he turned and walked further down the wall.

21

March 15

AT THE SOUND OF ST. LAMBERT'S BELLS, Andreas put down his tools. No one could predict what time the bells would sound, but when they did, everyone needed to come to the marketplace. It was the not knowing that put Andreas on edge. It was hard to plan your day when you never knew when a good chunk of it was going to be lost. Andreas walked up the hill to the central marketplace, searching for Elsbeth. When he arrived at the assembly, he spotted her standing with Ulrich, his hand resting on her shoulder. *Why does she still talk to him?* He strode over and stood on the other side of Elsbeth.

"Andreas," Ulrich said. "So good to see you. How's Peter?"

"Peter's fine," Andreas mumbled. "What's it today, another harangue from Rothmann's preachers?"

"No one seems to know." Elsbeth took Andreas's hand. "How's your day so far?"

"Bockelson ordered the carpenters to start working on support timbers for the tunnel walls," Andreas said. "I've been busy."

"Tunnels?" Elsbeth asked.

"The city has several tunnels built under the walls. We use them to raid the camps outside at night," Andreas explained.

"I had no idea," Elsbeth said.

"Not everyone knows about them," Andreas said.

"What's this?" Elsbeth said, eyeing a ragged-looking man being escorted into the marketplace.

"Herbert Rusher, the blacksmith," Ulrich replied. "He's in trouble."

Rusher was a massive man whose huge fingers reminded Andreas of sausages every time he saw them. His long dark hair hung down in oily strands over his face, obscuring his eyes. His head swung from one side to the other, glaring at the crowds as his captors pulled him by a chain toward the center of the market. Andreas winced. Rusher's face was swollen and puffy with a bruise surrounding one of his eyes. He was a pitiful, stumbling animal.

"What's going on here?" Elsbeth asked.

"I'm not sure." Dread filled Andreas.

A disturbance arose from the edge of the crowd as Knipperdolling, Tilbeck, Rothmann, Bockelson, and Matthys entered the square. They proceeded solemnly to the center of the market, people stepping aside to let them pass.

"They seem somber," Elsbeth said.

"Rusher looks terrified," Andreas noted.

Matthys and his companions made their way toward Herbert Rusher, who stood cowering, his eye on the approaching men.

"Dear God . . . " Elsbeth murmured. "What is this?"

Matthys stopped and raised his arms, leaned back, and looked toward the sky. A hush fell on the gathering, expectancy permeating the atmosphere. Everything stopped.

"Citizens, our brother has been led astray by Satan. Last night, possessed by an evil spirit, he called down the curse of God by blaspheming God's servants."

Murmuring built through the crowd, softly at first as people worked out what was happening, but then the buzzing grew stronger. Isolated voices rose from the crowd.

"Throw him out!"

"Cleanse us, Lord!"

"Deliver us from evil!"

Matthys shot his arms skyward. "I've prayed, but I need to ask you all, what shall we do with those who seek to destroy us? What did God do with those who disobeyed, with the people of Sodom and Gomorrah?"

"Cast him out!"

"Cut him down!"

Andreas cringed at the voices around him.

"Destroy him!"

"How dare he bring judgment on us?"

The accusations spread like tiny flames gathering tinder to themselves. Andreas noticed that many of those cursing Rusher did not even know the man. He was no one to them. But Andreas had worked with him in the tunnels, preparing obstacles to block entrance from outside if invaders ever discovered the tunnels. Rusher was known for questioning the leaders, but he was an honest man, a long way from evil.

"Punish him!"

"Out, Satan!"

As the tumult spread through the crowd, Andreas pondered how quickly the persecuted took up the stone against someone weaker. In a few minutes, a bellowing, belligerent mob was howling for the justice of God to fall on the blacksmith. If epithets were stones, the man would have been dead by now. Andreas lowered his head and groaned; Elsbeth squeezed his hand tighter. His own body surprised him when it started to shake involuntarily. *Why can I not be done with this?*

"You two might want to prepare yourselves." Ulrich rose on his toes to get a better look.

Matthys circled the blacksmith, alternately glowering back and forth between him and the crowd. Suddenly, the prophet stopped and screamed, "This enemy of God puked out curses against me! He pollutes us! If we let him live, we bring down the wrath of God on us all!"

Andreas's eyes shot to Ulrich; his mouth had turned up at the corners.

"We must rip up this noxious weed, root and all, and destroy it before it destroys us!" Matthys yelled.

Andreas noticed the carnivorous intensity in Matthys's eyes. "Rusher runs out of time," he whispered to Elsbeth.

"Maybe this is for show, and they'll throw him out like the others," Elsbeth said. "No one's been murdered yet."

"Oh, great prophet, surely your judgments are just and true, but please stay your hand for a moment!" Herman Tilbeck yelled, approaching Matthys.

The crowd settled, curious as to this new development in the drama.

"Throw him in prison, brother, and we can decide this later," Tilbeck pleaded. "There's no need for violence."

Matthys cocked his head, confused. Everyone remained frozen.

"Do you have a problem with God's will, Tilbeck?" Matthys demanded, rushing toward him. The veins in Matthys's neck bulged so clearly even Andreas could see them.

"Prophet, this man is guilty of betrayal." Tilbeck shrank back. "Perhaps we should hold a trial to confirm your judgments, so we can't be accused of injustice."

Matthys glared maliciously at Tilbeck, his face increasingly beet red in color. He motioned Rothmann and Knipperdolling to his side. After a few minutes of discussion, Matthys broke from his counselors and lumbered around the square. Andreas recalled this was the same quietness right before the order came to lower Elsbeth into the river. The longer Matthys walked, the more anxious he grew.

Suddenly, Matthys began screaming incoherently, running through the men and women, grunting loudly. After a few moments of lurching around, he stopped abruptly and calmly went back to Tilbeck. He hunched over Tilbeck, pressing his face into the mayor's brow. "Who do *you* think you are to oppose God's will?" Matthys challenged. Tilbeck squared his shoulders and drew himself up. "Have you taken leave of yourself? Are you mad? Who opposes God and lives to tell the tale? Arrest him!" Matthys commanded, pointing to Tilbeck.

For the next few moments, the only sound heard in the square was the sound of a crow cawing from the tower of St. Lambert's.

"You can't do that!" Tilbeck finally shouted.

"Shut up, or you'll share the blacksmith's fate," Matthys warned. "Take him to Rosenthal prison!" Matthys waved his hand dismissively and turned his attention back to Rusher.

Andreas heard someone murmur, "Who's he to imprison our mayor?"

A smattering of angry voices spread through the marketplace.

Andreas searched the faces around him. He held hope that perhaps this might turn out differently than other mobs he had witnessed, but Bockelson, standing next to the blacksmith, looked as if someone put his feet to flame. Bockelson's head moved quickly back and forth from Matthys to the crowd. His face contorted into a terrified mask as he sprang into action.

"No!" Bockelson screamed; grabbing a halberd from one of the guards, he shoved it into Rusher's back, blood spilling as the wounded blacksmith fell to his knees.

Gasps and screams echoed through the marketplace. Those in front backed swiftly away from the fallen man. Andreas stared at Rusher who was stunned, unsure of what had just happened. Rusher reached around to feel his back. When he brought it back to his face, he discovered his hand was covered in blood. Confused, the blacksmith looked back at Bockelson before he fell on his side, groaning loudly.

Elsbeth's body convulsed in short spasms as she collapsed against Andreas. "God, Andreas . . . Jan! What—?"

Matthys, awakened from his indecision by Bockelson's action, now struck quickly. Grabbing a double-sided ax from one of his guards, he plunged it into Rusher's back.

Bending over, Elsbeth vomited.

Everything moved slowly, as if happening in short little bits, dribbling out a piece at a time. Bockelson grabbed a pistol and ran up to the doomed blacksmith, pointing the barrel at his back.

"God has anointed me his servant. All who oppose me will suffer!" Bockelson yelled. He pulled the trigger, the hammer striking hard in the petrified silence of the crowd. When the shot was fired into Rusher, the crows on St. Lambert's tower flew off. Screams of both birds and people reverberated throughout the square.

A different shock overwhelmed Andreas's fear. He looked at Matthys, whose focus was on Rusher. Had he heard Bockelson say "Oppose me"?

Weeping and sobbing coursed through the scattering crowds as people grabbed onto one another and ran from the market. Matthys stooped over Rusher's body, grabbed his hair and pulled his face off the stones. He examined him and then gently put the head back on the ground. "Everything will be fine! He'll recover!" Motioning for his guards to come, he instructed them to take Rusher out of the square and back to his house.

Andreas knew that the blacksmith was not going to be fine. Matthys and Bockelson had murdered Rusher. What had been a tight circle around Herbert Rusher and his executioners began expanding outward like rings around a rock thrown into a pond.

"None of us are safe, none of us." Andreas's voice trembled.

"Why? Why did they do this?" Elsbeth cried.

"Why did Bockelson kill him, Ulrich?" Andreas demanded.

"I'm not entirely sure that went according to plan."

Elsbeth pressed Ulrich. "You knew about this?"

"I knew there would be punishment. Henry Gresbeck reported Rusher this morning. He called Matthys a shit prophet, and Matthys was supposed to render justice, but he faltered. Bockelson wasn't supposed to do that." Ulrich pointed to the pool of blood. "No one will question Matthys's authority now—or Bockelson's, for that matter."

"And you agree with this?" Andreas pressed.

"It was for the greater good. Rusher couldn't blaspheme and get away with it; there's always a price to be paid for disobedience."

"I need to find Ingrid and the others," Elsbeth said, edging away.

"Elsbeth . . . " Andreas called after her, watching her break into a run.

22

Evening

ELSBETH WAS IN NO MOOD for company when the knock sounded. Opening it, she found Ulrich on her doorstep. "How could you know about that and not warn me?"

"I only knew what had been talked about. Everything happened so quickly; I was as stunned as you were," Ulrich said. "Let me in, please, and we can talk about it some more. I need someone to talk to."

Elsbeth stood, implacable. "You seemed too calm out there."

"I thought maybe they would just make an example of Rusher by putting him in prison or throwing him out. It all went badly." Ulrich held out his hands. "Please, I'm not the villain."

Elsbeth lingered, not taking her eyes off Ulrich. Finally, she moved and motioned him inside. He entered her living room and reached out his arms. "I'm so sorry you had to see that," he said. "How can I help?"

"There is no help for what I saw." Elsbeth squeezed his hands and dropped hers away.

"Let's at least go for something to eat and drink," Ulrich offered. "Tell Rachel, Ingrid, and Ursula to join us."

"They're off to other things at the moment."

"But you shouldn't be alone," Ulrich said. "Besides, you told Andreas not to come until tomorrow."

"I *am* hungry. Let me get my cloak."

Within minutes, they were sitting in a small tavern on Ludger Street, commiserating over the blacksmith's killing. Elsbeth drained her first cup of wine in seconds, motioning to the waiter to refill it.

"So much blood, dear God," Elsbeth said, quickly finishing her second cup.

Ulrich reached out and took the cup out of Elsbeth's hand. "Don't drink too quickly; you'll make yourself sick."

"Sorry, I'm just trying to forget that horror."

"I understand the need, but we have the rest of the evening." Ulrich took her hand and stroked it. "Thank you for coming. You're a comfort to me."

"Ulrich," Elsbeth said, "about your story the other day."

Ulrich smiled. "The one about Andreas?" He threw up his hands. "Guilty. I was just having some fun at Andreas's expense. He can be so dreary sometimes."

"It's not funny. And besides, he told me you were the one who led that raid."

Ulrich reared back. "What? Me? Surely you didn't believe him?"

"Peter said you did; why would he lie?"

"Peter Droste has hated me for years. He has it in for me. He wanted me exiled because I questioned his decisions. In fact, I think he arranged my exile with the council. But I can't help it if I told the truth about him."

"What're you talking 'bout?" Elsbeth heard the slight slurring in her voice.

"When I lived there, he left the monastery almost every day. Sometimes he would even leave at night and stay gone until morning. What do you think he was up to? No one ever knew what happened to all the donations we got, but I wondered why the other orders were so much more prosperous than ours. I merely asked a few questions about him, and he took offense."

Elsbeth stared at Ulrich, waiting to see the knowing smile play on his lips, but he looked indignant. She waved her hand. "You always play with me. I don't know if I can believe a think—thing—you say anymore."

Ulrich took a sip of his cup. "Elsbeth, I do joke, and sometimes I spread stories for fun, but you also know I can be a serious man. Can you say I've done anything other than try and make your life better since we met?"

Elsbeth wished their food would come to temper the wine. "Frankly, I don't know what to think, or even whom to trust other than my friends."

"I would believe anything you told me, but there's so much I don't know about you. Like what brought you here?"

"It's a long, dreary tale." Elsbeth looked out the window.

"But I want to hear it. I want to hear everything. I love the sound of your voice, especially when it's full of righteous indignation." Ulrich rocked in his seat.

"Don't mock me." Elsbeth hit Ulrich on the shoulder.

"That was not my intent." Ulrich peered over his stein. "Let's start with Andreas. I don't know how you met. Tell me everything you know about him."

"He can be an odd one, but there's more ta him than you think."

And with that, Ulrich drew her out. It was pleasant having someone to talk to. She needed to talk with somebody, so she told him everything he asked, even about Andreas. Over dumplings and pork chops, he heard it all: how she and Andreas met; their journey to the city; meeting Bockelson; what life was like at Überwasser; even her confusion about the relationship with Andreas. By the time she told Ulrich she needed to get back home, she was as drunk as she had ever been. They stumbled their way back to her dwelling.

"Should I help you to your room?" Ulrich offered, escorting Elsbeth through the front door.

"I'll be fine. You cud sit wift mm . . . me."

Ulrich escorted her into the common room. The room was small but comfortable, with a sofa and a couple of chairs.

"Rachel? Ingrid? Ursula? Isss anyone home?" Elsbeth called upstairs to the bedrooms, but no voices sounded in response.

Elsbeth felt herself being guided onto the sofa, and she plopped her head on the back as Ulrich slid next to her.

"Elsbeth"—Ulrich gently caressed her hand—"is there anything I can do for you?"

"Mm…" she murmured. "Can you stop tha spinning?"

"No, but I can wait here until you're better."

"You said you had sumthin' more 'bout Andreas." Elsbeth's eyes closed.

"I did, but you should be sober to hear it."

"You should tell me now will I'm drunk. While, while I'm drunk," she giggled.

"Are you sure?"

Elsbeth snorted. "He keeps things from me, you know."

"I'm sure he does. He keeps things from everyone. Did he ever say why he left the order?"

"To fin' his parents." Elsbeth lifted her head off her chair briefly, only to lay it back again.

"Nothing about joining the Peasant's War?"

"Ulrich." Elsbeth cocked her head. "Do'n lie again. He's good."

"You can ask him yourself when you get the chance. Ask him if he was a part of the revolt. Didn't you meet down there? Ask him if he's ever been in a jail."

Elsbeth sat up. "Prison?" The spinning grew less intense, as logic fought its way through the haze. Andreas had never mentioned prison, but Ulrich seemed so convincing.

"I heard he'd been thrown in a dungeon for rioting with the mobs down in the south—him and his friends."

"Ulrich, you're . . . lying. Again. You're always lying." Elsbeth's face twisted in confusion. "How could you have heard sumthin' like that?"

Ulrich's hand caressed her arm. "Just ask him if it's true."

St. Lambert's bells sounded the tenth hour. Elsbeth rose unsteadily to her feet and went to open the window. Ulrich followed, standing behind her as she held her face outside to take deep breaths.

"Elsbeth, you are so beautiful," Ulrich whispered, placing his hand on her hip. "You could have any man in this city . . . " Ulrich lowered his head closer to her ear.

"Wha . . . arh . . . yew . . . doing?" Elsbeth heard her slurry voice, but it sounded as if it was coming from someone else.

"Nothing." Ulrich softly put his lips to her ear, moving his arm around her waist and pulling her closer to him.

"Ulrich . . . " Elsbeth straightened. "Not now . . . "

"Why not now? Life is short, Elsbeth." Ulrich's voice was comforting, alluring.

She leaned back slightly into him and felt his excitement against her. She was surprised by the desire that rose in her, the realization that at any moment she could be out of her clothes on the floor, wrapped around Ulrich. The image was like a slap to her face. "Ulrich . . . I can't."

"You can . . . you should. With all this pain around us, shouldn't we live? You deserve to have pleasure, Elsbeth," Ulrich persuaded.

Elsbeth turned to face him. She put her hand up against his chest, trying to create space between them, but Ulrich held her tight against him.

"Elsbeth, I want you. I want to take care of you." Ulrich's voice grew firmer. "I want you to take care of me."

"But . . . Andreas . . . "

"Andreas isn't here—I am. I'll always be here." Ulrich's voice grew quieter, softer.

Again, the desire to surrender, to give Ulrich what he wanted, overcame her. Elsbeth slid into a murky tide. The comfort of another body next to her felt good. Besides, Andreas was distant. *Who knows where he really is, what type of comfort he enjoys? No man has claim over me.* She looked at Ulrich's expectant face. Somewhere inside her she heard, "No!" She pushed herself away from Ulrich.

"I can't, Ulrich. I'm sorry, I can't," Elsbeth said, tears rising—tears of frustration, exhaustion, fear of how swiftly everything was changing.

"Did I have this wrong?" Ulrich's voice took on a harder edge. "I've been your best friend, Elsbeth."

"I'm grat'ful, but . . . too much. Please. I'm drunk." The fog dampening Elsbeth's mind lifted a bit more.

"Why did you lead me on?" Ulrich angrily demanded.

"I didn't." Elsbeth began to cry.

Ulrich reached out and grabbed her arm, pulling her toward him. "But you did, and you shouldn't reject those who only have your best interests at heart. You'll need friends now."

His tone frightened Elsbeth. "Let me go!" Elsbeth struggled to free her arm from Ulrich's grasp.

"I can protect you . . . I'm here—where's Andreas?"

"I can take care of ma'self," Elsbeth grunted as she tore her arm from Ulrich's hand. Scurrying to the other side of the room, her mind struggled to surface from its confusion.

They stood staring at one another, the sound of their breath keeping rhythm with the clock. Ulrich straightened up and smoothed his clothes.

"I could've taken what I wanted, but I find no pleasure in it."

"I'm sorry, Ulrich. I want to be your friend, but not like this." Elsbeth wondered if she could salvage something. "I care for you, Ulrich, I do, but . . . Andreas."

"Let's see how much help Andreas can give you." Ulrich stormed out the door.

"Ulrich . . . no!" Elsbeth called out as the door slammed shut.

23

March 16

MORNING'S COLD AIR SNAPPED her mind to some clarity as Elsbeth stood in front of her rowhouse. *Stupid.* She walked back every step made from the moment Ulrich showed up at her door. The moment when she knew she should've put down the wine, letting him into her house, his stomping out—she couldn't stop blaming herself. Considering the sun-dappled street and the play of light and shadow, Elsbeth questioned her decisions, finding no resolution to her anxiety. Perhaps there was still time to repair things with Ulrich. It was early and he'd most probably be at home. She grabbed her cloak and stepped outside when she heard Ulrich's voice.

"Good morning." He was standing in the shadows at the corner of the street.

Elsbeth placed a smile on her lips. "I'm glad to see you. I wanted to talk about last night."

"No need. You let me know where matters stand."

"Don't be upset, Ulrich. I'm not entirely sure about anything now."

"You may soon need me, Elsbeth, and when you do, I want you to remember last night."

Elsbeth felt his eyes boring into her, a vague and unknown danger looming behind them. "You are a dear friend," she appeased. "I hope not to lose that."

"And I hoped for something more." Ulrich wheeled away and headed for the market square. After a few steps, he abruptly turned and addressed Elsbeth. "I tried to warn you."

Absorbed in their exchange, it wasn't until he was out of sight that Elsbeth began to register the commotion around her. People were dashing up the street toward the market, being pushed by guards with spears. In seconds, she was caught in the crush, carried along with the stream of bodies. Was this a summons for more execution? Elsbeth couldn't recall bells being rung.

Pushed into the market square, Elsbeth spied bodies crowding in from every entrance. Matthys's men swarmed from side streets, pushing everyone toward the center of the plaza. Elsbeth was swept into the square by a multitude of men with weapons. Panic gripped her, rendering her unable to breathe. Pressed into more and more people, Elsbeth's head throbbed from the energy and terror surging through her. *Who dies today? Will he kill us all?*

"Everyone who has not been baptized, or who was baptized two weeks ago, must go to St. Paul's!" the guards yelled, herding everyone toward Cathedral Hill. As the crowd built, the bells sounded, increasing the confusion sweeping through the square. Elsbeth desperately searched for a way to escape, but she could not break free of the pressed huddle shuffling toward St. Paul's. Elsbeth glimpsed Ulrich walking alongside and arguing with one of the guards, pointing in her direction. He looked over at her for a moment but kept his distance.

Other crowds, mustered from the west side of the city, joined those flocked together on Cathedral Hill. All around her the sobbing and whimpering reached such a crescendo, they threatened to drown out the cathedral's bells. Loud wails pierced the air, heightening anxiety. Elsbeth shuddered as Matthys's retinue entered the square. She struggled to keep her wits about her, but her mind fled off in confusion. She wished the pounding in her head would stop.

"Those of you who have not had believer's baptism must go into the cathedral. Those baptized after the exile must join them! Now!" Matthys shouted.

His men shoved the crowd toward the doors of St. Paul's. Bodies stumbled ascending to Paradise Porch; others fainted, slumping on the steps. Several times, people tried to break through the phalanx of guards, only to be pushed back into line.

"Hurry, or you'll meet the fate of the blacksmith!" Like a demented shepherd herding sheep into a slaughter pen, Matthys yelled as he stood beside the entrance doors. Desperate bleating increased when escape became impossible. Fearing her sanity slipping from her, Elsbeth focused on staying calm even as she searched for some means of escape. At least she wasn't tied to a chair.

"You wicked snakes, you vipers and traitorous demons! Who will save you from the wrath to come? Throw yourselves on God's mercy and prepare for judgment!" Matthys harangued the throng staggering into the cathedral. Elsbeth stole a glance at him as she passed by. His pitiless eyes opened so wide, Elsbeth thought they were going to pop out of his head.

Entering the sanctuary, Elsbeth was stunned. Goats, pigs, cats, and dogs seemed at home as they stood mute at the procession of new creatures joining them. Elsbeth's mouth filled with sourness as the stench of a long-neglected stable sickened her. Broken statuary was scattered all over the charred floor, along with half-burnt books, works of art, blackened pieces of cloth—the debris of the earlier desecration bearing testimony to the relentless desire to destroy the past.

"Kneel!" The command came from Matthys who stood at the back of the nave.

A ball of fear hit her in the stomach as she looked for a place that wasn't covered with shit.

"Down! Quickly!" Matthys barked.

Elsbeth hit the ground, the cold, hard stone smacking into her knees, before a guard pushed her shoulder to the floor. Shit and urine, mixed with the charcoal smell of burnt wood, caused vomit to fill her mouth. *If I had not resisted Ulrich, I would not be here. If I had not turned away the priest, I would be at home. Must I always be prisoner to men's urges?*

"Repent, brothers and sisters!" Matthys picked his way among the bodies on the floor, a rising voice of terror. "If you love God, have no fear."

Sobbing replaced wailing as faces turned down into the stones in order that they would not see the sword coming for them. Elsbeth raised her head. The entire cathedral was full of prostrate bodies praying for deliverance. She crooked her arm and rested her face on it to keep her head from the cold stone. Shivering uncontrollably, her insides became runny, fluid, as if she might leak out of herself at any moment. She watched Matthys's boots step nearer and nearer.

"This one," he would occasionally say, pointing to a body on the floor. Every time he did this, the wailing grew more intense as people were picked up and taken from the cathedral.

"Our Father, who is in heaven . . . " Elsbeth heard the man next to her praying. On the other side she heard a woman whispering, "Hail Mary, full of grace . . . " She sensed Matthys's presence looming over her.

"Sister, have you had believer's baptism?" Matthys asked. In other circumstances, the voice would have sounded almost compassionate, but this only increased Elsbeth's dread.

She lifted her head to find Matthys eyeing her. "My lord, my parents had me baptized."

"Do you renounce this baptism of Satan and accept the water of true renewal?"

"I'm confused, Prophet Matthys," Elsbeth responded. "I do believe in Jesus and in Matthys his prophet; why must I be baptized again?" Elsbeth didn't know why she resisted; this shouldn't matter to her. She had told others she would accept baptism willingly if it meant saving her life. But that was before she had been backed into a corner, driven to a shit-covered floor. It was like being shoved back onto that damned ducking stool, where others got the say over whether she lived or died. She was sick of being at the mercy of others, especially when they used God to justify their weighing of her soul.

Matthys's eyes hardened. "Perhaps you need some time to ponder that." He motioned to the guards to come and remove her. When they took her out, Elsbeth expected to see a fire or nooses awaiting her; instead, the guards walked her to St. Lambert's. An unbroken line of spectators, stretched between St. Paul's and St. Lambert's, took in the victims stumbling past them toward an unknown fate. Elsbeth searched the streets for a glimpse of Ingrid, Rachel, Ursula, or Andreas—any friendly face. She found only Ulrich, chin resting in his upraised hand.

Just as they forced her into the side door of St. Lambert's, however, she spotted Andreas and Peter by the fish market, deep lines etching their faces as they focused on her. They were the last faces she saw before rough men dragged her into the sanctuary.

"Sit down and shut up!" a voice barked at her. The door to the nave slammed shut.

Hordes of people were already sitting on the floor. Others wandered aimlessly, talking in low whispers. Elsbeth's eyes adjusted to the darkness as she found a place against the wall where she could rest her back. People continued being thrust into the cathedral as the morning wore on, until finally, all the guards trooped outside. At twelve bells, Elsbeth heard the metallic clang of the doors being locked.

Six hours later, she was drowning in an ocean of hunger and desperation, spooked by a constant din of buzzing voices that sounded like irritated wasps, punctuated by sporadic screams and hysterical babbling. A specter stood just outside her mind, insistently demanding an audience, but she refused to invite it in. *No, spirit, you cannot have me today.* She desperately fought against being carried away by her emotions, though the fear permeating the room picked at her, seeking a way inside.

A woman crawled over to her and whined, "I wonder what it's like to die?"

"I don't know," Elsbeth said. "It's too early to think about dying." *Keep trying, wraith, but I will resist you.*

"Do you think I'll be forgiven for my sins?" the woman wept.

"I'm sure you will," Elsbeth replied. *I will not let you in.*

"Will it hurt?" The woman was insistent, holding onto Elsbeth like a beggar grasping her last piece of bread.

"Will what hurt?"

The woman sobbed. "When they kill us."

"They're not going to kill us," Elsbeth reassured her. *You may have taken her, but I will not yield.*

"Why else would they bring us here?"

"I'm not sure, but let's hope for the best." *Leave me, Satan!*

"I want to see my husband again. I lost him two years ago. Perhaps today is the day I'll join him," the distraught woman cried.

At that, Elsbeth started weeping. Images of her mother and her life in Jaberg filled her mind. Life might have been different if Mama had lived. She certainly would not have been in this place. Childhood memories overwhelmed her: playing with her sister and brothers, the smell of the wildflowers, the way that her mother's apple strudel tasted, the beauty of Lake Thun and the Alps—*That goddamn priest ruined my life.* Tears flowed as she scrunched closer to the wall.

Close to dusk, the cries of anguish started to die out, like roaring flames receding into glowing embers. Muffled sobbing and quiet prayers were the only sounds until an iron key in the door echoed like a thunderclap across the sanctuary. Torchlight filled the door opening, and Matthys walked in alone. People crawled forward, grabbing the hem of his robe. Others groveled and begged to be spared as he passed. Elsbeth was struck by how raw his feet were. No man wore sandals in this cold if he had a choice. *A part of him welcomes suffering.*

Matthys moved among them, crying, pulling people up and kissing their foreheads. He smiled benignly; the wrathful deity appeased. Occasionally, he would kneel to pray or talk with those who sat on the floor. Confused babbling grew louder the longer he whispered words of salvation.

Spying Elsbeth, he went down on his haunches and grabbed her hands. "Divara is praying for you." He pulled her to her feet. Elsbeth was weak in the knees from sitting so long, but she maintained her balance even as her legs trembled.

"I'm grateful," Elsbeth murmured, unable to think of anything else to add before he moved on to comfort and soothe the others.

After several more minutes, Matthys called out, "My heart is moved to mercy. I've interceded with God for your souls, and God has told me you are to be spared." The tension drained away from her body. Everyone in the room blubbered the praise of Matthys, the icy prospect of death melting into tears of gratitude.

Matthys took two of them, one in each hand, and led them out into the evening, motioning for everyone else to follow. It struck her as a bit too studied. People cheered as they saw their loved ones emerging from the church. They flocked to Matthys, kissing his hands and praising God as he smiled benevolently. Hymns of thanksgiving erupted throughout the marketplace.

Elsbeth looked around for the pot of water she was sure would be awaiting them, but she did not see one. She stood dazed—a statue—unable to move or focus on anything as a mixture of relief and horror nearly swallowed her. Then, the anger rushed through her. Matthys didn't need water. Her fists clenched up into balls. They had all been baptized into something far more powerful—fear. Total immersion. Emerging from this baptism, they were transformed into compliant citizens of the New Jerusalem.

Someone closed on her and Elsbeth turned, half-expecting to see Ulrich offering his apologies. Instead, it was Peter and Andreas, their faces furrowed in concern.

"Are you all right?" Peter took her arm, and Elsbeth burst into tears.

Crying freely, she grabbed them both around the neck. "No, but my body wasn't harmed." She swam for shore, trying to escape the suffocating ocean of terror.

"We thought they were going to kill everyone they took into St. Lambert's," Andreas said.

"That's what we all thought, too. I was not expecting to be released."

"It was horrible, waiting out here. Like slow death." Andreas's face pulled into a grimace.

"Elsbeth." Ulrich sidled up to them. "I'm so glad no harm came to you."

"Are you glad, Ulrich?" Elsbeth's voice was icy. Turning to Andreas and Peter she asked, "Peter, is the offer to stay in the guesthouse still open?"

"Elsbeth, are you sure this is wise?" Ulrich said.

Elsbeth regarded Ulrich. "I'll take my chances with people I can trust."

"I've only tried to help, Elsbeth." Ulrich pointed to the walls. "With what's outside, I'm afraid fate is coming for us."

"Ulrich," Peter said, "fate appears to us all."

"That may be, Peter, but some of you will never see it coming." Ulrich threw up his hand as he walked away.

Elsbeth called after him. "I never saw today coming, but you did."

Ulrich stopped and pivoted to face Elsbeth. Bowing slightly, he shouted over the tumult, "All the more reason to ask for your forgiveness, Elsbeth. I shall try to be a better friend going forward."

Peter took Elsbeth's elbow. "Let's get you out of here."

"Please." Elsbeth said, watching Ulrich as he disappeared into the crowd.

24

March 17

ELSBETH PUT DOWN HER bucket and wiped her forehead. The call for
dinner had just sounded, so she headed for the large wooden table where
the massive steaming pot of venison and carrot stew stood. The council
had decreed communal meals as everyone was assigned tasks to prepare
for the coming assault. Elsbeth looked forward to the meals; it was better
than shoveling cow dung up against the walls. Besides, Ingrid had been
assigned to her detail, and Elsbeth wanted to tell her why she didn't come
home last night. Filling her bowl with stew, she spied Ingrid at the end of
the table and joined her, plopping onto the bench with a grunt.

"Where were you?" Ingrid asked, spooning some stew on her bread.
"We were worried sick about you."

"I was caught up in the net yesterday; it was horrible. When I came
out of St. Lambert's, I made the decision that I couldn't stay with you all
anymore. I feel too vulnerable there."

"We'll take care of you." Ingrid reached out and took Elsbeth's hand.
"Come back."

Elsbeth cradled Ingrid's hand. "I know you would, but I've decided
to live in the Augustinian guesthouse. It's safer there, and it's closer to
Andreas."

Ingrid set down her spoon. "I understand, but I'm going to miss you
dearly, to say nothing of the others. You've been with me every day for
seven months now."

Elsbeth looked into Ingrid's limpid blue eyes and felt the water coming down her cheek. "I'm sorry, I'll miss you, too. But we'll still see one
another every day, and I can come and visit."

"I heard Überwasser is filling up with new refugees," Ingrid said, changing the topic.

"Not just Überwasser. Father Peter said the council told him he would also have to house refugees," Elsbeth said. "He's promised me I can stay in the guesthouse, though."

"Some days I miss our life in the convent," Ingrid confessed. "Life outside is harder than I thought it'd be."

Bells rang. "Goddamn those bells," Elsbeth muttered.

Everyone rushed to finish their meal before they headed to Cathedral Hill. Elsbeth pulled her cloak tighter, passing the dark spot of blood where Rusher fell a couple of days ago. She was beginning to understand why some in Münster believed that the energies of places entered deep into people. There were days she felt as if strange spirits wanted to possess her, to transform her into something dark. Turning the last corner before St. Paul's, Elsbeth heard her name called. Divara stood at the end of the street.

"Good morning," Divara said. "How are you?"

"Surviving. Barely."

"I'm sure things will settle down," Divara said.

The nonchalance threw Elsbeth. All the drama unleashed by Matthys in the last two days, and yet his companion seemed unfazed. How could she be so calm? "Rusher?" Elsbeth asked. "The scene yesterday? Doesn't it disturb you?"

"I suppose, but everything happens for a reason." Divara linked arms with Elsbeth and strolled toward St. Paul's. "I've missed you. Come see me soon."

"Of course, as soon as I can get the time." Elsbeth knew it was a lie. She feared Matthys so much that she would do anything to keep distance between her and the mad prophet. Being too close to power tempted one into collusion with it, but madness colonized everyone close to Matthys. None of them could be trusted.

"I understand; we're all busy," Divara said. "Jan says war is coming. All over the Low Countries people are rallying to our call to come and defend New Jerusalem. Thousands are on their way here." Divara leaned in closer to Elsbeth. "Christ comes quickly."

Studying Divara, Elsbeth pursed her lips, remaining silent. What could she say? Divara lived in a world Elsbeth could not inhabit. They entered the square as thousands of people stood, waiting to find out why they had been summoned.

"Come, visit me," Divara repeated, hugging Elsbeth. "I have to go now."

Elsbeth searched for Andreas and Peter. She mulled over the previous night when she stayed in the guesthouse. Had she done the right thing? She spotted them across the plaza. "Andreas!"

They joined her beside a stack of books about six feet tall piled up in the shadow of St. Paul's.

"What's this?" Elsbeth asked, pointing to the books, pamphlets, and heavy paper binders of court records stacked in the massive collection.

"Not sure." Andreas stepped out and walked around the pile. After a few moments of examining them, he returned and whispered, "They intend to destroy the past."

"What?" Peter's confusion echoed in his voice.

"Look at the books," Andreas said. "Theology, mathematics, physics. I even spied the Rule of St. Benedict in there."

Peering closer, Elsbeth noticed some books open with illustrated pages and gold leaf edges. These were among a pile of papers that were bound in leather. "What are those?" she asked.

"What?" Andreas said.

"Those books with the leather covers. They look important."

"They've gathered all the court records," Andreas said. "All the property documents—wills, deeds, all the accounts of the city are in that stack."

"They're not just going to destroy the past; they're going to destroy everything," Peter moaned.

"What?" Elsbeth asked.

"Without deeds, no man has a legal claim on his home. If they destroy all the contracts, no one really owns anything anymore. There'll be no way to prove any claim about property, goods, or money." Panic crept into Peter's voice. "Our entire economic life is being put to the torch."

Sheets from some of the ledgers swirled around in the wind as armed men threw still more books and papers onto the pile.

"Over there," Elsbeth said, pointing to the back of the cathedral as Matthys, Knipperdolling, Rothmann, Bockelson, and about two dozen guards came from the rear of St. Paul's and made their way to the gathering. Divara, aloof and distant, walked next to Matthys as they passed the circle of people waiting to find out why the assembly had been called. Matthys took his place on the steps of the cathedral and led the crowd in hymns. When the singing was over, he stood quietly. Anticipation built.

"Brothers and sisters," Matthys shouted, lifting his arms, "glory to God, who has given us a great victory over Satan."

Shouts and cheers resounded around the homes surrounding Cathedral Hill. "Matthys! Matthys!" Elsbeth resisted the urge to flee.

"God has given us this city because we've not been afraid to root out the idolatry that seduced the followers of Satan who once ruled here. God commands us to destroy all idols, and for this the whore who sits on the throne of Rome persecutes us. The evildoers hunt us down like dogs to kill us. We're not to trust this world, but our Father in heaven."

Those merchants still left in Münster pulled their soft fur cloaks around them in the chill, fingering their gold chains as guild members stood next to them, huddled together and raising fists into the early evening air.

"All this in front of you? It is the vanity of this world, and the god of this world desires it be planted in your heart. Everything here is an idol that consumes the soul with pride, greed, and covetousness." Matthys surveyed the crowd. "But now we will break this demonic hold on us. Today, we cast aside the gods of this world."

"So that your gods can rule it," Peter muttered.

"Did God say that we should enrich ourselves while our brothers and sisters are in need? Where in His holy word does God say we should have property and goods for ourselves while our brothers and sisters go hungry or have need of shelter? We are commanded to reject usury. But the evidence at your feet shows we have not obeyed. We have built a world of sin where greed reigns."

With each statement, the mob responded louder. Elsbeth scanned the crowd, wondering if anyone would protest, but all eyes were on Matthys, though she noticed that off to the side, a few of those in fine clothes were slipping off into the growing darkness.

"Let us look to God, the author and finisher of our faith! We must trust God rather than man! We must not put our faith in the snares and riches of this world." Matthys circulated back and forth in front of the crowd. "In the days of the Apostles, they sold all they had and possessed everything in common. We shall live as they did. They did not care about the vanity of knowledge or wealth. They cared only for the Gospel. When Christ comes, shall he find us grasping after our goods, or will we let go of them to welcome him with open arms? Do you think you can own things in heaven? In New Jerusalem, we shall live godly lives, not worldly ones. Will you serve God or Satan? As for me and my house, we choose to serve the Lord!"

To Elsbeth, it seemed his words had conjured up some malignant spirit that flew out of the crowd, borne by voices that howled against years of persecution and pain. Their cries carried upward to fill the sky like birds of prey stalking their victims before swooping down for the kill.

"We make a solemn promise," Matthys shouted. "We shall continue to send out messengers to all the surrounding lands to proclaim that this is a holy and free city where everyone will have what they need. The rich shall be humbled and the poor exalted. We will be fed and housed, and no longer shall it be 'mine' or 'thine,' but 'ours'!"

Boisterous, guttural, angry voices lifted higher and higher over the assembly, the frustrations of years set loose in a freedom that seemed more anarchy than release. Elsbeth was sure that if Matthys ordered it, they would have set fire to the cathedral, the entire city, to the armies arriving daily outside the walls, maybe even to themselves had he commanded—anything to burn to ashes the world of those who had sent them fleeing to this city. The God of no limits revealed himself again. Gazing in horror at the faces around her—masks of rage and ecstasy, merged in horrifying, open-mouthed orgasmic mindlessness—Elsbeth had no ability to understand this, no desire to. Her one thought turned to how she would survive. Absorbed in her escape plans, she barely heard Matthys scream out again.

"Idols!" Matthys yelled, pointing to the pile. "They lead us away from God. What does God want us to do with our idols?"

"Destroy them!" The cries rang out more robustly from the guilds than from the remaining merchants, who looked at one another, uncertain.

"Does God truly want us to destroy them?" Matthys exhorted.

"Burn it all!" the mob responded.

Matthys walked over to one of his guards holding a torch, took it, and circled the pile of books, waving the torch over his head. "In the name of the Father, I condemn these as the wisdom of this world. We renounce the forces of the Antichrist!" he yelled, putting the torch to the books and ledgers in front of him. The rest of the torchbearers stepped forward, pushing their burning sticks into the pile.

The flames danced up into the air, their embers floating away like small lights, disappearing into twilight. Elsbeth imagined that each light represented the prayers of hundreds of authors sparking up to heaven, pleading that their words not be lost in this desecration. Wonder, ecstasy, fear, even joy, marked people's faces as they stood in rapt attention around the growing fire. Elsbeth spotted Ingrid swaying, her eyes closed. Standing next to her were Rachel and Ursula, arm in arm, staring into the flames. Did they have no objections? A soft murmur settled over the crowd as those closest to the fire linked hands and made a large circle around the flames. All through the mob, hands clasped as a few voices started singing "A Mighty Fortress is Our God."

"Well, they may hate Luther, but they still love his songs," Peter said.

"Who's to say what songs we'll hear soon?" Elsbeth said, watching the fire roar brighter, the past flickering away on burning ashes. Turning, she made for the monastery.

"I've seen enough for one day." Peter turned to follow Elsbeth, as Andreas joined them, silence their companion on the way home.

❀❀

Later in the evening, the three climbed the steps to the promenade behind the monastery to check on the armies gathering outside the walls. The campfires of the Prince-Bishop's mercenaries were lighting up in an ever-increasing circle around them. The countryside seemed a dark, bottomless hole, a shadow surrounded by a band of lit fires.

"It's as if the stars have fallen to earth," Elsbeth murmured.

"And the universe itself holds us siege." Andreas finished the thought.

They watched as the enormity of the threat outside revealed itself with each new pinprick of light appearing in the countryside, the smaller fires pale images of the bonfire they left earlier. The contrast of light and darkness disturbed Elsbeth. The mercenaries outside seemed more threatening by their campfires than they did during the light of day. Despite her best attempts, fear crept into her alongside evening's chill.

"I'm scared," Elsbeth said quietly, as Andreas exhaled a long deep breath.

"We all are," Peter said. "But we must not lose hope, because if we do, we're lost."

25

April 3, Good Friday

NORMAL. IT WAS A MEMORY hard to hang onto. Still, Elsbeth tried. Without the memory of normal, life might simply float away. Untethered from her memories, she feared losing herself, like those who surrounded her. Walking in the mountains, picking flowers for teas, arguing with her sister and brother, even Papa in the time before Mama died—these were the images Elsbeth fought to hang onto, trying to weave them into a cloak that she could throw over herself and shut the world out. She existed in fragments, fighting to remember what normal used to look like.

Two weeks ago, refugees, needing to be housed, appeared at the monastery. Peter was gracious, though the visitors, given to hating Catholics, regarded him with a mixture of triumph and fear. It was an uneasy truce, but everyone tried to manage. It was the boys learning how to fire guns and girls dragging buckets of dung and mud to store by the gates that Elsbeth resented the most. Stolen childhood. She desired another world, a world where children were not sacrificed to the folly of their parents.

Still, life went on, and Elsbeth was particularly glad for this day as she and Andreas walked through town. Andreas and Jost had reconnected by working in the tunnels that ran out from Münster, shoring them up. Today was Jost's wedding day.

"How's work going in the tunnels?" Elsbeth asked.

Andreas stopped momentarily and drew a deep breath, then another, his hands going to his knees.

"Andreas?"

"They feel more tomb than tunnel. If not for Jost and the others, I'm not sure I could stay down there alone."

Elsbeth took Andreas's hand and squeezed it as they continued in silence.

"At least it's warmer." Andreas finally broke the silence.

"Jost getting married," Elsbeth mused. "Remember all his stories on the way here?"

"I only believed half of them. I never thought things would get worse." Andreas eyed the piles of furniture and goods placed in the streets by order of Matthys. "I guess all goods in common is now the rule of the day."

"Let's think about the respite of this day, love." Elsbeth rubbed Andreas's back.

"We do need a break from the struggle," Andreas agreed. "It is nice to see Jost married, though I'd rather Matthys were not the one blessing it."

"I wish Peter had come."

"Today's a fast day for him, and he keeps his piety no matter how much has changed."

A wedding was a small thing to hang onto, but Elsbeth clutched it to herself, this gesture of the mundane. Even amid the growing armies outside, life continued. Babies were born, people worked the fields inside the walls, and couples got married. Jost lived in the northwest sector, up by Jew's Gate. The celebration was being held at a tavern close to his home.

The tavern was decorated for a wedding day. Women in embroidered blouses and brightly colored skirts draping the ground stood in clumps talking with one another, and men in festive-colored jerkins and tipped hats with feathers laughed and celebrated. Sparkling cloth hung from the front of the tavern. Across the street, people decorated food tables with greenery and flowers. Walking over to them, Elsbeth and Andreas surveyed the feast. There were piles of roasted ox and venison, broiled chicken, fried pork chops, and fish—a carnivore's delight. Andreas grinned at the sight of strudels, sausages, breads, and dumplings that sat on white tablecloths.

"This is a bit of heaven," Andreas said.

"Or, at least a bit more like life is supposed to be. Let's go sit down." Elsbeth moved to the rows of tables set up for feasting. She spotted Bernard Knipperdolling and his wife sitting with Clara and Bockelson. Knipperdolling's wife looked sour, though Elsbeth thought her face was pretty enough, with clear blue eyes and blond hair streaked with grey tied back into a bun. Her lips were pressed together as her head swiveled back and forth on a jowly neck.

Matthys and Divara sat next to them, somber, yet serene.

"I want to say hello to Divara." Elsbeth touched Andreas's hand and headed for Divara, who rose from her seat as Elsbeth approached.

"Elsbeth."

She held Divara's eyes. They did not match the voice or the smiling face. Something in those eyes made Elsbeth stiffen.

"Divara?" Elsbeth whispered.

"We can talk later?"

"Of course, after the service." Elsbeth rubbed Divara's shoulder and slipped back over to Andreas, who sat waiting for the service to begin.

"How is she?" Andreas said.

"Something's wrong. Hard to know what for sure."

"I could say the same for Matthys. He looks about as excited as a stone." Andreas nodded at Matthys as the music started and the wedding party took their places.

An hour later the celebrating began. People strolled around the banqueting tables filling their plates with food, drinking and laughing while their children ran through the crowds. *It could be like any other day*, Elsbeth thought as she sopped the juices of her meal with sourdough bread.

"Hey, Jost, are you going to need any help tonight?" someone yelled.

"If he does, I'll give him all the help he needs," the bride shouted back, grabbing the groom's crotch and taking another swig of beer.

"Hey, Jost!" A man held up a thick sausage. "This might help." Peals of laughter rang out.

Elsbeth spied Divara talking with some other guests. She excused herself from the table and approached Divara on the edge of the crowd.

"Are you well?" Elsbeth asked.

"I'm not sure. Something's going on." Divara took Elsbeth's arm, steering her farther away from the crowd. "Jan's had another vision."

"What of?"

"I don't know; that's why I'm worried." Divara glanced over at Matthys, who sat at the table, picking at his turkey. "He and Bockelson have spent a lot of time lately locked away. My man grows more restless."

"Perhaps it's nothing," Elsbeth said.

Divara's lips disappeared into her mouth and her brows knit together. "He grows more distant."

Elsbeth had always thought of Divara as the strong one in the relationship, the grounded one. She was earth; he was a consuming fire, ready to burst into flame any moment. She had no sense of how to respond. They stood in silence until Elsbeth said, "Is there anything I can do?"

Divara gave a wan smile. "I have to go," she said, making her way back to Matthys's side and taking her seat next to him.

Elsbeth circulated through the crowd, picking up another plate of food before finding Andreas talking to a small knot of men.

"What's going on?" Andreas asked.

"I'm not sure. Divara's worried about Matthys."

Andreas motioned to where Knipperdolling and Matthys sat. "He looks horrible."

"I didn't think he could get paler, but you're right." Elsbeth studied Matthys. He was neither laughing nor offended at the profane jokes swirling around the table. He sat immobile, inscrutable, not interacting with anyone around him. Occasionally, Divara would lean in his direction to say something, but he barely acknowledged her presence. Elsbeth was looking directly at him when Matthys's head fell to his chest.

"What's this?" She nudged Andreas and pointed to Matthys.

"Is he drunk? Asleep?" Andreas asked.

"He hasn't been drinking, and I don't think he's asleep."

Matthys groaned loudly, his moans competing with the joyous sounds that hung in the early spring air. At first, only a few heard him because he was drowned out by laughter. But as those closest to him fell quiet and pointed in his direction, a pall fell on the celebration. Divara grew still, her eyes roving between Matthys and the crowd. Slowly, the wedding party turned their focus to Matthys's slumped head. Everyone stilled; Matthys's groaning grew louder. Divara leaned back, examining her husband. She glanced at Elsbeth and grimaced.

Divara reached over to touch Matthys's arm. The moment her hand brushed his skin, his head flew off his chest and snapped toward the sky.

"Why does he always do that?" someone next to Andreas whispered, as several people looked up at the clouds.

The wedding guests gawked as Matthys, pale as the white linen tablecloth, started shaking, his eyes rolling into the back of his head, revealing only bulging white circles. Suddenly, he tilted forward, falling face down onto the table, square into a plate of cabbage and leeks.

The loud and boisterous party froze. Everyone stared in horror at Matthys, his massive skull blending in with the cabbage.

"Andreas, what in God's name?"

"No idea." Andreas shook his head.

The jokes of wedding nights and future children evaporated into the spring air as an anxious silence spread over the tables.

Andreas glanced at Knipperdolling. "I can't tell if he's relieved or worried."

Elsbeth didn't concern herself with Knipperdolling; she kept her eyes on Divara, who took a sip of wine and looked directly at Elsbeth. Several people bowed their heads and prayed, as others scuttled away from Matthys.

"I hope God is not telling Matthys to kill today," Andreas whispered in Elsbeth's ear.

Matthys's head suddenly jerked up, a piece of cabbage falling off his cheek. He raised his hands and shouted to the sky, "Yes, Father, I hear you! But I beg you, let this cup pass from me. Not my will be done, but yours!"

Several people unconsciously reached for their throats.

"Your will be done! Your will be done! Your will be done!" Matthys shouted repeatedly, waving his hands. He lifted his gaunt, robed figure out of his chair and moved from person to person, kissing them all on the cheek, offering a benediction of peace. When he came to Andreas and Elsbeth, he smiled at them and kissed them both on the cheek.

"Peace be upon you," he said, before moving on.

He lumbered over to the bride and groom and embraced them, blessing their union. Turning to the rest of the crowd, he shouted, "God bless you and may peace be upon you! I must go do my Father's business!" Without another word, Matthys set out for the city center, Knipperdolling trailing after him. Elsbeth caught Bockelson and Divara looking at one another before Divara stood and trailed after Matthys.

26

Holy Saturday

ACCOUNTS OF MATTHYS'S PERFORMANCE spread like dye in water in taverns, homes, and on street corners. The city anxiously waited to see what it all meant, this business of Matthys and God's will. Standing in his living room, Bernard Knipperdolling watched as Matthys sat calmly between Divara and Bockelson on the long couch. Rothmann and the others worked hard to persuade Matthys to reconsider his vision, but Matthys dismissed their concerns. It was the first time since Knipperdolling had met Matthys that the man seemed to be at peace. Knipperdolling wondered if God really did speak to Matthys. If that was true, then the world itself was a vast mystery Knipperdolling would never understand. Rothmann's voice rose above the din.

"Prophet Matthys, how can you be sure this is what God commanded?"

"Gideon didn't have an army, and God gave him victory." Matthys shifted in his seat to face Rothmann. "Don't you trust God?"

Knipperdolling watched as Divara kept her eyes on the ground, not looking at anyone else. He wondered if Bockelson had talked with her about what was going to happen.

"That was different. This is different. You can't go out there," Rothmann pleaded. "Besides, when Gideon prayed for a sign, God gave him one."

"God gave me one, too. He told me Himself," Matthys explained.

"God told you to kill yourself?" Rothmann's voice went up in pitch.

"I have no other choice." The smile on Matthys's face as he answered their objections unsettled Knipperdolling. "My heavenly Father told me he would use me to deliver us from the hand of the Antichrist outside our gate."

Rothmann turned to Bockelson. "Do something. He listens to you."

"The prophet tells us what God speaks to him." Bockelson's shoulders lifted.

"Did God truly command this?" Divara asked, tilting forward to eye Bockelson directly.

Bockelson leaned over Matthys and gently took Divara's hand. Matthys barely registered the gesture, bowing his head and closing his eyes.

"God's ways are hard, Divara," Bockelson said. "We should not tempt God with our doubt."

"I'm not doubting God," Divara said, rubbing Matthys's shoulder. "Only whether the prophet has heard Him clearly."

"Brother Matthys is our deliverer." Bockelson stood up and moved to be next to Divara. He put his hand on her arm. "He'll save us; we should honor his sacrifice."

"I have more to lose than the rest of you." Divara kept her eyes on Matthys.

"Perhaps," Bockelson replied, stroking her arm, "but God restores to us what we give Him. God will provide for you immeasurably more than you can imagine. Besides, none of us know for certain that God has not called our brother to his task."

"This is a travesty. We can't let him do this!" Rothmann leapt out of his chair and addressed Matthys. "You can't go beyond the walls. They'll kill you."

"God will be with you all, no matter what," Matthys said, lifting his head. "Besides, why do you already have me dead? God is greater than you imagine, and He will do great things tomorrow."

"I'm sure God will do great things tomorrow, Brother Matthys," Bockelson said, one hand on Divara and another on Matthys. "You both must stay strong."

Knipperdolling noticed Divara's neck flush red at Bockelson's touch.

"David defeated Goliath. Gideon won a great victory with three hundred men. God will grant me a great victory tomorrow," Matthys rasped.

Knipperdolling felt compelled to speak. "Up to now, it's been skirmishes, games of back and forth. Perhaps they encircle us to scare us, make us fall prey to fear, but riding out is an incitement to attack. You could die."

"We've prepared for their assault," Bockelson said.

Rothmann's arms darted up. "You're sending this man to his death!" How could this possibly serve the will of God?"

"Ulrich, your thoughts?" Knipperdolling asked.

"Brother Matthys is a grown man; he knows his own mind," Ulrich said from his perch on a wooden chair in the corner of the room.

"Not my will, but my Father's will. If we desire Christ return to us, we must be faithful to him." Matthys's hands moved quickly back and forth along his thighs.

The clock ticked a few seconds before Knipperdolling spoke. "If he believes that God has spoken to him, there is nothing we can do to change his mind. He's riding out tomorrow whether we want him to or not."

"I must do my Father's will. That's what is best for us all." Matthys rocked in his seat.

Bockelson rose from the couch and walked toward the door. "At least our brother is willing to lay his life down for us. How many of you are prepared to do the same? Now, if you'll excuse me, I have some things I need to attend to."

"Wait, Bockelson, a word?" Knipperdolling said. Passing the others without a glance, he took Bockelson's arm, escorting him into the hall as babbling broke out behind them. They walked silently down the corridor to the main staircase leading to the bedrooms upstairs. When Knipperdolling grasped his shoulder, Bockelson stopped, hand on the railing.

"Do you think he'll go through with it?" Knipperdolling asked.

"I'm certain of it. We've talked of nothing else the past two weeks."

"How did he come to this path?" Knipperdolling asked.

"I just pointed out the story of Gideon; he's the one who had the vision."

Knipperdolling stepped back from his son-in-law.

"Don't look at me like that," Bockelson said. "This is not my fault. I only tell him to believe in himself. The visions are his, not mine."

Staring at Bockelson, Knipperdolling wondered what type of man he had welcomed into his home.

"He'll go through with this. You can't argue with God's will. Since he's resolved, we have plans to make." Bockelson held Knipperdolling's gaze. "Besides, tell me this doesn't solve our problems."

Knipperdolling leaned against the wall, considering the thought that life without Matthys would be much less complicated. "May God be with us."

"May God be with us, indeed," Bockelson said, walking up the stairs to his quarters and Clara Knipperdolling's waiting embrace.

27

Easter Eve Vigil

THERE WERE TIMES WHEN Jan Matthys was confused about his path; it was difficult to see. On those days, the voices were hard to understand. They were not voices, exactly, more like the high-pitched strings of a violin running scales incessantly up and down in the lightest, feathery tones; slivery whispers that suggested courses of action needing to be taken by faithful men not afraid of wielding God's scythe. At these times, he drifted down some long, dark tunnel that pulled him away from this world, haunted by a presence, a shadow of wolves, lingering just on the periphery of his mind. They sat on the edge of a thick forest, calling him to run with them, deeper and deeper into the darkness. Lately, the wolves were howling.

He spun around his room, twirling in ecstasy as he embraced himself. God had chosen *him*. Now they'd know he was powerful. God's chosen was not to be touched without a price to pay. The infidels would certainly pay it tomorrow. Sticking out his tongue, he touched his finger to the scarred remains of the hole twisted into him by the Dutch magistrates. Like Jesus, he'd suffered the humiliations of little men, heretics, and unbelievers, but tomorrow was his revenge. He walked among his dead enemies, boots slipping in their blood, as he slid across the thick wooden slats beneath him. Exhausted from his labors, he sat in his hard wooden chair as tears and laughter ebbed from him like pulsating blood leaking from a deadly wound. Vindication!

When Bockelson first brought the story of Gideon to his attention, he didn't make much of it, but the tale gradually wormed its way into his thoughts. God had given victory against overwhelming odds before, why not again? Why couldn't he be the new Gideon for God's oppressed people? God was mighty in power now, just as He was in ancient times. Gideon faced thousands of heathens intent on destroying God's people, but Jehovah gave him a great victory, defeating thousands with three hundred men. He wouldn't test God like Gideon; he wouldn't put a fleece out for a sign. He would obey the voices calling him to victory. One day, his name would be revered like Gideon, a tale told of faithfulness against all odds. He lifted his hands and wrote his imagined tale in the air: *Jan Matthys, clothed with the armor of God, mighty in battle, defeated the Antichrist of Westphalia.* Generations would read about this day. He smiled at the thought of the Book of Matthys, as the wolves sang seductively to him.

He adjusted the leather breastplate that Bockelson had brought him a couple of hours ago, grateful for all the help his friend had offered. Bockelson certainly thought his vision was divine. At least there was one faithful person who believed in him. He took his sword, flashed it in the air a few times, and sheathed it. God was a mighty warrior, crushing His enemies, and tomorrow God would rain down justice on those who made him suffer so horribly.

As he danced around the room, he imagined the celebrations tomorrow afternoon when he rode back into the gates, and the city saw their enemies scattering back to Hesse, Burgundy, Köln—wherever their father, the devil, had called them from. In a few short hours, he would make God, *his* Father, proud.

28

April 5, Easter

IT WASN'T RESURRECTION BUT death that enveloped Münster, draped like a Maundy Thursday black shroud over a stripped altar. Crowds lined the streets to St. Ludger's Gate, a smidgen of hope on their faces. Maybe God still worked in signs and wonders. Word had gone out through the city on Saturday: Matthys had received a word from God—he was the new Gideon for the New Israel. He would ride out and face their foes like Gideon did with a handful of men. It stirred imaginations, evoking Elijah facing the servants of Baal. Excited crowds formed a gauntlet of anxiety for Matthys to pass through before he moved beyond the city's walls.

"Madness, sheer madness," Andreas muttered as he, Peter, and Elsbeth took their places alongside the crowds waiting at St. Ludger's Gate. "How can people not see this for what it is?"

"People believe the things their fears tell them to," Peter said. "Suffering drove Matthys mad. Rather than allow others to control him, he controls this even if it leads to his death."

"So perhaps it will be over soon." Elsbeth brightened. "We can open the city and return to life as usual?"

"We still have Matthys's followers to deal with," Andreas said. "They believe they can defeat that army outside."

"With Matthys gone, the others will lose heart." Elsbeth rose on her toes, searching for Divara.

"Doubtful," Andreas said. "More likely Matthys becomes their martyr, and martyrs possess the power of their resistance."

"Listen," Elsbeth said. "He must be coming."

The steady clip-clop of horse hooves echoed down the street before they caught sight of Matthys, sitting on a white stallion, clothed in full armor. Carrying a shield and halberd, a sword at his side, Matthys towered above the spectators. The horse clomped along as Matthys struggled to balance himself, shifting so dramatically side to side that Andreas thought he would fall to the street. The horse's gait was slow, deliberate, leaving the impression that the unfortunate animal was trying to gain control over the unsteadiness on his back. A dozen men rode close behind, following their prophet into battle. Behind these, a singing crowd followed. Their hymns rose thin and pinched, more dirge than celebration.

Matthys approached the gate, and the harsh mechanical noise of chains and pulleys rose above the din of the masses. The inner-wall bridge was lowered, and the thick iron portcullis lifted as the crowds streamed up the outer wall.

"Are you going up on the wall?" Andreas asked Peter.

Peter sighed and nodded. "For all the good it will do. There are not enough prayers in the world for them." He followed Andreas and Elsbeth into the inner guardhouse, across the moat bridge, and then up to the wall, where people were already crowding the promenade, pointing at the siege ring.

In the distance, flags and standards of the bishop's armies fluttered high above their bone-white tents. It was so quiet from this height that Andreas could hear the barking of dogs and shouts of children playing in the camps. He wondered what life was like over there, where laughter sounded. Few laughed in New Jerusalem.

The horses hesitated as Matthys and his retinue urged them out past the outer wall. Reaching the end of the last bridge, the horses cantered out onto Miller's Hill, a low rise east of the gate. The errant knights of God stopped there, confused, uncertain about which way to go as their horses slowly wheeled around in place, waiting for direction. Matthys struggled to control his horse while holding onto his helmet and halberd.

Elsbeth pointed to the horizon. "Look."

Drawn by the call of the watch and the commotion coming from the lowering of the outer bridge, some of the mercenaries abandoned their campfires and meals, mounting horses to investigate. "Dear God, there are hundreds of them." Elsbeth's voice trembled.

Andreas observed the lines of horsemen saddle up. The sounds of armor clanking and hooves pounding the earth echoed in the air as people on the wall clutched one another. Piercing shrieks and groans lifted in the air as the horsemen moved into formation. Once in motion, the mercenaries shaped regiments swiftly; what seemed chaotic aligned into rigid symmetry. The voice of the horsemen's leader sounded over the open fields, and the mercenaries turned their horses toward the wall, then, the wave of crashing hooves broke as they rushed the field.

Andreas felt time itself was slowing.

"Will it be over soon?" Elsbeth asked.

Andreas grimaced. "It depends on how much sport they wish to make."

The thunder of the horses cresting the hill to meet Matthys and his men washed over the crowd. The citizens leaned over the wall as Matthys's horse, terrified by the noise, pirouetted around faster and faster. Then he reared back, almost throwing Matthys off. A gasp spread along the wall.

When he was a child, Andreas loved to watch riders at full gallop as they rode away from the city. The graceful way the horses bobbed up and down made it seem as if they could take flight, but no boyish pleasure comforted him. Soldiers rode now, their armor, shields, and swords glittered in the sun, creating flashes of white light that skittered around the battlefield. Looking at the two groups heading on a collision course, Andreas pictured a large creature hurrying to devour its defenseless prey.

Minutes later, cries of battle filled the air. The sounds of armor hitting swords, the bang of metal on wood, and terrified screams from all directions ripped a hole in Easter's hope. Six knights quickly surrounded Matthys, taunting him. Matthys unleashed a guttural roar, heard all the way to the wall. Swiftly, the soldiers drove him off his horse with their lances. Once down on the ground, they proceeded to toy with him, stabbing him with spears and swords, but leaving him alive. A quarter of an hour later, one of the horsemen delivered the fatal blow, separating his head with one massive stroke. They were more merciful to the other poor souls, killing them quickly.

The soldiers took Matthys's body and hacked at it as the throng on the walls screamed, cried, and roared in grief at the carnage in front of them.

"My God, why are they doing this?" Elsbeth cried.

"Life is tedious for mercenaries. They're having their fun," Andreas said.

When they finished dividing him up, the soldiers took pieces of Matthys's body and rode up to the walls. They heaved the bloody bits as far as they could at the onlookers, who dashed to the other side of the promenade to avoid pieces of flesh, bone, and blood landing around them. Other parts hit the wall, falling into the moat. The soldiers taunted the onlookers.

"Where is your prophet now?"

"Can you not find him?"

"Oh, wait, here he is."

"No, our mistake, he's over there."

"No, he's over here."

One of the horsemen grabbed Matthys's head, dripping with blood, and rode back and forth in front of the stunned crowd, so close everyone could see Matthys's open, terrified eyes.

Drawing his heaving horse up directly in front of St. Ludger's Gate, the man raised his trophy high. "Here's your David! I suppose it was Goliath's day after all! Repent of this foolishness. Let us be done with this farce. Your prophet is dead. You are free to come out and search for him if you like. But consider this: if you surrender today, Prince-Bishop von Waldeck will spare everyone in the city except for the ringleaders. Only open the gates and we'll take care of the rest."

Spurring his horse yet closer, he grabbed a spear from one of his companions, shoved Matthys's head on it, and drove it into the ground right beside the road leading into the city. After the knights formed a line along the wall, they stood silently before turning their horses back to their camp, laughing as one soldier waved Matthys's genitals above his head.

Those on the wall stood immovable, silent, struggling to comprehend the butchery. Elsbeth wept, burying her face in the folds of Andreas's tunic. Faint sounds of sobbing swept up and down the wall, as people held onto one another for comfort. Andreas wrapped his arm around Elsbeth and rubbed her back. He wondered if anyone entertained the knight's offer. He hoped so. It could all be over soon if they would accept that the mercenaries outside were too potent a force to be resisted. That would be the smart move, saving many lives.

"Let's go; the spectacle is over," Peter said, his shoulders slumped as he headed for the stairs. Elsbeth lifted her head from Andreas's chest, and they followed Peter down the steps and toward home. Along the way, they encountered men and women, children in hand, shuffling slowly through the streets, their faces masks of despair. Wails came from open windows throughout the city.

When they arrived back home, Peter brushed past the refugees milling around in the courtyard and headed for the refectory. "I'll meet you out back," he called as he disappeared into the kitchen. He joined Elsbeth and Andreas minutes later with three large steins of ale. He took his, handed the others theirs, and went out to the gardens. Andreas and Elsbeth followed and took their place on the bench beside him.

Peter remained silent, taking a drink and staring straight ahead.

"Peter?"

"Yes."

"About Matthys." Elsbeth's stein remained in her lap.

"Yes?" Peter took a long drink.

"Is he in heaven?"

"Why do you ask?" Andreas asked.

Elsbeth ignored Andreas and turned to Peter. "Do you think Matthys went to heaven?"

Peter continued to look out on the newly emerging flowers and herbs of his garden. He took several more gulps of his drink before answering. "I don't know. Grace extends far beyond our imagination."

"What about the story we're in now?"

"It's the same story, Andreas. We are loved, and if loved, forgiven."

"Are all forgiven?" Andreas pressed.

"As in Adam, all die; so in Christ, all shall be made alive."

"I appreciate your knowledge of Scripture, and I've always been attracted to your humanism." Andreas rubbed the back of his head. "But the Brethren of the Common Life taught you some strange doctrines. Answer me this, who is more forgiven: Matthys or the knights who cut him down?"

"Andreas, don't be an arse," Elsbeth broke in.

"No, it's a fair question," Peter said, turning to Andreas. "I don't know the reach of forgiveness, but neither do you."

Andreas nodded. "True, but if Matthys went to heaven, I'm not sure I want to be there. I can't imagine sharing eternity with the likes of him. From where I sit, the knights were doing God's will today."

"No one was doing God's will today. No one!" Peter's stein clanked against the stone bench; his face grew redder as he shook his head. "No one!"

"I'm sorry." Andreas put a hand on Peter's shoulder. "My frustration overcomes me."

They sat in silence for a few minutes before Peter responded, "We're all a bit on edge, yes? This is a dark day."

Andreas nodded and drained his ale. "I love you both, and I would give my life for you. Maybe that is what Matthys thought he was doing today, giving his life for his friends. I don't know. I've never understood God, though I thought I did at one time. Maybe we don't get what we deserve, but saint or sinner, Matthys got what was coming to him today."

Silence fell upon them until the ringing of St. Lambert's bells broke the quietness.

"Goddammit!" Andreas shouted to the sky. "Not now."

Peter lowered his head dejectedly as Elsbeth rose, taking their steins. "I'm not going," Peter said. "I'm too tired to take anything else today."

"We'll report back," Elsbeth said, heading to the kitchen.

Soon, Andreas and Elsbeth set off for Cathedral Hill. Just outside the monastery's gate, Elsbeth grabbed Andreas's hand.

"You were too hard on him."

"But we have these conversations all the time."

"He needs your support now, not your doubt. His life unravels, too."

"That's hard for me to imagine. I've always depended on his strength."

"Then don't tear him down."

"I'm sorry; that wasn't my intent," Andreas said, as they crossed through the marketplace. People with drawn faces and watery eyes surrounded them, all of them slogging along as if they were going to their funeral. The day of resurrection had turned into a day of death. It was as if they were all tied to a rope, pulled along against their will by a cord of grief toward yet another unknown horizon. Andreas imagined he could still smell the stench of body parts from earlier as he trudged along with the crowd. Was that odor also on those around him?

When they arrived at Cathedral Hill, the men who had once served Matthys directed everyone to the courtyard between St. Margaret's and St. Paul's. Thousands of people milled about, despondent in the face of the unwelcome summons. The dusk of evening was slipping in slowly as the sun set behind St. Paul's.

Elsbeth tapped Andreas on the shoulder. "Is that Bockelson up there?"

She pointed to the second-story row of windows of St. Margaret's. Bockelson stood by one of the arched windows, dressed in a long white robe. Framed in the two windows on either side of him stood

Knipperdolling and Divara, as if they were in a triptych set into an altar-piece. The light of candles and lanterns from behind them lent an air of mystery.

"What's this?" Andreas wondered. "What could they possibly be up to?"

"The light makes them look almost angelic."

Divara flashed a quick smile at Elsbeth.

"She's not unhappy," Andreas observed.

"We don't know her state," Elsbeth cautioned. "Is she up there because she wants to be?"

For the next hour, all stood mute, benign statues watching over the city. Torches were lit throughout the square. It was just like waiting for a play to begin. Time passed, and people turned to leave when Bockelson threw up his arms.

"People of Zion!" Bockelson shouted.

"*Zion?*" Andreas mouthed to Elsbeth.

"I've come to offer you comfort and a word from the Lord of Hosts. We despair, we mourn, and we grieve our prophet. But God has called him to rest. Today was the will of God. Who can stand against what God ordains?"

An excited buzz rippled through the crowd as Andreas whispered in Elsbeth's ear. "Rubbish. God didn't ordain that. Matthys chose his fate."

"Shh," Elsbeth warned. "We don't know who stands close by."

Andreas glanced around, searching for guards while Bockelson called for quiet.

"God Himself," Bockelson proclaimed, "visited me eight days ago and told me our prophet would die today—"

Angry protests erupted from the gathering. Next to Andreas, a man spit on the ground. Others raised their fists, shaking them at the window.

Bockelson thrust his hands to the sky. "Listen! Please listen! I speak the truth! God revealed to me that our dear prophet had become too vain, too proud, even disobedient."

People stopped shouting. Their prophet, disobedient? They considered this for but a moment before the yelling resumed.

"God commanded!" Bockelson shrieked in such a high-pitched voice that it silenced the tumult. "He commanded that our brother go and face the armies of our enemies alone, but he took others with him. He led them to their death today. Holy Scripture says that King Saul defied God's command by not falling on the Amalekite. God spoke to me and said that Matthys had become proud like Saul." Bockelson spread his arms. "And when Saul defied God, his throne was taken from him and given to David—"

Andreas stiffened. A smattering of conversations broke out around him.

"Surely no one believes this?" Elsbeth whispered in Andreas's ear.

"We believe what we want." Andreas kept his attention on the windows. "Scream out 'God says,' and this crowd becomes mindless sheep."

As the rumbling below him grew quieter, Bockelson yelled, "When I received this vision, I was in Brother Knipperdolling's house! He can confirm what I'm telling you! He'll testify that I'm telling the truth!"

All eyes shifted to Knipperdolling's window. Knipperdolling raised his palm to the crowd as if to bless them, then waved his arm to Bockelson. "Jan of Leiden speaks the truth! I was skeptical when he first told me what was to happen, but when it came to pass that Matthys was martyred, I had no other choice but to believe. Bockelson told me it would happen. It's as he said. He's been chosen to lead us out of this wilderness into the Promised Land."

"Glory to God!" someone standing right behind Andreas yelled.

Andreas glanced back. The voice belonged to one of Matthys's personal guards. A string of ringing cries erupted throughout the crowd. Andreas noted each face—all members of Matthys's flock.

"Interesting," Andreas said under his breath.

"What?" Elsbeth asked.

"Look around at who's yelling approval—they're all Matthys's men," Andreas observed.

"Brothers and sisters, God also told me that we are no longer citizens of Münster!" Bockelson cried, his upraised arms against the light behind him casting an enormous shadow. "We live under God's rule. Münster was our home in the flesh, but we seek a heavenly home, one fit for our Lord's return! Glory to God who has given us a new Jerusalem, a new Zion!"

"Why Zion?" Elsbeth asked.

Andreas shrugged. "No idea."

"I was asleep just moments ago," Bockelson continued, "when Matthys himself came to me and spoke: 'Do not be afraid! God will work through you as He worked through me! You must be obedient and not disobey as I did. God has told me you're to take care of Divara and give me peace knowing she will be cared for—'"

At this, Knipperdolling started, surprise marking his face. He leaned over to face Bockelson and Divara.

"Well, this is unexpected." Andreas caught the warning on Bockelson's face as he glanced at Knipperdolling.

"For a moment," Bockelson continued, "I believed this was my own voice I was hearing, but it was so insistent, I could not resist."

A man standing beside Andreas and Elsbeth began shaking. Others sobbed. Up in the window, Knipperdolling glowered at Bockelson before he turned his attention to the crowd. "Friends!" Knipperdolling shouted. "The prophecy God gave Bockelson has come true, and I cannot keep it to myself any longer!" He threw up both arms. "All hail our new prophet, Jan of Leiden!"

Hours ago, gruesome death had plunged the city into despair. Moments earlier, uncertainty and fear choked everyone. But now, they saw a glimmer of hope. Maybe God had not deserted them. Maybe Christ tarried for a reason. The chants began slowly, but they picked up quickly, driven by the expectation of something new.

"Bockelson! Bockelson! Bockelson!"

They chanted his name, ready to take their suffering and lay it at his feet in the hope that he would bear it away from them, would give them something to live for. Anxiety and terror faded as they continued chanting his name. Men and women grasped hands, locked arms, kissed, hugged, and collapsed in relief. Screams of wild laughter pierced the night air. They huddled next to St. Margaret's, reaching up the walls toward the three figures that stood with arms outstretched.

A couple of women beside Andreas slid their blouses from their shoulders, breasts swinging as they danced.

"Grief takes a peculiar form in Zion," Andreas observed.

Others began sliding out of their clothes, grabbing hands, and making small circles to dance. Laughter broke out as they grabbed onto one another. God was still with them. They had not been forsaken.

"They're drunk on God," Elsbeth marveled.

Andreas studied the pale, naked bodies drifting around him. "No, they're drunk on their delusions. They prefer lies to the truth."

"Evidently," Elsbeth said. "Look." She pointed to Knipperdolling and Divara as they joined Bockelson at his window. Divara and Bockelson locked in an embrace as Knipperdolling, his face dour, looked on.

29

April 6

ELSBETH WOKE WITH DIVARA on her mind. Was Divara a part of this? Had she conspired with Bockelson? The questions came incessantly. She got out of bed, pulled her blue woolen dress over her head, put on her head covering, and slipped out of the monastery. Expecting to find her at Knipperdolling's, Elsbeth rounded the corner and saw her standing outside his door, enjoying the cool spring morning. She no longer wore her usual white robe; instead, she was dressed in a beautiful light-green velvet dress with gold aprons and silk taffeta arms. Against her black hair, the outfit accentuated her beauty.

Divara flashed a welcoming smile. "Good morning."

"I tried to get to you yesterday . . . after Matthys fell . . . but I couldn't reach you." Elsbeth lowered her eyes.

"Yes, it was horrible." Divara frowned, but quickly brightened. "It ended well, though."

"Walk with me?" Elsbeth invited.

"I'd welcome that. Wait just a minute." Divara darted back inside and reappeared with a shawl draped around her shoulders.

They walked through the marketplace and continued wordlessly to Überwasser Church, where workmen, hanging by ropes on the roof, were attempting to pull down the church's tower. The men scurried like ants over an anthill, picking, chipping, clanging with picks and hammers. Some, on ropes, swung from one side to the next, chopping at the foundations of the tower. Elsbeth and Divara watched for a bit before Elsbeth put her hand on Divara's shoulder.

"I'm so sorry about Matthys."

Divara took her hand. "Thank you. His end was not as fine as his beginning."

"I'm not sure I understand . . . "

"When he first started preaching, he was alive, on fire, glowing with passion. He was like a sponge, soaking up whatever I'd tell him."

Elsbeth nodded.

"It wasn't long after he started preaching in the streets that the authorities took him. He was not the same after he left their prison; something about him was broken."

The workmen continued their destruction.

"He told me," Divara continued, "that although he was married, I was his wife 'in the spirit,' but I wanted to be his wife in the flesh—"

A massive piece of metal hit the ground. The women jumped.

"Save all the lead and copper!" one of the men on the ground shouted to his companions. "We're going to need it for bullets and cannonballs."

Divara took Elsbeth's arm and guided them into the park beside the church. "He wasn't an attractive man, but he was true, and I believed we were joined somehow. I trusted him, and he needed me. It felt good to be needed that much."

"Did he need you or your body?"

Divara laughed. "Well, he wanted my body, but it wasn't the most important thing for him." Elsbeth heard a distance creep into Divara. "But then he was different."

"Different? How?"

"He changed once we got here," Divara said. "I mean, he was always moody, but here . . . "

"Münster changes everyone." Elsbeth's thoughts grew gloomy.

"He had power he never had before, but his anger couldn't stand the freedom. Or, at least, that's how Bockelson explained it."

Elsbeth stiffened. She wasn't going to bring up Bockelson, but now that the subject had arisen, she couldn't resist. "About Bockelson . . . what was that last night?"

Divara didn't answer. She held her hand up to her eyes, examining the men hovering around the tower. Elsbeth kept silent, wondering if she had pushed too quickly.

"God gave me another man to take care of me," Divara finally said, smiling broadly.

"It's good to have people who will take care of us, but don't you want to be able to take care of yourself? I feel safer if I make my own decisions.

What happens if we're left on our own?" The questions poured out of Elsbeth. "I've never been on my own; have you ever lived alone?"

"No," Divara said, an odd look on her face. She was silent as a few more pieces of copper fell to the ground. "I went from my parents straight to the convent and then right to Jan. And now I'm with my other Jan. I've never really been on my own. Is any woman ever on her own? Jan said he needed me."

"You do know Bockelson's already married?" Elsbeth couldn't help herself.

"Yes, but so was Matthys. This is no different. God has called me to be wife to both, regardless of their other women. They didn't support the calling; they weren't true wives. God gives us what we need, and Jan needs someone who believes in him."

"But what of Clara Knipperdolling?"

Divara leveled her eyes at Elsbeth. "As for her, that was for convenience, to win Knipperdolling's favor. Jan doesn't love her. They don't even share a bed anymore."

"I didn't mean to offend," Elsbeth apologized.

"Sometimes they doubt themselves so much, I have to stand them up," Divara disclosed. "God can be a burden. I've seen the toll God takes on those who follow Him. I'm called to comfort God's prophets."

"But do they comfort you?"

Divara grabbed Elsbeth's hands. "Yesterday was a sign of Jan's desire to take care of me. We're very close. That's why he did it."

"Did what?" Elsbeth was confused.

"Said I was to be cared for. I'm pregnant, Elsbeth. I have a child coming."

"Is it Matthys's?" Elsbeth blurted out, hands flying to her mouth.

"Who else? When Jan first told me Matthys was called to sacrifice his life, he promised me he would look after me if anything went wrong. Bockelson has loved me since he first joined us. I see it in his eyes."

Dumbfounded, Elsbeth found herself unable to respond.

"It was not a bad thing yesterday. Jan served God, and now he's free of his suffering. Besides, he was so old. Bockelson will make a better father."

Elsbeth searched Divara's eyes for a sign of madness, or fatigue—anything that might help her make sense of the woman in front of her.

"You can't tell anyone yet, not even Andreas," Divara pleaded.

"I'll keep your secret," Elsbeth promised. "But what kind of future can a child have here? Those armies outside grow itchy."

"Jan told me that thousands of people are coming to our side," Divara said. "They're gathering all over the Low Countries to march here. He promises me one day I'll be a queen. I rather enjoy that idea. You could be one of my attendants!"

Elsbeth drew her arms around herself and stepped back. Something in those shining emerald eyes made Elsbeth uneasy. Maybe it was how she assigned her to servant status without blinking, or how easily she had gotten over yesterday's horror. Did she really think she was going to be a queen in this city? What lies had Bockelson fed her? Whatever it was, Elsbeth sensed she was vulnerable because of Divara. Staying on this woman's good side was going to be important.

30

April 16

LEANING AGAINST THE WALL across from St. Giles's Gate, Andreas watched people trickle in and out. He was unsure of the rules that governed the flow of people in and out of the city. Yesterday, emissaries from von Waldeck came through this gate on their way to Knipperdolling's house. Maybe things were relaxed enough for him to pass through now. He took a deep breath and stepped over to the gate.

"Sorry, I can't let you pass." The guard stopped Andreas before he could walk through.

"Others pass, why can't I? Back by nightfall, I promise." Andreas held up his hand.

"I have my orders. I can't let you leave the city."

"Is there any harm in my leaving? Do I wrong anyone by taking a walk outside the walls?"

"I'm only following orders."

"Whose orders?" Andreas demanded.

"Leave, Andreas, or I'll arrest you." The guard turned brusque, pointing to the other side of the street.

Andreas wondered how far to push it. Others were clearly leaving without any problem. How was this possible? Waving to the brusque guard, Andreas made for home, but before he turned down his street, Bockelson sped by him, arms flailing around his slender naked body, a couple of dozen people trailing after him. Curious, Andreas fell in with them.

Unlike the hysteria of earlier demonstrations, Bockelson trotted quietly along, occasionally grunting. When they arrived at Überwasser,

Bockelson stopped, threw back his head, and screamed as if he were in agony. He pulled his head down, looked mutely at those around him, and dashed for the city center until they reached Knipperdolling's house. Everyone gathered in a circle around Bockelson as he motioned for something to write with. A man from the crowd produced a pen and scrap of parchment, which Bockelson grabbed. Scribbling, he finished his message and shoved it back into the hands of the man who had given him pen and parchment, motioning that the man should read the note.

> God has taken my voice and soon strikes me down. In three and a
> half days, as the prophet John proclaimed, I will come back to life,
> and speak the Word of God.

People wailed loudly after the message was read, and Bockelson promptly collapsed face down on the cobblestones. Andreas knelt and shook his shoulder.

"Jan," Andreas said quietly, "what's this?"

Bockelson didn't move, didn't speak; he hardly breathed. Andreas stood up and looked at the fearful faces of the women and men staring at Bockelson. Glancing back at his naked body, Andreas pondered what lay behind this ploy. Before he could form an opinion, Knipperdolling's doors opened and several men emerged, grabbed the fallen man by the shoulders, and dragged him inside as the door closed behind them.

"At least we only have to wait three and a half days for the next act," Andreas said. No one responded, but a young boy and girl dashed out from the gaggle of people in front of Andreas. They appeared to be about ten years old.

"Don't mock the prophet," the little boy with sunken eyes warned.

"We're going to report you to the authorities," the girl threatened.

"So, this is how things are in Münster now? Children become spies?" Andreas said. "I only meant that we have a set time to know God's will, nothing more."

"You sounded as if you mocked," the boy accused.

"Well, go on, then; we'll let the elders sort it out. But if I were you"—Andreas took a step toward the children—"I'd be careful about accusations."

The children narrowed their eyes. He headed home, contemplating the last few weeks. An uneasy calm had settled over the city, but tensions, like cracked ice on a lake, ran under the surface. Matthys's followers grieved, and Andreas had overheard some grumbling about the burning of the records and deeds. Those who lived in Münster before the refugees arrived grew angrier about having to leave their doors unlocked and their goods being common property for whoever wanted them. There were no private places anymore.

Andreas worked over in his mind what Bockelson was up to. Had he heard how bad spirits were in the city? Did he know that in the taverns there was talk of opening the gates to the Prince-Bishop's armies? Bockelson must have realized his authority was in question, that he didn't carry the weight of Matthys. Leaving the marketplace, Andreas doubted whether this new theater could save Bockelson from the doubts about him that spread from street to street, house to house.

31

April 20

For the next three and a half days, scores of people stood in front of Knipperdolling's house, constantly praying and holding candlelight vigils. When the time arrived for Bockelson's resurrection, Elsbeth, Andreas, and Peter joined the thousands of other onlookers who waited to see what the next act brought.

"Behold, the prophet!"

The shouts directed their attention to Knipperdolling's door. It flew open as Bockelson, still naked, was pulled outside and carefully placed on the grey stone street. Several women rushed to him and started stroking his back.

"They've wanted to get their hands on him for some time; now they have their chance," Elsbeth quipped.

"Three and a half days—right on time," Peter said.

Others approached Bockelson, forming a circle around him. Suddenly, as one of the women's hands lingered on Bockelson's flank, he raised himself up on one elbow, rolled over and sat up. He looked at the woman whose hand now rested in his crotch, smiled, and lifted her hand off before he stood up.

"A cloak," someone in the crowd yelled.

A man took off his coat and walked over to Bockelson, placing it around his shoulders. It stopped at his thighs, his legs and bare feet poking out the bottom.

"How long have I been like this?" Bockelson rocked unsteadily, trying to keep his balance.

"Three and a half days—just as foretold of the witnesses in Revelation," one of the men who had carried him from Knipperdolling's shouted, setting off a round of cries and excited voices.

Bockelson motioned for quiet. "I've had a vision!" His hands flew toward the sky.

"Hallelujah!" It was one word, but it echoed through the square as everyone responded.

"God took me up to heaven and told me He still desires to restore His kingdom here!"

"Glory to God!"

"Hallelujah! Hallelujah!"

"I've been commanded to tell you something else significant, too. Something important!"

The cries turned softer; expectant faces hung on Bockelson's words.

He spread his arms. "From this day forth, no longer shall we be known as Münster. No longer will we use the name given to us by the world." People in the crowd looked at one another. "From this day on," Bockelson cried, "we are Zion!"

"Zion? That's the word he used the night Matthys died," Andreas said, turning to Peter.

"As in the ancient days of Israel, God wishes to restore all things, starting with us, because we have been faithful," Bockelson said. "There is to be no council anymore. Councils are not of God."

"Who will rule us then?" one of the men standing behind the circle of women yelled.

"We'll have twelve elders, just as Israel did," Bockelson replied. "And God has chosen me to pick them."

Andreas glanced over at the small group of men closest to Bockelson; Knipperdolling and Rothmann were whispering to one another. "They don't seem entirely surprised by this." Andreas turned to Elsbeth.

"Divara mentioned something earlier about becoming a queen," Elsbeth said. "I wonder if this has anything to do with that?"

Bockelson motioned to Rothmann, holding a piece of parchment and pen, to his side. The two huddled together, Bockelson speaking quietly as Rothmann wrote furiously on the paper until Rothmann's pen stopped, his face looking like a knife had plunged into him.

After several minutes of heated discussion, Rothmann walked away from Bockelson.

"Men of Zion, God has given Bockelson the names of the elders who are to rule us. Step forward as I call your names!" Rothmann yelled. "Herman Tilbeck, come here!"

The crowd murmured.

As the other names were read, Andreas noticed that all the chosen ones were close to Bockelson's inner circle. Finally, Rothmann came to the last name. His eyes darted from the page to Bockelson before bending his head back to the list. A rustle stopped him, however. Knipperdolling, who had not yet been called, strode out toward the circle of called men. Rothmann shot him a glance and read someone else's name. Knipperdolling's eyes widened as he froze, unable to move.

Bockelson held out his hands, shouting, "I have also been instructed by God that we must have someone who bears the sword of righteousness against evildoers. Anyone who disobeys the commandments of God will be cut off, body and soul, from Zion."

Heads turned toward the ground; the only sound an awkward clearing of throats. No one wanted to be the executioner. A man with a huge sword stood next to Bockelson and handed it to him. The blade alone looked to be almost four feet with a jewel-encrusted handle. Andreas recognized it from the cathedral treasury. Bockelson put it on his shoulder and began circulating among the people, stopping occasionally until moving on. He went through almost the entire crowd before he stopped in front of Knipperdolling. A smile covered his face as he held out the sword to his father-in-law, nodding at him to take it. Knipperdolling's hands remained at his side, fingers flexing.

"Anyone who questions the wisdom of Zion or its elders," Bockelson shouted, keeping his gaze fixed on Knipperdolling, "will see the wrath of God coming at them through the hands of our brother, Bernard Knipperdolling. The sword of the Lord for the people of Zion!"

Knipperdolling, anger glinting in his eyes, kept his hands by his side.

Andreas wondered if the sweat running down his face was from desperation or a desire to harm Bockelson. "I saw that look once in a fox that had been run down and cornered by dogs," Andreas said out of the corner of his mouth.

St. Lambert's bells pealed the hour as Bockelson remained standing in front of Knipperdolling. Putting the blade on his shoulder, Bockelson held out the handle, silently urging him to take it. Knipperdolling, fists forming, glared at Bockelson. The market was absolute stillness, the only sound the echo of the bells and the chirping of birds. Everyone stared at

Knipperdolling until he held out his hands to take the sword. Bockelson beamed with joy. The crowd broke out in cheers and applause.

"No one stands above Bockelson now," Andreas said, "not Rothmann, not Tilbeck, and certainly not Knipperdolling. He's clever, this one."

"This takes an unwelcome turn," Elsbeth said.

"Peter, I don't suppose we could convince you to reconsider leaving?" Andreas asked, observing the look of devastation on Knipperdolling's face.

"No, though if you and Elsbeth can escape, it might be for the best," Peter said.

Andreas heaved a sigh and glanced at Elsbeth, who took his hand and squeezed it. "I'll try another gate right now if you wish," she said.

"Perhaps later," Andreas said. "Peter needs more persuasion."

32

April 22

"THEY DIDN'T LOSE MUCH TIME, did they?" Elsbeth studied the list that appeared three days after the elders had been chosen. New decrees hung on every pole in the city.

"Apparently we're all *Israelites* now." Andreas's head shook as he read the list of new laws.

"Dear God," Elsbeth exclaimed as her eyes scanned the first few lines of the new proclamation:

Whoever curses God shall be put to death.
Whoever curses the ruler shall be put to death.
Whoever curses her husband will be killed.
Husbands shall have complete control over their wives.
Whoever locks their door shall be put to death.
If anyone holds back wealth from Zion, they will suffer death.

"What *doesn't* get us killed?" Elsbeth exploded in anger as she continued down the list. "No one is innocent according to this! The elders can execute us under any pretext."

Andreas and Elsbeth became even more incredulous as they read the rest of the laws. Peter walked across the street and joined them. "How bad is it?" he asked.

Andreas moved aside to let him see. "Worse than we imagined."

Peter took out his glasses and put them on, trying to focus on the printing. "It appears they wish to organize the city by the Bible." He took a deep breath and exhaled. "Or, more specifically, the Old Testament."

"It goes beyond that," Elsbeth said. "You can be killed for gossip, anger, lying, swearing, slander, envy—how would they even know about

179

that last one? Look—criticism of Bockelson is punishable by death."
Elsbeth read for a few minutes more. "Idle conversation? You can be executed for that? I'm surprised they can't kill you for breathing."

"Don't suggest it," Andreas said.

"Look here," Elsbeth steamed. "All meals must be taken in common, but men and women now have to sit at separate tables. And if you
complain about the food, you'll die." She continued going down the list.
"Women must keep their head covered and not wear their hair down?
You can't even fish without their permission." Elsbeth stormed off down
the street, pivoted quickly, and stamped back.

"There are some things in here that are meant to be practical," Andreas said, "though no one can live under this law."

"That might be the point—" Peter said.

"Shit! No garments with holes? No new fashions?" Elsbeth ranted as
her finger traced a line down the decree. "This is madness!"

"They want to control your body first. If they discipline your body,
they get your conscience in the bargain," Peter said. "They want total obe-
dience, and this is how they'll get it."

"It looks as if justice will be swift in Zion." Elsbeth pointed to the
bottom of the flyer.

Peter and Andreas looked to where her finger was pointing:

> The elders of Zion will sit in judgment every day but the Lord's
> Day, from 6–8 in the morning and 1–3 in the afternoon.

"If they keep to this rule, then Knipperdolling's going to be a busy
man," Peter said.

"This is outrageous!" Elsbeth spewed. "How is this better than what
they lived under before? Were Catholics really worse than this?"

"I did not find it so," Peter said.

"I'm sorry, Father. That didn't sound the way I meant it."

"I'm not offended. This is a predictable path. It repeats itself
continually."

"Pardon?"

"Power. Those outside want to maintain their power, and now those
inside want to consolidate theirs. They define each other in the process.
When God gets dragged into the mix, it only heightens the stakes. The
enemy must become Satan, the forces of darkness. That way you justify
your own atrocity."

"Then we're doomed," Elsbeth muttered.

"Perhaps not," Peter said.

"Those outside will pillage us, rape the women, and cut us down for the sheer joy of killing," Andreas broke in. "Von Waldeck gives them license to do it, and they'll be regarded as heroes for it. We are stuck between them and the tender mercies of Zion. If we can't leave, we'll have to fight with Zion or lose our lives, so I'm with Elsbeth on this. We're doomed."

"Oh, God." Elsbeth slumped over, grabbing her knees. "If you talk to a single stranger who comes into the city, you can be executed." She stood up and stalked back down the street, cursing, throwing her fists in the air.

"Have you tried the gates again?" Peter asked Andreas.

"Yes, as has Elsbeth," Andreas replied, watching her box the sky. "Neither of us can pass. I suspect we are more prisoner than guest."

Elsbeth strode back to Peter and Andreas. "We need to plan for ways out of this."

"Do you have any ideas?" Andreas asked.

"Other than staying alive until this madness is over?" Elsbeth fumed. "No, but we must walk very carefully, lest we end up at the end of Knipperdolling's sword."

Thinking about the armies preparing to attack outside, and now the danger growing inside the city, Andreas wondered if Elsbeth might have been better off in Bern.

33

May 22

THE BOOM OF SHELL on city wall hit Andreas at the same time the vibrations rippled through his body, knocking him to the floor of his room. He sprang to his feet and hurried to the courtyard. Trying to gather his wits, he met Elsbeth and the other residents running from their quarters into the courtyard.

"Stations, everybody. Hurry!" a voice shouted above the chatter of hysteria. They had been training for this day for weeks, joined by some of the mercenaries who left the camps and joined their side, but nothing prepared Andreas for the shock when the first cannonball hit the wall.

Elsbeth cowered as a cannonball flew into a house across the street, sending splintering shafts of wood and stone flying. "God!" she screamed.

"We'll survive this, but we need to go—now!" Andreas grabbed Elsbeth in his arms. They held one another tightly a few seconds before rushing to their stations. Elsbeth had been assigned to defend Cross Gate while Andreas had been working at Jew's Gate in the northwest sector. They dashed into the street and ran for Elsbeth's station. Andreas held out his hand and grabbed her arm as they arrived at Cross Gate.

"I love you," he said. "I'll see you tonight."

"If we live that long," Elsbeth shouted as she mounted the stairs.

Andreas waited for her to reach the top of the wall before dashing off for Jew's Gate. He had been working there the past three weeks, while hundreds of peasants outside the walls had been forced by von Waldeck to drain its moat. That part of the city was on a slight rise, so Andreas knew that the invaders' plan was to divert the river and let the area drain, creating a clear path to the wall. Every night, as the peasants worked under their wooden shields to move dirt and build new channels for the water, Andreas and his companions would rain down arrows and bullets on them; but no matter how many workers they killed or wounded, the plan was gradually succeeding. The moat had been turned into a marshy area where wood planks and large woven mats could be placed to allow attackers access to the wall. If the wall was breached, the gate would open, and the city would fall. Andreas, caught between defending a city he wished would fall and the fear of what followed if it did, thought every day about how to survive.

Boys with muskets and ammunition ran past him, headed in the opposite direction, their childish voices raised in excited shouting. Andreas envied them their innocence. He wished he could hide in that childish unknowing. By the end of this day, those voices, if they spoke at all, would sound much different. Looking up, Andreas saw several arrows falling from the sky. He curled up into a ball and hit the ground while the metal tips of the arrows clanged against the street. When they stopped, he rose and ran on, marveling that the barrage had not hit him.

Nearing the gate, the sulfurous smell of gunpowder stung his nose as he climbed up to his station. The defenders were busy returning fire, but for every shell they launched out toward the siege line, several more fell on the city. It was a nightmare of fire and thunder. Shaking, Andreas delivered shells to the cannons sitting out on the section of the promenade that jutted out into the countryside.

"Move the shields!" his captain ordered.

Andreas and several other men pushed the woven stick shields alongside the cannons. He wondered how much good the shields did. They had been constructed with the purpose of hiding the cannons from view while other, more obvious, shields on the wall served as decoys.

As the morning passed, his arms and legs became weights, dragging him down, enticing him with thoughts of sleep. His mind, sharp at the beginning of the attack, wandered into fantasies of escape, rendering him unable to calculate the sound of the shell with its likely target. The next cannonball hit only a few feet away. Andreas collapsed to the stone walkway, his head hitting rock, knocking him out. When he came to, he crawled to the city side of the wall. Leaning against it, bodies came into focus, their mouths opening and closing, but silence gripped him. He shook his head, trying to make himself hear again.

Stone fragments exploded up in smoke and rained down fire mere feet from Andreas. Several men collapsed onto the promenade as the blast reverberated down Andreas's spine. *I must get back to work.* He staggered to his feet and examined his body, sure he would see blood, but to his surprise, he was not wounded. Engrossed in his own survival, he barely noticed when several flaming arrows hit the windmill on the promenade. The wooden building smoked for several minutes before bursting into a ball of flame.

Men with leather buckets threw water on the fire as more flaming arrows landed around them. The smell of charred flesh seared Andreas's nose, and a defender beside him took a flaming arrow to his thigh. The cloth-tipped arrow sparked into flames just before a bucket of water doused him. Though Andreas could see the man's tortured face, he could not hear him screaming.

As Andreas slogged from one task to the next, the weight of battle pushed his body to exhaustion. Glancing around at the havoc, he desperately struggled to find a place within that he could hold onto before he lost his grip on sanity. When morning passed into afternoon, the ringing in his ears was slowly replaced by shouts and blasts, muffled at first, but gradually growing more distinct. As the shelling subsided, Andreas saw one of his men perched precariously on the top of the wall's ledge, screaming out into the fields. They were the first words he had heard in hours.

"You goddamn bastards! Goddamn you! Go to hell! You'll burn, you shit-filled sons of whores!" The man on the ledge tore open his shirt. "Come on, you bastards! Come and get this with your own hands if you have the guts!"

Several of the man's friends pulled him off the wall right before bullets chipped the mortar where the screamer had stood.

The captain of the gate waved his arms toward the streets. "That's it for now. They're softening us up for later. Go home and get some rest, but report back here in a couple of hours."

Andreas climbed down and plodded home. Entering the refectory, he found Elsbeth listlessly eating bread and broth, her face laden with worry. When he called her name, she leapt to her feet and rushed over to him, throwing her arms around him, sobbing.

"I never thought I would see you again. We heard Jew's Gate was taking the worst of it!" Elsbeth cried.

"It was bad, terrifying," Andreas said, his skull still throbbing. They held one another as Peter came out of the kitchen.

"You need to eat. It's going to be a long day," Peter said.

Andreas took a seat beside Elsbeth. A couple of dozen people sitting at the long tables were sharing reports of how their section of the wall fared against the morning's onslaught. A bowl of broth with chunks of pork and onions appeared in front of Andreas, along with some bread and cheese. He rapidly spooned the soup into his mouth.

"I thought I was going to die." Andreas coughed up some filmy sulfurous muck. "A shell fell so close to me, I lost my hearing for a time. My ears are still ringing."

Elsbeth took his hand in hers and put her forehead on it. "I was terrified you weren't coming back."

"So was I."

Peter sat down beside them and started spooning broth out of his bowl. "Von Waldeck is wearing us down."

"But shouldn't we hope for him to succeed?" Elsbeth asked. "Would that not mean freedom?"

"Not if we die because of it," Andreas replied. "If they gain the gates, they'll not stop to ask who is here freely and who stays under coercion. Everyone in the city is in peril."

"Then what hope do we have?"

Andreas heard the shakiness in Elsbeth's voice. "Perhaps we can convince the soldiers we were kept here against our wills."

"How likely is that?" Elsbeth said.

"Claim sanctuary with me," Peter offered. "They may kill me, too, but they'll at least think twice about killing a priest. I suspect they'll want to turn me over to von Waldeck."

They sat silently until Elsbeth pushed back from the table. "I have to go rest," she mumbled and excused herself.

Peter looked at Andreas as he finished his bread. "She needs you."

Andreas nodded, rose, and headed for the guesthouse, where he found Elsbeth lying on her bed, staring at the ceiling.

"It was awful out there," Elsbeth said.

"Yes, it was."

"Did you lose anyone?"

"No. Bullets and shells flying everywhere, a few wounded, but no one died."

"I thought we would lose some, but everyone survived. I could've died today so easily." Elsbeth began weeping as Andreas lay down beside her. She rolled onto her side and moved her body next to his. Andreas smelled the dank smell of mud, sweat, and gunpowder.

"Hold me; I'm so tired." Elsbeth's voice grew fainter before she slipped into sleep.

"You're stronger than you know," Andreas whispered, as her body slackened and her breathing grew heavier.

❀❀

Two hours later, Andreas and Elsbeth arrived at Cross Gate. He gripped onto her like it might be the last time they saw each other.

"No matter what happens, I love you," Elsbeth said, heading up the stairs.

Andreas put his fist over his heart and headed for his post. Mounting the stairs, he found his companions leaning over the wall.

"What's going on?" Andreas asked.

"Listen—they're drunk," the captain said.

Andreas went to the wall, glanced down, and saw soldiers stumbling around, taunting the men on the wall.

"Hey, heretics, do you know what we're going to do to you when we break into your city?"

"How many women do you have in there anyway? When they've had men from Gelders, they won't want you anymore."

"We can't wait to break you. Then your women will get to find out what real men taste like."

"How much money do you have in there? They tell us we'll be rich when this is over."

One of the men beside Andreas raised his arquebus to shoot. "No!" the captain yelled. "Don't waste your ammunition. We'll need it if they get to the inner wall."

"But it's the perfect moment. They're too drunk to shoot straight," the shooter said.

Just then, one of the mercenaries pulled down his pants, turned to the wall, and took a shit.

"Please?" the shooter beside Andreas begged.

Before the captain could respond, a shot rang out as the man fell to the ground, shot in his backside. His companions quickly pulled him back to their campsite.

"That ought to shut 'em up," the shooter said, as the men on the wall collapsed in laughter.

Everyone settled in to see what would happen next, but for hours no sound came from the mercenaries. Andreas and the others played cards, talked, and waited for signs of action from outside.

"What's going on over there?" Andreas finally asked.

"They must've passed out. God knows they've been drinking enough," the captain answered. "I guess the attack isn't coming today."

Andreas was grateful for the reprieve. He took in the approaching evening. The thin red slip of sun on the horizon looked like an arch dipped in crimson cloth as twilight settled in. The men on the wall, relieved that the assault was not coming, talked among themselves, sharing stories they had heard at lunch about how things were going at other gates. The respite lifted spirits until, at the cusp of dusk, shouts erupted from the drunken mercenaries.

"Attack! Hurry! We're late!"

"For God and Gelders!"

Andreas and the others pushed their heads over the wall and squinted toward the field along the moat. Below them, several dozen men rushed the wall. Stumbling in the knee-deep muck, they fired wildly, the bullets pinging against the walls.

"They're not carrying mats!" Andreas shouted.

"What the hell?" The captain was puzzled. "Where're their mats? Stupid! Fire on them, now! Quick, move the cannons to fire. Step fast!"

Andreas looked down at the men stuck in the swampy mess below him. *There was no reason for this attack. What are they doing?* Only mats would have allowed them decent passage to the wall.

"To arms!" the captain repeated.

Bodies in motion snapped to action, shooting arrows and guns down on the hapless men flailing below. Hundreds more voices arose from other parts of the camps along the siege line, and soon mercenaries ran to the aid of their entrapped comrades, though they, too, quickly became glued in the sticky mud left by the drained moat.

Screams of men taking bullets and arrows pierced the evening air. When the moon just crested the horizon, Andreas bent over the wall. Dozens of men, stuck in mud, their bodies slumped forward like marionette puppets whose strings had been cut, groaned as life ebbed from them. He could not see much more than that in the moonlight, but he shuddered at the thought of their suffering.

The retreat signal sounded. Those not dead, or stuck, trudged back to their camps. "We've won!" the captain cried. "I don't know why they attacked, but we've won this round."

"Hallelujah!" voices around Andreas began shouting.

"Praise God!" others joined in, singing hymns and praising God for deliverance.

Andreas searched the horizon, waiting for torches and troops to appear. *What the hell just happened?*

34

May 26

BERNARD KNIPPERDOLLING STUDIED the milling crowd in front of him. Their celebrations of von Waldeck's defeat pierced him since it meant his worst nightmare had come true—that sack of shit Bockelson was now unassailable. Holding the winnowing sword of Zion on his shoulder, he watched the mob gathered in front of the elders of Zion. The city had been summoned to the market to witness Zion's justice, and Knipperdolling, though he was only a cog in a greater machine, had his part to play. Stepping back, he took his place at the end of the elders' morning tribunal. Buzzing arose as a ragged and disheveled man was brought before the tribunal and tossed on his knees in front of his judges. Jan Bockelson took his seat on the largest chair in the middle of the judging table.

"Are you the one they call Gert the Smoker?" Bockelson leaned forward, addressing the unkempt man.

"Yes," Gert replied, eyes flitting about.

"What's this smoke that continually surrounds your face?"

"It's a novelty, my lord," Gert offered, pulling an ornately carved pipe out of his pants pocket. "It's called tobacco."

"It offends, but no matter, we have no laws against it . . . yet," Bockelson said. He turned down his face. "You and your friends are here for another matter." Bockelson pointed to the six men surrounded by guards standing behind Gert.

"When you and your gang were carousing last night in the tavern, did you grab our brother's wife?"

"Yes, but I was only trying to get her attention," Gert croaked. "I wanted more ale, that's all."

"But her husband says you fondled her . . . in lust." Bockelson rose from his chair and stepped down to the street to stand over the prisoner. "We can't have this behavior in Zion. God would be displeased if we allowed it."

Tears poured down Gert's face as his head turned from the crowd of witnesses to the judges. "I swear, there was nothing lustful in my reach."

Knipperdolling picked up a sharpening stone from behind him and rubbed it slowly along his blade, his face intent on the wooden block and straw in the street. The mixture of excitement and revulsion swirled around inside of him, his stomach churning.

"Why would you do that?" Bockelson's voice was kind. "Take what wasn't yours?"

"My lord"—Gert shook so hard he had difficulty speaking—"I'm so sor-sor-ry. I had some drink and for-got-got myself."

Bockelson circled Gert. "Have you heard of prostitutes in our city?"

"Pardon, my lord?"

"Whores. Have you heard of them here?"

"Yes, my lord. I've heard mention of them."

"Are they used by your companions?"

Knipperdolling suspected that at this moment Gert wished he and his companions had never deserted the mercenary armies of von Waldeck and come into the city.

"I don't know, my lord, maybe. I've heard of such things."

"If you had a wife of your own, do you think you would still make our women whores?"

"No, my lord, but I don't make them whores now." Gert kept his eyes on Bockelson's feet, following their steps.

Bockelson's mouse. Knipperdolling's stone stopped.

"I'm sorry, but it's better to perish than lose your salvation," Bockelson said. He turned back to the gathering of elders sitting under the arcade. "This disease needs to be cut out from among us, so that we may not lose favor with God."

"Kill him!" a chorus of women's voices rang out.

Bockelson looked silently at the elders who all nodded their heads in unison.

"Please, no!" Gert yelled. "This isn't right. I've fought for you, my lord, for Zion!"

Two men took Gert and pushed him to his knees beside the wooden block. They forced his head onto the grooved part as Gert screamed.

Knipperdolling stepped around him and approached from behind. Gert lifted his face to Knipperdolling.

"Don't look at me! Turn around!" Knipperdolling commanded.

Jeering and shouts of encouragement, mixed with the women's screams, enveloped the mob. Knipperdolling drew his sword over his head and with both arms swiftly brought it down, barely missing a clean cut. Gert's head stayed attached to his body just long enough for his screaming to linger in the air for a couple of seconds. His pipe tumbled out of his hands and onto the street. Knipperdolling raised the sword quickly and hacked at the neck one more time before the head rolled off the block into the straw. After it was over, Knipperdolling stumbled away, his face ashen. He hated his life.

The headless body slumped on the block as Bockelson walked over to it and called for quiet. "We will not survive if we don't have discipline!" he bellowed. "Law and order must be maintained. If we don't pull together, fight the devil inside as well as outside, we'll not taste victory. Those outside our walls fight for the love of money—the root of all evil—but we fight for the honor of preparing a home fit for Jesus!"

The roar from the crowd drowned out Bockelson's next words, so he let the noise recede before he spoke again.

"We must prepare ourselves, Zion. Satan's armies outside desire our death, yet God is greater. Continue in goodness and obey your elders and the law. We can't afford to lose any more good men. We need all those we have to defend against the coming attack." With that, Bockelson turned to the six companions of Gert the Smoker. "But these are not good men and must suffer the same fate as their leader." Bockelson shouted. "Take them to Cathedral Hill, tie them to posts, and use them as target practice for our archers."

As relieved as Knipperdolling was that his day was done, he pitied the men who were going to die for no other reason than the whims of Bockelson. Why had he ever taken that viper into his house?

Turning to the elders, Bockelson said, "Go get Rothmann. Meet me in City Hall within the hour." Knipperdolling glimpsed Bockelson gazing at him. "You're needed as well, executioner. And bring your sword."

❀❀

An hour later, Knipperdolling stood as the elders sat chattering around a massive oak table in City Hall. Tilbeck and Bockelson were flanked by several of the Dutchmen he had chosen for council. Knipperdolling's eyes went to Ulrich, standing in his usual place, looking out the window.

"Ahh." Bockelson cleared his throat. "I've been in prayer about this for a while, brothers. I believe the time has come for us to face our plight. We're far from the one hundred and forty-four thousand souls prophesied in Revelation. Our sisters number six thousand and are not being taken care of. It can't have escaped your notice that there are three of them for every man. They need husbands. Rothmann believes, and I concur, that God is calling for a restitution of the full Word of God. I've had a vision that God desires us to take plural wives so that the women won't come to shame."

Coughing and scuffling of chair legs stilled into silence, followed by outbursts around the room. Knipperdolling saw a brief glimpse of hope that his problem might get solved.

"I never said that!" Rothmann jumped up, his hands gripping the table. "This is not the restitution I was talking about. How could you even consider it?"

"You're the one always going on about how too many women are wearing the trousers," Bockelson retorted. "Didn't you say just the other night that women lead men around like bears on a chain—that they hold us hostage through sex?"

Rothmann sheepishly sunk back into his chair. "But that was before the laws of Zion were passed. It won't be that way now."

"Consider this," Bockelson responded, "have not men lost their role here as head of the household? With so many sisters in need, don't we have to provide for them? Every woman should have her own husband, but if they are three times our number, how is this to happen? We must find another way to take care of them. Besides, lust is causing us to lose some of our best soldiers to the heathens outside. Will Christ return to a city wallowing in lust? If each woman has a husband, then righteousness is ours. In the bonds of matrimony, we restore the rightful position of man as head of the household."

"And what about the women who are already married?" Rothmann regained his footing, leaning further over the table. "Whose husbands left them here when they were exiled?"

"They're married according to the flesh. We live by the spirit in Zion," Bockelson said.

Knipperdolling ran a sharpening stone along his sword, trying to get rid of the last traces of Gert's neck. He wondered if anyone in the room would be interested in the story one of his serving girls told him that morning about finding Bockelson in bed with two women. *By the spirit, indeed.*

"But polygamy?" Rothmann slumped into his seat.

"No one ever said doing God's will would be easy," Ulrich said quietly, his eyes on the street.

"It's biblical, Rothmann," Tilbeck broke in. "It's in the Word."

"But that was in the age of the patriarchs." Rothmann waved his hand in protest.

"You're the one who's been preaching that we live in the restitution of all things. This *is* of the spirit. It's merely the logical conclusion of your own theology," Bockelson argued.

For several seconds, the only sound in the room was the steady scraping of stone on metal. Rothmann looked around the table at the elders of Zion; none openly joined him in opposition. His hand touched his neck.

"This goes too far," Rothmann protested.

"That's why we need you," Bockelson replied. "Someone's going to have to convince the city to obey God's new command."

"Someone will need to convince me first," Rothmann countered.

Bockelson rose and went to the lectern in the corner of the room. He took the Bible that sat on it and brought it back, tossing it on the table with a loud pop. "Then let us begin, because I would rather you do the convincing than Brother Knipperdolling," Bockelson said, his head turning to Knipperdolling, who stared back mutely at his prey.

35

June 18

ELSBETH QUICKLY WORKED her hoe over the ground, pulling out the weeds that grew in between the squash, carrots, and beans. The city was trying to take care of the crops and prepare for the winter, though everyone was anxious about the rumors that another attack was close. Elsbeth had stopped imagining a life outside of the walls, her hope fading with every new attempt to leave thwarted. She'd work for her friends, but she cared nothing for Zion. A slamming door grabbed her attention. Startled, she found Ingrid rushing toward her, her body coiled in anger.

"Ingrid—" Elsbeth dropped her hoe.

She put up her hand, stopping Elsbeth. "They . . . Bastards . . . Divara—" Ingrid stopped to catch her breath.

"What's the matter?" Elsbeth asked.

Ingrid grabbed Elsbeth by the shoulders. "I hate them, every goddamn one. I hate them all."

"What is it? What's wrong?"

"They sent . . . that poor . . . girl to von Waldeck," Ingrid stammered.

"Who?"

"Hille Feyken."

Divara's studies about Judith and Holofernes flashed into Elsbeth's mind. Ingrid was not making sense; Elsbeth had just seen Feyken yesterday, but she was dressed in noble's clothes, with her hair braided and bejeweled. She thought it odd at the time but kept about her business.

"Wait, who sent her to where?"

"I don't know—Bockelson? Rothmann? Someone sent her out to the Prince-Bishop." Ingrid spit at her feet. "She took a poisoned shirt with her, who knows where she got that, to offer the Prince-Bishop as a gift. Rachel said she heard that Abbess Ida's brother, who's high bailiff for von Waldeck, arrested her."

"When did this happen?" Elsbeth asked.

"Yesterday. She was imprisoned and might have been set free because she's so young, but some arse from the city who knew of the plot snuck out to warn Ida's brother that Hille meant the Prince-Bishop harm."

"Who would do . . . ?" Elsbeth dropped her head. *Judith? Divara!* It was a horrific thought, and Elsbeth felt sick for even considering it. "You don't think—?"

"Yes, I do," Ingrid cut in. "Who else? Remember how Divara said we might need a Judith one day? After the traitor betrayed Hille, they made her put on the poisoned tunic meant for von Waldeck. Those goddamned bastards killed that poor girl."

Elsbeth stood up and walked out toward the wall. Could it really have been Divara? The more she stood in the garden, trying to work it out, the angrier she grew. The rage started as a small ball in the pit of her stomach, but soon it swelled up, taking away her reason, her speech, her good sense. She stormed back into the monastery, with Ingrid on her heels.

Twenty minutes later, they were standing outside Divara's, Elsbeth banging on the door with her fist. Divara answered, looking puzzled.

"Elsbeth, Ingrid, what's wrong?"

"Did you send her?" Elsbeth shouted. "Did you?"

"Send who?" Divara said.

"Feyken. She went over to the camps. Where would she have gotten that idea?"

"Come on in, we can talk about this inside," Divara said, motioning the women into the house.

"No! Answer my question—did you talk her into this scheme?" Elsbeth's hands moved to her hips.

Divara leaned on the doorframe. "Am I responsible for how she acts? The last I heard of her, she was in Knipperdolling's living room with Jan and Rothmann."

"What if it were your daughter? Would you be so calm? Damn, Divara." Elsbeth stepped away from the door.

Elsbeth saw it all in her mind's eye. An impressionable girl sitting in a group of women, feeling important, included. She hears the story of Judith, perhaps for the first time. It sits there, working its way around in her mind, until one day an elder, maybe even Bockelson himself, invites her in for cake. A few moments of innocent conversation before the one question idealistic children everywhere find irresistible—would you like to serve God? "Why, yes, but who am I to do such a grand thing?" That is what she would have said, and then perhaps they would have offered sweet praises of how she was perfect for this mission, *called* even. Later, she would have stood in front of her mirror as she dressed to go to the enemy, confident in her ability to seduce a man. Did not the young men fall over themselves to be next to her? Her husband was always saying how beautiful she was, how grateful he was to have her. This couldn't be much different. She would have ridden out of the gate pleased that God had chosen her for this task, the joy of saving her people from the Antichrist filling her very soul.

"Elsbeth, please come inside and we can talk about this," Divara pleaded. "I have some cakes and milk."

Elsbeth stared at Divara, her mouth agape. She shook her head slowly, anger fading into disappointment. Now she had her answer—the God this woman and her people served had no limits, no place He would step back from. This God was fine with child sacrifice. No angel stayed the hand of Abraham this time. Hille Feyken lay dead in the camp of the enemy, and everyone involved was the worse for it. Feyken had lost her life; they had lost their souls. Elsbeth's shoulders slumped as she pivoted for home.

"No! Elsbeth, please come back!" Divara shouted, but her pleas fell on deaf ears as Elsbeth and Ingrid picked up their pace.

36

July 17

ROTHMANN SHUFFLED HIS PAPERS, eyes darting back and forth from the crowd to the pulpit. Elsbeth noticed he spent a long time clearing his throat. His lips pressed together as he looked out over the congregation. Women crowded down at the front, looking as if they were ready to leap up to the pulpit with the slightest provocation. Ingrid, Rachel, and Ursula stood next to Elsbeth, along with Peter and Andreas, all eyes locked on Rothmann.

"It is the creation story that calls for our attention today." His voice was steady, but his hands flew in constant motion. "We read in Genesis that among the very first commandments that God gives to man is that he should be fruitful and multiply. Do we believe this is the living Word for us?"

Heads nodded assent.

"So, the Word lives today as it has since the foundation of the world. Brothers and sisters in Christ, have we not been called by God to be the new Israel, a light to the Gentiles and the heathen?"

Elsbeth twisted around to find Divara and Bockelson in the back of the church.

"This has been our destiny, to be the beacon that shines throughout the empire, calling all those hounded and persecuted to come and find rest. Many of you found rest here, have you not? Yet Christ has not come to us. What prevents his coming?"

Voices murmured, the expectations of wounded souls looking for healing.

"To truly prepare the way for our Lord's return, we must become an Israel fit for the Messiah," Rothmann continued. "If we look at the patriarchs and kings of Israel, we find that they had many wives to help them follow the command to be more fruitful. Abraham himself had two wives, Sarah and Hagar. Jacob had two wives. Solomon had many wives and concubines. Why would God allow this in ancient times and not today? Do we dare question their righteousness? Is our Lord not the same yesterday, today, and forever?"

Elsbeth glanced at Peter and Andreas, their gaze fixed on the floor.

"If God does not change, then what has happened that we do not live as the Israelites did? St. Paul commands every woman to have a husband and every man a wife in order that they not burn with lust. So, we find that God wants us to be married and to look after one another. We leave our sisters in mortal danger"—Rothmann looked at the group of women on his left and opened his palm toward them—"if we do not do everything in our power to take care of them." Murmuring spread throughout the gathering. "We must look after those who have no husband in order that they not be tempted."

Waves of chatter rolled in, softly at first, but then a tide filled the cathedral. Elsbeth located Knipperdolling on the opposite side of the cathedral, standing with his wife and Clara, who looked as if she were on the verge of tears.

"So, we have the witness of Scripture that we are to be fruitful and multiply." Rothmann's voice grew more urgent. "We have the example of the kings and patriarchs, who had multiple wives and concubines, and we have St. Paul who said every man should have his own wife. But what do we have in Zion? We have hundreds of brothers and sisters who have come into the city unmarried and remain that way. We have married women whose husbands have deserted them."

The communal waters were being stirred into muck. The rest of the congregation wore puzzled looks, not quite sure how to respond. People crossed their arms, and the women below Rothmann had stopped moving. Everyone waited as he paused before continuing.

"Thanks be to God, we have Holy Scripture as our guide. We are the new Abraham, the new Jacob, and the new Solomon, living in the New Jerusalem, the new Zion. The new covenant has surpassed the old. We live in the freedom of Christ and are dead to the law."

The murmuring stopped when Rothmann came out of the pulpit and stood on the steps leading to the altar.

"*We* are the *new* Israel. It is no longer the kings and patriarchs who are allowed these freedoms. We were meant to multiply and populate the earth with the elect. St. Paul said if a man wants to be a bishop, he should be the husband of *one* wife, but who among us wants to be a bishop?"

Laughter awkwardly echoed throughout the sanctuary.

"No one I know," a voice called out. Boisterous laughter followed.

Rothmann smiled. "Well, if no one wants to be a bishop, St. Paul must have meant that having more than one wife was a common practice."

Elsbeth noticed Rothmann's eyes turning to Bockelson, who nodded approvingly. "Why do we not follow the Bible? Are we afraid of the full Gospel?" Rothmann raised his arm. "Listen to me, Zion. God has revealed that He wishes to restore to us the former glory of Israel, the purity of the true Law. We should not make whores of our sisters and daughters. If we leave them without husbands, is this not what we do?"

Elsbeth noticed Peter looking at the floor, shaking his head. Similar gestures swept through segments of the congregation. Even some of Rothmann's preachers stood with arms folded, their faces masks of mute indifference. Others walked toward the front of the church in anticipation. Elsbeth took Andreas's hand.

"We must not leave our widows bereft. Marriage is an honorable estate and adultery should be held in contempt. How shall we avoid such a state when there are over six thousand women in Zion but only two thousand men?"

A man and woman in front of Elsbeth abruptly spun around and stalked out of the church. Rothmann stopped. They were quickly followed by several more couples. There was an uncomfortable silence, broken only by a crying baby as the rest of the congregation waited in anticipation.

"We must preserve the sanctity of marriage," Rothmann began, a hint of hesitation in his voice. "We must follow the will of God, or else we will be given over to our enemies. We are called by God to be an example of faithfulness to the world. They will look at our families and marvel! There will be no more widows, no more orphans. We shall look after one another."

Elsbeth glimpsed Rachel and Ursula grabbing hands. Peter and Andreas moved their eyes from the floor to Rothmann.

"In the coming days, I will be teaching at City Hall so that you may know this is the true word of restitution."

Elsbeth took in Knipperdolling and his family. Deep blue veins rose on his neck. "They look miserable," Elsbeth whispered to Andreas.

The service ended in clamor as people rushed to the rear exit, fighting about what they just heard.

"This is what happens when you let foreigners in."

"How dare he even suggest my husband can have more than one wife?"

"How can this be God's will?"

"We'll be the laughingstock of the empire."

"This is wrong. We need to stop this."

"But it's biblical. How can we go against the Word of God?"

"It's polygamy! This goes too far!"

Elsbeth and her friends walked past the buzzing groups quickly, not stopping to talk to anyone. Ingrid, Rachel, and Ursula waved goodbye and headed to their quarters, as Elsbeth, Andreas, and Peter walked back to the monastery.

Peter spoke first. "That was unanticipated."

"That's one word for it," Andreas said.

"Madness is the word I'd choose," Elsbeth said. "Did you see Knipperdolling? I thought he was going to explode."

"If the city doesn't accept this, Bockelson's authority will be threatened," Andreas said.

"So, Zion falls apart because of men's cocks? Fitting somehow." Elsbeth drew shocked looks from her companions. "What? Is it not the truth?"

"Indelicately stated, Elsbeth, but probably accurate," Peter admitted.

"I'm sorry. I just feel my blood boil at what they ask of us." Elsbeth glanced at Peter. "Father Peter, you look troubled."

"I was thinking that you two have some decisions to make," Peter said.

"Decisions?" Elsbeth asked.

"What if they're able to convince the city that this is God's will?"

"Do you think that's possible?" Andreas asked.

"Anything is possible now," Peter said. "The reason there's any resistance to this at all is because a handful of people still live in the reality of Münster and not the fantasy of Zion. Those raised here won't easily accept this, but the refugees have been willing to accept almost anything their leaders feed them."

Silence fell between them as they continued for home.

"I suppose, if you think about it, there's a logic to it," Andreas interrupted the quietness.

"Logic?" Elsbeth scowled.

"Consider. We are assuming that someone wants access to more women—or at least, that's what you said, Elsbeth."

"Yes, but—"

"Hold on, let me finish," Andreas said. "We know from Gert's execution that the mercenaries who deserted and came inside have been causing some problems. And we know that there are women in the city who risk their lives to take care of these men's, uh, urges."

"They're called whores," Elsbeth said. "You don't have to be so delicate."

"There are hundreds, maybe even thousands of widows," Andreas continued. "Your friends from the convent . . . how many of them are living without men?"

"Some of them don't need men."

"If you wanted everyone to live a godly life, you'd do exactly what they're doing. This solves the problem of how to take care of all the women."

"I think I may actually be more cynical than you are," Elsbeth said. "This is all because Bockelson means to have both Divara and Clara without challenge, and, if the stories about his appetites are true, more besides them."

"There may be many motives at work here," Andreas said, "but the more I consider it, the more I wonder if order is what they want, not access to more women."

"You may be right," Peter said. "This revelation takes care of several of their needs."

"And yet, I'm sure the women won't be allowed to have multiple husbands," Elsbeth muttered. "Besides, the women in this city are fierce; they don't need anyone's protection."

"All the more reason to make sure they're under their husband's control," Peter said.

"I take your point," Elsbeth conceded.

"Regardless, if our speculation is right or wrong, like I said before, you two have some decisions to make. Sooner would be better," Peter said.

"Pardon?" Elsbeth said.

"Assume they get their way," Peter said. "What then?"

Elsbeth grew more uncomfortable as she started to contemplate the future.

Andreas, who had been lost in thought, raised his head. "Women won't get the choice. Men will do the choosing. Women will probably be forced to marry whoever asks them."

"Oh, God . . . " Elsbeth groaned as the implications sank in.

Arriving at the monastery gate, Elsbeth pushed it open with such force that it slammed against the wall. She stomped through the common room and out into the backyard. Andreas and Peter followed and watched as she stormed to the wall, where she tramped in a circle. After her steps slowed, she returned, walked past them without a word, and disappeared inside. Minutes later, she returned with a single stein of ale and sat down. She took a long quaff. The only sound heard in the next several minutes was Elsbeth's belching as she finished her mug.

She finally spoke. "You're right. We have some decisions to make." She rose from her seat and poured the last few drops from her stein on the ground. "I'll see you two later." And with that she was off.

Andreas and Peter exchanged confused looks.

Thirty minutes later, Elsbeth sat on the couch in her friends' common room as Ingrid, Ursula, and Rachel gathered around her. They sipped their cups of wine as Elsbeth shared what she had worked out.

"We need to be ready for what comes next," Elsbeth said. "We should expect anything."

"What do you think that might be?" Ingrid asked.

"We may be forced to marry any man who asks us."

"They can't do that!" Rachel and Ursula exploded simultaneously.

"How are they going to enforce that?" Ingrid wondered. "Can they get away with this?"

"They do anything they want," Ursula complained. "No one wants to be on the wrong end of Knipperdolling's sword."

"Can they make us do *that*, though? Can they really force us to take men not of our choosing?" Ingrid asked.

"Yes, which is why we need to be ready," Elsbeth answered. A wave of gratitude for the enormous love she shared with these women swept over Elsbeth.

"I would rather die than marry one of those fools," Ursula said.

"Then we must see that it doesn't come to that," Elsbeth said.

"But how—what can we do?" Ingrid said.

"It may seem crazy . . . " Elsbeth waited.

"What? What might seem crazy?" Ursula asked.

"We'll have to wait to see what kind of laws they post first, but if they do what I think, we must be prepared to slip through their noose." Elsbeth took a deep breath and looked at her friends. "If they make us marry, I'm thinking that Andreas should marry all of us."

They gawked at Elsbeth as if the Virgin Mary had suddenly appeared in their room.

Ingrid laughed out loud. "You can't be serious."

"I am. If you think it through, you'll see the wisdom in it." Elsbeth stood and went over to the fireplace, resting her arm on the mantle. "Mine is the only body that will actually be in his bed, but if he marries us all, no one else can force our hand. We still remain free from them."

The others sat, stunned, exchanging glances.

"Will Andreas agree to this?" Ingrid broke the silence.

Elsbeth shrugged. "I'm not sure, but he loves me, and I know he cares for you. He may need a bit of persuasion, but I think he sees the matter as it is. He knows what will happen if a decree comes down. He won't want to lose me to another, and he might unless he agrees to this."

Ursula and Rachel shook their heads as if they had just been told to step in a pot of fire.

"Will we have to live in the monastery?" Ingrid said. "We like it here." Her hand ran over the sofa covering.

"Probably, but you are vulnerable here. There's room in the guest-house with me. Andreas stays over in the monk's quarters for now, though if we were all married, I suppose he would move in with us. I would enjoy your company. And I think he would take some pleasure in keeping you all from worse fates." Elsbeth smiled at her friends. "Well?"

"And Father Peter, would he agree?"

"That man is not like most priests," Elsbeth replied. "He'll under-stand; he sees things clearly."

"As a last resort . . . and only if Andreas is willing," Ingrid said hesi-tantly, putting down her cup and standing to stretch, "but I hope they don't push it that far."

Elsbeth hugged Ingrid, and Rachel and Ursula joined the embrace. Elsbeth held her companions tight. "Let's hope it doesn't come to this, but if it does, at least we have a plan."

37

July 19

"'ALL EXISTING MARRIAGES are to be dissolved.'" Elsbeth read the notice placed for display. Her finger went down the list of new rules. "'All single women, *without exception*, are to take husbands.'" Elsbeth groaned. "This is ridiculous."

"But expected, yes?" Andreas said, his eyes scanning the notice. "'Women whose husbands have left the city are considered widows and must take new husbands.'"

"'The elderly women are to be assigned husbands if no one takes them,'" Elsbeth read.

"'If a woman is childless,'" Andreas followed, "'a man is free to find new wives to be fruitful, and if a wife becomes pregnant, the husband can take one or more additional wives.'"

"'A woman must not defraud her husband by withholding intercourse,'" Elsbeth continued. "Now we get to the point of it."

Andreas shook his head, clasping his hands behind his head.

Elsbeth pointed to the bottom of the sheet. "Women are to be given one warning, and if we are disobedient, then we suffer the sword."

"Dear God—" Andreas muttered. "Is that Ulrich coming our way?"

"Good morning, friends. Isn't this wonderful?" Ulrich hummed as they faced him. "I love this city, something new every day."

Andreas drew closer to Elsbeth and draped his arm around her.

"I don't mind saying that I'm very excited. I never really needed to be married before." Ulrich smiled, looking at Elsbeth. "But now that I can have as many wives as I want, it increases the possibility of finding someone I can tolerate."

"There have to be limits, Ulrich," Elsbeth said.

"No, read *all* the rules. There are no limits. A man can have as many wives as he desires and can provide for. Zion's men are going to be very busy."

"And this makes you happy?"

"It does, Andreas, it does." Ulrich laughed as he continued down the street.

After he faded from their view, Elsbeth said, "It's uncanny how he appears out of nowhere."

"Elsbeth, we need to get married," Andreas blurted out.

"Andreas?"

"I'm sorry to be so blunt. I thought this would go differently, but we don't have the luxury of flowers and sweet words. I love you and don't want to lose you to another because they're the first to ask. We need to get married today." Andreas gestured at the rules. "I fear Ulrich intends to have you one way or another. I think he's going to use this to try to take what he wants."

"This went differently in my mind," Elsbeth sighed, "but I won't marry you unless . . . "

"Unless what?"

"Unless you marry Rachel, Ingrid, and Ursula as well." Elsbeth raised her eyebrows.

Andreas snorted in laughter, until he realized Elsbeth was not smiling. "But . . . why?"

"They don't want to be married, but Ulrich and others keep sniffing around their quarters. They think he means to have them all, plus me. They hate this decree because it makes them vulnerable. If you marry us, you protect us from worse fates."

Andreas's face puckered as his hands went to his hips. "You've obviously already discussed this without me."

"Don't pout." Elsbeth wrapped her arms around him. "We only worked out a plan. We hoped we would never need to use it. You're free to say no."

"I'm not so sure I have that option. Where will we all live? Do we have to move in with them?"

"I'm hoping Peter will let us live in the guesthouse. It's safer here and there's room for everyone." She released Andreas and they joined hands.

"Is that what you wanted to see your friends about the other night?"

"We talked about it. They're willing."

"Well . . . I . . . uh, think . . . it's . . . brilliant," Andreas said. "Though I hoped that when we finally did this, it would've been in better circumstances."

"One more thing—*you* don't live in Zion. We're going to be married, and we'll be faithful to one another. Don't think you have license. The others pretend for their freedom. With us, it's another matter."

"You didn't really think . . . ?" Andreas pulled back slightly.

"I wanted to be clear. Now, we need to hurry before Ulrich makes his move."

"Go gather your friends and meet me on Cathedral Hill."

Elsbeth's eyes widened. "This very minute? We can't wait until this afternoon?"

"We don't have time to waste. What if someone is up there now, asking for Ingrid's hand? Ursula's? We must step quickly," Andreas said. "Peter needs to agree to this as well. I'll seek his permission and you find the others."

An hour later Elsbeth, Ingrid, Ursula, and Rachel met Andreas on Cathedral Hill where Rothmann stood in the middle of the square approving marriages. Old men pulled young women, their faces locked in horror, by their arms past Rothmann as he proclaimed them married. Young men linked arms with two or three women and paraded past Rothmann, who pronounced his blessing. Some couples were more conventional, the women shyly holding flowers, the men dressed in clothes a bit finer than the usual peasant blouse and vest over plain knee plants. In other groups, several of the men wore felt hats with peacock feathers, and some of the women had dressed themselves in whatever finery they could scrounge.

"Dear God," Elsbeth said, noticing one of the women in a group of four standing in front of Rothmann. She was dressed in a long black gown, veil covering her face. "This is lunacy."

"Then let us join the dance." Andreas grabbed Elsbeth and the others to fall in with the marriage processions as they approached Rothmann.

"Andreas, are these your brides?" Rothmann asked.

"Yes, I want to marry these women and make them my responsibility."

Rothmann grinned and nodded as Bockelson walked over. Studying the women grouped around Andreas, a smile grew on Bockelson's face. "Well done, Andreas. God is pleased you've accepted this burden." He gave Andreas a playful nudge.

"Look." Elsbeth pointed at Ulrich, who glared at them from his perch on one of the second-story porches fronting St. Paul's Square.

"I don't think this day goes the way he hoped." Andreas waved at Ulrich.

"Andreas, are you ready?" Rothmann asked.

Andreas glanced past Elsbeth at Ursula and Rachel, who held onto one another, looking radiant. Ingrid's face was a mask of boredom, but when Andreas glanced at Elsbeth, a smile spread across her face.

"In the name of the Father, I pronounce you all man and wives," Rothmann intoned. "Go in peace, be fruitful and multiply."

"We're married." Ursula cackled, flinging her arm around Rachel.

Amid Ursula and Rachel's laughter, Andreas took Elsbeth's hand and squeezed it. He couldn't remember the last time he was happy. He wondered if he ever had been.

38

July 30

KNIPPERDOLLING PUT DOWN HIS CARDS. "Quiet! Does anyone else hear that?"

Bockelson, Rothmann, and the others playing cards around the massive oak table in the council's chambers stopped and cocked their ears just as the doors to their room burst open and a group of armed men broke in and surrounded the table. Chairs scooted back and steins were knocked over, but they were surrounded before they could get up. Knipperdolling recognized the man at the head of the invaders, Henry Mollenheck, a friend of the murdered blacksmith, Rusher.

"Stop, or we'll kill you where you sit!" Mollenheck commanded.

"Mollenheck, have you lost your goddamn mind?" Knipperdolling said.

"You're all under arrest." Mollenheck ignored Knipperdolling. "Take them downstairs and throw them in the cells."

Knipperdolling looked at the men standing with their swords, halberds, clubs, and guns. Most of them were deserters from the mercenaries outside. "I hope you brought more than these discarded knights, Mollenheck." Knipperdolling reached over and grabbed his stein, taking a large swig.

"I have enough for the task," Mollenheck said. "When everyone hears you're in jail, they'll rally to me and throw you and the other traitors out to von Waldeck."

"When the city hears I'm in jail, they'll come to kill you and your men." Bockelson laid the cards still in his hand on the table and leaned back in his chair.

Mollenheck's leg swept out the back legs of Bockelson's chair causing him to crash to the floor. "You bastard," Bockelson yelped.

"What do you want, Henry?" Knipperdolling asked.

"I don't want my daughters to be made whores by your sewer saints,"
Mollenheck said. "Rusher was right—the Dutchmen are shit prophets,
and I was stupid to ever believe you knew what you were talking about.
Jesus returning here. How could I ever have believed any of it? Even after
you killed Rusher in the square, I still thought maybe you were right."

"This isn't going to help." Knipperdolling tried to placate Mollenheck. "Call off your men and perhaps we can resolve this. Your daughters
don't have to marry men they don't want."

"Take them downstairs!" Mollenheck barked. "Tomorrow their
heads will be on von Waldeck's lap, and we'll be free."

"I'll have your balls in my hands by sunrise," Bockelson taunted, as
he and the others were gathered up and herded downstairs to the city
council's cells.

Mollenheck followed them. "Go to hell, you bastard. It's your cock
that'll be nailed on von Waldeck's walls tomorrow. You goddamn Dutchmen have ruined us."

Knipperdolling, Rothmann, and Bockelson were put in one cell
and the others were put in the other one beside them. One lone chair,
slats askew, sat in the corner of Knipperdolling's cell. He considered the
hard simplicity of the chair and shivered. Memories flooded into him of
another prison, another hard chair. His breathing grew shallow as he rapidly paced his cage. Outside their cells, Mollenheck's men carried silver
goblets, golden bowls, and other objects from the treasury underneath
City Hall. Minutes later, men with uncertain feet meandered down the
hall, oblivious to their prisoners.

"They're drunk." Knipperdolling directed Rothmann and Bockelson's attention to Mollenheck's recruits. "Stupid fools."

"They're not here for us; they're here for the treasure," Rothmann
observed. "This is good for us. They're not listening to Mollenheck."

Knipperdolling moved over to the ground floor windows and lifted
himself up. "Help! Help! We've been betrayed."

Bockelson and Rothmann joined him in yelling out to the streets.
Boots appeared outside the window, and a man went down on his knees
to peer inside the cell.

"Get help! We're under attack!" Knipperdolling yelled, not knowing
whether the man outside was one of Mollenheck's guards or a citizen of

Münster. "Call the city to arms." When the man arose and ran off, Knipperdolling hoped he wasn't running to Mollenheck. Moments later, when Mollenheck appeared outside their cell, Knipperdolling's hopes sank, but Mollenheck was too busy trying to restore discipline to his men to worry about his prisoners.

"Stop looting, goddammit!" Mollenheck shouted. "We have to secure the building."

"It appears you don't control your men," Bockelson shouted down the hall, as Mollenheck made for the wine cellars. "Let us go and you can still save yourself."

Mollenheck jumped back to the cells. "I've already sent someone to open the gates, so the one needing saving here is not me. Rusher's going to be avenged."

Knipperdolling, still holding out hope he could persuade Mollenheck to call off the raid, shouted after the retreating man. "One more chance, Henry. We can all go home and sleep in our own beds if you call this off."

Bockelson nudged Knipperdolling in the side and silently shook his head, drawing his finger across his throat.

The ringing of St. Lambert's bells broke through the chaos, signaling with clarity that the man outside the cell had not been Mollenheck's. Knipperdolling and his companions went to the windows, where the chants outside were growing in strength.

"Death to the traitors! Death to the traitors!"

Knipperdolling heard the thudding clank of iron wheels on stone, indicating that cannons were being moved into position. This was followed by the occasional shot from a wheellock pistol and the steady beat of clubs and halberds being pounded on the streets. He went back to the cell door, expecting to see Mollenheck and his men coming to kill them, but the hallway was empty, and desperate muffled shouting sank downstairs into their hallway. The heavy oak doors of City Hall were slammed shut right before cannon balls hit, sending dust and mortar onto Knipperdolling's head.

"I don't think this is going as Mollenheck hoped," Bockelson said. He held up his finger. "Listen . . . they cry for blood."

Knipperdolling couldn't work out why Mollenheck had not come back to kill them. It made no sense, but a stranger appeared outside the cell with keys to unlock the gates, and the prisoners slipped out the back of City Hall to join the crowds standing in the acrid sulfur air of gunpowder smoke. Knipperdolling was preparing to address those attacking City Hall when Bockelson stepped in front of him and called out in a loud voice.

"Kill the traitors! Kill Mollenheck!"

Another cannon shot boomed into the humid July air, blasting open the oak doors. Men poured quickly through the door, weapons ready as they pursued Mollenheck and his mercenaries upstairs to the council chambers. Knipperdolling winced at the screams coming from the building, until minutes later Mollenheck and his men were pushed out of the building onto the portico. The defeated rebels stumbled over the stone fragments loosened by cannon fire and stepped down into the street. A rock flew from the crowd into the side of Mollenheck's head, knocking him back, followed by another that drove him to his knees, a trickle of blood running down his forehead. Mollenheck struggled to raise his hand.

"Hear me," he croaked. "Bockelson's a viper, and no one's safe from him. He's brought us to ruin. Kill him before it's too late."

A crowd of women descended on him, biting, kicking, and clawing his body in a frenzy of rage before a shot rang out. Knipperdolling looked over at Bockelson, who held a pistol. Bockelson strode over to where Mollenheck lay on the stones.

"Did your men steal from our treasury?" Bockelson demanded. "Did they?"

"That was not our intent," Mollenheck cried. "The plan was to ransom you and free Münster from your poison."

Bockelson wheeled around and threw his hands up in the air. The crowds quieted.

"They're nothing more than common thieves who wanted to steal our wealth and betray us to the Antichrist, von Waldeck."

"Death to the traitors! Death to the thieves! Death to the snakes!"

Knipperdolling knew the night's ending and the work that lay ahead of him. Looking at Mollenheck as he slumped to the ground beneath the flying fists of the women beating him into silence, Knipperdolling regretted that Mollenheck's men had not been more disciplined and struck Bockelson down when they had the advantage.

❖ ❖

The next day, Knipperdolling walked among the bodies, trying not to slip in the mud and blood that saturated Cathedral Hill Square. He examined the heads of his childhood friends. He choked back his pity, trying not to betray his anger. It had worn him out, the hours spent chopping, cutting, and dismembering. He stared at Mollenheck's headless body. He had always liked the blacksmith, but the man had left him with no choice. If he didn't perform his duties, he was going to end up like those at his feet. The cries and screams of those not killed with the first blow troubled him, a reminder of all he hated about what his life had become. He despised killing his friends. He hated the looks on their wives' faces when he missed a clean cut because he was tired. But most of all, he loathed the small thing in him that took its dark pleasure when he started swinging his blade. The blackness that penetrated him in those moments gripped him with the knowledge that he was a prisoner to both life and death, each one pulling on him, calling for total allegiance. He stared at Mollenheck's bruised and bloodied head. Sadly, the one head he truly wanted to see on the ground was not there. Knipperdolling stared at Bockelson, who was occupied giving orders. Soon, he hoped, the head he really desired to feel on the edge of his blade would be his.

39

August 12

THE AUGUST HEAT SUCKED OUT Andreas's breath as he worked his hoe back and forth in the garden. The image of Knipperdolling hacking at men's heads, his iron-shod boots kicking them into graves, lingered. Given how the suffocating heat drained Andreas, he wondered how Knipperdolling kept his strength through so many executions. The more he tried to escape the memory, the faster his hoe went. He would never forgive Bockelson for making everyone witness the slaughter of Mollenheck and the rebels.

Weeding beside him, Peter took off his hat and wiped the sweat that dripped down his forehead. "I'm not sure how much longer I can last."

"We're almost done for today."

"I don't mean the garden, Andreas. I don't know how much longer I can take the strain."

Andreas put down his hoe and retrieved a jug of cider from the porch. Returning, he took Peter's arm. "Here, let's rest a minute."

They found a place in the shade and sat down, contemplating their work. "You have so many plants in here," Andreas said.

"They all have a purpose." Peter's eyes lost their worry as he looked at the roses, lilacs, cyclamen, columbine, aquilegia, and other plants he cultivated for elixirs, teas, and poultices.

"Why do you keep those separated from the rest?" Andreas pointed to a corner of the garden.

"Oh, that's cowbane, mandrake, henbane, and the like. You must be careful with those. They can kill a person if they're not handled wisely," Peter warned.

"Aren't those plants that witches use?"

"Some of the wise women use them, but they're not witches. A cunning person uses whatever nature gives him. There's nothing evil or against God in them."

"Who taught you these things?"

"Does it matter?" Peter shot a sideways glance at Andreas.

"I guess not, though it does make me curious . . . how you came to this art."

"I've learned from books or sometimes from wise women who would teach me things," Peter said, wiping his brow. "Occasionally I tried things on my own."

"But why plants and herbs?"

"I use anything God gives to heal. Sometimes I need to use these before I can work on what's really troubling people."

"And what troubles *you*, Peter?" Andreas had sensed Peter's anxiety these past several days.

"I fear I'll die in this siege." Peter sighed and looked out at the wall.

The heaviness Andreas heard in his voice conveyed how much Peter lost by admitting this. "It wouldn't take much to end it. One well-placed spear or knife would do the job," Andreas said. "Wouldn't it be better for one man to die than all of us?"

Peter's mouth thinned. "Where did that get Mollenheck?"

"Mollenheck lost his nerve. If he'd killed Bockelson when he had him, you and I might be free. I've thought about doing it myself."

"Doing what?"

"A stone to Bockelson's head, a knife in his side," Andreas answered. "I could do it. I don't sleep well as it is, so I wouldn't lose much over him."

Peter shifted on the bench and looked directly at Andreas. "Listen to yourself, and for once please keep your mouth shut. Don't argue with me."

"I wasn't—"

Peter raised his hand, cutting Andreas off. "I've struggled as you do. Don't you think I've killed men in my mind? I understand your anger." Peter stood and walked through his garden, fingering his plants. "Don't you think I've thought about making potions to kill my enemies? It would be so easy."

"But Peter—"

"No! I'm not finished. Since you came back, you've been my calling. I remember when you first came to us as a child. You were so fragile, you cried yourself to sleep every night. But you had something inside of you that fought on behalf of the other boys."

Andreas sat quietly, unsure what to say.

"You were more forgiving to Ulrich than I could've been. You had a huge heart, but it's shriveled in you."

Andreas's throat grew tighter.

"Since you've returned, I've spent countless hours praying for your soul because, my young friend, what defines us in the end is what we give ourselves to. If you give yourself to hate, you will wander the earth a lost and hungry soul."

"It's so hard. I used to believe. Maybe I still do somewhere deep inside me." Andreas paused, looking out on the fields. "How can I believe when the evidence in front of me"—Andreas spread his arms out, pointing to the city—"argues otherwise?"

"Andreas, God suffers the same as you. God is not out there, but in here." Peter pulled his hands to his chest. "God bears the wounds you carry. You must believe me. I don't know many things, but I know this to be true."

"You have some strange doctrines. How did you ever escape the inquisitor's examination?"

"There is only one real test." Peter stood in front of Andreas and put his hand on his shoulder. "Life is our test and the only one we have is the one in our hands. Don't let your enemies define you. Let love shape you instead."

"I do love, Peter. I love you, I love Elsbeth, and I used to love this city." Andreas's voice choked. "I love you for forgiving me my flaws and not losing faith in me."

"Andreas—"

"The rest of life, though? How can I love the stupidity around me? How can you?"

"How can I not? What else is there? Hate? Revenge? I can't live in that world, Andreas. You shouldn't, either."

Andreas lowered his head, fighting back tears. "But I don't know any other world."

"Then you must create one." Peter eased his body onto the bench beside Andreas, putting an arm around his shoulders.

"I'm not sure Münster allows me that option."

"Then we must make sure that we find you a place that does."

40

August 28

THE FIRST SHELL CAME early in the morning, pounding the outer wall, sending stone flying away into the moat and jolting the terrified citizens out of restless slumber. Seconds later, there was another as screams echoed in the hallway outside Elsbeth's room. Leaping from her bed, Elsbeth threw on her clothes and dashed out of her room to find Rachel, eyes widened, screaming.

"What devilry was that?" Rachel cried, as Elsbeth ran to her side. The two of them rushed to the refectory where about a dozen people stood, preparing for the battle ahead. Andreas, Ursula, and Ingrid were packing food into sacks. Peter was in the corner, setting up places for the wounded and filling jugs with ale. Jars and bottles sat on shelves, each of them containing a different colored liquid that Peter had mixed together over the last couple of months.

Rachel stood staring at the ceiling, afraid of moving. A cannonball hit the inner wall, loosening dust from the monastery walls as they shook.

"Aieeeee!" Rachel shrieked as her hands covered her head.

"Steady, everybody," Andreas declared. "We'll get through this if we keep our wits."

"I lost mine with that last blast," Ingrid gasped.

"Is this the end?" Rachel cried.

"No, not if we can help it," Ursula said. She kissed Rachel on the forehead. "But we have to move fast."

Another shell slammed into the inner wall behind the monastery, causing more mortar and dust to fall.

"We've survived this before; we'll survive this again," Andreas called out.

Skin growing prickly, Elsbeth struggled to steady herself as Andreas took her hand.

"I've got to get to my station." He leaned over and kissed her. "I'll see you later."

She looked at him, smiled wanly, and caressed his face with the palm of her hand. "Make sure you do."

They ran outside to find everyone streaming out of the surrounding buildings, running toward their tasks. The constant training since the first attack had prepared them well. Elsbeth fought the voice inside urging her to run back to her room and hide. Clammy and sour, the oppressive heat drained her as she ran to St. Ludger's Gate. Goosebumps emerged up and down her arms as anxiety surged through her, propelling her forward. Thunder from an approaching storm mixed with the sounds of shelling, making it hard to tell how close the cannonballs were landing. Shells whizzed overhead into the homes and churches nearby, creating showers of stone debris and dirt when they hit.

An almost simultaneous flash of lightning followed by excruciating noise tinged her hair. She fell to the ground as a bolt of lightning struck a roof across the street. Grey slate tiles flew up, then came slicing into the ground, sticking up like tiny headstones. She heard screaming behind her and turned to see an unfortunate man sprawled out, pulling a piece of jagged slate from his thigh. Collecting herself, Elsbeth rose and staggered over to him, helping him to his feet. After mumbling his thanks, he limped away, as she made her way to her station.

All around her, people worked with a fierce energy. Men hoisted timbers to shore up St. Ludger's Gate, which was splintered by cannon fire. Children piled up dung and mud against the holes in the wall. Running up the stairs to the promenade, Elsbeth found Rachel, Ingrid, and Ursula with dozens of other women placing copper cauldrons filled with boiling lime at the edge of the promenade wall.

Others stacked up the wooden wreaths they had prepared. Elsbeth had spent days wrapping hemp around the wreaths and dipping them in tar and resin. Should the attackers reach the tops of the walls, the women were to take the wreaths, set them on fire, and use the iron poles to drape them around the invaders' necks. Elsbeth wondered if she could do it when the moment came.

Amid the chaos, Elsbeth heard a voice below her. Moving to the city side of the wall, she saw Bockelson ride up on a horse, yelling exuberantly up to the defenders. "Courage! Courage! God will give us the victory if we stand strong! There's a better life to come, so fear not! We'll defeat the Antichrist and all those who make war on the saints!" His horse cantered back and forth, momentarily rearing up on his hind legs.

"For Zion and Jehovah!" the people on the wall shouted. Bockelson raised his sword. He shouted again and spurred his horse on to the next gate. Watching him gallop away, Elsbeth marveled. She hated this fight, but watching Bockelson and the way people responded to him made her feel like a warrior. Matthys never inspired anyone.

Returning to the other side of the wall, Elsbeth stole a glance at Ingrid, who was busy setting up the iron poles to handle the wreaths. Ingrid glanced back at Elsbeth and smiled right before the bullet caught her in the throat. A spray of red mist flew from Ingrid's mouth as her contorted body spun around and slumped to the ground. Elsbeth heard herself scream.

The next shell threw Elsbeth off the promenade and onto the stairs. She lay stunned, rendered deaf by the blast, but clinging to the stairs so she wouldn't fall to the street. Regaining her wits, she pulled herself back to the top of the wall and slumped on the walkway. *If I can just sleep, it will all be over when I wake up.* Raising her head off the stones, she saw Ingrid prone on the ground, her chin and neck covered in streaks of red. Stunned, Ingrid stared at Elsbeth, her eyes frozen open.

Rachel and Ursula scrambled beside Ingrid, trying to staunch the bleeding while Elsbeth crawled in their direction. Ingrid's eyes grew vacant as blood gurgled from her throat, her mouth frozen in a grimace. Elsbeth finally reached her companions.

"Ingrid . . . " Elsbeth cried.

Ingrid groaned. "Mama . . . Mama."

Elsbeth, Rachel, and Ursula sobbed as they all stared helplessly at Ingrid. She coughed out a small bit of blood, and blinked a few times before her body went limp, her eyes locked open.

"We need to get her down from the wall," Rachel sobbed.

"Grab her feet; I'll take her head," Ursula commanded as she cradled Ingrid in her lap, her white apron growing dark where Ingrid's head rested.

Smoke rose from burning houses as Elsbeth stumbled to her feet. Dirt and grime stuck to her skin like a second coat of filthy flesh. Her lungs choked with grief and fear as she drew in deep breaths. Nothing made sense anymore. She could not remember why they were there, how her day began, or the night before. She stared at Ingrid, and the only thought she had was that she needed to get her off the wall. Grabbing Ingrid's feet, she helped the other women carry her down the stairs, passing a line of women running pots of lime up to the defenders.

They carried her across the street to a patch of grass, where they all collapsed into weeping. Elsbeth heard herself crying, felt tears running down her cheeks, but in her mind, she found herself back home in Jaberg, walking through fields, helping herd the cows back into the barn, resting on soft grasses, and watching clouds change shape. Everything around her slowly faded away as she journeyed to a world where no one could touch her. She was a little girl again, untroubled by wars and the madness of adults.

Happy and protected in her new world, she did not hear Rachel or Ursula call her name, nor feel them lead her back home. Instead, she and her sister laughed together down by the river. She did not feel Rachel and Ursula put her in bed, nor hear the call for Peter to brew medicine. When the cup was placed in her hand, she thanked her mother for being so kind before she drank it and fell into a deep sleep.

It wasn't until she heard Andreas call her name that the world she had escaped into crumbled away. She found herself lying in her bed as Andreas sat beside her. Rachel, Ursula, and Peter stood in a half circle around her, concern and worry etched on their faces.

"Oh, thank God," Rachel sighed.

Andreas took her hand. "Elsbeth?"

Elsbeth looked around the room, disoriented. The rest of the morning came creeping back into her memory, beginning with the horror on the wall. Elsbeth's hands covered her face. "Ingrid?" She could barely get the word out.

"Gone," Andreas answered and smoothed her hair.

Elsbeth stared at the ceiling, listening to Ursula and Rachel cry. She slowly grew aware of the soft comfort of the featherbed under her, and the way the light fell in the evening shadows. It seemed as if parts of her were waking up separately. Rising on one elbow, Elsbeth looked at Rachel and Ursula. "I'm so sorry," she whispered.

The two women nodded and took Elsbeth's hands. "We were afraid we almost lost you out there today," Rachel whispered.

"When the shell knocked you off the wall, we thought you were going to fall to your death," Ursula said.

Elsbeth looked at Andreas, who squeezed her hand tighter. His face was filthy, and dried blood stained his shirt. She fell back on the bed and stared at a crack in the ceiling. "What happened? How did I get here?"

"When we took Ingrid to the street, you sat down and curled up into a ball. We tried to get you to speak to us, but you kept rocking, not responding. We had to leave Ingrid and bring you back here," Rachel explained. "We thought Peter might know what to do."

Tears traced down into Elsbeth's ears.

"I'm afraid today was only a hint of what's to come," Peter warned.

"They didn't try to take the city?" Elsbeth was confused.

"No, it was just a round of shaking us before their assault," Andreas said.

"I don't know if I can last through another attack."

"We don't have the luxury of avoiding it, I'm afraid," Rachel said. She wiped Elsbeth's face with a cool damp cloth.

"I can't go back up there," Elsbeth moaned. "I'm not strong enough."

"We'll have to take our stand on the inner walls from now on." Andreas reached over and brushed the hair away from Elsbeth's eyes. "Bockelson's passed word that we're to let them have the outer defenses and draw them in. We'll attack from on top."

"I can't." Elsbeth's fingers touched the bruises on her body.

"We have to fight if we want to survive," Andreas said. "Either we win, or we're at the mercy of von Waldeck's armies." He stroked Elsbeth's arm gently.

Elsbeth closed her eyes. *I won't be able to survive another day like this one.* When she opened her eyes, her friends' worried faces mirrored the spasms of fear vibrating through her aching body.

41

August 30

THE ROILING THUNDERSTORMS KEEPING Andreas awake intensified as dawn's first light smudged the horizon. Watching lightning streak across the sky like angry fingers reaching for something to grasp, he felt the ferocity of the storm pass into his body, every loud boom a reminder of the day that lay ahead. For the last three days, the bombardments had been constant, wearing the city down, but although the walls shook and the gates splintered, their defenses were holding. But with each new sunrise, the ring of soldiers drew closer to breaching the walls.

Andreas reached for the memory of last night and the comfort he and Elsbeth found in one another's bodies. It had been as if they were both caught in the grip of a force, a desire to *live*, even amid so much death. The power of that urgency flowed through them, leading them to seek a sanctuary in one another's flesh. After, in the silence between thunder and lightning, Elsbeth had asked Andreas if he thought they would survive. He could only stroke her back in reply. Sometimes the only thing that made him want to endure was the feel of Elsbeth's body in his hands or the sound of her laughter in his ear, though it had been weeks since he had heard that.

Now, in the dim greyness of morning, shells floated lazily toward Münster, leaving graceful smoking arcs in the sky, until, with a start, Andreas realized one was heading in his direction. He dove away from the window just as a cannonball slammed into the monastery wall, sending chunks of mortar and stone falling to the ground as dust filled his lungs.

Elsbeth screamed in terror as she sprang from the bed and grabbed Andreas. "I can't do this! I can't!" she screamed.

"You have to," Andreas assured her, holding her tight against him. "We both have to."

"Goddamn bastards, every goddamn one of them, inside and out. I hope they all go to hell!" Elsbeth yelled, quickly slipping into her grey linen dress. She tossed the apron over her dress, slipped into her worn leather shoes, and followed Andreas to the refectory.

When they arrived, Peter was tending the leg of a woman brought in last night, as others in the room prepared for battle. Andreas had not made much of an effort to learn about the people who had come to live there, but he admired their courage. They were on the wall every morning, waiting for the next attack. Desperate, they had nowhere else to go.

Peter looked up from his patient. "Come back home," he implored Andreas and Elsbeth.

"We'll do our best," Andreas said, grabbing his bag.

"No thanks to those bastards," Elsbeth muttered.

"Just come home," Peter repeated.

Elsbeth grabbed her satchel as Rachel and Ursula joined them. They ran swiftly to their stations at St. Ludger's. Andreas had asked to be assigned there yesterday. At least now he could keep an eye on Elsbeth. But when he climbed up to the promenade, the sight that greeted him made his stomach turn. Hundreds of soldiers were already surging through the outer wall, carrying ladders, grappling hooks, and battering rams.

Two main forces, one from the east, the other from the south, approached the walls. The mercenaries pulled massive wicker mats into the marshy areas so they could cross over the muddy terrain. Thunderstorms had been constant the last several days, and despite the best efforts of the attackers, they kept slipping in their attempts to gain a foothold. Arrows and boulders rained upon men trying to place barrels of gunpowder at the gates of the inner wall, holding them at bay.

Soldiers with grappling hooks and ladders slipped in the mud and fell into ditches of thorns and brambles. Stuck and unable to move, they struggled to free themselves as their companions crawled over their bodies in an attempt to keep moving. Those hampered by the mud and thorns fell victim to arrows and bullets, their bodies piling up on top of one another like dolls thrown away by bored children.

The waves of mercenaries grew more relentless as the morning passed. Andreas continued moving shells to the top of the wall, but the stairs grew harder and harder to climb. Pain gripped him in his back as fire ran down his spine into his leg. The sound of ladders thudding against the wall and the sight of grappling hooks sailing over his head focused his attention on survival. If the invaders gained the wall, everyone would die. Looking down the promenade, he found Elsbeth running back and forth, frantically filling the cauldrons with more boiling lime.

"Cut the rope!" a voice shouted above the noise, diverting Andreas's attention to the two timbers suspended from ropes positioned out from the walls. Two massive logs swung into one another, smashing a ladder and crushing several climbers, as the rest dropped to the ground. Long hours helping build that apparatus had not been in vain.

His clothes, wet from rain and sweat, clung to him, tempting him to lie down and fall asleep even during battle. Fatigue's sweet temptation sounded. Would it be so bad to die? Andreas fought the desire to sit down and rest. He grasped the image of last night with Elsbeth to remind him of what he fought for.

"Below! Below!" A man between Andreas and Elsbeth pointed to the ground.

Several men were placing ladders beneath Elsbeth's position. Andreas moved toward her, but a grappling hook flew over his head, clanking to the other side of the promenade. The hook snaked to the wall, lodging in between the slots carved in the stone, the rope drawing tight. Andreas drew his sword and chopped at the rope until he cut off the hook. After tossing it into the city, he turned back, trying to locate Elsbeth.

He found her with several other women holding long iron poles pushing up against the steaming cauldrons. They spilled the contents off the walls, sloshing hot oil and burning lime over the climbers. Anguished howls competed with the sound of thunder in the distance. He was about thirty yards from Elsbeth, close enough to see her widened eyes and open mouth when she turned to him. She shook her head slowly before going back to help fill another pot.

Turning back to his duties, Andreas helped the men closest to him place a huge boulder on the wall, rolling it right to the edge where a ladder had just appeared.

"Not yet . . . not yet. Let them get on the ladders first!" one of the captains commanded. They waited a few seconds as the soldiers mounted the ladders. "Let it go!" the captain yelled. Andreas leaned out to see the falling boulder split the ladder into pieces, throwing several men to the ground.

"For Zion and God!" the defenders shouted as they lifted more boulders.

The constant chaos and relentless motion of war pulled everyone into its embrace with an inexorable momentum. Andreas was so focused on helping his companions hoist boulders or cutting down anyone who gained the top of the wall, that it took a few seconds for Elsbeth's screams to finally break through. Glancing down the wall, he discovered Elsbeth holding a pole with a flaming ring around it. She draped it around a soldier struggling to lift his leg over the wall. The defenders pushed the ladder away, but Andreas saw the soldier's horrified face before he disappeared. The smell of burning flesh and singed hair wafted along the wall.

Elsbeth leaned over the wall and spilled vomit onto a couple of the men below her. Taking her apron, she wiped her mouth and quickly returned to lighting more wreaths. Engrossed in Elsbeth, Andreas never noticed the soldier coming over the wall behind him until he heard Elsbeth scream. He spun to find the man bearing down on him. Picking up the nearest rock, Andreas hurled it, striking his attacker in the head, knocking him back. Rushing forward, Andreas threw his body into the man's chest. They tumbled to the stone walkway, the soldier's breath escaping when Andreas landed on top of him. Taking advantage, Andreas dragged him to the edge of the wall to throw him off, but his body betrayed him, rendering him unable to avoid the man's knife jerking into his arm and slicing into his chest. Two defenders ran to him, grabbed the man, and tossed him over the wall into the city, his body thumping on the cobblestones below.

Staggering to his feet, Andreas caught Elsbeth, her hands clasped to her face, staring at him. Following her eyes, he discovered his blood-soaked shirt. It was then that he felt the first twinge of pain, but he waved to indicate he was fine and returned to the edge of the wall in case any more ladders appeared. Reaching inside his shirt, he gingerly explored the cut, and was relieved it wasn't worse. On the ground below, hundreds, maybe thousands of bodies, lay in the mud as far away as he could see, their limbs contorted by slow agony or quick death. It had rained so heavily earlier that puddles of water covered many of the bodies so that only an arm, a leg, or a torso was showing. Hours had passed since Andreas and the others joined battle, but in the flurry of activity, Andreas hadn't registered the time. As he stared all around him, time itself seemed to crawl to a stop.

Against all odds, former nuns, tailors, bakers, goldsmiths, and blacksmiths were beating back trained military men. They fought with a ferocity Andreas had not thought possible. He stood as bullets flew past him and cannonballs hit the wall below his feet. Deadly havoc enveloped him, but Andreas slipped into an odd serenity, as if he were invincible, untouchable. Immersed in the chaos of smoke and screams, he straddled the boundaries of fate, vulnerable to the thin edge of life and death.

The terror he saw was not on the faces of those defending Münster; rather, the fear was in the eyes of their enemy. Hardened warriors of dozens of conflicts lay dead in the mud, while on the wall, men and women moved unceasingly, repelling every invader. *Who knows? Perhaps God did choose sides.* A strange warmth surged through Andreas; he felt more alive than he could ever remember. He had slipped beyond the fear of death. He wondered if this was what the mystics experienced when they passed beyond the line separating this world from the next. He was at one with everything—the mercenaries, the citizens of Zion, the rain, lightning, the air—he was a part of it all, life and death rolled up into one huge *gift*, held out for him to embrace. It was sublime.

His epiphany so overwhelmed him that he almost didn't hear the bugles calling for retreat, the shouts coming from all up and down the wall. The sounds of trumpets, flutes, drums, and artillery that had marked the day's beginning fell silent, leaving the plaintive sound of defeat to haunt the dead and comfort the living. Relief flooded Andreas as he caught Elsbeth's eye and made for her, his arms held out. The soldiers and knights still beneath the wall turned away from the city and dejectedly lurched back to their camps, stumbling through the valley of death formed by their fallen comrades.

42

September 3

AFTER THE ANTICHRIST IS DEFEATED, what more is there to be done? It had been four days since the dolorous sound of the bugle, four days since the people on the wall watched in stunned silence as the arrayed power of the empire turned tail and staggered back to contemplate how great a humiliation it had suffered.

For their part, the citizens of Zion climbed off the wall exhausted. There were wounds to heal, deaths to grieve. Peter had been busy after the final battle, binding cuts, smearing salve on gaping holes in the body, and setting bones with planks of wood. Even though they were victorious, the whole city seemed to be walking with a limp. That is how it goes when Jacob wrestles God. You are never the same once God smacks your thigh out of joint. *Who is like unto God? Who can resist His mighty hand?* They had done their part—spilled their blood—now it was time for God to deliver on His promises. Come, Lord Jesus. Do not tarry.

Expectancy hung in the air like early morning mist as the tattered company of Christ filled the market and surrounding streets, sharing stories about how things went on their part of the wall. No one had been spared the frantic mercenaries trying to mount the walls, the incessant arrows, bullets, and shells. The final attack was launched on every gate. This September morning was tinged with a hint of autumn, the air fresher than it had been for days. No sulfur hung in the sky, stinging throats and eyes. Sunlight bathed the landscape, projecting shafts of light onto the shadowed streets, as small groups stood together, talking. Later, they would tend to the fields and take whatever crops they could to survive the winter. But for now, all that mattered was a bit of time together.

Wandering around the market, Elsbeth hugged anyone she encountered, joined in a moment of joy at being alive. Mothers held their
children with maternal tenderness, but when Elsbeth glimpsed the tiny
faces, she grieved the fear that met her gaze. What would they remember
about these days? Stolen childhood marked them going forward. Elsbeth
had her own scars to tend.

Surveying the marketplace, her attention was drawn to the small
knot of men standing with Ulrich outside Knipperdolling's house. They
were crowded around one of the last refugees into the city, the goldsmith,
John Dusentschuer. He was a short, gnomish man, who walked with
a pronounced limp. Every time Elsbeth encountered him, he wore the
same brown leather jerkin over a dingy green blouse. His knee pants and
hose were always black, matching his unruly beard and hair. She tugged
on Andreas's sleeve, pointing as the goldsmith nodded to his companions
and headed into the center of the marketplace.

"Behold, the greatness of God!" Dusentschuer yelled.

Everyone froze and looked around them, some looking
up . . . searching.

"What now?" Andreas placed a hand on her shoulder as Peter joined
them.

"I'm not sure," Elsbeth answered, grimacing at the goldsmith's raspy
tone. Too much like the priest back in Jaberg.

"Citizens of Zion, God has spoken! We've been given a great victory
by God's own hand. Who else could've brought us this?" Dusentschuer
yelled. "Listen to me! When our faith was waning, who rode among us,
encouraging us and calling to us to stay strong?"

"Bockelson!" Several voices echoed throughout the marketplace.

"It was indeed Bockelson!" Dusentschuer yelled. "In prayer this
morning, God revealed to me that we have been faithful, and He finds us
almost a kingdom fit for His return."

"How come God never speaks to us like this?" Elsbeth asked.

"We don't work for Bockelson," Andreas said.

"Evidently God does," Peter quipped.

The crowd around Dusentschuer grew still as he cried out. "I be-
seeched God, 'We are a kingdom without a king. We need a king to rule
over us!' I prayed, asking, 'Who shall be our king?'"

"Bockelson!"

Elsbeth noticed the elders, standing to one side, calling out Bock-elson's name. Walking slowed, voices quieted, as the crowds drew to Dusentschuer like iron filings to a magnet.

"God has raised up among you a man to finish the work of the king-dom so that Christ might return," the goldsmith called. "Jan of Leiden, where are you? Present yourself!"

A path formed from Knipperdolling's door to where Dusentschuer stood, brown teeth locked in a silly grin. Under Knipperdolling's arcade porch Bockelson stood, looking about in confusion. He was dressed very plainly in brown knee pants with plain white hose and a simple white shirt with ties up the front, his head unadorned with a hat.

"I'm here! Who needs me?"

"Jan of Leiden, deliverer, step forward!" the goldsmith shouted.

Bockelson sauntered toward the goldsmith, the crowd following each hesitant step. His head went from side to side, his mouth locked open, his face a mask of incomprehension.

"He really is quite the actor, isn't he?" Elsbeth whispered to Andreas, who silently nodded.

"But . . . but . . . I . . . I'm not worthy!" Bockelson called out, his arms held up as he arrived at the goldsmith's side.

"Do not tempt the Lord your God. Kneel!" Dusentschuer yelled.

Elsbeth studied Bockelson as he looked helplessly around the square. Dusentschuer strode over to Rothmann and took his sword. He pointed it at Bockelson, motioning him to the ground.

"I have received a vision from Jehovah. You are to rule this city—indeed, the entire world—with this sword until God comes to take it Himself."

Bockelson threw himself prostrate at Dusentschuer's feet. "As God wills."

A vial of oil was placed in the goldsmith's hands, and he poured some of it on Bockelson's head.

"Zion, who has delivered us from our enemies?" Dusentschuer shouted. "Who slayed Goliath and freed us as David delivered Israel? Behold, God has given us a king just like Israel had—King Jan!"

"At least we see why he dressed plainly," Elsbeth whispered. "He didn't want to get his clothes dirty."

Andreas snorted. "The man knows how to deceive. Always has."

At first the gathering stood in silence, chirping birds and crying babies the only sounds heard. People exchanged puzzled looks, until a solitary voice cried out, "Long live King Jan, the savior of Zion!" Slowly, the chant picked up until the mob filled the square with shouts of "Long live King Jan! Long live King Jan!"

The goldsmith reached into a bag at his feet and pulled out a golden crown and a golden chain attached to a golden apple with two miniature swords piercing it. A scepter, sword, and some golden rings quickly followed. Dusentschuer placed rings on every finger of Bockelson's hands.

"I'm too young. There are others in the city more worthy than me," Bockelson protested, walking through the crowds before stopping in front of Rothmann and his wives. "Brother Rothmann, you should be king. You're a wise man."

"No, Your Majesty. God has chosen *you* to be our king," Rothmann grunted.

Elsbeth concentrated on Rothmann's pinched, stone-like face. Whatever this was, Rothmann was not a willing participant.

Bockelson swept around in a circle, his arms opened wide. "David was young when he killed the Philistine. We also have slain our Goliath!" He fell to his knees, crying, "I will accept this burden because the sheep need a shepherd."

"Indeed," Andreas muttered, "how else shall they be sheared?"

"Shh," Elsbeth chided. Then she saw her—Divara—partially hidden behind some of Bockelson's soldiers.

Bockelson got to his feet and motioned for quiet. "Zion, God revealed to me this morning that this moment would come. I didn't say anything because I thought it must have been my own pride. But this, *this* is confirmation. God even had our brother Dusentschuer prepare the symbols of royal rule." Unexpectedly, Bockelson's knees fell to the pavement as he flicked his hands in the air and shouted, "Not my will, but your will be done, O God!"

The crowd surged toward Bockelson, several of the larger men linking arms to form an impromptu seat. They knelt as two of the guards lifted Bockelson up on his throne of arms and hands. Teetering in his seat, Bockelson clutched the shoulders of his admirers as they bore him around the marketplace.

A clump of Überwasser's former nuns glared at Bockelson.

"Not everyone is convinced." Elsbeth directed Andreas to her former friends.

"Perhaps not, but with Knipperdolling and that sword on his shoulder, no one's going to dispute it," Andreas responded.

"Who needs more power than Bockelson already possesses?" Elsbeth said, her eyes on Divara.

"Beautiful day, isn't it? One could even say it was fit for a king."

"Morning, Ulrich," Elsbeth mumbled, not bothering to turn around.

Ulrich gestured toward the masses of people clustered around Bockelson. "I swear, it's something new every day, isn't it?" He laughed before lowering his voice. "I was sorry to hear about Ingrid; I always liked her. Is there anything I can do?" Ulrich's hands rested on Elsbeth's shoulders.

"No," Andreas snapped.

"I only offer comfort."

"You're kind, Ulrich," Elsbeth said. "But we'll let you know if we need anything."

"Of course," Ulrich said. "Oh, and by the way, Andreas?"

Andreas remained silent.

"Word is that the king may have need of you."

Andreas twisted around to look at Ulrich fully.

"Don't look so surprised." Ulrich laughed. "A king needs a throne, and you're still a woodworker, the last I heard."

"Did you have anything to do with this?" Andreas demanded.

"Me?" Ulrich held up his hands. "No, but I saw the list being drawn up of artisans, and your name was at the top of woodworkers."

"How could that be?"

"I don't know." Ulrich's shoulders went up as his hands expanded outward. "Apparently, the king heard you were talented, but rest assured, he didn't get that from me."

Shouts from the crowd drew their attention back to Bockelson, who had taken off his outer clothes and was standing in the center of the marketplace. Some of his guards appeared, each one holding something to adorn him: velvet knee breeches, red-and-yellow striped hosing, a red velvet vest, a white linen blouse with puffed sleeves, a magnificent burgundy coat, silk shoes, and a red-and-yellow striped codpiece.

"That is one insolent bag," Elsbeth noted, as the men fashioned the codpiece on Bockelson.

Dusentschuer approached and put the scepter into Bockelson's hand, a crown on his head, a sword in his other hand, and draped a magnificent thick gold medallion around his neck. He stepped back, admiring his handiwork.

Bockelson, clutching scepter and sword, raised his arms and proclaimed, "I am given power over all the nations of the earth. God has granted me the right to use this sword to smite all those who complain about God's reign." He rotated to face the entire crowd. "To anyone who is tempted to choose wrongly, you should obey God's chosen servant, lest you lose your head!"

The buzz stopped and silence fell on the market. Bockelson continued to twirl slowly. "Brothers and sisters of Zion," he roared, "I do not deserve this honor, but I will serve you as your king until Christ returns!"

"Elsbeth?" Startled, she pivoted to find Divara standing a few feet away.

"Divara." Elsbeth wanted to slap her, but the look on Divara's face and the size of her belly revealed the woman had her own burdens to deal with.

"I miss you," Divara said, hands clasped, resting on her belly. It was a simple comment, though there was so much longing in the statement that it took Elsbeth by surprise.

"I've been busy." Elsbeth's arms pulled tightly into her body.

"Where is my queen? Where is the queen of Zion?" Bockelson's incessant bellowing interrupted their moment.

Divara looked in his direction and turned back to Elsbeth. "I have to go. Please, come to me. I need you." With that, she was off to join the celebrating Bockelson. The Antichrist of Westphalia had been routed, and it was carnival time again in Münster.

43

September 24

Elsbeth placed the mandrake and poppy, along with the marigold plants, in her basket. Peter also needed some monkshood for pain, as well as mugwort to treat the parasites another one of his patients had picked up. She finished her task and went back inside. All the refugees who had lived there were gone now, having moved into houses that opened due to casualties from the last assault. The only people remaining at the monastery except for Peter and a couple of his patients were she, Andreas, Rachel, and Ursula.

Andreas had been summoned by Bockelson shortly after he was declared king and pressed into service as the royal woodworker. He told Elsbeth he hated working for the incessantly demanding Bockelson, though the extra rations he brought home were welcome. At least they were left in peace at the monastery. Elsbeth was grateful for that small mercy as she entered the refectory and handed Peter her basket.

"Thank you, dear," Peter said. "There is someone in the reception room waiting for you."

Elsbeth washed her hands in the pail on the refectory table. "Who?"

"Divara," Peter replied. "I have no idea why she's here."

Wiping her hands on her apron, Elsbeth hesitated before going to the reception area. When describing the desires of Bockelson's wives, Andreas had told her Divara's demands for furniture exceeded the others. She made her requests take place over others, making his life difficult. Elsbeth thought Divara probably made everybody's life more difficult. *Why is she here?* Elsbeth entered the reception room to find Divara waiting on a sofa, a basket of bread sitting on her lap. Her voluminous green velvet dress covered her swollen belly, and her hair was tucked under a firm black hat crowned with strands of silver. Even pregnant, Elsbeth thought that she looked regal. She stood in silence until Divara lifted herself off the sofa and spoke.

"How long will you be mad with me?"

Elsbeth crossed her arms and pulled her lips in before responding. "It is hard to forget the image of that poor Feyken girl."

"Please believe me, that was not my fault. She might have heard me tell the story in our study, but I never said a word about it to her directly. She went to the elders with the plan all on her own. She convinced them to let her go. Ulrich convinced the others she could save us."

"Ulrich? He was part of it?" Elsbeth pondered that idea.

"Yes, of course. His counsel is always heeded by Jan."

"But you're the one who said that we may need a Judith. I heard you," Elsbeth accused.

"That was Feyken who said that, and besides, does that make me responsible for how the story was used? Do you imagine I gave the orders? Do you think I talked Jan into it?"

"If not you, then who?" Elsbeth moved to the wall.

"I don't know, Elsbeth, but surely you don't think me capable of pushing that poor girl to go out there? I was furious when I heard it."

Elsbeth crossed her arms and tightened. Perhaps Divara really didn't have anything to do with this, other than teaching the story, but she had seen a side of the woman that concerned her, made her want to keep her distance.

Divara held out the basket. "Please take this."

Elsbeth reached over and silently accepted the offering.

Divara exhaled in relief. "I was hoping you'd not turn me away."

"It's difficult for me because you're with them"—Elsbeth motioned toward the palace—"and they are murderous. I'm fearful of expressing myself to you, lest I find Knipperdolling's sword against my neck."

"You have nothing to fear from him. Knipperdolling is obedient to his king."

"Be that as it may, I do wonder what goes on in that house of yours."

Divara maneuvered herself onto the couch, placing her hands on the worn green cushion in order to lower her body to the seat. She patted the space beside her. "Then sit and let me answer your questions."

What are the consequences of rejecting a queen with power? Why couldn't life be simpler? Elsbeth sighed and took her place next to Divara, setting the basket at her feet.

"How do you stand it, sharing him with others?" Elsbeth asked, thinking of Andreas's stories about the competition among the queens.

"I am the chief queen, though others sometimes challenge me. One of them, Elizabeth Wandscheer . . . do you remember her?"

"Yes," Elsbeth said. "The woman was spirited, as I recall."

"Too spirited for my taste," Divara said. "I can't trust her."

"Wasn't she the one who was put on trial recently?" Elsbeth recalled a couple of weeks ago when Wandscheer was brought one morning to the elders for judgment. She was tall, blond, and beautiful. Her father had brought her before Bockelson because she would not heed his orders. She had been forced to marry a decrepit, gnarled old man after the decree on polygamy, but was caught trying to escape from her husband. She was forced to return, but her husband died shortly thereafter. Though there had been no inquiry, suspicions remained about the manner of the old man's death. Things went from bad to worse when she was forced to marry again, only this time the husband was the very picture of ugliness and contempt. Rumors swirled that his character was as horrible as his appearance. She adamantly refused to live with him, which earned her a September morning before the elders for her insolence. Elsbeth recalled Wandscheer's haughtiness as she, her father, and would-be husband stood before the king as he examined them, going back and forth from one to the other. Elsbeth could still remember the conversation.

"Sister, would you marry this man freely?" Bockelson asked.

"I would rather sleep in the bushes or fields than in this man's bed." Wandscheer held her chin high.

The king laughed, looking to his counselors and back at her. "It doesn't have to be that bad, surely. You don't want that kind of life."

"I would rather marry a goat than that sack of skin and boils," she shot back. Elsbeth remembered the laughter.

Bockelson and Wandscheer went back and forth, but she would not give an inch. Elsbeth had told Andreas at the time that if she were Wandscheer, she, too, would rather die than take that "sack of skin and boils" for a husband; the man had a propensity for violence. There were worse things than death and having to marry that man was definitely one of them. The king formally forgave Wandscheer and told her she could come and live in the palace. A short time later, she became Bockelson's tenth wife and, as Elsbeth was now learning, Divara's chief rival for Bockelson's attention.

"She conspires to take Jan away from me," Divara said. "She lies constantly about me with the other women. I could lose my place."

Elsbeth froze, not knowing how to respond. Divara started crying, tears dripping onto her gown. Elsbeth's hand went to Divara's shoulder, and the woman leaned into her and wept. "How can I help?" Elsbeth asked.

Immediately, Divara brightened, wiped her eyes, and said, "I need you to come and help me take care of the baby when it's born. I don't trust the others to care for an heir they haven't brought forth themselves."

How *does* one reject a queen? Why had her tears dried so fast? Elsbeth realized this wasn't a request she could spurn; there was a subtle, vague threat lurking in the shadows. Elsbeth's mind clouded. She shook her head, trying to think clearly. Trapped. Elsbeth's mouth curled upward in acquiescence.

Divara clapped her hands and threw her arms around Elsbeth's neck. "Thank you. I hoped I could win you back."

Elsbeth returned the embrace, but though Divara's hands were light on her back, Elsbeth felt them constricting her, squeezing her ability to distance herself from the danger wrapped around her.

44

October 3

RUNNING HIS HAND DOWN the long wood board was a small but satisfying pleasure. Andreas loved the way smooth wood felt against his fingers. The piece he held was ready to fit into Divara's cradle. When Bockelson had offered him the position, Andreas had not wanted to accept it, but he couldn't refuse. The extra rations that came with his work were important, especially given the number of people Andreas had to feed, but at what cost? Some days he was hopeful that the empire would just forget about them. Perhaps one morning, everyone would awake to find no guards manning the blockade, and they could just walk away. It was a foolish hope, but he held onto it. Attentive to his wood, Andreas didn't notice someone had entered his shop.

"Good morning, Andreas," Ulrich murmured from the shadows. "It's been months and we've still not shared an ale. Perhaps now we can rectify that?" Ulrich took a few more steps into the shop.

"What do you want, Ulrich?"

"So guarded. I came by to see how my old friend is doing."

Andreas's gut constricted. "What do you want?" he repeated.

"Why are you always so curt with me?" Ulrich explored the shop, poking at the cabinets, curios, and other unfinished pieces. He picked up a chisel, studied it, put it down, and picked up other tools as he moved along Andreas's worktable. "How's your life these days? Getting enough to eat?"

"I'm fine; why are you here?"

"That's good to hear. It has to be hard for you . . . all this." Ulrich waved his hand in the direction of outside.

"What do you care how things are for me?"

"I do care about your life—I care very much."

The unctuous tone irritated Andreas. "You haven't answered my question."

"We've never really talked since you returned." Ulrich leaned back on the worktable, bracing himself with his arms.

"What would we have to talk about?"

"How about life in Zion?"

"What about it?"

"Don't you find it fascinating?"

Andreas put down his plane. "What is any of this to you?"

"Remember when we were novices? All the nonsense we were fed about God and Jesus and faith? It always seemed so stupid to me. I went through the motions because I had to. I hadn't figured out what my next move was. But my God, look around you; true believers surround us. This is the world they create. This is their city of God."

"No, this is the city of fools," Andreas muttered, hoping no one was eavesdropping outside the door.

Ulrich moved in closer, whispering, "Yes, but we get front row seats to the carnival." He lightly tapped Andreas's shoulder. "You're no fool. You know how this is going to end—as it always does: flames, death, slaughter unimaginable."

"Ulrich, is there a point here? I'm busy."

"Don't you find it exhilarating to see men being set free to do whatever they desire?" Ulrich's eyes shone as a grin spread across his face. "Besides, in the end, this *is* God's world, isn't it? Aren't they closer to God than they've ever been?"

"What are you talking about?" The worms in Andreas's mind stirred to the call of their master.

"Remember your Scripture, Andreas. This is the way the world ends—destruction, death, the end of life—all so the reign of peace may flourish. God comes to the world to cleanse it of the unrighteous. Not quite the baby in the manger this time, is it?"

"I suppose that may be what some men believe, but I left all that."

"Oh yes, you're an unbeliever." Ulrich chuckled. "I've heard there are some like you walking the earth."

"From what I can tell, you're one, too, Ulrich."

Ulrich leaned over the table and came so close Andreas could feel his garlicky breath on his face. "Oh, Andreas, that is where you are so very wrong. I do believe."

"In what? In what do you believe?"

"My way of thinking may not fit with what passes for belief in their world." Ulrich nodded toward the door. "But I left that behind when I gave up the desert."

"What do you mean, Ulrich?" Andreas was angry at himself for being so curious.

"I haven't had time to tell you about my adventures after I left Münster, have I? I've tried, but you rebuff me." Ulrich pouted. "Why is that?"

Andreas knew a trapdoor was being opened, but he couldn't stop himself. "Ulrich, we live different lives; some people aren't meant to be friends."

"Did you know I went south when I left here?" Ulrich ignored him. "As fate would have it, I ended up in Mühlhausen. You know the area? I think so. Met some . . . um, interesting people. They were doing God's work, sweeping out the garbage, stirring the righteous to slaughter. I ended up one May morning in Frankenhausen with my friends."

"God, Ulrich, you were there?" Andreas was stunned. The story of Frankenhausen was well known. In 1525, one of the most fanatical preachers, Thomas Müntzer, had drawn a peasants' army to his side that had rampaged through Thuringia and surrounding areas. The nobles banded together and fielded an army that decimated the rebels in a slaughter that even Luther sanctioned.

"Yes, that poor, doomed army of fools armed with their swords, knives, and sticks. I saw it all. I watched as the peasants cheered the morning rainbow. It was on their flags, you know, the rainbow. It was their symbol of a new world after the old one was swept away. Didn't God give Noah the rainbow as a sign He wouldn't destroy again? What the peasants didn't know at the time is that the armies of the nobles saw the same rainbow as a sign of God's favor."

"The peasants were destroyed. How did you survive?"

"I headed for the tree line when the first shells fell. I watched it all. It was butchery."

"And you weren't caught?"

"No, by the time the princes had their way, there was only a field of crushed, moaning men. Those deluded souls could only lie there defenseless against the birds plucking their eyes out."

"Why are you telling me this, Ulrich?"

"Because, Andreas, I want you to understand. I stumbled among the dead and dying that day, peering into their eyes, or at least the ones that remained, and nothing . . . *nothing* stared back at me. It was an epiphany. God is death. Death *is* the way of God. Why else would the world be as it is, animals preying on one another to live?"

The worms stirred to the call of their master, burrowing deep into Andreas's mind, rendering him incoherent. "No, there's more—"

"What more, Andreas? Is it not true that at the end of the world there's nothing but blood and death? I saw the end; I know the truth now. I don't know about the God you or your friends serve, but I serve the living God, great in might and terror."

Andreas stared back at Ulrich, mouth agape, unable to respond.

"Consider it, my friend. How many have died because God commanded it be done? It's a thing of beauty, really. You read the revelation of John when you were younger. You know at the end of the age the Whore of Babylon sits on her throne and the saints make war against her. The nations worship her and her power. They bring their empires to her and lay them at her feet, without a thought for God."

"But the whore is the enemy of God," Andreas protested.

"Yes, but even knowing it to be so, we put everything, even faith, at *her* feet and proclaim, 'Who is like unto you?' The whore is *violence*, Andreas, and we are so intoxicated by her charms, we can't stop humping her even though we know we shall die. She's the last whore. According to God's word, it's the saints—with God's approval—who commit mass murder in the end. It's how God puts all things right."

Andreas stood rooted, captive to the sermon being preached. He tried to think of refuting it, something that would assure him Ulrich was wrong, but it cut too close to the bone, too near his own thoughts.

"Can you imagine it? In the last days, destruction rains down on the earth and a third of the world perishes. What imagination did it take to even conceive that? Shouldn't we admire it?" Ulrich moved around the room, preaching to saws, planes, and pieces of wood. "And you know what's even better? That horrible vision of destruction came from the one who was called the beloved of God. Did he get it wrong? Who can ever look at God as the God of love, knowing that in the end He destroys it all?"

"No! There are those who love!" Andreas's shout surprised him. "They don't worship at the altars of power. There are those who care for the souls of others."

Ulrich put his hand on Andreas's shoulder. "I know, Andreas, I know," he comforted. "It's a hard truth to face at first, but look around you. Where are they now? Show me one who follows the way of grace or the mercy of nonviolence. Rothmann? Bockelson? Knipperdolling?"

"You can't use those as your examples—they're all half mad."

"They're not mad. They're the true believers. Rothmann locks himself away for hours, writing his hopelessly sincere theological treatises about the restitution of the Kingdom of God, but to what end? Knipperdolling? Yes, he's devout, no doubt, but how has faith helped him, other than leading him further into captivity to his own ambition? Bockelson? He's plunged so deep into the ocean of delusion, he's drowning. I think he's even come to believe his own lies. No one, Andreas, no one in the Kingdom of Zion cares about the Prince of Peace."

"Peter does."

"I doubt it. When it comes down to it, he'd kill to stay alive," Ulrich said. "Why do you think he grows those poisons?"

Andreas shook his head. "There's no sin in medicine or self-defense."

"That proves my point. God is whatever you need Him to be to survive."

"No one's going to survive this."

"Some will, I assure you," Ulrich promised. "Anyway, I'll make sure to keep you and your wives and the priest here until the end."

"Keep us here?"

"Why, yes. I've kept you all with me this whole time." Ulrich smiled.

Andreas gawked at Ulrich. "You've . . . kept us?"

"Oh, stop sputtering, Andreas. Why do you think you remain? Why weren't Peter or you exiled? Why couldn't you leave when you tried? How do you think you got this job? Did you think it was because of your carpentry skills? I was the one who recommended you to Bockelson."

Andreas's mind clouded. "You're behind all of this? That's not what you said earlier."

"Put it this way. You, Elsbeth, and the priest are here because I convinced people you belonged here, even if it was against your will."

"I'm not your prisoner," Andreas shot back.

"Prisoner is such a harsh word. I prefer *guest*. I had hoped we'd become friends again. I think we share more than you realize."

"I doubt that."

Ulrich tilted his probing eyes toward Andreas. "Are you sure? I heard you tell Rothmann you were there when they killed Michael Sattler. As chance would have it, I came through Rottenburg shortly after Sattler's execution. Everyone was talking about a couple of heretics who had killed their guards and escaped. Know anything about that?"

"No, why would I?" Andreas felt Ulrich's cold curiosity.

"Oh please, Andreas, don't mistake my interest. Actually, I admire what you did. I believe we should do everything we can to make those who cross us pay for their betrayals. If it *was* you . . . " Ulrich edged a bit closer. "You can tell me. You're among friends."

"You're not my friend."

"But I'm trying to be. We used to be close, you and I." Ulrich's voice went cold. "And I would be closer to Elsbeth if it weren't for you. I yielded so you could have her. The least you could do would be to grant me some respect for that favor."

"You lie! Whatever game you're playing, I won't be your sport."

"Andreas." Ulrich's amusement spread over his face. "You've been my sport since the day we met. When you turned against me, I hoped I would one day be able win you back. You still have time to come over to me. I can grant you the desires of your heart. I have influence with the right people. It's one of my gifts. People like doing things for me. I let them, of course. It makes them happy, and I like making people happy. You would be so much happier if you realized I'm not your enemy. I'm your truest friend in this city. In fact, your survival may depend on me."

"I can take care of myself." Andreas picked up a chisel.

"Ah yes, well, that would probably be true anywhere else. But here your situation remains precarious." Ulrich walked to the door, pausing before he left. "Of course, I can also talk to my friends about letting you slip out if you still want."

"Why would you do that?"

"I told you, I'm not your enemy. I can say the word, and you'll be relieved of all this tomorrow. There are ways out for you."

"Why would you do that for me?"

"Why can't you accept that I care for you? But I should be clear, only you can go, not the rest."

"Let the others go instead. I'll stay here. Besides, what are they to you?"

"No, the offer is that you must leave. I'll look after Peter and Elsbeth when you're gone."

"My place is here."

"Noble, but foolish. What do you think Elsbeth or Peter would do if I made them the same deal?"

"What does it matter?" Andreas slumped against his worktable.

"It was good seeing you, Andreas. I hope you'll consider my offer," Ulrich said, stepping out into the street.

Looking down at his white knuckles clenched around his chisel, Andreas dropped the tool back on the table.

45

October 10

ULRICH'S TAUNTS REMAINED IN Andreas's head. Was escape impossible?
Franz von Waldeck had pulled his mercenaries, but he left a siege ring
around the city, stifling any movement in or out. Those discovered trying
to escape earned an appointment with Knipperdolling's blade, but that
did not dissuade Andreas from searching for any path out of the city.
Andreas turned over Ulrich's visit continually, pondering his intentions.
Distracted, he only heard the screaming as it passed by his shop.

He peeked out his window just as Knipperdolling sped by, foaming
at the mouth, eyes shadowy and troubled, beard soaked in spit. He didn't
have on the fine clothes and jewelry he usually wore, but something more
akin to sackcloth, clinched at his ample waist, held there by a piece of
string. Andreas stepped out of the shop into the area where Knipperdolling stopped. A small crowd quickly formed around the raving merchant.

"Repent!" Knipperdolling bellowed continuously, grabbing anyone
passing by. Andreas moved to the crowd, and Knipperdolling immediately fell upon him, grabbing his shoulders in his thick hands and crying,
"Repent, brother, for the Lord is at hand."

"Are you well?" Andreas asked, frightened by the gleam of madness
in Knipperdolling's eyes.

"Repent!" Knipperdolling bellowed in response before he took off
toward the market, the crowd trailing after him.

Andreas shut the door to his shop and followed along until they
reached the marketplace. He found Elsbeth standing under an arcade,
watching the procession.

"Elsbeth!" Andreas waved her over.

Elsbeth joined him. "What's going on? I was up here getting some material, now this?" Elsbeth pointed to Knipperdolling.

"Not sure, but if past displays are any sign, we won't have long to find out."

They trailed Knipperdolling and his gaggle out of the marketplace and onto Cathedral Hill, where Bockelson and his wives sat on a large wooden platform. When he was announced as the king of Zion, one of the first things that Bockelson had ordered was a throne placed on a large outdoor platform just outside the gate of the most beautiful house in Münster, which Bockelson had taken to serve as his palace. Andreas created the throne, but others had built a platform large enough to hold the king and his sixteen wives. Most every day Bockelson and his wives filled the platform so he could hold court or pass judgment on some poor fool who displeased the king. Thousands were jammed around the platform as Knipperdolling pushed into the crush of people.

"Repent! Repent!" he cried incessantly, moving from person to person, grabbing their arms, and spitting on them. At one point, he spun so quickly through the crowd, he toppled off-balance onto the street.

Jumping up, he dashed close to the throne platform as Andreas and Elsbeth took places about twenty feet away from the throne. Knipperdolling spit in the face of the man standing next to them. "The Father has made you holy, receive the Spirit," he intoned, continuing to spit on those gathered close by. Flecks of saliva hit Andreas in the face as Knipperdolling traced a cross in the air every time he spit on someone.

When his mouth ran dry, he blew on those closest to him, raving, "Receive the Holy Spirit." Scurrying through the crowds, Knipperdolling frequently stopped, bending down, grabbing mud, spitting on it, and rubbing it into people's horrified faces, screaming, "You are healed! Receive your sight!" Those who didn't scatter stood rooted, curious to see what came next.

"Is he possessed?" Elsbeth turned to Andreas with widened eyes.

"I'm not sure what he is." Andreas glanced at Bockelson sitting under his purple velvet-covered canopy, watching impassively. With each minute that Knipperdolling's manic display held the crowd's attention, the king leaned further forward until he was at the edge of his throne.

"You're all healed!" Knipperdolling ran among them. "We've been living in the kingdom of the blind! All of us are blind! Behold, I give you sight!" Knipperdolling kept smearing mud on faces as he edged closer toward the steps of the platform. He gurgled incoherently for a few minutes before he leapt up the steps to where Bockelson and his wives sat. Andreas was impressed that Knipperdolling's porcine body moved so quickly. Before anyone could stop him, Knipperdolling danced to the front of the platform. Grunting like a pig in heat, he pirouetted around, arms raised, hands drooped, shifting his weight from foot to foot as he lumbered back and forth before the captivated audience.

"I saw a bear dancing like that once in a cage in Bern," Elsbeth offered.

"Um . . . " Andreas stayed focused on Knipperdolling, who twirled his hands over his head. He danced toward Bockelson, flailing awkwardly in front of the throne, grabbing his crotch, and laughing madly.

"This is how I dance in front of the whores and sluts of court when I call them to dance with me. Bockelson, come and dance with me," Knipperdolling jeered. He motioned Bockelson forward, waving his arm in invitation. "You like to dance, don't you? You dance so well with the ladies before you take them to bed."

Bockelson's mouth opened, his face twisting into a mask of outrage.

"What's this? What game is he playing?" Elsbeth wondered.

"A very dangerous one," Andreas said.

Bockelson, now on the very edge of his throne, yelled, "Knipperdolling, come to your senses! Have you been possessed by a devil? What evil spirit has come over you?"

Knipperdolling continued skipping around in front of the king, thrusting his crotch forward over and over. "I *have* been possessed by a spirit, *King Jan*—the spirit of truth. Let's tell the truth, shall we?" Knipperdolling laughed crazily as he shimmied behind the throne. Peering around one side of it, he rested his arms on Bockelson's shoulders, grinning at the assembly. "Would any of you be interested in the truth about our *king*?"

Everyone stood frozen, absorbed in the spectacle before them. Andreas sensed the performance had moved beyond play, beyond the puncturing of pretension, past the space of reversal that carnivals celebrated. This was something entirely new, marked by rapt faces focused on the stage. They had all become part of a play whose ending had yet to be written.

Knipperdolling shifted his face to the other side of throne. "I know some truths about him I would love to tell you." Stepping out and strutting in front of the throne, Knipperdolling swiveled his pelvis back and forth in front of Bockelson, guffawing as his contorted face jerked next to the king's. Knipperdolling quickly swung his ass around and farted in Bockelson's face. "Do you like the smell, *Your Majesty*? I made it especially for you. Of course, everything smells like shit these days, doesn't it? You should be used to the fragrance by now."

"Careful, Knipperdolling. I have my limits," Bockelson warned through clenched teeth.

"I don't give a shit," Knipperdolling retorted, turning his attention to Bockelson's wives. "Oh, look! I see you have all your lovely wives here today." He danced to the far side of the platform and moved down the line of women, kissing them, reaching around to grab what he could, and pronouncing a blessing upon each one. When he got to Divara, sitting next to the king's throne, he fixed Bockelson with a malicious grin.

Suddenly, Bockelson threw himself out of his throne onto the ground.

"What's this?" Elsbeth groaned. "Trying to grab the act back?"

"This mockery is no act," Andreas said.

Knipperdolling grabbed a sword from one of Bockelson's bodyguards and returned to his splayed body. Screams rippled through the square as Knipperdolling pulled Bockelson to his knees and clutched him tightly against his chest. Knipperdolling raised the sword up to his neck. "Oh no, you won't fool us with your actor's tricks today," Knipperdolling shouted. "Look everyone—the king's fool and the fool king. Give us your conscience, and we'll give you hell. I made him a king and he makes me a fool."

Knipperdolling pushed Bockelson away as the king glared at his tormentor.

"What's the matter, *King Jan*? Afraid we'll let out your secrets? How you keep the best food, shake the sheets with the best women? How much you lie?"

Bockelson stormed off the platform and into the palace courtyard. Visible through the ironwork gate, the crowd watched him pace furiously back and forth while Knipperdolling took a seat on the throne, his legs crossed, hands resting on the ornate arms, occasionally waving as if he were dismissing the crowds.

Knipperdolling rose from the throne and sidled to the edge of the platform. Raising his hands, he bellowed, "God has spoken to *me*. Yes, just as God speaks to Bockelson. What? You thought God only spoke to him? God speaks to us all. Why does God just speak to *him*?"

"So much contempt," Elsbeth whispered to Andreas.

Cupping his ear, Knipperdolling yelled, "Hear what God has spoken to *me!*" He traipsed back and forth across the stage. "Bockelson is to be your king *in the flesh*, but I'm to be your king *in the spirit*. Burn the Bibles, for we no longer live in the flesh but the spirit. Aren't we beyond the law here? We can do whatever we please, can't we, *Your Majesty*?" Knipperdolling yelled over his shoulder in Bockelson's direction.

Andreas's gaze went to Bockelson, dazed in his courtyard, until he stormed back to the platform, mounting the steps and making for the throne, but Knipperdolling scurried to it first and plopped himself into the massive oak chair with velvet covering and canopy.

Bockelson leaned toward Knipperdolling and snarled, "You have one last chance. Stop this and I'll let you live."

"And if you slay me, shall you stand? You gave me the power of life and death in this kingdom of fools. Who was swinging that sword while you were swinging that tiny thing between your legs? Who else will do your dirty work for you?"

Bockelson faced the crowd. "Brother, you're not in your right mind," he shouted. "Allow your king to help you." Bockelson reached out to Knipperdolling as if to embrace him, but Knipperdolling danced away.

As he strode from one end of the platform to another, Knipperdolling cried out in a singsong voice, "What is madness or sanity anymore? Murder is God's will? God's will is murder? Who would King Jan have us kill today?"

Bockelson finally motioned for his guards to seize Knipperdolling, who skipped along the edge of the platform, winking at the crowd. The first guard approached cautiously, unsure of what to do. Knipperdolling looked his way and sneered, "Are you here to do the *king's* bidding? Watch out or next you'll have to murder for him."

Caution vanquished, three other men leapt forward and secured Knipperdolling, pulling him off the platform. His arms flying out as they dragged him away, he lifted his head and howled, "Münster, oh Münster, how often would I have gathered you under my wings to protect you like a mother hen protects her chicks, but you would not! Beware the wolf in sheep's clothing!"

The last thing everyone heard before the silence was Knipperdolling's shrieking laughter as they carried his shaking body into the palace.

46

October 13

"Something's going on, I'm sure of it." Elsbeth spooned barley into her mouth, hating the grainy bland taste of it. "There's too much activity up at the palace."

"Every day we're told to expect the seventh trumpet to sound, and every day, nothing." Peter pushed his bowl away. "They use Armageddon to keep us off-balance. At least when the bells of St. Lambert's rang, we knew to gather."

"I don't see how you go up there." Andreas shifted the conversation. "That place seethes with intrigue."

"Do I have a choice?" Elsbeth plopped her spoon into her bowl. "Divara pulls me to her rooms to fret constantly about the other queens. Wandscheer is maneuvering Bockelson into her bed and away from Divara. Given his reputation, you can hardly blame her for her fears. I comfort where I can, but she turns colder to me."

"That house is a snake pit." Andreas's spoon worked around his bowl. "And I don't like you being around Ulrich."

Elsbeth put her hand on Andreas's arm. "I think Ulrich's wives are keeping him too busy for him to be scheming about us."

"Have faith—" Peter began, before being interrupted by a blaring noise outside.

"Well." Andreas cocked his head in the direction of the noise. "I'll wager no one thought the last trumpet was going to sound like a cow horn."

Elsbeth jumped up from her seat. "I'll go get Rachel and Ursula."

Andreas gathered up the bowls and cups as Elsbeth made for the guest quarters.

Moments later, Elsbeth, Ursula, and Rachel came into the refectory. "Let's get to the assembly." Elsbeth threw up her hands. "Jesus awaits."

The cow horn was different enough to change expectations. Men in armor slogged along in the morning gloom, women and children, arms full of weapons, trailing after. No one dared to remain home for fear of being discovered by the men that Bockelson sent to scour everybody's houses once assemblies began.

"Could this be it?" a woman asked her husband as they passed by. Elsbeth looked at Andreas and shook.

Bockelson's soldiers shepherded the mob toward the center of the market as they arrived. Entering the plaza at St. Lambert's, Elsbeth was glad to see that bonfires had been lit to ward off the morning chill. She and her companions made their way over to a fire to warm themselves. Hands held over the flames for warmth, Elsbeth noticed that the fires created pockets of light and shadow, a reflection of her life.

They stood for hours, uncertainty growing with each stroke of the bells. The elderly stood among the young, children alternately crying, shouting, and sleeping. Some wore their finest clothes; others, little more than a plain pair of pants with a waistcoat or vest. Most women were in a simple dress. Some of the older people, tired of standing, sat down on the plaza. After the cathedral bells rang the eleventh hour, a blast of trumpets heralded the king's servants. They entered the marketplace two abreast, dressed in uniforms of red pants and yellow shirts with red stripes running down the front. Bockelson followed on a white stallion, held by stable hands in purple tunics and white trousers with purple stockings. Behind the king, the royal bodyguard of thirty-two men rode ceremoniously into the market astride magnificent horses.

Bockelson barely acknowledged the expectant stares as he rode past, newly polished steel armor gleaming from underneath his cape. His golden crown rested atop his head, and a page walked at his side carrying a helmet. Erect in his saddle, a sword in one hand, Bockelson kept his eyes straight ahead, processing solemnly into the square.

"All hail the king of thieves," whispered Andreas.

"Shh," Elsbeth cautioned.

Divara followed Bockelson in a coach while the king's other fifteen wives marched slowly behind her. Arriving at the throne platform built for the market square, he slipped off his horse, ascended to the stage, sat, and bowed in prayer. He maintained his pose as his generals and their soldiers cantered into the square. Hundreds of soldiers on horses surrounded the market, their standards fluttering in the slight breeze of an October morning. Anticipation hovered over the market, accompanied by the irregular clacking of hooves and snapping of fabric. Elsbeth thought the scene would have been almost pleasant, except for the fact that everyone there expected it might be their last day on earth.

The king's chief general, Gerlach von Wullen, mounted the steps of the platform, walked past the throne, and faced the crowd. Dead silence met his upraised hands.

"Citizens of Zion!" von Wullen shouted. "Our Lord Jesus Christ has called us together this day through our king, Jan of Leiden. We have come to fight the last battle foretold by the prophet John. Are you ready to defend unto death the Gospel of our gracious Lord?"

Amid a loud din of voices, weeping rose all around Elsbeth as families bade goodbye to each other.

"By your presence, you have shown yourself worthy of the Kingdom of God, and your majesty is grateful for your willingness to lay down your lives. Hear me, Zion! Though we wait for the last day, today is not that day—"

For a second, the energy of the crowd faltered; discouraged gasps erupted from all corners of the square.

Von Wullen acknowledged the moans by nodding, but then he smiled and threw his arm to Bockelson. "The Lord came to our king this morning and said he should test you to see if you are willing to give your lives for Christ. You have passed the test. We are well pleased to see you here today. To reward your faith, we have prepared a feast for you to enjoy."

Food. Salvation. Relief washed over the crowd like an ocean over the shore at high tide, sweeping away their fear and replacing it with gratitude.

"Hosanna!"

"Long live King Jan!"

The king's servants quickly moved wooden tables into the plaza. Leaving the platform, Bockelson mounted his horse and silently rode out of the square as tables and benches were set for the feast, the fear dissipating from the relieved crowd. On the edges of the square, smoke rose from bonfires set to cook pigs and other game. Hesitantly at first, people took their places on the benches as drinks were brought out to them.

A short time after everyone was seated, Bockelson reappeared in royal garb: a dark purple blouse with green stripes around the cuffs, red and white hose, woolen knee pants, and his scarlet cape. Circulating among the throng, Bockelson and Divara played host, talking and celebrating as they helped serve the large plates of food set on the tables. Roasted pigs, slabs of beef, chickens, and venison—every type of meat not seen in the city for weeks graced the tables in abundance. Local beer and wine, imported from the south before the blockade, flowed freely as everyone toasted their good fortune. Bockelson approached the table where Elsbeth, Andreas, and Peter sat.

"Hello, friends. I hope this is to your liking?" Bockelson took a sip from his jewel-encrusted chalice.

"Thank you very much for your generosity, Your Majesty." Andreas raised his mug.

Bockelson regarded him quietly for a few seconds. "Please stay after the first meal; I'm rewarding the court with a special feast." Shifting his attention to Peter, Bockelson said, "I see you've joined us. I'm so glad you've found the true way."

"I do give thanks to God for your generosity." Peter raised his stein. "To your good health."

Bockelson smiled and raised his chalice. "And to yours as well." After taking a drink, he turned to Elsbeth. "And you, my dear. How are you?" His hand rested lightly on her shoulder.

"Grateful, Your Majesty." Elsbeth forced a smile before Divara's pinched face appeared behind Bockelson.

"Elsbeth!" Divara snapped. "A word?"

With a furtive glance at Andreas, Elsbeth quickly rose and followed Divara to the edge of the crowd where the queen rounded on her and sputtered, "You? I thought I could trust you."

Elsbeth recoiled. "What are you talking about?"

"Truly? You haven't seen the way the king looks at you when you're at court?" Divara challenged. "And just now, I saw him touch you."

"That was unwelcome, Divara," Elsbeth insisted. "I would never do anything to betray you."

"You're no better than Wandscheer and the rest of those bitches." Divara put her hands on the back of her head and walked away. "How could I have been so stupid? You're all out to take my place."

Elsbeth stood frozen, terrified that her next words might be her undoing. "Divara, I swear to you, I serve you, only you," Elsbeth assured.

"I am Andreas's woman, no other. I am only at the palace because you asked me."

Her gaze focused on the horizon, Divara's head shifted back and forth. "Even if that's true, I can't trust you anymore. Jan asks about you, how you're doing, when you're coming to me." Divara paced away from Elsbeth, moving in small circles before returning. "Stay away from the palace and Jan. Don't even talk to him. I don't want to hurt you, but if I have to I will."

"But what about the baby?" Elsbeth asked. "Who'll take care of her when she's born?"

"I have maids who can help me, older women who won't draw Jan's attentions." Divara rubbed her stomach. "Besides, I'll soon be free of this burden and can take care of Jan's needs again."

Burden? Elsbeth's thoughts often turned to having children. Her children would never be a burden. "Divara, please reconsider," Elsbeth pleaded, but inside her the weight of a thousand stones lifted. Divara was giving her a gift, and though she would protest it to allay any suspicions of disloyalty, she was relieved not to go back.

"No," Divara replied. "This is for the best. I was foolish thinking we could be close. This way, at least I won't have you for a rival."

Inexplicably, tears came to Elsbeth's eyes. She had no words, no gestures, only the realization that Divara's world had closed in on itself, creating an unassailable fortress of fear and suspicion. Elsbeth's confusion turned to pity and compassion as she held Divara's eyes. *She's caught in a cage and can't get out.*

Elsbeth held out her arms. "Divara . . . "

"No!" Divara held her arms at her sides. "If you leave me alone, I'll not harm you, but if I see you around the king, I'll make you sorry." And with that warning, Divara strode over to Bockelson, who was entertaining some more guests.

"What was that about?" Andreas asked, as Elsbeth returned to her seat between Peter and Andreas.

"Divara's banished me."

"What?" Andreas shook his head.

"She's trapped. Everyone's her rival now, not to be trusted. She thinks me capable of betrayal."

Andreas tipped his head at Divara. "The choices she makes are always . . . peculiar."

"She's not stupid, but I think she likes being queen, even if that goat has his other wives. Her desire for status takes its toll."

"That type of desire always does," Andreas said.

"How can she put up with these disasters?"

"We experience them every day."

"I'm not talking about Münster, Andreas. I'm talking about Matthys and Bockelson."

Andreas took Elsbeth's hand. "There's nothing to be done for her. She'll have to live with her path."

Elsbeth watched as Divara flitted from table to table, laughing and smiling. "Yes, just like the rest of us, though I'm sick of having to live with the ones made for me."

"An understandable sentiment." Peter pushed up from the table to stretch. "I'm going back home. I'm an old man in need of rest. I'll see you two later."

The afternoon passed as everyone feasted, but when evening fell, torches were lit and Bockelson and Divara took places at the head of the main table as servants placed plates of bread and chalices filled with wine in front of them. When everything was prepared, Bockelson held up a loaf of bread and shouted, "This is the body of Christ given for you, just as today you were willing to give your body for him. Eat this to remember the death of Jesus!"

Taking the chalice, Bockelson lifted it high. "And this is the blood of our Lord Jesus, shed for us. Just as you were willing to give your life for him today, he gave his life for you. Drink this in remembrance of his willingness to die for us all!"

As Bockelson held the cup and bread above him, Rothmann's pinched face loomed behind him; Elsbeth's hand went to Andreas's shoulder as she directed his gaze. "Now that the king has become a priest, I guess there's no need for ministers."

"He looks like Jesus returned but didn't know who he was," Andreas observed.

Guided by Bockelson's servants, everyone formed lines and moved slowly toward the king and queen, who held the bread and wine. Women, men, and children all took a piece of bread from the queen's hand, dipped it into the wine cup Bockelson held, and pushed it into their mouths.

Elsbeth was so focused on the ceremony, she hardly noticed Andreas tugging on her sleeve. "Look!"

Bernard Knipperdolling, wearing ragged black clothes, stood in line, his daughter Clara behind him, hand on his shoulder.

"Damn," Andreas said.

Knipperdolling moved docilely with the rest of the crowd toward the bread and cup. His face was bruised and his right eye swollen, but from the haunted look in his eyes, Elsbeth knew that Knipperdolling's worst wound lay within. "He won't be a problem for Bockelson anymore," she murmured.

"Crushed by mercy—what a horrible humiliation," Andreas whispered into Elsbeth's ear.

Knipperdolling, eyes turned away from Bockelson's smiling face, took a piece of bread, dipped it into the wine, and shoved it into his mouth.

As the celebration ended, Bockelson stood on the table closest to him and took off his regalia. He put his ten rings and scepter on the rough wooden table, followed by his crown and the golden apple. After he removed all his jewelry, Bockelson held up his hands.

"I've sought to lead you!" he shouted. "But I'm not worthy to be your king. I will die for you if God wills it, but I'm not fit to lace your shoes. I've failed you and God. I've failed to punish the godless and the evildoers. The Antichrist outside still threatens us. You should choose someone worthier." Bockelson wept. "Please forgive me and at least allow me to be your humble servant after we choose a new king."

Andreas rolled his eyes. "Is it possible he's truly mad?"

"I've entertained that thought," Elsbeth said. "But I think he's—"

Just then, the goldsmith Dusentschuer yelled, "Zion, listen to me! God has told me that we must send out apostles to call for reinforcements and preach the Gospel to the heathens who surround us."

Confused looks passed through the crowd. Some of the men put their mugs on the tables and stood, nervously shifting their feet. Anxiety and anticipation permeated the feast.

"By our faithful witness," Dusentschuer continued, "the armies of Christ will come to our side if we go out and help recruit them. If you hear your name called, go gather a pack from your house and come back here immediately. You're to leave the gates tonight and tell the world outside the great things God is doing in Zion. Proclaim that all are welcome to the wedding feast of Christ. Just as Jesus sent out apostles to spread the good news, you will call all those outside to come feast in Zion."

Wives congregated around their husbands, trying to wall them off from being taken away. Dusentschuer read several names quickly. When they were announced, the men looked stunned, desperation written on their haggard faces as wives huddled ever closer to them. Then several names from the council of elders were read, their faces growing noticeably paler.

"These are the most powerful men in the city," Andreas said. "What's his game?"

Elsbeth warily eyed the soldiers forming a ring around the men. "From the looks of things, they weren't expecting this."

When the goldsmith finished reading the names, he tore the parchment into pieces and tossed it into the wind. "If you refuse the command of God, you'll be scattered to hell this very night." The goldsmith stood up on a bench, spread his arms wide, and shouted, "King Jan, where are you?"

"Here," replied Bockelson, sitting right below the goldsmith.

"I knew there'd be farce," Andreas snorted.

"Rise, King Jan." Dusentschuer's voice trembled. "The Most High has revealed to me that He has placed you on this throne to restore righteousness to a fallen world."

While the goldsmith spoke, he took the regalia off the table and ceremoniously placed them back on Bockelson's body. His hands shook as he placed the crown on Bockelson's head. When he finished, he stepped back and threw up his arms. "Behold, the King of Zion who will cleanse the world of evil and usher in the thousand-year reign of God!"

Bockelson, oozing humility, faced the crowd. "We have heard the Word of God. We have celebrated the Lord's Supper, and we have learned that our salvation is very close. We began this day in fear, but we are ending it in hope and joy. Let us go home and renew ourselves for the days ahead. Thanks be to God!"

"Let's go, Andreas," Elsbeth sighed. "We don't have to stay any longer."

"We can't go," Andreas reminded her. "Remember the offer of another banquet? We have to stay."

Elsbeth groaned. "Damn, it's too much."

Artisans, soldiers, queens, and their servants milled around and talked with one another while the chamberlain directed servants to remove the old settings and cover the tables with beautiful cream-colored damask tablecloths. Silver plates and candelabras appeared, placed with utmost care. Fresh barrels of wine and ale were greeted with wide grins.

As evening's shadows crept into the market, Elsbeth noticed Bockelson constantly leaving and returning to his seat, his body twisting in jerky movement. He gulped his wine and slammed it back on the table with every trip away from his chair. Bockelson's attention focused on a stranger whom his soldiers had placed right beside the king as the second feast began. The visitor was a slight man, dressed in simple brown pants, and a soiled beige blouse with a black woolen vest. Bockelson's eyes darted from the stranger to those gathered around the table as he paced back and forth behind the man.

Finally, Bockelson spoke. "Friend, your clothing seems strange to me. We've not seen your kind in the city for some time."

The man kept eating his turkey leg, not responding. One of the guards tapped him on the shoulder, and the stranger looked up. The soldier motioned to the king who loomed behind him.

"Oh, sorry. I'm but a prisoner." He brusquely wiped his mouth with his arm. "Your guards brought me here tonight for some reason, though it escapes me."

"Perhaps, like the parable of the wedding feast, they've called everyone to come and join the celebration, even those not originally invited." Bockelson's lips spread into a smile as people put down their forks and knives.

The man continued working on his meal, drinking wine and belching. "Maybe they thought I would convert to the *true* faith." He grinned and looked around to see if anyone else was amused.

Divara slid down the bench away from the prisoner.

"Ah, and if you don't mind, what is *your* religion?"

"I believe in drinking and whoring, though not necessarily in that order." The man laughed at his own joke.

"How is it that you come to the feast of Christ without proper attire?"

"I didn't come to this whore's wedding willingly. I was brought here against my desire. But since I'm here, I'm grateful for the wine and food. You may be a heretic, but you treat your prisoners well." The man held up his cup, half toast, half request for a refill.

"Bockelson picks a fight," Elsbeth whispered to Andreas. "To what end?"

"Not sure, but I wouldn't want to be in that seat." Andreas nodded at the stranger.

"Get up, jackal!" Bockelson demanded. "Who do you think you are to defile Zion and her king?"

The prisoner gnawed on his turkey leg before responding. "*You're* a king? Does God make pimps into kings now?"

Elsbeth didn't see where the sword came from that Bockelson swung over his head. She was paralyzed by the slow glide of the blade above the man's head, the startled look on his face as he dropped his turkey leg, the blade descending into his neck. The victim's head bounced across the table and landed on the ground opposite Divara as his lifeless body slumped beside his plate, blood leaking onto the tablecloth.

Bockelson motioned to his soldiers to remove the body. He strutted in a tight circle, pounding his chest. "I *have* rid the world of the godless. This is but a foretaste of what is to come for those who oppose God's chosen. Let this be a sign to you that we must not shirk our responsibility to cleanse the earth of the wicked! I promise you this day I will free this city from our enemies by Easter! May God take my head as I have taken this heathen's if this does not happen!"

Grabbing his silver chalice and holding it over his head, Bockelson shouted, "To Zion!"

Elsbeth watched a smile play out on Divara's lips as she lifted her cup to her mouth and took a long gulp. She reached her hand up to Bockelson, who grabbed it and pulled her up, slipping his arm around her ample waist.

Amid the severed head and bloodstained tablecloth, the entire company, save Elsbeth and Andreas raised their cups and shouted: "Hail to our God and His king!"

"Next Easter ought to be interesting." Elsbeth picked up her cup and drank.

"Yes, if any of us are still alive." Andreas drained his mug of ale.

Elsbeth, her gaze fixed on Divara's smiling face, merely nodded her head.

PART III

47

March 28, 1535, Easter Day

ANDREAS SAT AT THE REFECTORY TABLE, contemplating the specter of emptiness. He knew now that hunger is a wily and tortuous enemy. It counts on its victims not wanting to die, hanging on to the last shred of hope for survival. At first, it incessantly twists your gut into knots, but then it gets much worse. The emptiness relaxes its grip just long enough to make you think it's gone; then, when it returns, it's far more virulent than before. He thought about the people he had seen crawling on hands and knees, eating grass or searching for snakes and bugs, or the stories he had heard of those who had stolen at night into the homes of the dead, returning to their families with enough meat to last another day. Hunger was omnipotent, relentless, like God, a destroyer of worlds.

It had been five months since the last feast of Zion, time enough for the city to sink to its knees and beg for mercy. Hunger gripped everyone, even more firmly than fear of a murderous king. Because he built lovely things for Bockelson, Andreas was fortunate enough to take home extra rations in his tool sack at the end of the day. The rest of the city, however, fared poorly. Sawdust had been disappearing from Andreas's workshop for weeks. People were coming at night and taking it to mix with their barley so they might relieve the emptiness that gnawed at them. Elsbeth had reported seeing women chipping the plaster off walls and cooking it with water to give their babies "milk." A shroud of aching emptiness covered everyone—except for Bockelson and his court.

Bodies piled up relentlessly in the streets every morning, as howls rang out of windows and gatherings. Death stalked Zion leading to rumors of spirits roaming the streets at night searching for victims. The rapacious spirits were said to appear as wise women forecasting a horrible fate for all. Though Andreas didn't believe in the tales and ghost stories, he felt as if some malevolent spirit was sucking life from the city.

Listless emaciated bodies of those wandering mad in the streets the night before, stumbling like confused drunks, would litter the sidewalks the next morning. It was the children's bodies that always left Andreas weeping. Tears flowed when he saw their lifeless forms splayed on the ground, bereaved mothers sitting beside them, too weak to cry. Corpses Andreas saw in the morning would not be there when he returned home in the evening. He often wondered where the bodies went, what happened to them.

Hope had been higher last October when Bockelson's chosen "apostles" stole out of the city to rally others to their cause. But the stories filtered back that all the men had been captured in neighboring towns and immediately killed. All that is, except for one, Henry Graes, who had been found a couple of days after last October's feast, grey and half dead, curled up against St. Ludger's Gate. He was brought inside, hailed as a hero for escaping von Waldeck's soldiers, and became part of the king's inner circle. But when Bockelson sent him on another mission on New Year's Day to rally believers to Zion, Graes went straight to von Waldeck with reports about the city. He had been a spy all along, planted by the Prince-Bishop to gather information.

Just a few nights ago, Graes had posted a letter on St. Ludger's Gate urging the city to free themselves from the beast Bockelson before he destroyed them all. It circulated before Bockelson got word of it, sparking talk of rebellion, or at least opening the gates for von Waldeck to take back the city. When Bockelson found out, he seized the letter and doubled his guard.

Still, Andreas thought, this was Easter—the day of reckoning. Bockelson had some promises made at October's feast to keep. Andreas desired no resurrection, but a dead king suited him.

"Love, are you well?" Elsbeth, in a simple grey smock, shuffled across the refectory. Her already thin frame had become skeletal over the last few months, and the laughter in her voice had gone flat. Andreas worried about her constantly.

"I'm fine, just trying to gather my strength." He went into the kitchen to fetch her some porridge. The extra ration of oats they received had kept them alive through the winter, but even that grew smaller.

"Do you think Bockelson makes good his promise?" Elsbeth sounded oddly upbeat.

"Doubtful, given his lies," Andreas replied. "Peter tells me to have hope."

"Hope for what?" Peter asked from the kitchen.

"Bockelson's death?" Andreas muttered.

Elsbeth lifted an eyebrow as the bells of St. Lambert's rang.

Groans filled the room as they rose and shuffled for the door, heading for the marketplace. Just outside the monastery, they encountered a man leaning against a post. His shirt hung loosely on a taut frame, skull and skin indistinguishable, his face twisted into a gruesome smile. Teetering toward them, he held his finger to his mouth, inviting them to share a secret.

"Do you want to see something?" the wasted man whispered.

Andreas, Elsbeth, and Peter stared mutely at him, their eyes pained and moist.

"Watch." The man raised his shirt, revealing the bare remains of a human being. Putting his finger to his stomach, he cackled, "I can touch my backbone."

Andreas pulled his companions away, but he could not spare them from the gruesome spectacle of other skeletal figures lumbering alongside them, their pallid bodies shambling toward yet another judgment day. A crowd half the size of the previous October gathered to await Bockelson's latest performance. From the looks of the waxen and gaunt bodies, Andreas was pretty sure no one was going to find the king's theater charming.

The blare of trumpets sounded.

A disturbance grew behind the throne platform as Bockelson stumbled into the crowd wearing sackcloth. His face was covered in ashes, and he wailed loudly, though no one paid much attention. Wandering among the listless spectators, beating his chest and moaning, he tried to rouse emotions, but people just stood aside mutely to let him pass. After making a circuit through the square, Bockelson mounted the stage and staggered to its front.

"Saints of Zion." Bockelson flicked out his wrists. "Last year, I promised on a blood oath that I would lead this city to deliverance by Easter, or I would willingly forfeit my life. I have been in prayer and fasting for days, approaching the throne of grace that God might see fit to deliver us. God gave me an answer, and I must confess to you today that I have failed."

"Surely he . . . " Elsbeth started.

"I was too proud and arrogant when I made those promises to you," Bockelson continued. "I had not received approval from God for my vow. My compassion for you was great, but God told me I was deceived. God desires to save souls, not bodies. He wants to save all your souls for heaven, for what does it profit a man to gain the world but lose his soul? Because of your faith, God revealed to me that you are all saved!"

A cadaverous figure beside Andreas fell on his knees and groaned. Andreas tried to help him to his feet, but he waved him off and lay face down on the stones, whimpering, "No hope . . . no . . . rescue."

Andreas turned to the stage where Bockelson paced. "I have sacrificed myself in prayer and fasting for you, dear children. God has accepted my prayers on your behalf. You are saved! Go in peace!"

With a final squint at the crowd, Bockelson started to leave.

"You're not true!" a man who resembled more clump of hair than flesh shouted.

Stopped short, Bockelson glared at the man. He motioned to his guards to take the hirsute man away. Surveying the emaciated bodies beneath him, Bockelson said, "I only care about you, my children. Have faith and we shall shortly be free. Don't be like the traitor Graes."

"False prophet!" a shrill scream echoed over the market.

"I just told you that you're saved. Now please, rejoice and return to your homes." Bockelson raised his hand and waved as if shooing an insect.

"You vowed if the city wasn't free, God would take your life," the woman persisted.

Bockelson's head went from his guard to the woman as they pushed through the crowd to arrest her.

"Liar!" the woman screeched as she was dragged away. "You sit on a throne of shit!"

Bockelson sneered at the rest of the worn faces in front of him. "Is there anything else anyone wants to say?"

"Well, go on, Andreas, surely you have something to add?"

Andreas flinched at the sound of Ulrich's voice over his shoulder. Since their discussion in the woodshop, he had managed to mostly avoid him. "Why are you even here, Ulrich? I thought you would've left by now."

"I can't leave. Not anymore. We're all prisoners. You of all people should know that." Ulrich rose on his toes to observe the gathering. "There still may be ways out, however."

Andreas, mindful of an earlier offer, went alert at Ulrich's remark.

"How? What do you mean, 'ways out'?" Elsbeth asked.

"No doubt you've heard about the letter Henry Graes posted?" Ulrich started.

"Most have heard of it," Andreas said.

"It's caused quite the stir at court." Ulrich's eyes darted from Elsbeth to Bockelson. "The king thinks everyone is out to betray him, and he's working on something, though even I'm not sure what it is."

"You put us on a puppet string again." Andreas's face flushed and his hands clenched.

"No, I'm only trying to help." Ulrich looked directly at Elsbeth. "I've been a good friend to you both, if in ways you're not aware of."

"Saints, wait upon the Lord, I will set you free in the next couple of days!" Bockelson's voice rang out as all eyes turned to him. "I promise you can go very soon."

The haggard, raggedy crowd looked mutely at the king before turning their shoulders and heading back to hunger's misery.

Ulrich looked at Andreas, Elsbeth, and Peter. "When I get word of what he intends, I'll come to you."

48

April 2

"ANDREAS CAN FOLLOW LATER." Ursula folded her clothes and put them in a dingy linen sack. "I just hope my mother and father will take me back."

"They may take you." Rachel looked at the floor glumly. "But I doubt your father will have me in the bargain."

Ursula touched Rachel's cheek. "Let me take care of that."

"Elsbeth?" Rachel said.

Elsbeth sat motionless on the bed. "I'm fine, really. It's just . . . "

When Bockelson first announced that women, children, and old men could leave the city, Rachel, Ursula, and Elsbeth discussed it for hours. At first, Elsbeth had resisted the thought of leaving Andreas. She feared she'd never see him again. But he had been adamant—she was wasting away and if she could, she needed to leave. They decided to go to Ursula's house in Wolbeck. Andreas would find them there when he could escape. Peter agreed with Andreas—Elsbeth should get out while she could. Through her tears, Elsbeth prepared to flee.

Ursula and Rachel huddled around her. "He'll come. He's a resourceful man."

"Hello, is anyone here?" They were all startled when Ulrich called out from the reception hall.

"Remember when we had locks on doors?" Rachel complained.

"Why is he here?" Elsbeth headed for the reception hall, the others following along.

When they arrived, Andreas and Peter were already talking with Ulrich.

"Elsbeth, Rachel, Ursula, please listen to me," Ulrich pleaded. "You can't go out there today."

"Another lie, Ulrich?" Andreas challenged.

Ulrich held up his hands. "Please, I know I play games, but this one time, you must listen to me. You have to stay here today."

Elsbeth regarded Ulrich, looking for the hint of a smile that he toyed with them. No amusement marked his face.

"We're leaving," Rachel said. "Don't think about keeping us here."

"If you value your life, you won't leave," Ulrich urged.

"What's your motive here?" Elsbeth asked. "Why don't you want us to leave?"

"Because they'll cut you down outside those gates," Ulrich warned.

"But the letter from Graes promised us we'd be spared," Rachel argued.

"That was if you turned over Bockelson. Without him, they'll surely kill you," Ulrich declared.

Elsbeth didn't know what to believe. She was only going because Andreas had begged her to, but her heart wasn't in it. Her eyes swung to Andreas, who concentrated on Ulrich.

"We're leaving no matter what you say, Ulrich. You give us no reason to trust you. Besides, here we might as well be dead. We won't last another month if we stay." Ursula returned to her room to get her satchel. Rachel followed close behind her.

"Why should we believe you?" Elsbeth turned to Ulrich.

"Have I not kept you both alive, looked after you all these months? I know you think me awful, but I'm telling you, Elsbeth, don't go outside the gates today. If things go well, I'll take you, Andreas, and Peter outside tomorrow."

Elsbeth pondered her next move as Rachel and Ursula returned with their satchels.

"Elsbeth?" Rachel asked. "Coming?"

"Andreas?" Elsbeth looked back and forth between Ulrich and Andreas, who held his chin in his hand. "Thoughts?"

"Don't go. Not today," Andreas finally said. Elsbeth nodded in agreement.

Ulrich exhaled, relief washing over his face. "Thank you."

Ursula tenderly hugged Elsbeth. "Sorry, but we're resolved. We'll wait for you in Wolbeck." Hugs were exchanged all around as Ulrich stood by himself.

"We need to get moving," Rachel said.

Everyone left the monastery and headed for St. Ludger's Gate, except Ulrich, who headed in the opposite direction.

"What do you think?" Elsbeth asked Andreas, as they trailed behind their friends.

"I don't know. His voice was so urgent. It would be his best lie yet," Andreas mused.

The air was warm and dry on Elsbeth's skin. She looked at the pink and light-blue hues of the morning sky. Maybe this was the end of the misery. By the time they reached St. Ludger's, crowds had already gathered, milling in front of the gate, smiling, eager for the bridge to come down. Elsbeth was struck by the fact that everyone leaving had worn their best clothes, though the brightly colored fabric of dresses and tunics could not hide the wan faces and frail bodies beneath them.

"Come and find us." Ursula grasped Elsbeth's hand.

"I will," Elsbeth promised. She threw her arms around Ursula and Rachel, weeping as she held them in a fierce embrace. "Now, go—" Elsbeth released them and pushed them toward the gate.

"Andreas, Peter, please come as soon as you can," Rachel said, as she and Ursula grabbed hands. "Tomorrow, if possible."

"As soon as we can," Andreas assured them.

Soldiers formed a line and herded the refugees through the massive stone gatehouse onto the bridge over the inner moat. Those remaining in the city walked past on either side so that they could climb the walls and bid their family and friends farewell. After Elsbeth mounted the steps and took her place beside Peter and Andreas on the promenade, she saw Bockelson standing down the wall with Divara, her daughter cradled in her arms.

"Why has Bockelson come to see them off?" she asked Andreas.

"I'm still surprised he allowed it, but if it's true that there is safe passage, we leave tomorrow."

An irrational jolt of joy overwhelmed Elsbeth. Freedom. Tomorrow. She spotted Rachel and Ursula locked arm in arm and called out. They smiled and waved as the outer bridge lowered and the portcullis rose.

Just then, Bockelson started screaming: "Snakes! Traitors! Demons! Leave here! You are cast out into darkness!"

Elsbeth gripped Andreas's arm. "He curses them? It was his decree that they could leave."

Bockelson strutted back and forth on the promenade. "Go to hell! God has no part of you!"

Pushed by the guards, those gathered at the gate crowded onto the road beyond the outer moat. Ditches filled with brambles and briars, and fields with no cover made escape on anything other than the road impossible. The refugees crushed together, inching along the path toward the nearest guardhouse. Drawn by the commotion, the guards came outside with bows, arrows, and guns in hand. Elsbeth grabbed Andreas's arm with a cry. She screamed as the soldiers raised their weapons and fired on the crowd moving toward them.

Chaos erupted, with people screaming and scattering to avoid the assault. People ran back toward the city only to find the portcullis down and the bridge tilting up toward the wall. Stuck between a closed city and bored soldiers looking for a little sport, the refugees froze. Elderly men were the first to fall, collapsing in a hail of bullets. In the silence that followed as soldiers reloaded their weapons, arrows flew from archers. Those not immediately killed or wounded fled off the road in a panic and scattered into the muddy fields and ditches on either side of the road. Women bundled their children next to them, enveloping them in arms that became pockmarked with red from bullets and arrows. Children pushed away from their mothers and ran blindly through the thickets that tore at their bodies.

Wailing, mixed with Bockelson's curses, permeated the morning air as loved ones fell. Searching for her friends, Elsbeth's eyes widened in horror as Rachel spun around, struck in the shoulder, and fell onto a patch of bramble. Ursula, already waiting in the field below, clawed her way back to Rachel and dropped to her knees, draping her body over her. Elsbeth didn't even hear the gunshot that hit Ursula, but her body went limp as blood poured from her neck, soaking her and Rachel in red.

"No! No! No!" Elsbeth threw back her head and screamed.

Andreas tried to shelter her from the carnage, but Elsbeth would not avert her eyes. Though she had fallen apart with the death of Ingrid, today she wanted to remember everything: Bockelson's caterwauling curses, the sight of her friends dying, and the anguished wails of those beside her. She wanted the betrayal, the dead children, and the horror of this slaughter seared into her mind. She locked it all away inside, knowing that one day she might need to draw on the fierce strength of anger and revenge to survive. Bockelson left the wall with Divara, their daughter pressed closely against her chest, following in his wake. All Elsbeth could hear was sobbing and random gunfire, an occasional anguished shout lifted to the heavens.

Moments later, Henry Gresbeck joined Elsbeth and Andreas. Gresbeck's dark hair was matted, and his beard mottled with dirt. His yellow, cracked fingernails gripped the wall as he stood staring at the dead bodies piling up below. Elsbeth took him in, remembering when he looked more robust, his pleasant and round face always ready to smile. Now he trembled, shaken and as pale as the dingy white linen shirt he wore, his mouth locked in a scowl.

"Gresbeck?" Elsbeth asked. "Are you well?"

He rubbed his eyes, his fingers wet. "Something must be done."

"Yes," Elsbeth growled. "The sooner the better."

Stunned by the carnage, they all stood rooted until one of the king's guards, Johann Nagel, known to all as Hansel Eck, approached the three of them. "Gresbeck, a word?" the short, squat man asked. "In private?"

Gresbeck looked at Eck, confused. "Sure," he responded, as they moved to an empty spot on the wall.

"What do you think those two have in mind?" Elsbeth asked.

"What does it matter?" Andreas replied.

"I don't know. Did you notice the look on Gresbeck's face?" Elsbeth watched the two men walk down the promenade, away from the crowds. Glancing one more time at Rachel and Ursula, Elsbeth clinched her face. "I want to go." She headed for the stairs.

Thirty minutes later, Elsbeth, Andreas, and Peter were back at the monastery, collapsed on benches in the refectory.

"Ulrich . . . God, he saved our lives." Elsbeth broke the silence.

Andreas disappeared into the kitchen.

"It is unexpected," Peter conceded.

Elsbeth teared up. "I almost didn't heed his warning. I would've met their fate."

Andreas brought out a plate of cheese and bread with a few slices of raw turnip and one small piece of pork. He returned to the kitchen and retrieved three mugs of ale, placing them on the table. "It's hard to believe Ulrich was our savior today."

"He keeps his virtues well hidden." Peter grabbed a turnip piece and started chewing.

"Whatever Ulrich's virtues may or may not be," Andreas said, "I think we should concentrate on figuring a way past the guards."

"Then what? Be cut down like they were?" Elsbeth cried. She put her head in her hands, slumping on the table.

"Whatever is to be done, you two may need to do it without me."

"Peter." Andreas reached out his hand. "We'll get through this."

"You and Elsbeth, maybe." Peter coughed. "But you must consider the possibility that I won't make it. I grow weaker."

Elsbeth examined Peter. His complexion had grown sallow, his face drawn, and the grey had overtaken the reddish brown in his hair and beard. He had been their rock; life without him seemed impossible. "Father, none of us are thinking clearly. Don't talk like that. It makes me think you've given up hope," Elsbeth chided.

"I always have hope, but there's a part of me that grows curious about the mystery."

"What mystery?" Andreas asked.

"You know . . . what comes next."

"And if there's nothing?"

"Then I won't know it, will I?" Peter smiled at Andreas, who looked exasperated.

"But what about hell?" Elsbeth asked. "Not that you have to worry about that, but I fear it."

"I can't say one way or the other about hell, Elsbeth—or heaven, for that matter. But if hell exists, well, I was taught the *resignatio ad infernum*."

"What?" Elsbeth asked.

"The resignation to hell," Andreas answered before Peter could respond. "It's a faith that loves God so deeply that even if God puts you in hell, the love for God can't be quenched. The idea is that true faith goes beyond the hope of a reward or fear of punishment. To love God even though He condemns you is purer than a love that desires heaven over God."

"Very good, Andreas." Peter sounded delighted.

"But who possesses that type of faith?" Elsbeth asked. "Why would they want to?"

"There are some," Peter replied. "They've taught me a great deal."

"Peter Droste, the mystic," Andreas said without a hint of sarcasm. "It's part of the air he breathes. It's his legacy to me. I can't let go of God because of him, even though I believe God has let go of me."

"Perhaps it's time you did let go of God."

"Peter?" Elsbeth scrunched up her face.

"I'm only saying what he knows deep inside. Our most noble journey can be the one where we take leave of God, for God's own sake."

"I'm lost," Elsbeth pleaded.

"We all are, except for him." Andreas pointed to Peter. "Peter has always held . . . um, *peculiar* beliefs. He's hesitant to talk about them, but it's one of the reasons I trust him. Mystics see the world differently."

"I realize you can't walk my path, Andreas, but I've been hoping you would pick up some things in the last year. Maybe I've snuck in the back door?" Peter smiled.

"Don't be smug, Father; it doesn't become you," Andreas teased.

Elsbeth moved over to Peter and draped her arm around him. "Don't listen to him. He can be irritating at times."

Andreas drew back in mock offense. "Me?"

"Your self-righteousness doesn't prevent love from breaking through," Peter said.

Silence fell on the room as Andreas leaned back and crossed his arms. "If that's true, my friend, love could start by giving us a way out of this hell."

"Andreas!" Elsbeth scolded.

"No, Elsbeth, he's right." Peter held up his hand. "At moments like this, it's hard to hold on to hope. My own grasp is slipping. But you two must hold on a bit longer." Coughing, Peter rose. "I'm tired. I need to rest."

Andreas stood and hugged Peter. "I need you, my friend. Don't give up."

"I'll never give up, Andreas, but I feel as if the sands of my hourglass are running out."

Elsbeth came over and put her arms around the two of them. "Then we'll turn the hourglass back over."

49

May 23

THE SACK OF BONES floated toward Henry Gresbeck. She, like the others, drifted aimlessly through the streets, untethered to life, waiting for the end to come. Some nights when he walked to his post on the night watch, the soon-dead would pass him and collapse, falling into a heap, gurgling with ungodly voice. Feeling his own ribs, Gresbeck looked down at his bony and translucent fingers, the blue veins visible beneath the skin. It reminded him of cheese he used to enjoy. Even though he received extra provisions for being part of the guard, it wasn't enough to feed his family anymore. Their lives were dribbling away.

The night before, his neighbor had asked him if he wanted to share some leather he was boiling for dinner. He dripped some candle tallow on it so it would go down easier. Gresbeck refused the offer, though he was impressed that the man wanted to share what passed for food. No one shared much of anything these days, even the horse dung they gathered after the king's men rode through town. When he saw the vomit stains outside his neighbor's stoop the next morning, he was glad he had resisted.

The crying of his own children wounded Gresbeck the most. His wife and mother tried to calm them, but hunger picked away at his clan, one piece at a time. He had to act. On his way to Cross Gate tower, he wondered how he had let himself be so taken in. His dead friends, the blacksmiths Rusher and Mollenheck, still weighed heavily on his mind. Everything had gone awful after the night they shared guard duty. He should never have told Matthys that Rusher called him a shit prophet. The guilt had burned deep into Gresbeck ever since the blacksmith's murder.

A gaunt figure hunched over a fire called out to him as he drew close to Cross Gate.

"Do you want any?" The man held out a plate of cooked horse dung.

"No, and if you eat that, you'll probably die."

"I'm already dead, so at least I'll have a full belly when I go." The man shrugged and went back to tending his fire.

Gresbeck walked on, thinking about what he needed to do in the next couple of hours. He had to be careful. He started dropping notes over the wall a couple of weeks ago. He didn't know if the soldiers outside would get them, but much depended on finding a partner outside to aid him and Hansel Eck in their plan to betray the city to von Waldeck. The time for caution was over. If Gresbeck took no action, his family was going to die. He had to trust someone, and Eck seemed as likely a candidate as any. Eck was never really one of the true believers, but Bockelson was fond of him. Short in stature, he played the fool for the king's enjoyment, but he was not someone to mess with.

Entering Cross Gate tower, Gresbeck mounted the circular stairs to the guardroom on top of the wall. *Eck better be there.* When he reached the top and didn't see him in the guardroom with the others, he rushed outside and found Eck standing on the wall, taking in the storm on the horizon.

"I should never have deserted and come over to this den of insanity," Eck said.

"Why did you leave?"

"Hard to recall." Eck shrugged his shoulders. "A warm bed? A fiery woman? Seemed like a good idea at the time."

"Are you sure you want to do this?"

"I could die by Bockelson's whim any second. Something has to be done."

Gresbeck looked at Eck. He stood just a bit over five feet, his bristly beard shooting out all over his barrel chest. A black leather vest sat snug against his torso, and a wide-brimmed leather hat rested on top of a mass of unruly black hair. Gresbeck had seen Eck fighting off much larger men last August, his eyes crazed with brutal intensity as he swung his sword, knocking invaders off their ladders. He was a fierce warrior. Gresbeck hoped he had chosen well. Both their lives depended on it.

"Are you ready?" Gresbeck asked.

"Do you think your friends got your messages? I would hate to end up dead in a ditch tonight."

"If we don't do this, we're going to end up dead anyway. Your being captain of the watch has given us an opening; let's just hope our luck holds."

Lightning flashed across the sky as thunderstorms shook the countryside. The first smell of rain was followed by waves of water flying into them. They hurried inside the tower where most of the night watch huddled together, trying to avoid the wind-swept rain coming in through the windows.

"Horrible night, eh?" Gresbeck said.

"No real reason to stand watch, is there?" one of the guards asked.

"If you don't want to do your duty, fine," Eck retorted, "but I've work to do. Gresbeck, you're coming with me."

"Why? What did I do?" Gresbeck protested.

"I just love your company." Eck emphasized his sarcasm. "Step to it. We'll take the first look around and then let these girls have at it when we're finished."

The men laughed, took off their cloaks, and moved away from the windows closer to the fireplace. One of the guards called out, "Where're you going? I thought you were supposed to be on the wall."

"We'll be back shortly. We're going to go tell the others below to stay inside tonight and then we're going on a short patrol. No one's going to try and breach the gates on a night like this," Eck said.

Coming out of the guardhouse, the two men walked to the outer gate where six other men recruited by Gresbeck waited.

"We have to move quickly. It won't be long before we're discovered," Eck whispered. Pulling a key from his tunic, he unlocked the door beside the gate bridge.

They stole through the door and onto the small ring of land between the outer moat and wall.

"There's no other way, so let's get to it." Eck waved them on. The deserters waded into the moat and slogged to the other side, where they paused to debate their next move.

"We should go toward the closest guardhouse. That's where the soldiers from Cleves are. I addressed my messages to them, so they should be expecting us," Gresbeck declared, breathing heavily.

"What? No. We need to go in that direction," Eck responded, pointing to a field that looked easier to navigate than the thorn-filled ditches leading to the guardhouse.

"No, Eck, trust me. We must go where I say. It may look harder, but it's shorter and our best chance is with the people I've already tried to contact."

"But we have no idea whether they've received your messages, do we? Go where you want, Gresbeck. We're going in this direction." Eck and the others ran across the road, heading west.

"Hey, brothers," a voice high up on the wall called. "What're you doing? Come back inside!"

Gresbeck looked up to the top of the wall. Several of the watch shouted for them to return. "Shit," he said.

"Come back! We won't tell the king if you return now!" The cries grew louder.

Gresbeck searched in vain for Eck and his men, thinking to join them, but he could not spot them anywhere.

"Don't you remember what they do to deserters? They're going to kill you! Come back! We'll prote—!" Claps of thunder drowned out the yelling.

Gresbeck froze, caught between two worlds. Any choice now probably meant death. He scurried along the bottom of the rampart below the guardhouse, looking for a clear path over the ditches and, if possible, past von Waldeck's watch. The moon disappeared again, leaving him to feel his way through a pitch-black landscape.

Crawling into a ditch of briers, he curled up in the mud as the rain beat down on him. His hands spasmed first, followed by uncontrollable trembling. Even in the cold rain, sweat beaded on his face and under his clothes. It had been a stupid idea; now he was going to die in a ditch, alone, never seeing his children again.

"Hey! Look here!" a voice shouted directly above Gresbeck. The man held a torch out over the ditch and peered down. "Look, there's a big worm crawling in the mud. Is anyone's gun loaded?"

"No, don't shoot it. Where's the fun in that? If we shoot it, we can't play with it."

Gresbeck, horrified, listened to von Waldeck's soldiers above him debate his fate.

"Let's take it prisoner. We'll return it to those bastards inside when we've had our fun," another guard chimed in.

"What fun? It's not like it's a woman."

"It could be one tonight."

Gresbeck curled tighter into a ball, as their laughter grew.

His only way out was to convince the guards that they needed him. "Wait! I was a soldier! I was like you!" Gresbeck shouted. "I have some news for your master. Pull me up, and I'll make sure you're rewarded."

"Shut up! We'll decide what to do with you, traitor," a harsh voice shot back.

"I wrote your leader I was leaving the city! Didn't you get my messages?" There was a moment of silence as Gresbeck prayed.

"We never heard anything about this. Don't try and talk us out of our sport."

"Arrest me and I can give your master the city," Gresbeck begged.

A pole slipped through the thorns toward him. "Take this. We're not going to kill you yet, but you better have something good for us, or we'll chop you up into little pieces and toss you back over the wall like we did that bastard Matthys."

Gresbeck grabbed the pole and tugged it. Covered in mud and dread, he held the pole as they pulled him through the brambles until his body cleared the obstacles and slid onto the top of the hill. Stumbling to his feet, he found himself surrounded by a ragtag gang of soldiers, suspiciously eyeing his mud-covered form.

"Remember my warning," the harsh one barked, shoving a piece of bread into Gresbeck's hands. "Tell the truth, you live; lie, and we'll kill you."

An hour later, the captain of the watch scrutinized Gresbeck from his rickety wooden chair, a bowl of stew in front of him. Weakened from his lack of food and exhausted by fear, Gresbeck was grateful that his captors had brought him directly to their captain.

"You're a lucky man. We've killed everyone else caught trying to escape. Some of my men said you had something of value for me?"

"Before I tell you, did you kill any other men tonight?" Gresbeck asked.

"I'm the one asking the questions. That's none of your concern," the captain shot back, ladling another large spoonful of stew into his mouth. Spit formed on the inside of Gresbeck's cheeks, filling his mouth until he couldn't stop swallowing.

"There were others with me; their leader was a short, trollish man named Johann Nagel, but we called him Hansel Eck."

"Little Hans?" The captain chortled. "I remember him from his days with us." The captain studied Gresbeck for several minutes and then called for his guard. "Go down the line and see if anyone else was taken or killed in the last few hours. Report back to me if you hear of anything."

The guard went to complete his mission as the captain turned back to Gresbeck. "You told my men you could give them the city; I'm all ears."

"There's a section of the wall that's vulnerable to attack," Gresbeck said. "Give me a piece of paper and a pen."

The captain waved his hand; minutes later, paper and pen were on his desk. Gresbeck took the pen, slumped into a chair, and hunched over, scratches from the pen coming faster as he drew a crude picture of Münster's fortifications. "Here." Gresbeck pointed. "At St. Giles's Gate, there's an alcove that a raiding party could use to stand unobserved while they prepare to take the walls. The wall can be breached with a small raiding party and then, if you're lucky, you can take the tower guard and unlock the gate while the city's asleep."

The captain's mouth hovered between a smirk and disdain. "I'm going to turn you over to my superiors, Gresbeck. But I'm going to ask them to bring you back to me if they find out you're lying, because I want the pleasure of killing you myself."

"You're not alone in that desire, but we can only take advantage if we move quickly. Bockelson knows we're gone by now. If we can gather forces within the day, we'll be able to catch them with their defenses down."

A fist slammed on the table. "Quiet, Gresbeck!" Stew spilled to the surface. "Don't argue with me. You're going to Count von Dhaun. He'll know what to do with you."

Staring at those drops of soup, Henry Gresbeck wept as he thought of his wife and children. What if his betrayal had been for nothing?

They hauled him outside and put him in a cart. He was so miserable he barely felt the bumps as they slid in the muck to Wolbeck. It seemed like an eternity before Gresbeck was standing in the reception room of a prison. The room was bare, save for a table and couple of chairs. Before him sat Count Ulrich von Dhaun, whose two massive sideburns dropped down to a bare chin, and Wilhelm Steding, who sat stiffly straight in his chair. Dressed in their dark grey military uniforms, they struck fear into Gresbeck as he withstood their barrage of questions.

"How many weapons do they have?"

"Why did Bockelson send those people out?"

"Will they fight?"

"Where do they store their cannons?"

"How can you get into the gate?"

The questions were unremitting, repetitious, trying to catch him in a lie. But Gresbeck answered each one in as much detail as they asked for. During the interrogation, his legs buckled as he slid to the floor.

"I need some food," he moaned.

"Get him something to eat," von Dhaun ordered one of his men. "Now, while we wait, tell me again why it is I should believe you."

"I want to save my family," Gresbeck croaked. "They're starving to death. Everyone is. That's why I left, but we need to move quickly."

Von Dhaun opened the door to the next room. Gresbeck saw a large board resting on a table. There was a pile of clay-like mud on the floor. Beside the mud lay sticks and nails. Gresbeck looked at his captors and then back into the room.

"What's this?" Gresbeck asked.

"You're a smart man; you can figure out what we want," von Dhaun said.

"You want me to make a model of the city?" Gresbeck asked.

"Very good," von Dhaun said. "If you ever want to see your family again, show us how things stand inside: where the armories are, where the king sleeps, how the guards are concentrated. You can eat first, but then get to it."

Staring mutely at von Dhaun, Henry Gresbeck was pinched between the guilt of knowing how much his family was suffering and the overwhelming relief that a full stomach was closer than it had been in months.

50

June 11

IN THE END, what had it all been worth? The question haunted Peter Droste as he lay in his bed, pondering his life. Walking around the monastery earlier that day, he recalled his time in the order. Was it the right decision, becoming a priest? So much missed: the pleasure of a woman's company, the laughter of children, the small satisfactions of family life. This place had been a family of sorts: keeping daily office, common meal, study, the homes he visited for pastoral care, the people he treated over the years—these moments shaped him.

Then there was Andreas. *Andreas.* When he left years ago, Peter was surprised by the depth of his grief. He had sensed Andreas's confusion for months, had seen him grow less involved, less present, so it was not a total surprise when he went missing. Still, it wounded him to think he had failed Andreas so badly. Peter questioned if it wasn't also a wound to his pride, an offense to his confidence that he could help anyone. Ulrich. Had he been wrong about him? Misjudged him? If it weren't for him, Elsbeth would be dead. Maybe a spark still flickered somewhere in that darkness? So engrossed in his thoughts, he barely registered it when the door to his room creaked open and the intruder slipped in.

"Ulrich, I was just thinking about you," Peter said calmly. "What brings you to my room at this hour?"

"I was hoping to catch you asleep," Ulrich whispered. "But no matter."

Peter quietly took in Ulrich, dressed in black down to his soft leather shoes, as he grabbed a chair. He pulled it up beside the bed, took a seat in the shadows, and crossed his legs, his hands resting in his lap.

"You didn't answer my question." Peter finally broke the silence.

"What do you think brings me here?"

Hearing the joy in Ulrich's voice, Peter jolted up. He had not noticed the rope and strips of cloth in his hands when he first came in, but spying those, he knew his hope in Ulrich was misplaced. Why hadn't he put the water pail in front of the door to warn him of visitors? But what could he have done anyway, weakened as he was?

"You can put those away, Ulrich." Peter pointed to the rope and strips of cloth in Ulrich's lap. "There's no one close enough to hear me. Besides, did you imagine I'd scream and thrash around as if it were going to make a difference? There's not much left here for you to take."

Ulrich hummed. "No matter, there's enough for me."

"Given your warning to Elsbeth, I'd hoped you might've found something good inside of yourself to nourish."

"I have other plans for those two. I won't be denied my satisfactions. You lasted much longer than I thought you would. I'm glad nature didn't finish the job before I got the chance."

"Old age has not robbed you of your revenge, Ulrich, though the satisfaction you feel puts your soul in peril."

Ulrich grunted, shot out of his seat, and pulled Peter out of his bed, dragging him to a chair across the room, tying his hands, pulling the rope until it cut into Peter's hands. "You're so smug. Why aren't you fighting? Don't you fear the angel of death?"

Peter fought the fear that welled up in him. "Tell me, Ulrich, was it like this with your parents?"

Ulrich kicked Peter's chest so hard the chair tipped over to the floor, knocking Peter's head against the wooden boards. Ulrich lifted the chair back up and leaned into Peter's face. "Who the hell do you think you are?"

"I'm the man you're going to kill," Peter gasped. "But that doesn't answer my question. Was it like this the night you killed your parents?"

Ulrich struck him again, holding onto the back of the chair with his free hand. "What does it matter to you?" He stalked away from the chair, stood on the other side of the room, and continually rocked on his heels as he moaned.

"You sound troubled."

Ulrich rushed back to Peter and leaned in. "Well, what do I have to lose? When did you know?" Ulrich's quick breaths warmed Peter's face.

"I was never totally sure, but the more I got to know you, the more I wondered what happened to them. It was a good story you told about the plague. If anyone could believe that, it would be me, but I guess you knew that. The thing was, you never seemed to *grieve* them. That was my first clue that you were not entirely unhappy they were gone." Peter hoped his voice hid his terror. He did not want Ulrich to have the memory of his fear as a trophy.

"Why should I mourn them?" Ulrich sneered. "They were in my way. Besides, you should've received some of the beatings I endured. You might not be so goddamn judgmental then. I did what I had to do to take care of myself. I have a right to defend myself."

"It was nothing of the kind," Peter challenged. "When you were brought here, you showed no signs of being tormented."

"I thought I was finally free when I put that pillow over their heads. I never realized I was trading one prison for another."

"You could've left. Others walked away from us."

"That was in my mind, but I needed money, a plan. I was working on it, but then you intervened and had me thrown out, you bastard," Ulrich seethed. "At the time, I hated everyone involved, the council and you. And I still hate you for the humiliation."

"You had a role in that."

"But you didn't speak up for me. You allowed them to disgrace me." Ulrich straightened up and looked down at Peter.

"Are you happy about this?" Peter shifted the conversation.

"Yes, very. I've waited for this a long time." Ulrich's teeth glinted in the moonlight.

"I'm not talking about my death. I mean Münster, the world you've created."

Ulrich circled Peter, shaking his head. "I didn't create this world. I wish I had, but I can't take credit for this. It was beyond my abilities."

"Don't be so modest; this was well within your reach," Peter objected. "You came to take your revenge on the city, yes?"

"Certainly, though events took a turn even I didn't anticipate."

"Still, it was fortunate for you that the city went mad."

"Münster rejected me—they got what they deserved," Ulrich started. "I deserve to protect my honor. Yes, my parents were the first, but there've been others who've wronged me. Should I just let that pass? Give in to injustices? No! The bodies of those who spurn me litter the land. Do you want to hear my confession? It won't end with you, either."

"I'm sure that's true."

Ulrich bent down closer to Peter. "The man with all the answers, the wise one, now helpless before God's true and obedient servant. How fitting."

"In your world, perhaps, where God justifies murder." Peter raised his voice, hoping someone could hear him.

"What did I do that God hasn't done countless times? Doesn't God cleanse the world continually, wiping away all sin? What about all those stories of infidel death? The Canaanites and Amalekites slaughtered to satisfy Yahweh? And the followers of God are the ones who carry out the murders! Why am *I* not chosen? I, too, cleanse the earth of the heathen. What about the great flood, the death of the first-born? Is this not what God desires—a pure world? I've only helped to cleanse Münster of all its impurity."

"But not all its monsters."

Ulrich punched Peter in the stomach, knocking the wind out of him. "Is it my fault? The chaos they carry?" Ulrich growled. "Is that *my* fault? I only help to bring about what they desire. If they didn't secretly adore violence, I wouldn't be able to exist. But then," Ulrich paused, "perhaps, *priest*, neither would you."

Peter took a deep breath, fixing Ulrich with his gaze. Time was running out, but he held onto the hope that Andreas and Elsbeth might have heard noises.

"You regard me with judgment." Ulrich broke the silence. "But all the hate, the violence, and death that enters the world comes from their hands, not mine. Not mine! I merely suggest that what they do, what they desire, is God's will. I can't be blamed for that. Emperors *and* popes have been doing it for ages. They've proclaimed for centuries that their wars are just; why not mine? Outside, they believe they're exterminating the unbelievers for a pure world. Here, they believe in a just revolution. Why should the empire or the Church be the only ones with license to murder? And who am I to tell them differently? I only bring them the truth. I'm a prophet, the harbinger of the new order."

"You're no prophet. There are hundreds, thousands just like you. Münster's not unique, either. There'll always be others driven by delusion and lies."

"No!" Ulrich's face twisted into a mask of anger. He stormed behind Peter, bent down, and whispered in his ear, "*I* am special. I am special to *you*. *I* am the most special thing in *your* world."

Peter sat mute, not moving a muscle, his eyes focused on the wall.

Ulrich stepped in front of him. "Why don't you beg for mercy? All the rest did. Aren't you afraid?"

"What man's not afraid of dying?"

"I'm not," Ulrich asserted.

"Well, I'm sure you'll have a chance to test that soon."

Ulrich smacked Peter with the palm of his hand, drawing a trickle of blood from his mouth.

"Don't worry, I'll be merciful," Ulrich whispered, wiping the blood from Peter's cheek and lip with his finger.

"No, you won't. You're not a merciful man. Your life is destruction and death. You've given yourself to the spirit of annihilation, and how long do you think you'll last in the grips of that master? You've deceived yourself, Ulrich, but it's not too late. There's still redemption . . . even now."

"I don't want your redemption," Ulrich sneered.

"And that grieves me; your wounds destroy you."

"I don't need your pity. When the sun rises in the morning, the world will not mourn one less priest. The world will always have its priests."

"I may die soon, but you died a long time ago, even if you still haunt the earth." Peter coughed. "You're not the prophet of a new world, though you may have a hand in the destruction of this one."

"You're mistaken, priest," Ulrich jeered. "I'm a prophet of a world you can't imagine—the age of man without his God!"

"No! You're the blade that gashes the souls of men, luring them to destroy all that graces the world. There's nothing grand in murder, no matter if the rulers of the world indulge themselves in that lie forever."

"The delusion doesn't need to last forever, just a bit longer. Don't worry, though, at least you won't have to see your friends suffer."

A flash of fear sparked across Peter's eyes; an involuntary gasp escaped his mouth.

Ulrich let out a breath of relief. "Ah, finally, at last."

"No, Ulrich. There's no reason for that; it's senseless."

"At least now I'm able to take some pleasure in this."

Ulrich wrapped his hands around the long piece of cloth he brought. He sauntered around to Peter's back once again, wrapped the cloth around his neck, and whispered in Peter's ear. "Consider the sight of me over them, their fate in my hands. Think of Andreas begging me for their lives as I hump Elsbeth. Do you think everyone is as strong as you are? They won't be, I guarantee you. Come then, *Father*, and join the mighty chorus of those who praise God Almighty."

"Lord Jesus Christ, into your hands I commit my spir—"

Peter gurgled as the cloth wrapped tighter and tighter around his throat. His legs kicked as Ulrich's knuckles grew white with exertion. Finally, his body went limp and slumped in the chair. Ulrich untied him, carried him to his bed, and covered him with the blanket, making sure everything was set back in place.

Making for the door, Ulrich paused and sidled back to Peter's body. He spit on his fingers and traced the sign of a cross onto Peter's forehead before slipping out into the night.

51

June 12

St. Lambert's bells sounded six as Andreas got out of bed. Outside his window, a brilliant pink and azure sky painted the morning.

"My love?" Elsbeth rolled over toward him.

"I can't sleep anymore." Andreas leaned over and kissed her forehead. "I'm going to fix some broth."

Coming into the kitchen, Andreas half expected to see Peter, but there was no sign of him. He peeked into the chapel, his office, and stepped outside, but found no sign of Peter. Returning to the kitchen, he set the fire to cook some broth. *Peter doesn't usually sleep late.*

"Where's Peter? He's usually up by this time of day," Elsbeth called from the refectory.

Andreas poked his head out of the kitchen. "I'll have food in a minute."

Tossing some oats in the pot, Andreas was grateful to have some food for the day. When the porridge was hot, he ladled it into bowls and brought them out into the refectory, placing one in front of Elsbeth. They ate in silence, Andreas too absorbed in his thoughts to talk. He could not shake the feeling that something was wrong. When he finished, he rose from his seat. "I'm just going to look in on Peter. We should've heard from him by now."

"Do you want me to go, too?"

"No, I'll be back in a minute."

Walking down the hallway toward Peter's room, Andreas called out, "Peter? Are you up? It's time to eat." He knocked gently on the door. "Peter?" Hearing no answer, he entered the room. "Oh, God, please. No!"

Andreas dashed to the bed where Peter lay, his eyes frozen open. Andreas grabbed his hand and, feeling the coldness, recoiled. Everything inside him turned to liquid as he sank to the floor, his head falling on the down and straw mattress. He wasn't sure how long he was there before he heard Elsbeth calling.

"Is everything all right?" Elsbeth appeared at the door and bent over.

"Dear God, not Peter," Elsbeth cried, taking Andreas's hand as he wept.

Elsbeth rubbed Andreas's back, but he did not feel her as he waded into a river of grief. Darkness enveloped him, wrapping him in arms of numbness. He vaguely noted the striking of the hours and the shifting of shadows and light as the day progressed. At some point, Elsbeth's hand lifted off his back, and he heard her take a chair by the bed. He fought the overpowering nausea that clutched at him, pulling him deeper into grief.

Andreas drifted into his memories of Peter and stayed there until he became aware that St. Lambert's bells were tolling the ninth hour. He stirred, opening his reddened eyes to look at Elsbeth. "Why? I . . . why Peter?"

Elsbeth sat silently, her watery eyes offering no answers.

Andreas groaned as he clutched his knees.

Moving to his side, Elsbeth rested his head on her shoulders.

Closing Peter's eyes with his fingers, Andreas stood and drew the blanket off his body. "We should bury him out back, beside his garden. This place has been his life," he said. "We should do it quickly before anyone hears about this and comes to scavenge."

Elsbeth suddenly vomited a bit onto the floor. "Oh . . . sorry . . . it was just the thought."

"I'll carry him downstairs," Andreas volunteered. "Maybe you should rest while I dig."

"I'll help. Give me a minute to collect myself."

Andreas bent down to put Peter over his shoulder when he noticed that Peter's wrists looked chafed and swollen. "Elsbeth, look at this." Andreas pointed to the skin around the wrists. "Why does he have these marks?"

"What marks?"

"See how much redder his hands are on the outside of his wrists?"

Elsbeth leaned in for a better look.

Andreas examined Peter closer. "How'd he get this bruise on his cheek?"

"Perhaps he fell and then made it to the bed," Elsbeth offered, before the bells rang.

"Goddamn!" Andreas reared back and shouted. "Not now!"

"We'll bury Peter when we get back. I'm worried about being missed. I don't want anyone poking around here today."

Andreas placed the blanket back over Peter's body, covered his face, and held Elsbeth for a minute. "It's just us now," he sighed, wiping the tips of his fingers across his eyes.

"We'll be back shortly. Then we can take care of Peter." Elsbeth steered Andreas from the room and out into the street.

They stumbled along with the emaciated masses heading toward assembly, a desiccated corpse with many limbs, trudging toward the grave. The pale, worn bodies drifting toward Cathedral Hill bore vacant stares. Leather-like skin hung off them in tiny wrinkles. Looking neither left nor right, people plodded forward, their heads hung down toward distended bellies. Andreas and Elsbeth arrived at Cathedral Square just as the king and his court entered.

"Citizens of Zion, your king!" the guard yelled.

Bockelson strode toward the center of the crowd. He alone among them looked healthy and well fed. Everyone else had acquired the same pallid greyness of a cold February morning sky. Bockelson paced in front of a woman kneeling on the stones.

Elsbeth pulled on Andreas's arm. "It's Wandscheer."

"What's she doing here?" Andreas wondered.

"I'm surprised she's lasted this long," Elsbeth said. "Divara hated her accused her of trying to replace her for Bockelson's affections."

Elizabeth Wandscheer was hunched on all fours, a greasy mess of hair covering her face. She tried to blow it out of her eyes, but it kept falling back.

"Zion!" Bockelson shouted. "Our sister has been disobedient to her king. I've long been patient, but today we put her fate in front of you."

"Don't listen to him! He's a fraud!" Wandscheer shrieked. "He seeks out debauchery the way a pig loves slop. You're running out of chances to stop him! He's killing you! We'll all die if you don't do something. Someone, kill him, kill him now and let's be free!"

"Do you see? Do you see what I have put up with?" Bockelson yowled. He stormed over to her, grabbed her hair, and jerked her head back, pulling her up on her knees. "I'm your king. I will not be disrespected."

"You disrespect all of us, *Your Majesty*." Her tone was venomous. "You make our daughters whores, and our sons murderers." Wandscheer turned directly to Knipperdolling. "You can do something about this!"

"You see? You hear? Is there any doubt why this woman kneels before us in judgment?" Bockelson's agitation grew as he circled Wandscheer. "She drives me to madness!" He thrust his torso down toward her.

"Then you did not have far to go!" she jeered. "Beware of this viper you've let into your midst. I most likely die today, but death is preferable to life with him. Kill him now before he kills you!"

Small knots of people formed, glancing at Bockelson. He reached over to Knipperdolling and grabbed his sword. He swung it over his head, holding it high above him, lips pulling away from his teeth, a feral intensity shining through his eyes. Lifting on his toes, he brought the full weight of his body down with the sword as it sliced through Wandscheer's neck. The blow was so savage, Wandscheer's head flew off quickly, but her body remained upright for a second before sliding to the ground. The crowd, a few yards away from Wandscheer's body, stared mutely where her head lay, blood leaking into the crevices of the street, and turned their apathy to the king.

Bockelson exploded, cursing and stomping on her body. "Do you see what you made me do? Goddamn witch, do you see what you made me do?" When Bockelson tired of kicking her, he slowly danced around her body, humming. He motioned to Divara, imploring her with his hand to leave the other queens and join him. Divara passed her daughter to her servant and hastened out to take Bockelson's hand.

"Dear God." Elsbeth's hand on Andreas's arm turned pale. "Look."

Andreas followed Elsbeth's prompting. Despite her solemn look, there was a hint of a smile on Divara's face as she stood over Wandscheer. His arm grew sore from Elsbeth's grasp.

"She's happy she won," Elsbeth whispered.

A softly sung *Alleluia* arose from Bockelson. He and Divara both invited the other wives to come and join them. The cowed women shuffled over toward the corpse and slowly grasped hands, forming a circle around Wandscheer. Bockelson's queens exchanged furtive glimpses, their eyes darting back and forth as they danced around Wandscheer's body.

Bockelson sang as Divara picked up the harmony.

"Who is this woman?" Elsbeth whispered.

"The woman she's been all along," Andreas said. "The mask slips sometimes, but you knew what she was capable of."

"I had hoped I was wrong." Elsbeth watched the *danse macabre*. "If I didn't believe in hell before, I do now."

Slowly, people shuffled away, until only a few witnesses remained. Tears welled up in Andreas. It was Peter he mourned, not Wandscheer, but he was mindful that tears can lead to much suffering. He grabbed Elsbeth's arm. "Let the dead bury the dead. We have work to do."

Elsbeth nodded, but then she pointed to Ulrich heading toward them.

"My God, that was horrific," Ulrich said.

"Yes, it was," Elsbeth replied, walking away with Andreas, but Ulrich matched their pace.

"I noticed that Peter was not here. Is he well?"

Andreas stopped and glared at Ulrich. Anger and grief churned in him, clouding his judgment. He wanted to lash out at something. He thought about the marks on Peter's wrist as he searched Ulrich's eyes. *Are you capable of this? Is this taunting I see?* Andreas shook his head, trying to break the spell.

"Ulrich, why don't you come with us and say hello yourself?" Andreas heard the loathing in his voice and fought back the urge to wrap his hands around Ulrich's throat.

"Maybe later. I have some work to do." He motioned toward Wandscheer's lifeless body. "Perhaps I'll come by this evening." He bowed and returned to Bockelson's group as Andreas watched him intently.

"You don't think . . . ?" Elsbeth's eyes narrowed.

"Hard to know what to think anymore."

"Come on, Andreas." Elsbeth pulled Andreas along. "We need to go tend to Peter."

52

June 23

UBIQUITOUS SUMMER STORMS ROILED the countryside with lightning strikes, blanketing the sky with grey clouds thicker than sun could penetrate. A streak of lighting and clap of thunder simultaneously lit up the room and rattled the walls of Peter's lantern-lit office as Andreas and Elsbeth sat, going through his papers.

"God, that gives me dread," Andreas said.

"Me, too. It reminds me of cannon fire." Elsbeth studied one of Peter's letters. They had spent the last several days pouring over his journals, records, writings, and letters.

"What are you looking for, exactly?"

"I don't know, clues about his life?" Andreas leafed through Peter's journal. "Maybe I'm just trying to hang onto him a bit longer. I still can't reconcile things in my mind." Andreas stopped and read for a minute. "He was murdered, I'm sure of it."

"We've been going through these papers for days. What kind of evidence are you looking for?" Elsbeth stood up and put her hand on Andreas's shoulder. "If we don't do something soon, I'm afraid we're not far behind him." Her exhausted face was pale and shallow, thinned almost beyond recognition; life itself was draining from her eyes.

Andreas gently squeezed Elsbeth's hand. "Agreed. No one's in charge and the king and his court stay out of sight, hiding in their palace. Perhaps the guards won't stop us if we try to leave. We can go to the tunnel at St. Mary's Gate tomorrow morning before the sun comes up. If there're no guards, we'll sneak out that way."

"Don't you think everyone would be flying out of those tunnels if they weren't guarded?

"Do you have another plan?"

Elsbeth's face clenched in concentration. She frowned and shook her head.

"We don't have anything to lose at this point. Maybe we'll get lucky." Andreas brushed her cheek with the back of his hand.

"Perhaps, but if there are guards, we'll not get out, unless we're prepared to take action. If we're going to try tomorrow, I've got to rest." Elsbeth stood, wobbled, and grabbed the back of a chair to steady herself. "Coming?"

"I'll be there in a minute. I found something I want to take a closer look at."

Andreas turned his attention back to the desk as Elsbeth closed the door behind her. He thought about all the debates he had with Peter in this office. Something inside him had changed with each conversation. It was hard to grasp at first, but he always seemed lighter, less burdened after one of their meetings. One day, he realized that he no longer woke up in a cold sweat, looking down at his hand expecting to find a poker. All those visits had been healing him and he never even realized it.

Peter said to him once that his vocation, the reason he became an Augustinian, was the care of souls. He wasn't interested in power or influence like other orders. He only wanted to heal people, body and soul. Andreas leaned back. *You were a damn fine healer, my friend.* Picking up Peter's journal, he opened again to the last entry:

> *June 11, 1535, Anno Domini*
>
> *Everything in this world is penultimate, but we make it ultimate. We stand at the door of grace with the gift of every breath, but we waste this gift as we drive the stake of the penultimate into the ultimate. Acts of faith now lead to the death. Demonic alchemy. Perhaps the day will come when we see that all that which divides us is nothing compared to the love that calls us to one another. The madness surrounding me concerns power, not love. The Lord Himself was not immune from destruction by these forces. He warned about them. Everyone falls into the temptations of power. Is this true? Even if there is nothing left after this life, I will serve love rather than hate. I'm scared. I don't know how much longer I have, but I am grateful for Andreas. He has traveled far since he returned home. The blessing of Elsbeth has been no*

small thing. She has been as much a part of his healing as I have.
They are all I have left. Keep them when I am gone.

Andreas wiped his eyes, tore the page out, folded it, and put it into his tunic pocket. He thought about what tomorrow would bring, whether this was his last night on earth, the losses he had known. How was he going to protect what was left? Andreas heaved a breath and went to join Elsbeth, knowing he would not be able to sleep.

53

June 24

CANNON BOOMS JERKED ANDREAS out of a deep sleep. Elsbeth sprang up beside him, confused.

"That was not thunder." Andreas leapt out of bed. Elsbeth flopped back onto the mattress. "It came from inside the city."

"What now?" Elsbeth struggled up.

"Let's stick to our original plan and get to St. Mary's tunnel." Andreas stuffed his feet into his boots. "If the armies have broken through, it's our only chance to survive."

"Can't we stay here and hide?"

"If they're attacking and succeed, they'll kill us." Andreas threw Elsbeth her clothes. "We need to go, dear. Now!"

Groaning, Elsbeth slipped her dress on, secured the apron, and put on her boots. She grabbed Andreas and pressed up against him. "No matter what happens, I love you." The wetness of her eyes dampened his shirt and vest.

"I love you, too, but we're going to find a way through this." Andreas held her tighter before letting her go.

They stepped outside and immediately encountered dozens of armed men running toward the city center.

"What's this?" Andreas called out.

"Von Waldeck's bastards have broken through."

"This way." Andreas pointed to the ring road. "We must avoid the marketplace. If this is an attack, our only chance rests on not getting caught in the crossfire."

Elsbeth nodded, and they ran toward the western side of town. Gunfire and shouting echoed from Cathedral Hill, and women's howling voices sounded from the wall's promenade. Everyone they met on the street grasped weapons, dashing toward the market.

"We need to hurry." Andreas grabbed Elsbeth's hand and pulled her toward St. Mary's Gate, where the screaming of frenzied women competed with pealing church bells and cannon fire.

"God, they sound like the shrieking of the damned," Andreas said, running faster.

"That's because they are." Elsbeth struggled to keep up.

Surrounded by chaos, Andreas questioned his choices. Maybe Elsbeth had been right. They should have hidden in the root cellar at the monastery. There would be no reason for anyone to look there. They could explain themselves later. Lost in his thoughts, he almost didn't register that they had reached St. Mary's Gate.

"Shh," he cautioned, positioning them against the wall of a building across from the gate. "Can you see anyone?"

They searched up and down the street, listening to the shouts coming from St. Giles's Gate.

"To Waldeck! To Waldeck! Münster is ours! Charge! Charge! Hurry! Hurry!"

A mixture of fear and relief surged through Andreas as he watched the soldiers coming into the city. As the invaders approached the sides of the buildings, chairs, warming bricks, pots, pans, stones, and numerous knives rained down on them from the windows above.

"They've broken through, Andreas. It's done!" Elsbeth sobbed, grasping his hand.

It was the last thing Andreas heard before he fell to the ground, unconscious.

Elsbeth screamed as Ulrich Schlatter's club headed for her.

❋ ❋

Andreas opened his eyes to a throbbing head, his cheek resting on rough stone. He couldn't remember why his face was on the street. Gingerly, he sat up. "Elsbeth!" Silence. Staggering to his feet, he tried to work it out. The last thing he remembered was checking for guards at St. Mary's. Elsbeth! Swiveling in a circle, he saw she wasn't there. Where was she?

Panic gripped Andreas as he fought back horrible thoughts. Ulrich! Who else? Why?

Noticing the open door of the guard tower, Andreas ran across the street. The tunnel! The more he thought about it, Ulrich was the only option that made sense. If he were wrong, he'd never see Elsbeth again; if he were right, it might already be too late. He burst into the tower room. Two guards lay dead on the floor, a bloodied sword beside them. The door to the tunnel was open. Ulrich was taking her out of the city! That had to be it. He shook the cobwebs from his head and searched for a torch, but there was none. He was going to have to search the tunnel in darkness. His mouth went dry.

Andreas felt his way down the circular stairs to the tunnel floor. His throat constricted the darker it became, as if fingers were closing their grip around his neck. He couldn't see a thing, so he put his hands on the damp wall, feeling the dirt, stone, and timber, his legs growing heavier with each step. Months ago, when he was in the tunnel, he was overcome by the feeling that he was suffocating. Jost had to carry him out just so he could breathe. He didn't have that luxury now. If Ulrich had taken Elsbeth and was trying to escape, he could not let his fear stop him.

The air was cold and musty, smelling of mold and death, but the dank darkness helped Andreas's mind clear. Nevertheless, his feet grew sodden, sloshing through the puddles of the black passageway. The more he scuttled along, the less hopeful he became. *What if I'm wrong?* His thoughts paralyzed him. *Give up. This is hopeless. They're already gone.* Resisting the overwhelming urge to turn around, Andreas stopped and listened for a sound, anything to give him some hope. *Wait! Was that a noise ahead?*

"Elsbeth!" he yelled. Standing still, breathless, he waited for a noise, a light, anything that would give him hope. *Was that Elsbeth?*

He moved forward, desperate, continually feeling the timbers on either side of him to guide his footing. He slipped and fell onto the muddy floor, his back soaking in the mud. Getting up, he was disoriented, confused by the absolute darkness. He was sure he heard her voice. Turning in the direction of it, he hurried on, terrified that he would be too late.

"Elsbeth!" he shouted. No reply. Seeing a dim glow ahead, he plunged on toward the light. He no longer cared if he lived or died. He only wanted to find Elsbeth.

Drawing closer to the light, he slowed down, wary. Whatever it was up ahead had stopped moving. The burst of hope that accompanied the light was crushed when he saw Elsbeth's prone, still body splayed in the wet mud of the tunnel floor.

"No!" Andreas cried, sliding to his knees, reaching for her. A torch rested on the side of the tunnel wall, illuminating her face, which was unresponsive to his cries. His hand was inches from her when a sharp pain exploded in his spine.

"God, you never learn," Ulrich grunted as he drew his club back again.

Though the first blow stunned him, Andreas moved quickly, raising his arm to deflect the next strike. Ulrich crouched over him as Andreas tried to stand up on the slick floor. Ulrich swung again, his club smashing into Andreas's leg, dropping him back to the ground.

"Goddamn—" Andreas yelled as he flailed, trying to hit Ulrich somewhere, anywhere, but Ulrich had all the leverage and Andreas could only scuttle away. Ulrich kept pounding his club against Andreas's legs in short strokes, making it hard for him to get up.

"Christ, Wagner, give up already. Your bitch is dead, and you'll soon join her. Accept your fate and go like a good boy."

"Go to hell!" Andreas staggered to his feet and rushed Ulrich, throwing him against the wall. Ulrich clubbed Andreas in the back and side, while Andreas swung wildly. The effort of trying to hit Ulrich caused Andreas to slip again on the muddy floor. Ulrich was on him in seconds, beating him relentlessly.

"It didn't have to be like this," Ulrich railed, bringing the club down on Andreas's exposed pelvis. Andreas screamed in pain and writhed away. "It'll all be over soon, Wagner, and then you can join Peter and your whore." Ulrich grabbed Andreas's feet and pulled him back toward the torch. "You should've been my friend like I wanted. I reward loyalty."

Andreas's hands frantically searched for anything he could hold onto to avoid being dragged back to where Ulrich would have more room to maneuver. His strength drained away. *She's gone. Maybe I should give up.* His eyes flitted to Elsbeth, but her body was not there. *Where'd she go? Alive!* Renewed, Andreas struggled to free himself, kicking Ulrich in the groin. Ulrich yelped with pain and reeled back.

"Why can't you just die like a good boy?"

"Bastard!" Andreas cried, as Ulrich rose as high as he could to bring the club down, but Andreas dodged the blow and staggered to his feet, throwing his body into Ulrich, who lost his club. Ulrich struck back with his fists, but Andreas kept pushing him, hoping not to pass out.

"It's over," Ulrich snarled. "Die with some dignity, you bast—"

Andreas heaved harder, pressing Ulrich against the door that swung closed on the other side.

"Goddamn! Goddamn!" Ulrich howled.

Andreas knew Ulrich would not be prepared for the spikes slamming into his back and plunging into his body. Ulrich had never worked down here, so he didn't know that iron doors fashioned with spikes had been placed to slow attackers should they discover the tunnels. Preoccupied, Ulrich did not see Elsbeth standing on the other side of the door, waiting for Andreas to push him closer before she slammed it against Ulrich's body.

Rendered immobile on the grid of stakes penetrating his back, Ulrich let loose a wail that filled the tunnel. Elsbeth stood on the smooth side of the door, holding it tight, making it impossible to pull away as Andreas held Ulrich firmly by the shoulders.

Caught hanging between Elsbeth and Andreas, Ulrich yowled in fury. "You bitch! Whore! Who do you think you are?"

"It's no bitch who takes your life," Elsbeth wheezed as Ulrich's body jerked in agony.

They held him until the screaming turned into whimpers. He labored to pull away, but with each thrashing of his body, his resistance grew weaker. Finally, he stopped wiggling and hung limply, helpless as an animal on a butcher's hook.

Elsbeth let go, slipped around to Andreas's side, and picked up the torch, holding it to Ulrich. "For Peter, you sack of shit." Elsbeth spit in Ulrich's face.

Ulrich stared back at them, blood running from his mouth. "You still serve me."

"We will never serve you," Elsbeth shot back.

"But you do, or at least my mistress. We all serve her now. Violence has joined us together. The whore takes us all in the end," Ulrich gurgled, choking on his blood.

"Perhaps," Andreas said, his face inches from Ulrich's, "but today we're the ones who survive."

Ulrich's eyes glazed over as his mouth twisted into a grotesque grin. "For now." His voice went silent as he slumped on the spikes.

Andreas and Elsbeth crouched down, gasping.

Muddy sweat dripped from Elsbeth; her face was coated with a brown sheen. "After he knocked you out, he clubbed me. When I woke up, he was dragging me through the tunnel, but then he hit me again when he heard you calling my name."

"How did you know about the door?" Andreas staggered to his feet and pulled Elsbeth up.

"I saw it when I came to." Elsbeth wept. "What do we do now?"

"We have to go forward, though death may be at the end of the tunnel." Andreas cupped Elsbeth's face in his hand.

"Whatever it is, at least we'll be free today—one way or the other." Elsbeth stroked the back of Andreas's head.

Heaving a deep breath, Andreas picked up the rapidly fading torch, grabbed Elsbeth's hand, and they slowly made their way through the tunnel to the exit beyond the walls.

54

June 26

FRANZ VON WALDECK'S COACH rumbled through St. Giles's Gate, accompanied by all the pageantry a Prince-Bishop commanded. Companies of soldiers in their dress uniforms trotted alongside as the carriage bumped and shook its way through the streets. Von Waldeck contemplated his city. The jewel of Westphalia was desolate—its proud towers demolished, its beautiful buildings pockmarked with shells and bullets, and its once firm streets now rugged from lack of stones. The beautiful linden and oak trees he loved to sit under as a boy were gone. Little remained of his precious home, and the desolation in his heart matched what his eyes beheld. He pressed his handkerchief close to his nose, trying to block out the stench of corpses and mottled blood staining the streets.

He turned his attention to the report of his generals. The slaughter must have been awful. More than a thousand traitors shot, stabbed, and slain; hundreds more were severely wounded. Von Waldeck glanced outside his carriage at the ambling, shuffling shadows of human beings meandering through the streets. One of them gazed back at him, holding up his hand, pleading for food. Von Waldeck sighed. *What a goddamn waste. How could people be so crazy as to pull the world down upon their own heads?* His carriage neared the cathedral; his generals, Steding and von Dhaun, stood at attention, waiting.

The horses pulled to a stop, and von Waldeck maneuvered himself out of the coach to greet his commanders. In his mind, he still looked the robust and vigorous man who first took the crown of Prince-Bishop, but his girth now distended the waistcoat and pants that used to fit him in younger days. His straggly beard failed to hide his jowly chin, and the black hair falling from his head could not disguise his receding hairline. His thick fingers grabbed the coach as he let himself down and maneuvered to face his commanders.

"Well done, gentlemen." Von Waldeck coughed, dabbing his handkerchief at his mouth. "You'll be rewarded for your service."

"There are also these, Your Eminence." Steding pointed to the box beside him.

Von Waldeck eyed the massive chest full of gold jewelry and coins. He reached in and pulled out a coin with Bockelson's image on it. "Hmmm," he murmured, turning the coin over and over in his hand. "And Tilbeck? Rothmann? Did you find them?"

"Tilbeck's dead, Your Eminence," Steding said. "But we haven't located Rothmann yet. The last anyone remembers seeing him was the day we took the city. We never found his body, even on our house-to-house searches. I'm sure it's only a matter of time, though. It would've been impossible for him to escape."

"I want him, Steding. Make sure your men leave no door unopened, no closet undisturbed, no cellar untouched. I want him most of all."

"Yes, Your Eminence."

"And Knipperdolling," von Waldeck asked. "Where is he?"

"In prison. We caught him hiding on the top floor of some woman's house. She was hiding him there until he could escape, but when we announced what was going to happen to anyone caught hiding fugitives, she gave him up promptly," von Dhaun said.

"And the mad Dutchman? Where might he be?"

"In Rosenthal prison." Steding grinned. "Would you like to see him?"

"Oh yes, very much."

Moments later, the three of them were standing in Bockelson's cell. Von Waldeck examined the pitiful creature in front of him. Bockelson was dressed in a tattered and filthy red cape, a white blouse, and dirty yellow pants with red-and-yellow striped hose. His face was swollen and discolored from beatings, and his hands hung down in front of him, tied to chains.

Clutching his handkerchief closer to his nose, von Waldeck circled Bockelson, scrutinizing him from every angle. *This man is a fraud, a rat from the sewer.* Under the weight of inspection, Bockelson raised himself to his fullest height. Von Waldeck could not see how this wretched creature had managed to bankrupt him and make him the laughingstock of the empire. How had this *thing* held his forces at bay for so long? He examined Bockelson, hoping to find something, anything, that would indicate that this madman was worth the trouble.

"And are *you* a king?" von Waldeck sneered.

"And are *you* a bishop?" Bockelson retorted.

"You've cost me dearly."

"You cost yourself," Bockelson parried. "You could've left us alone. We were no threat to you."

"But you were. If we had let you have your way, the entire empire would've crumbled. We couldn't have that."

"We did you no harm," Bockelson insisted, glaring at von Waldeck.

"You did!" von Waldeck shouted, pushing his face as close to Bockelson as he could before the stench overcame him. "You took what did not belong to you. You tried to take Münster. That belongs to us."

"All things belong to God—Zion, even your precious empire," Bockelson countered. "When the world persecuted us, it gave up its claim to our allegiance. If you had left us alone, there would've been no need for us to defend ourselves."

"But you left the faith!" Von Waldeck's face pressed closer, too angry to care about the stench any longer. "We don't have the luxury of indulging your fantasies. Barbarossa and his pirate armies ravage the Mediterranean; Suleiman and the Turks keep lapping up to the gates of Vienna like waves of the ocean churning up the shoreline. Charles and Francis conspire to tear each other to pieces. Luther and his minions rip apart the world. And all the while that goat sitting on the throne in England threatens God's own order, our Holy Mother Church. You with your fanatics, you would destroy the Holy Roman Empire with your . . . your . . . damnable heresies."

"It is *not* holy. Not as long as it hunts down the servants of Christ. You left us no choice but to defend ourselves. We only wanted to practice our faith and protect the brethren." Bockelson turned his back on von Waldeck.

"You won't manipulate me, Bockelson. I'll have my satisfaction. *I* will be the hero in this story, *not* you. Those who value order over anarchy will remember *me*, not you. The order that God demands must be respected. Even as we speak, your kind are trying to distance themselves from you."

Bockelson looked over this shoulder at von Waldeck. "What are you talking about?"

"They have a new leader, Menno Simons. He's telling his followers to put away violence and follow the way of peace. We'll be vigilant anyway, though, in case the Mennonites rise up against their masters. I can promise you that."

"Until you stop killing the faithful, you'll suffer God's judgment."

"Ah, yes, the killing of the faithful. Well, consider how many you killed. How many did you lead to an unnecessary death?"

"But I was the king, by God's design—"

"You were deluded. Mad!" Von Waldeck bellowed. "You arrogated for yourself the power of life and death."

"I made you tremble, though," Bockelson taunted. "I made them all tremble. How many of those trying to make their way here did you and your kind kill? Why shouldn't we have the same powers you do?"

"Because we have the armies."

"I had one, too. It would have been larger without your meddling."

"Which is precisely why we acted, you idiot!" Von Waldeck's hand drew to his sword. "All those thousands who tried to make their way here to join your folly? Their blood is on your hands. There's nothing worse than a true believer with an army."

Bockelson looked at the ground for a minute and then raised his head, his tone less testy. "But we did have true faith, not that superstitious garbage the Antichrist of Rome spews."

"It doesn't matter. Did your faith make you any different than that which you hated?" Von Waldeck peered down at Bockelson. "I suppose in the end we at least understand your choosing violence. What we don't understand are those who don't fight back . . . what they're after, I just don't know."

"So, do I die today?"

"Oh, God no." Von Waldeck flashed a wry grin. "I've earned the pleasure of watching you suffer the way you tormented me."

"I could yet be of some help to you." Bockelson raised his chained hands and moved the iron collar around to relieve the sores on his neck.

"And how would you be able to help me?"

"You need money. Why not put me in a cage and parade me around your domain as an example of what happens to those who cross you? I'll be your prize pet. You could charge people to come and see me. You would make more money off me than you could from church offerings or new land taxes. Everyone will want to see the monster of Münster. Throw the rest of us in cages and put on a show. It can't fail."

Von Waldeck gawked at his prisoner. "You mock me. You can't be serious?"

"You pay back your creditors and restore your good name, all the while watching me suffer."

"Have you lost your mind? You're not negotiating your life with me. Have you no shame?"

"Do you?"

"Do I what?"

"Have any shame?"

Von Waldeck stormed away, resisting the urge to pummel Bockelson. Pacing for a few seconds, he stopped. "I've no intention of making you my show, but I do want to thank you."

"For what?" Bockelson's face clenched in confusion.

"For the idea about the cages. I like that one. Very much."

"What?"

Leaving the cell, von Waldeck smiled, pleased with the puzzled look on Bockelson's face.

55

January 22, 1536

BLOOD. SCREAMS. DARKNESS. DRIFTING down into the murkiness, Bernard Knipperdolling slumped against the iron spikes on the inside of his collar, hoping they would puncture his neck and release him from terror's grasp. But just when he thought death's merciful release was at hand, he felt himself being pulled away from his desired oblivion by two men, one on either side, who grabbed his shoulders and hoisted him up.

When Bockelson started screaming, Knipperdolling had let his weight go, hoping that he could kill himself before the hooded man with the tongs turned his attention to him. Now, as his eyes fluttered open, everything he'd tried to escape confronted him—the pitiless crowds, Bockelson's screams, and the pole he was chained to. He looked over at Bernard Krechting, the brother of Bockelson's chancellor, already dead and limp in his collar. Lucky bastard.

Knipperdolling shivered as warm piss streamed down his leg. Standing before him were those who had been exiled from Münster and had filtered back, reclaiming what was theirs. The last six months had been occupied with repairing the damage to their homes and fields. Trees had been planted, holes patched, and souls mended. Husbands and wives were reunited, though there were many widows who still grieved their losses. Münster was shaky, but it was healing. The executions were meant to bring a sense of relief—the casting out of demons.

Those exiled of two years ago stood below Knipperdolling, their faces cold masks of apathy. Their mute indifference stung him worse than their fury would have. No mercy, no understanding that he had tried his best to help those less fortunate. He had only wanted to give the city its freedom, protect it from the powerful taking what they wanted and throwing scraps back to the mob. Or, at least, that was what he had thought he was doing. Now, he wasn't so sure.

When had the demon entered him? Was it when von Waldeck's predecessor cuffed him to an iron boot? The day he realized he enjoyed the power of the sword? When had that moment come where he ceased to be human and became something more elemental, more primal in his desire to rule others? How many lines had he crossed before he ended up here? Did the demon enter him when Bockelson crossed his threshold? He let that snake into his house, offered him his daughter. All brought to ruin. "Clara! Oh, God, please forgive me, Clara!" Knipperdolling lifted his head and wailed, a howling born of remorse, but when his eyes fell back on the crowds in front of him, they stood indifferent to his spasm of suffering confession.

Memories of his life flowed through him: running through the streets, watching the mummers perform in the market, his first drink, his first woman. Tears mingled with the blood on his neck. This was all his fault. He could have broken the chain of fear that wrapped around him when Matthys showed up. He should have ignored Bockelson when he lured him to the brothels and bathhouses. How could he have trusted a goddamned Dutchman?

Knipperdolling glanced at Franz von Waldeck sitting on his second-floor balcony, adorned in leather-and-steel breastplate over military garb with a helmet in his hands and a thick velvet purple cape draped over his shoulders to keep out the cold wind that swept through the streets. Knipperdolling kept his eyes on von Waldeck to see if he would acknowledge his suffering, but the Prince-Bishop only had eyes for Bockelson.

It was then that Knipperdolling became aware of how quiet it had grown. Bockelson wasn't screaming anymore. Cold sweat beaded up on Knipperdolling as he watched the executioner slipping and sliding across the bloody platform to get to him. His sobbing turned to whimpering. No more time.

His mind raced back to his six months in the iron boot. What humiliation. That wound fed the spirit of revenge. He could have starved it, but he vowed he would make them pay—make sure that no one had power over him again. Revenge was the path that led him to this morning, to the executioner beside him, glowing hot tongs in his hand.

Clara, forgive your papa. Münster, forgive your son. God, forgive me. Knipperdolling searched the market once more, hoping for understanding. Beyond the sea of suffering faces, he took in City Hall, St. Lambert's, his beautiful home. Suddenly, everyone around him disappeared and he was a child, running through the market stalls, playing games of hide and seek.

❀❀

It had to be done. It was necessary to send the message. No one stands against empire and Church and gets away with it. Order demands its sacrifices. The cold morning fog had been miserable, settling in on those gathered to bid their deceivers farewell. When the cart first rolled into the marketplace, Franz von Waldeck took pleasure in the confused and terrified looks of his enemies. Putting Knipperdolling and Bockelson in the same cart, their hooding eyes regarding one another with contempt, seemed fair justice. Von Waldeck only wished it had been Bernard Rothmann, not Bernard Krechting, who served as the appetizer before the main course. Von Waldeck eagerly watched as Knipperdolling searched the crowds, looking for compassion. No one met his desperate gaze with so much as a smile.

It had taken three hours to complete; each man tortured for one hour, as the law required. The screams were hard to take at first, but it was surprising how quickly one became used to it. Their bodies had been put in the three cages after they were executed. Von Waldeck thought Bockelson was brilliant for suggesting them. He would have thrown their bodies in a shallow grave; he just didn't have the imagination for something so creative. Those cages were going to serve as a warning beacon for ages to come. This is what happens when you forget your place; this is your fate if you rebel.

The cages floated in the air as pulleys hoisted them to the steeple of St. Lambert's. Von Waldeck followed their ascension. There was almost a grace about the way they floated up, even though weighted down with corpses. He pulled his ermine-trimmed collar tighter around his neck as the throngs below huddled in silence while the cages were secured to the steeple of St. Lambert's. The only Münster tower spared from iconoclastic fury now held the cages of the counterfeit king and his accomplices. That which they tried to destroy would be their final resting place. Von Waldeck sucked in the irony. His eyes went from St. Lambert's to City Hall. He would run things now. Münster had lost its freedom. He regarded the cages, still swinging slightly. *Don't cross us, or we'll take our pound of flesh, piece by bloody piece.*

56

Erfurt, May 29

THEY CAME MOSTLY WHEN she slept, but sometimes even in her waking hours. Some faces smiled, others contorted in agony. They wore the visages of those connected to her: her mother, her father, childhood friends gathered by the river, Ingrid, Rachel, Ursula, Ida, even Andreas—all the souls who'd become woven into her life. When they appeared, she tried to honor each one, to allow them all a voice, but it was excruciating. Their tales were too painful. Ulrich's visitations were the ones she dreaded the most. When he troubled her dreams, Elsbeth heard her own screams and jerked out of sleep gasping, feeling as if she had been drowning. Even with her new life firmly in place, the old one still haunted her. The scars remained raw, hard to heal. There was a place inside her that was so torn she feared it could never be repaired.

When she first heard about Divara's execution, darkness settled deep into her for weeks. She wasn't sure why. Was it guilt or grief? She wondered if Divara's daughter were alive. The girl would need a home, but Elsbeth was not inclined to be of any help. Sometimes it felt as if Divara herself had a hand on some invisible place inside of her, pulling her down into the void. No one could save the child or the mother.

She and Andreas had barely been able to save themselves, slipping out of the tunnels, past the blockhouses. All the soldiers had rushed for the city, and no one remained to stop them as they fled. It had almost been a year since they reached Erfurt, and Andreas's friends had helped him start a woodworking shop. Elsbeth worked with some of the wise women, learning their craft. She studied as much for her own healing as for those who would come later. She knew she had to get better, stronger. Her son was going to need her.

Reaching down into the sack tied to her chest, Elsbeth stroked his head, laughing as he grinned at her. He would know what normal was if she had anything to say about it. She would not offer him up as a sacrifice to a pitiless God. She prayed he would not be swept away by the rivers of madness that had taken so many others in her life. There were powers in the world stronger than her, but she would fight and claw them away from her son with her last breath. Elsbeth's pulse quickened as her body tensed. Calming herself, she remembered a comment that Peter had once made. She couldn't recall what it was they had been talking about, but he had mentioned something about heaven being found in every small, seemingly insignificant moment of life. *The exquisite beauty of the mundane.* When her son's tiny fingers grabbed onto hers, she knew exactly what he was talking about. Her son's touch contained worlds of healing.

Andreas interrupted her thoughts when he entered the kitchen, his face registering delight that she had prepared some of his favorite Thüringian sausage along with bread, cheese, and ale.

"Someone in the shop today reported a rumor that Rothmann was seen in Denmark." Andreas reached for his baby boy.

"Peter, say hello to Papa," Elsbeth cooed. She no longer instinctively flinched at Rothmann's name, no longer cared about what had happened to him, whether he died in Münster or not. It had been a long time since he had visited her dreams.

Elsbeth watched Andreas take their son out of his sack, cradle him in his arms, and walk outside into the late May sunshine. He sat down on a bench and propped the boy on his knee, gently bouncing him and singing a song. The baby laughed with delight.

Elsbeth came outside and sat next to them, resting her head on Andreas's shoulder. They were finding their way to one another a bit each day, repairing the damage done in Münster. Enjoying the majestic sight of Erfurt's cathedrals, smelling the wild honeysuckle growing outside, and feeling the sun on her skin, Elsbeth sensed somewhere deep inside her a place opening, an appreciation for how each minute of life, good or bad, carried within it an infinite possibility of grace. *This is how God comes to us—not in fire or flood, but through love.* Love was the parable of God. Love had saved her. It was love that helped her forgive, encouraged her to reconcile with all those faces who appeared to her, enabled her to know forgiveness. The love of Andreas, of her mother, of Peter, of her friends, of her cherished son—all were gifts of healing given to her in the midst of darkness. She prayed she would become a gift as well, a healer.

Andreas put his arm around Elsbeth's shoulders and pulled her close to him. He kissed her forehead and stroked her arm. It may have seemed a small and insignificant gesture compared with the grand designs of Church and empire, but for her, this day, it was enough.

HISTORICAL NOTES

WE KNOW THE PAST as contested interpretations and Münster lends itself to a host of narratives. What were the forces that coalesced around the insurrection? Was it religiously motivated? Driven more by class interests, or boiling over of long pent-up frustrations with the power of empire to determine the lives of its citizens? Most likely, several factors went into the events that pulled people to Münster, but certainly religious motivation played the largest role, though it was not as much the religion of the theologians as it was popular religion that influenced what happened in Münster.

One of the most interesting forces in popular religion of the sixteenth century was expectation of Christ's return. The apocalyptic images motivating people did not come from theologians or church authorities, as much as they came from artists like Albrecht Dürer or church art inside cathedrals. Images of a world populated by devils, angels, and the end of days shaped the imagination of millions of people in the sixteenth century and continue to do so. This was a huge aspect of the Münster insurrection, but it was not the only one.

By the time Bartholomew Boekbinder and William de Kuyper, the two Dutch prophets sent by Jan Matthys, arrived in Münster on the eve of Epiphany in 1534, most of the pieces were in place for the debacle to come. The city was riven by different factions, in part driven by Bernard Rothmann and his followers' desire to the see the Word of God prevail over its foes, but also by months of social ferment among various power centers in the city. Münster was not immune from the disruptions that were shaking the Holy Roman Empire. This, unrest had been over a decade in the making.

Starting with Luther's preposterous performance at the Diet of Worms in 1521, where he appealed to individual conscience over centuries of accepted authority, through the Peasants' War of 1525, the world must have seemed as if it was crumbling under everyone's feet. This tumult came to a head in a decisive battle in 1525 in Frankenhausen. Thomas Müntzer, leader of the peasants, was an early proponent of Luther who turned against the reformer. Müntzer embraced radical ideas about theology, leading to radical ideas about peasants, nobility, and the obligations between them. He gathered peasant armies and pillaged the countryside around Thuringia until the nobles finally struck back, egged on by none other than Luther, who sanctioned slaughter of the upstarts in his pamphlet, *Against the Murderous, Thieving Hordes of Peasants*. Even though the ferment had spread throughout southern Germany and parts of Switzerland, it the peasant's defeat at Frankenhausen that took the wind out of their revolution's sails.

Müntzer was partly, motivated by his interpretation of the book of Revelation and other apocalyptic texts found in scripture. His belief that the world must be prepared for the return of Jesus found resonance throughout Europe. In this way, the city of Münster was not unique, and Rothmann and Matthys were not alone in their speculation. Apocalyptic anticipation had raised the temperature in many pockets of Europe. Expectation of the end times caused mass demonstrations of odd behavior in numerous cities throughout the empire. Münster experienced to a more intense degree what was happening elsewhere.

Expectation of Jesus's return animated many other aspiring prophets and theologians, one of the most influential of whom was Melchoir Hoffman, another peripatetic preacher who traveled throughout the empire, spreading his apocalyptic visions. Like many of the most radical reformers of the 1520–1530s, he moved quickly past an early admiration of Luther to the world of the Anabaptists. Hoffman's embrace of a prophecy about his future imprisonment led him eventually to Strasbourg, where he commenced preaching that Christ was returning to earth in 1533 and that Strasbourg was to be the New Jerusalem.

This is where two central characters of Münster's story enter the picture, for both Jan Matthys and Jan Bockelson were followers of Hoffman. Matthys, a baker in Haarlem, was converted by Hoffman in the 1520s and quickly became a leader of Dutch Anabaptists after Hoffman's imprisonment. Matthys baptized Jan Bockelson, who would become his successor in Münster after Matthys rode out on his ill-advised sortie against the siege armies of Franz von Waldeck. These two argued that Hoffman had been mistaken: Münster would be where Jesus would establish his new kingdom. Thousands of people would follow that call to flock to the New Jerusalem, a place of freedom where they could follow their consciences without fear of reprisal from both Catholics and Protestants.

Their ability to gain power in Münster was paved by the ongoing iconoclasm of Rothmann and the ambitions of the cloth merchant, Bernard Knipperdolling. While these two were joined by significant numbers entering Münster, not all the city council welcomed the radicals. Acutely aware of the Peasants' War and the chaos of mobs burning down castles and pillaging the countryside, the city council tried to hold the tensions between guilds and burghers, lay and clergy, in some order, but when expectations of cleansing fires are stoked, the flames often leap out of control. Such was the case with Münster, whose fall into the hands of the extremists was years in the making, but days to completion. Once they grabbed control in January of 1534, until the fall of the city in June of 1535, charismatic leaders were able to hold power through the force of apocalyptic expectation and religious terrorism.

It is difficult to get an accurate read on what really happened in those sixteen months. The two closest accounts of Münster come from authors who were unsympathetic to what followed after January 1534. Hermann von Kerssenbrock's *Narrative of the Anabaptist Madness: The Overthrow of Münster, the Famous Metropolis of Westphalia,* is rich in historical detail about the city, its past, physical description, and nature of citizens. However, von Kerssenbrock was exiled from the city early in 1534. Henry Gresbeck also wrote an account of the events in Münster, but from a position of hatred for all he and his family had experienced. *False Prophets and Preachers: Henry Gresbeck's Account of the Anabaptist Kingdom of Münster* is the only true eyewitness account we have of what happened inside of the city, but it is colored by Gresbeck's perspective. Is it even possible to obtain an objective account of the insurrection?

As scholars have approached the siege of Münster, the interpretations have ranged from sympathetic to horrified, and there is certainly enough to justify the full spectrum of views. What is hard for many to grasp is the role that the religious imagination played in the insurrection. The tropes, metaphors, and images that shaped identities in the sixteenth century had striking actors: God, the devil, angels, and saints were not remote figures, but readily at hand. This makes certainty about motivations difficult to fix. I do believe that Rothmann was sincere in his desire for the restitution of God's kingdom, Matthys was a wounded and broken man who desired revenge on those who harmed him, Bockelson was a conniving and duplicitous opportunist, and Knipperdolling nursed his own wounds and resentments, not the least from being imprisoned by von Waldeck's predecessor, Frederick von Wiede. What is harder to assess is the depth of authentic religious conviction. This is true for several reasons, not the least being how clever humans can be at hiding true motivations from themselves.

It is true that most people in this age were shaped by Christendom, shaped by theological and social ideas, to act as they did. We would misread them too quickly if we slapped the label "fanatics" on them. Christianity had formed them to behave in a way that had concrete effects. Münster can be understood as a rational reaction to an empire that outlawed and persecuted religious dissidents. One of the few things that Catholics and Protestants agreed on was that killing Anabaptists was necessary. Given the empire's persecution and slaughter of those trying to make their way to Münster from surrounding areas, self-protection was certainly warranted. People pushed to the wall fight back with the only weapons they have sometimes, even if those weapons are rhetorical.

One of the more interesting aspects of this event was the aftermath and its role in moving future Anabaptists to a more rigorous non-violent stance. It was documented that Peter Simons, who may have been the brother of Menno Simons, was one of those killed attempting to make it to Münster. Menno Simons was a Catholic priest when the debacle in Münster ended, but it was the violence of the revolutionary Anabaptists that partly pulled him from his rectory to lead a disillusioned and disheartened flock in Münster's aftermath. His leadership would repair much of the damage, and through him the Anabaptist movement would grow and strengthen, to the point that the term "Mennonite" would become one of the most recognized names in the Anabaptist communities going forward.

It was far more difficult than I anticipated deciding which parts I could cut out. So much rich history was left in the deleted file that at times I felt I was doing the story injustice. The conflicted background of the city's fights with ecclesiastical authority was years long. At one point, the city launched a daring Christmas Eve raid on the Prince-Bishop's quarters at Telgate in 1532 to take hostages. Compounding this conflict, others, like the Wassenberg preachers, appeared in the city looking to stir the pot. These could not all be included and needed to be cut to keep the book focused.

I was fascinated with how contemporary the events of Münster could seem. For example, women's agency in this story tracks what happened in the city. From the promise of new freedoms to the Patriarchy asserting itself, the stories of women's responses to the unraveling of the city are revelatory. For the reader interested in this, Jonathan Grieser's "A Tale of Two Convents: Nuns and Anabaptists in Münster, 1533–35" found in the *Sixteenth Century Journal* XXVI/1 is an interesting look at convent life in the city. Once freed, many of the women took power in their own way until the new masters instituted more control over them than existed before the insurrection. For example, there is a fascinating account of a group of women shouting down the Lutheran priest on Sunday morning at St. Lambert's, and then disrupting city council meetings with riotous behavior. Flinging animal excrement at city council was perfectly fine when Rothmann, Bockelson, and their gang was out of power, but when they took control, women's dissent against authority was quickly quashed.

There are perennial questions hanging in every age that vex us. What role should religion have in government? Given that you cannot separate a person's conscience from their participation in the political order, what role should religion play in constructing that order? When the righteous seek to take over political systems to establish their religion as the sole source of morality, we are all endangered to some extent. Religiously fueled insurrections are not just a thing that happened in the sixteenth century; they are a very present challenge throughout history. We are seeing echoes of Münster in our own age, when many religious communities, fearful of shared power and social claims, have given up on more democratic politics in their pursuit of absolute power. In that regard, the cages of Münster do have a warning for us today—the desire for purity is a totalitarian agenda that brings great harm into the world. We ignore these lessons at our peril.